Praise fo...
of Johnn...

...t Johnny D. ...

...e of Re...

...a bygone

...Wilkinson,
author of *Oblivion's Altar*

"Filled with vivid characters and action as fast as a gunfighter's draw. Johnny D. Boggs has written an exciting work of fiction that looks at how life in the dangerous American West in the late 1880s could turn ordinary people into heroes and outlaws—and back to heroes again."

—Stef Donev, author of *The Wild, Wild, Wild West Stunt Show*

"Boggs is a master. Every page brings surprises, every chapter crackles with action."

—Bruce H. Thorstad, author of *Deadwood Dick and the Code of the West*

"Woven with actual people from the past . . . a fine snapshot of history."

—Sandra Whiting, Spur Award–winning author of *Charity*

"Boggs's narrative voice captures the old-fashioned style of the past and reminds a reader of the Western legends of yesteryear."   —*Publishers Weekly continued . . .*

"An entertaining Western in the classic mold . . . with interesting stuff on the weaponry of the times." —*Booklist*

"A rib-tickling story filled with traditional Western action."
—*Roundup*

"Action from the first page to the last. . . . The reader has to decide which is the best: the action, the characters, or the setting. This combination is so winning that to make a choice is impossible. Just enjoy it all." —*Rendezvous*

SPARK ON THE PRAIRIE

A GUNS AND GAVEL NOVEL

JOHNNY D. BOGGS

A SIGNET BOOK

SIGNET
Published by New American Library, a division of
Penguin Group (USA) Inc., 375 Hudson Street,
New York, New York 10014, U.S.A.
Penguin Books Ltd, 80 Strand,
London WC2R 0RL, England
Penguin Books Australia Ltd, 250 Camberwell Road,
Camberwell, Victoria 3124, Australia
Penguin Books Canada Ltd, 10 Alcorn Avenue,
Toronto, Ontario, Canada M4V 3B2
Penguin Books (N.Z.) Ltd, Cnr Rosedale and Airborne Roads,
Albany, Auckland 1310, New Zealand

Penguin Books Ltd, Registered Offices:
80 Strand, London WC2R 0RL, England

First published by Signet, an imprint of New American Library,
a division of Penguin Group (USA) Inc.

First Printing, May 2003
10   9   8   7   6   5   4   3   2   1

For the Langendorfs—
Dan, Laura, and Grace

"Laws do not persuade because they threaten."
—Seneca, *Epistulae ad Lucilium*

Prologue

*"Teach us the road to travel, and we will not depart
from it forever. For your sakes, the green grass shall
not be stained with the blood of the whites. Your
people shall again be our people, and peace shall be
our mutual heritage."*
    —Satank, Medicine Lodge Treaty negotiations, 1867

May 7, 1871
North Fork of the Red River, Indian Territory

Satank accepted Maman-ti's pipe and smoked. More than a
hundred warriors had gathered around the council fire to listen to the words of Maman-ti, the gangling warrior who
could almost touch the clouds, who had not forgotten the old
ways like some of his people who called themselves
Gai'gwu but acted like cowardly *Tehannas* and Mexicans.
Satank passed the pipe to the fool Satanta, a good provider, a
good speaker and, at times, a good man to have by your side.
Satanta would have been stronger, though, if he would learn
that open mouths draw flies. The middle-aged warrior liked
the sound of his own voice. Satank preferred silence.

Satank had never been impressive looking, especially
now that his weary bones forced him to stoop. His hair
showed more gray than black, and the young ones, not to
mention a few old, whispered when he passed, leading the
big horse carrying the strange bundle. He wore a thin mustache, contrary to the customs of *Gai'gwu,* The Principal

People on Earth, sported ragged, spartan chin whiskers, and had been shot in the mouth twenty-four winters ago, all combining to render his face far from handsome. The bluecoats despised him, as did Old Stone Head, the Indian agent. So did many of his own people. Yet all respected or feared him, for he wore the red elkskin sash, and that was enough. He was *Koiet-senko.*

He came to hear Maman-ti because it was expected of him. Satank led the *Koiet-senko* Society, limited to the ten bravest warriors of the tribe. Having seen seventy winters, Satank had proved his courage long before Maman-ti or Satanta were born. Yet he had also adopted the ways of peace after hearing the white leaders during the Timber-Hill Winter at the place the white-eyes called Medicine Lodge. His speech had moved many in the audience to tears, had even earned praise from accomplished talkers like Satanta and Ten Bears of the Comanche. He had meant what he had said, too, for Satank never lied.

The *Tehannas* had lied. Like all white-eyes.

He thought back to The Winter The Horses Ate The Ashes and the white man in Kansas named Peacock. Satank had been impressed and awed with how white-eyes communicated with turkey scratches on paper and had asked Peacock to give him a letter that would introduce him to other white-eyes so he could trade with them. Peacock had obliged, and Satank excitedly rode off to try this new kind of talk. But when he showed the letter to a wagonmaster on the Santa Fe Trail, the white-eye beat him savagely with a blacksnake whip. Later, Satank learned the letter Peacock had written did not praise Satank as a friend but called him a beggar and a thief, the worst Kiowa ever born, and said to teach him a lesson rather than barter with him.

Satank had ridden back to Peacock's fort with ten good warriors and killed everyone inside, including the lying little Peacock. That had given him much pleasure.

Peace had not been easy, not for a *Koiet-senko,* and the white-eyes, from Stone Head to the bluecoats nearby, did not make things easier. They demanded that the children of The Principal People—and those of the Comanche and Kiowa-Apache—shun their heritage, pray to a squaw called Jesus, learn the white-eye language, both spoken and written, and dress like white-eyes. Maybe this was how things had to be. Satank did not know. But the whites were insulting, treating warriors like children, and shaming them all—men, women, boys, and girls—by telling them that they had to forget their old ways, forget the buffalo, the raids into Texas and Mexico, the Ten Grandmothers, and all the ways of The Principal People.

Satank would not do this. He would not live as a white-eye, with no honor, no love for the hills and creeks. He would not dirty his hands like some plowman. He detested the taste of the white man's beef, so hard on the few teeth he had left, and longed for buffalo. He wanted to feel the wind in his hair as he rode into battle, and he was not alone in this, yet he would not break his word—until *Tehannas* killed his favorite son.

That had happened last spring. His second son had ridden off to Texas to steal horses and mules, the way a good warrior should. Yes, Stone Head would be angry, would say the Kiowas were not living up to their end of the treaty, but what did Stone Head know? He was a Quaker, what Satank considered the weakest of the white-eye tribes. So Young Set-añgya had crossed the Red River, to be killed by some *Tehanna.* His friends, who would never become *Koiet-senko,* had left Young Set-añgya in Texas. Mad with grief, Satank, riding alone, had followed the path the young braves had taken, found his son's grave, wrapped the bones in a blanket, bundled them tightly on the back of a fine blood bay stallion, and brought his favorite son home.

He talked to Young Set-añgya often, invited friends to share a pipe in his son's lodge. Many thought him crazy, and maybe he was: crazy that he had ever believed the white-eyes, crazy that he had ever believed The Principal People could follow the white man's road, crazy that he thought he could live in peace. He, a *Koiet-senko*.

So he listened to Maman-ti, and he liked what he heard.

Only a few moons ago, Maman-ti had led a band of The Principal People and their allies into Texas, where they had killed four black men hauling supplies. The black men's scalps made poor trophies, and the warriors had pitched them on the road, but they had captured good livestock and grain. Now Maman-ti wanted to lead another raid, a raid promising much bounty, much glory. Who would come with him?

"What of Kicking Bird?" asked Ádo-eete, the young brave called Big Tree. Satank saw much in Big Tree, saw more than a little of a younger Satank. Big Tree had proved his bravery time and again, might likely someday replace Satank as leader of the *Koiet-senko*—if only he would stop listening to Kicking Bird, Satanta, and Stone Head the Quaker.

"Kicking Bird talks of peace, and that is his right," Maman-ti answered. "His wives do not go hungry. Stone Head and the long knives make sure he eats well while we starve for food and for the old ways. Big Tree, you have shared my vision. You know the white man's road means death. Let Kicking Bird travel that path. Perhaps the road of Maman-ti leads to death, too, but if so, at least I shall die *Gai'gwu*." Maman-ti approached Big Tree as he spoke and placed both hands on the young man's square shoulders. "Ádo-eete, my brother, will you ride with me?"

"I will ride," the warrior answered.

Maman-ti moved over to Satanta, asked the same question, heard the same reply. Now he stood in front of Satank.

"Grandfather, will you ride with me?"

He felt the stares and knew the raid Maman-ti planned depended on his answer. Words from Big Tree, Satanta, and Maman-ti carried weight, but not the power of Satank's. He might be a crazy old man, he might not care about his personal appearance, but no one questioned his courage, and when he painted his face for war, others were quick to join him.

"I will ride," Satank answered. He felt like a true *Koiet-senko* once more. Maybe in Texas he would take the Great Journey to the next life, but if so, at least he would join Young Set-añgya. It would be a death befitting a warrior such as himself. He would die with honor, a leader of The Principal People, or he would live. In either case, the *Tehannas* would pay for killing his son. He would have his revenge.

Part I

Part I

Chapter 1

"I do think the people of Texas have a right to complain, only their complaints are now against the troops who are powerless, but should be against the Department that feeds and harbors these Indians when their hands are yet red with blood."
—General William T. Sherman

May 17, 1871
Salt Creek Prairie, Texas

He hated everything about this damned state. The wind . . . the desolation . . . everything. Water would taste like a horse's iron shoe at one hole and be pure brine at the next. And, damn, the heat. How could anyone live in this climate? It wasn't humid like Ohio, not even like Washington or Virginia, but here it never seemed to cool off. You'd step outside at first light and feel as though you had just walked into a roaring furnace and someone had slammed the door behind you. By noon, your head had been baked like a hotcake left on the griddle. By dusk, you were so worn out and sick you didn't feel like eating and dreaded going to bed because you knew it would be just as steaming, if not worse, by morning. A thousand bugs would crawl up your ass in a minute if you weren't careful. Hell itself couldn't be as miserable as Texas. Maybe that was why he hadn't seen a soul, only a few abandoned homesteads of crumbling adobe and charred chimneys, since leaving Fort Belknap at six this morning.

Most of all, however, William Tecumseh Sherman disliked Texans, or Texicans as they liked to call themselves out here. All they had done during his tour of the state's frontier settlements and military posts was complain about the lack of Army protection. Kiowas did this. Comanches did that. Livestock run off. Homes pillaged and burned. Women and children abducted or their brains bashed against cottonwoods. Back during the War for the Suppression of the Rebellion, he had heard Texans cursed with fear and respect as the worst at killing and the hardest to kill, like those wild secessionist boys with John Bell Hood's First Texas Brigade. Tougher than a cob and wild as, well, Indians. Still, Sherman would be hard-pressed to call them fighters these days. Complainers? Yes. Fighting devils? Not by a damn sight. Indians, the settlers railed. The Army had to help them.

Leaning forward, he peered through the choking dust at the rolling nothingness that passed by monotonously as the military ambulance bounced uncomfortably over what out here passed for a road. The curtains had been rolled up to allow a breeze through the wagon, but inside it remained stifling—and it was not yet noon. He spotted a conical hill to the north—trees, scrub, and grass greening from recent rains—but there was not a bird, not even a lizard or a snake, anywhere. Too hot, he figured. For anything.

"Indians, my ass," he said.

"You say something, General?" Inspector General Randolph Marcy pushed back a black slouch hat and stretched, careful not to wake the two sleeping junior officers sitting across the aisle.

How anyone could sleep in this jostling torture-contrivance, in this heat, Sherman hadn't a clue. Marcy had been in this man's army for just about forty years, and Sherman usually enjoyed the old man's company, but the gray-haired, mustached joke-spinner had been quite reserved on this trip, shaking his head as if he believed the far-fetched stories of the settlers and pointing out the ruined homesteads, blaming Indians.

"Nothing," Sherman replied, leaning back.

Marcy pulled a pewter flask from his coat pocket, unscrewed the top, and took a quick pull. He offered Sherman some of the brandy, but the general declined, having never been much of a morning drinker. If, however, that little mick driving the ambulance hit one more boulder, or if the sun didn't dip behind a cloud soon, he might accept Marcy's generosity.

"How much farther to Fort Richardson?"

The inspector general looked outside as if there were any landmarks a body could recognize in this godforsaken blight, then pulled a silver watch from a vest pocket. "Be late afternoon, is my guess, General." He returned both flask and watch. "Interesting country, isn't it?"

"So is Hell, I warrant."

Marcy had been stationed in Texas before the Rebellion. Maybe a man had to live here before he could appreciate it. Sherman shook his head, pushed up his hat, and patted his coat and vest pockets for a cigar. He found one, bit off the end, and struck a match against the uncomfortable wooden bench that served as a seat. The ambulance lurched suddenly to the left, waking the two sleeping colonels. Sherman dropped the match and grabbed the door for support.

"Hey, John Wilkes Booth!" he yelled, pounding the top of the wagon. "Watch the road, you damned assassin."

He swore again, removed the cigar and put it back in his coat pocket before turning to the inspector general. "Randolph," he said, "hand me your damned flask."

May 17, 1871
Rock Station, Texas

Jimmy O'Neal wrapped the reins around the brake lever and leaped off the ambulance, trying to open the door for his distinguished passengers. Too late. Sherman scowled at him and shoved a cigar into his mouth. "Six years ago," the general said, "I could have had you shot for high treason, son, the way you drive this buggy."

"Yessir. Sorry, sir."

Sherman smiled suddenly and lit his cigar. "I'm joshing you, O'Neal. Anyplace I can wash this dust off me?"

The driver nodded toward a well in front of the decrepit limestone cabin that once had been the center of a booming mail station. O'Neal would have almost sworn on a stack of King James Bibles that the general had liquor on his breath.

O'Neal and the station hands had watered the team and harnessed the mules again before he spotted the dust. The two helpers, Mexican teenagers, turned to see what held the driver's attention. They muttered something in Spanish and quickly headed for the lean-to near the corral, where they had shed their chaps and hardware before tackling the hot work. One pulled a massive Colt Dragoon from a shabby holster, and the other grabbed a shotgun leaning in the corner. O'Neal decided they had the right idea and backed toward the ambulance, climbed part of the way up, and lifted a Henry rifle from the boot.

Sherman's escort of seventeen Tenth Cavalry buffalo soldiers had also seen the travelers. They stopped tending their lathered mounts and began fingering their Spencer carbines nervously.

O'Neal let out a sigh when he could make out the riders and returned the rifle to the boot. The Mexicans stared at him, wondering. Apparently, he could see better than both of them. That didn't surprise him. When you drove wagons across this part of the world, it paid to have keen eyes. "Cavalry," he told them. *"Soldados."* They understood, also relieved, and put away their weapons before returning to work.

The buffalo soldiers relaxed, but only briefly. A gray-bearded sergeant barked an order, and the black troopers fell in, standing at attention to greet the arriving horsemen.

It was a good-sized patrol. Between fifteen and twenty troopers with a string of mules behind them. O'Neal quickly recognized the leader's mustache and Dundreary whiskers.

Second Lieutenant Robert G. Carter, Fourth Cavalry. One of those West Point boys stationed at Fort Richardson, probably ordered to give Generals Sherman and Marcy a proper escort to Jacksboro.

Sherman stepped out of the cabin, followed by his aides. The general still smoked his cigar, but he had gotten smarter, removing his vest and coat and loosening the cravat around his collar. One of the feather-headed colonels behind him carried the discarded clothing.

Carter raised a gauntleted right hand, and the troopers reined to a halt behind him. He swung down from the saddle, hurriedly brushed alkali dust off his blouse to make himself as presentable as possible, and marched to the Army brass standing in the shade near the station building. The second lieutenant stopped sharply, clicked his heels, and fired off a perfect salute, introducing himself to Sherman like some ass wipe West Point plebe.

Old Billy Sherman returned the salute, then pumped the lieutenant's hand like a papa welcoming home his prodigal son. Carter didn't seem to know what to expect. He began spitting out some more orders and such, welcoming the general and his staff, conveying the compliments of Colonel Mackenzie back at Richardson and expressing what an honor it was for him to meet the general and serve as his escort to the fort. Sherman nodded, pitched his cigar into the dirt, and walked to the troopers, who were busy watering their mounts and themselves.

Corporal Charlton—J. B. to his friends—walked up to O'Neal and held out a square quid wrapped in a faded blue bandana. *God love a damnyankee soldier,* O'Neal thought as he unwrapped the tobacco and bit off a substantial chaw.

"See anything 'tween here and Griffin?" the corporal asked. Charlton was a young man, not even twenty-five, but his weathered appearance made him look like a veteran of the war—the Mexican War, that is.

O'Neal waited until he had worked the tobacco into a comfortable position in his mouth before answering. "Some turkey vultures circling near Belknap and a snake sunning hisself on the Brazos. Why?"

Charlton spit at a beetle, missed, and shrugged. "Heard some of the injuns is actin' up."

"Didn't see any signs."

"Too bad." He laughed dryly. "The citizens of Jack County is wishin' the Kiowas or Comanch would do somethin' while Gen'ral Sherman's in Texas, show him just what they gotta live with out here."

O'Neal shrugged and spit. He hit the beetle and smiled. "Can't say I blame them none. Sherman hasn't been too impressed so far."

"Yeah, I know. Injun raid would help things a mite—lessen, o' course, you was the ones they decided to hit."

Sherman, O'Neal saw, was shaking his head. "Thanks for the offer of your mules, Lieutenant, but mine are fresh enough," the general told Carter. "Your horses, however, are worn out. You won't be able to keep up with us. Rest them here, then come in at your leisure."

Carter shuffled his boots. "Yes, General, but . . ."

"Don't fret, Mr. Carter. I will personally thank Colonel Mackenzie for his kindness, and"—he patted Carter's shoulder—"for sending out such a fine-looking detachment for my safety. My compliments to you and your men. Now, if you'll be so kind as to point out the right road. . . ."

Charlton snickered and whispered to O'Neal: "Young Mr. Carter's gonna catch pure-dee hell from Mackenzie back at the fort. The colonel was plannin' a two-cannon salute to greet Sherman. Now the gen'ral's gonna sneak in without any fanfare."

May 18, 1871
Fort Richardson, Texas

Sweat darkened the back of Peter Lynn's boiled blue shirt as he stood beside his friends and neighbors, waiting for his

chance to talk to Sherman, to speak his mind, let the general
know what was going on here in Texas. Right now, W. M.
McConnell was reading the petition he and Henderson Horton had drafted, pleading for the Army to help.

They had gathered in front of the commanding officer's
quarters, using a live oak for shade. The Army brass sat at a
table brought out of the adjutant's office, flanked by a couple
of guards while the townsmen stood or squatted on dead and
dying grass. To Peter Lynn's surprise, the fort looked abandoned. No troopers drilled. No sergeants barked orders. Even
the horses in the stables on the opposite side of the post had
fallen silent.

"One hundred and twenty-nine citizens have been killed
in Jack County by Indians over the past twelve years, General," McConnell said. "Twelve of those in this year alone,
and, General, it's not even June, sir. We've lost cattle and
horses, barns and homes. We've lost friends, family. It's a
small county, sir. If we don't get help, there won't be anyone
left here alive."

Sherman nodded politely. McConnell handed him the petition, and he glanced at it briefly before passing it on to General Marcy. Lynn knew they were getting nowhere with the
Army.

Sighing wearily, McConnell turned and looked at his
neighbors, searching faces. His eyes settled on Lynn. "Peter,
you tell General Sherman what you've seen. God knows,
you've been hurt more than a lot of us."

He shifted uncomfortably, aware of everyone staring at
him: friends, soldiers, General Sherman. Lynn cleared his
throat, apologized, and stepped forward, stalling. He was a
thirty-year-old cowboy. What did he know about talking to a
four-star general? Well, that's what he came here for, wasn't
it?

"We moved here in 'fifty-six. I pushed cattle mostly,
saved up and finally got a place of my own. Good land, in the
Keechi Valley." He stopped, thinking.

"Go on," Horton said.

"Well," he continued, "earlier this year, me and Mr. Harrell, Albert Harrell that is, we were out looking for strays. I was on a jenny of mine; Albert, he rode a good bay mare. Anyway, we looked up and saw about twenty-thirty-forty Indians. I remember one of 'em was wearing a beaded jacket, remember that clear as yesterday. Well, we ran. Couldn't stand them off, not just the two of us. I fired once, but my pistol jammed, so I shucked it. To lighten the load. I was riding a mule, you see. Albert, God bless him, he could have left me alone, but he reined in that mare of his just ahead of me, kept telling me to whip that mule, whip that mule. And I did, yes sir.

"Well, that red buck with the pretty jacket rode right up to me—Albert, he pulled his pistol and fired, but the Indian ducked underneath his pony. He had a long red lance, and he up and speared my jenny. When the Indian rose, Albert fired again. I swear I saw the beads fly off that jacket, but it didn't seem to even hurt that buck. But he did back off. God, I remember those bucks yelling. Haven't never heard anything like that before. I figured my mule was played out, but she kept running. Albert fired till his gun was empty, kept those Indians back, and then we saw Mr. Atkinson's house. His was the closest shelter, you see. We jumped off our mounts, raised dust, and Newton—that's Mr. Atkinson, General—he opened the door and barred it once we was inside. Those Indians rode around the house a spell, then got bored, I reckon, and disappeared."

He stopped, adding as an afterthought, "My mule died, sir."

McConnell patted Lynn's wet back and told Sherman, "Peter eventually had to sell out. He had a good ranch, a good future. Now he's back punching cattle for somebody else at twenty-five a month and found."

Sherman's small hands patted his coat pockets. He found a cigar, thought better of it, and placed it beside a note pad on the table in front of him. "One dead mule, gentlemen," he said, "does not constitute a federal emergency."

A low rumble started among the crowd of settlers. "Tell him about your sister, Peter!" J. R. Robinson shouted, and the men of Jack County fell silent again.

"That was in 'fifty-eight . . . April," he said. He cursed himself silently as a tear rolled down his cheek.

"They hit the Cambren place first. Folks say white men were riding with the Indians."

"Damned comancheros!" Robinson interjected.

Lynn nodded. "Mr. Bill and his boys were in the field working when Miz Cambren called them in for dinner. She and her daughter saw them swarm over the hill. They killed the two boys in front of her. Sent an arrow through Mr. Bill, killed him. Then they went in, took the rest of the kids and Miz Cambren. We found her and one of her little boys on the other side of the mountain. They had rammed a spear down the boy's throat till he died, and then Miz Camb—" He couldn't finish.

"Well, I guess after they looted the Cambren place, they hit my brother-in-law's, Tom Mason. It's only about a mile down the crick. Mary was my sister. They had two younguns. My pa—his name's Issac, General—he found Mary and Tom later. For some reason, the Indians didn't hurt Mary's two boys, Tobe and Milton. Pa found them crawling over Mary's body. The younguns were covered with blood. Pa, he saw there wasn't a thing he could do for Mary and Tom, so he cleaned up the little ones and took off for Mr. Bill's. He saw what had happened there, yelled out if anyone was alive. The Indians had left Miz Cambren's other kids, little Mary and Dewitt, behind after they killed Miz Cambren and the little boy. Again, I don't know why they didn't keep the kids. Indians will do it most times. Anyway, little Mary took her baby brother back to the house. Pa found them there, hiding in the root cellar.

"A bunch of us went after the murderers, but we never found them. Lost the trail. But I bet you they come off the reservation and lit a shuck back there. Ma and Pa have been raising Tobe and Milton. Milton was just a baby, not even a

year old, and Tobe was only three. I don't think they really
remember what happened, and I thank God for that. Same
with little Dewitt Cambren. But Mary Cambren? She hasn't
uttered one word since the raid."

He stopped, wiped his eyes, stared at the soldiers in front
of him. Marcy, the inspector general, looked moved. So did
Colonel Mackenzie. Even still, however, Sherman didn't
seem convinced.

"And they killed ol' Britt Johnson and them other darkies
back, what, December?" someone said.

"January," McConnell said solemnly. "Britt was a good
boy, too. They butchered them poor boys, then tossed away
their scalps a few miles up the road."

The crowd's rumbling erupted now. "You gotta do something, General!" . . . "Where in God's name are those red
niggers gettin' their guns? That's what I want to know!" . . .
"It ain't right, the Army protecting those butchers. They steal
our livestock, kill our women, kidnap our babies to raise as
their own, and all they have to do is cross the Red River and
the damned government feeds and protects them!" The
voices soon became so vehement, so loud, that Lynn couldn't
understand a word.

Colonel Mackenzie finally stepped forward and banged
the butt of his revolver on the tabletop. It took a while, but
the crowd finally fell silent.

"Gentlemen," Sherman said, rising from his seat and
sticking that cigar in the corner of his mouth. "I appreciate
your time, your zealousness. I understand your concerns and
sympathize with your plight. I can't, however, promise you
anything but this: When I get to Fort Sill, I will investigate
your charges. If stolen stock and children are being brought
to the reservation, they shall be returned. Thank you, and
good day."

Lynn followed the angry crowd as it left the post. He had
a pretty good idea where most of them would be going. Hell,
he needed a drink, too, so he'd join them. Something to wash
down the dung he had just been served by General Sherman.

As he pulled himself into the saddle, J. R. Robinson asked, "Well, what do you think?"

"Waste of time," he answered.

"Amen," someone added.

Sherman woke with a start, trying to remember the nightmare but having little luck. The midnight haze enveloping his mind lifted, and he made out the blares of a trumpet, soldiers barking orders, cursing, horses whinnying, traces jingling. He felt like he was standing on the banks of the Tennessee again at Pittsburg Landing. Colonel Mackenzie had offered the use of his personal quarters, but Sherman had declined. That's why he had brought canvas, he told the commandant. He looked across the Sibley tent, saw Randolph Marcy curled up like an infant and sawing logs like an Ohio drunk. Sherman sat up, pulled on his boots, grabbed his hat, and stepped into the night air, almost knocking a pockmarked private onto his hindquarters.

"Sorry, sir," the trooper said. "Colonel Mackenzie begs pardon for the intrusion but asks if you could join him at the hospital immediately."

He grumbled a reply, and the soldier sprinted away. Sherman felt wet, downright cold, even. He looked up, realized that, hell, it was raining. Raining in Hell. Who would have believed it?

"General, this is Thomas Brazeal," Mackenzie said, pointing at the pale, shivering man on the cot, his right foot heavily bandaged. The post surgeon was giving the man a shot of brandy as the colonel continued. "He and this gentleman over there"—Mackenzie pointed at a tall gent standing in the corner, wrapped in blankets, trying to warm himself by the stove—"I'm sorry, but I can't recall your name."

"Hobbs Carey."

"My apologies. They say they were attacked by Indians this afternoon at Salt Creek Prairie."

Sherman scratched his beard. The colonel looked at the wounded man and surgeon, waiting for the doctor to nod and let him know it would be all right for Brazeal to talk.

A New Yorker by birth and a career soldier by circumstance, Ranald Slidell Mackenzie was not quite thirty-one years old. He had never wanted to be an Army man. Mackenzie's father had died when Ranald was only eight, and his mother had moved the family to New Jersey. Ranald hadn't known what he wanted to do. His brothers, like their father, had made careers in the Navy, but Ranald got seasick on a wharf. He tried reading law, but that bored him, so at last he earned an appointment to West Point for no other reason than to help his mother. That was in 1858.

Four years later, Mackenzie found himself a second lieutenant, graduating first in his small class, and in the middle of a war. To the surprise of the entire Mackenzie family, Ranald included, the young officer found he had a passion for the military. Rebs shot two fingers off his right hand at Petersburg, and by Appomattox he had been wounded five other times and had been breveted a major general. After the surrender, he earned a commission as colonel of the Forty-first Infantry, a colored unit, where he felt forgotten until happily transferring to the Fourth Cavalry in December of 1870. Down south at Fort Concho, he had whipped the troopers into fighting shape. Now, thanks to bad timing on the part of some stupid Indians, and a stunned general-in-chief, Mackenzie knew he was about to go to war again.

The doctor removed the empty glass of brandy from the weak man's hand and signaled the colonel.

"Mr. Brazeal," Mackenzie said, "tell General Sherman exactly what happened."

The teamster painfully slid into a seated position on the cot, keeping his wounded leg on the bunk. "We're with Captain Warren's train, General."

Mackenzie explained. "Henry Warren has a contract to haul supplies to forts on the Texas frontier, sir."

"That's right." Brazeal grimaced, clutching his leg. When

the pain subsided, he went on. "There were twelve of us hauling corn, including Nathan Long; he was our boss. We were at Salt Creek Prairie late yesterday afternoon when, God, there must have been three hundred of them. Indians. Swarming, shouting. We put up a fight, but there was too many of them. I got hit. Arrow and bullet, practically the same place. Most of the boys were cut down before they knew what was happening. Then we saw our chance, made a run for the trees near Cox Mountain. God, General, if you could've heard our boys screaming." He collapsed, exhausted.

Shaking, the teamster named Carey stepped away from the stove. "A big storm blew up. I guess that's what saved us. Me and Tom here and three others were all that made it. We walked, Lordy, I reckon twenty miles till we came to a ranch. Anyway, we borrowed a couple of horses—most of the boys were wounded, but Tom here got the worst of it—and rode here. You gotta help us, General."

Mackenzie said he had already ordered "boots and saddles" and now awaited the general's orders.

"Where is this place where they were attacked?" the slack-jawed general asked after a minute.

"About four miles from Rock Station, sir," Mackenzie answered.

"Jesus. That could have been . . ." He paused, glanced at Brazeal and whirled to face Mackenzie, his face firm now, eyes angry, the shock worn off.

"Colonel, I want you to go to Salt Creek Prairie at once, report what you find, and pursue those hostiles. Have your adjutant send word to Colonel Wood at Fort Griffin, tell him to send as much cavalry as he can spare to rendezvous with you at . . . pick a likely spot."

"The Little Wichita headwaters."

"So be it. Now get me something to write with. I'm putting these orders down so there will be no questions. I take full responsibility. I'm authorizing you to enter the Fort Sill reservation if need be, and if you overtake those bastards

anywhere within forty miles of the Red River, you can and
will attack. If you lose the trail, continue to Fort Sill. I'll be
there, mister, waiting."

He moved to the wounded teamster, stared down at him in
silence, then looked up at Hobbs Carey. "Those bastards will
pay, mister," Sherman said. "I promise you that."

Ranald S. Mackenzie stroked his bushy mustache to hide
his smile.

Chapter 2

"*There could be nothing more appalling, heart rending or sickening to the human senses than the spectacle which was witnessed when our command reached the scene of the Salt Creek Prairie massacre.*"

—Robert G. Carter, *On the Border with Mackenzie*

May 19, 1871
Jacksboro, Texas

Water poured off his hat brim as Thomas Ball reached inside the india rubber poncho and withdrew a handkerchief from a coat pocket. He blew his nose, returned the handkerchief, picked up his grip and crossed the muddy street, leaving the sign that had greeted him on the courthouse door soaking in the monsoon.

COURT CLOSd Today

Jack County would take some getting used to, he told himself as he maneuvered across the quagmire with a barely detectable limp and headed for the Wichita Hotel and breakfast, ignoring two cowboys snickering at him while they lounged in front of the Green Frog Saloon. Jacksboro was the county seat, even had a spartan but efficiently built two-story courthouse, and the presiding judge for this session, Charles Soward, was known for his punctuality. Court was to have been called to order at nine o'clock today, and Thomas Ball had to defend a client accused of horse stealing. The man was guilty as hell but had paid Ball's retainer without haggling and seemed a friendly sort when he wasn't in his cups and coveting other people's livestock.

In his thirty-four years, Ball had never seen anything like this. Court canceled on a whim? No warning, no instructions given to officers of the court. The torrential downpour reminded him of Virginia, but little else about this strange state did.

He had grown up in Northumberland County near the Chesapeake Bay, had graduated from The College of William and Mary and been admitted to the state bar in 1858. Then came the war, and he found himself a lieutenant in the Forty-seventh Virginia Infantry. After the surrender, like so many other Southerners, he became increasingly restless. Practicing law among ruined homes and defeated people quickly lost its appeal. So in 1869, he kissed his parents good-bye and headed west.

Texas, he had been told, was a great place to start over, and Thomas Ball settled in Weatherford. Only it turned out that a lot of attorneys at law had chosen Weatherford for a new home, so early this year, heeding Judge Soward's advice, he had packed his bags again and traveled northwest to Jacksboro, where he hung his shingle in an office behind the Wichita Hotel.

He liked Jacksboro and Texicans even though some of them could be crude, and many would joke at his fancy wardrobe and ask him what was it like to be part of the landed gentry back in uppity Virginia. It was true that his family came from old stock and that he had never lacked anything growing up; however, if they bet he wouldn't last six weeks on the frontier, they quickly learned otherwise. He had seen more than his share of hard fighting in Virginia during the war and had spent months rotting in that hellhole the Yanks called a prison at Point Lookout. What's more, he knew his law and would argue vehemently and passionately for his case, his clients, his sense of justice.

He ducked inside the hotel and headed to the dining room. Men filled the lobby and saloon, their voices excited, downright angry, and he slowed down to listen, finally stopping, ignoring the water pooling beneath him on the hardwood floor. He had skipped breakfast this morning, too busy working on his opening statement and plans for defense, and his growling stomach had sent him to the Wichita. Now, however, he forgot all about breakfast and began removing his poncho, listening.

"I mean to have the men responsible brought to justice," came the staccato voice from the center of the lobby. "That much I promise you." The man was having trouble speaking, fighting through the mob surrounding him. Ball hung his poncho and hat on a deerhorn rack and moved closer. "Damn it, people," the voice suddenly cracked. "Would you give me some room!"

The Texicans parted, and Ball immediately recognized wiry, red-bearded William T. Sherman. He remembered that the general had spoken to several residents yesterday. Ball knew that most Jack County people voiced concern over recent Indian depredations, but his case had consumed all of his attention, and he had forgotten all about the celebrity visit until now.

"That ain't what you said yesterday," cracked a rancher Ball did not know.

"Yesterday is history," said Sherman, breathing easier now, fishing in his pockets for a cigar. "I have ordered Colonel Mackenzie to pursue the hostiles, to cross the Red River and enter the reservation if necessary, and bring back the leaders of this horrible, tragic affair. I have instructed Colonel Wood at Fort Griffin to put all his available cavalry in the field and rendezvous with Mackenzie's troops. Right will prevail, gentlemen. This I promise you."

While Sherman began answering questions, Ball studied the faces, trying to recognize someone. He headed for W. M.

McConnell, then saw another figure in the corner of the lobby, a handsome, dark-bearded man talking to a young woman who sat in a chair and kept dabbing her eyes with a handkerchief. Ball didn't want to intrude, but the woman was beautiful and the man was Judge Charles Soward, so he veered toward them.

Presiding judge of the Thirteenth Judicial District, Charles Soward was a native Kentuckian who had just celebrated his thirty-fifth birthday. His family had moved to Missouri when Soward was still a teen, and Soward had been admitted to the bar in Canton shortly before the war erupted. After the surrender, he, too, headed for Texas, settling in Sherman in November of '67 before moving to Parker County three years later after Governor Edmund J. Davis appointed him judge of the district comprising Parker, Jack, Palo Pinto, Hood, and Johnson counties.

Soward saw Ball approaching, touched the woman gently on her shoulder, and greeted Ball.

"You heard?" Soward asked.

"No, sir," Ball said. "I saw the note on the courthouse door, came here for breakfast. What's going on?"

"Indians hit Henry Warren's wagon train yesterday on the Salt Creek Prairie. Killed Nathan Long, and I don't know how many others. Under the circumstances, I thought it best to postpone proceedings today. We'll reconvene at eight a.m. sharp tomorrow. I sent the bailiff to your room, Thomas. I'm sorry he missed you." Soward's voice flowed as smooth as Kentucky bourbon, and the judge stroked his beard momentarily before his penetrating eyes increased their intensity. "Plead your client guilty, counselor. I'll give him an easy sentence. This county is about to explode, and I won't dilly-dally over some silly waddie sowing his oats and full of John Barleycorn." Soward looked past Ball. "I need to talk to General Sherman, get a few particulars." His eyes fell back on Ball. "If I may impose on you, Thomas." He didn't wait for a response, simply steered Ball over to the sobbing woman.

"This is M. J. Shelley, friend of the family." The woman

looked up with a sad, false smile. "M. J., this is counselor Thomas Ball, new to Jacksboro but a fine gentleman from Virginia and a late officer of the Confederacy."

Ball reached to tip his hat, forgetting that it now hung, sopping wet, across the lobby. "My pleasure, ma'am," he said.

"Thomas, will you escort Miss Shelley home?" Again, Soward didn't wait for Ball's reply. "Go on, M. J. This is no place for a lady. There's nothing for you here, nothing you can do. I'll be in touch. I'll let you know about Samuel once I hear something."

"It's funny 'bout a damned injun," said the cowboy standing next to Ball at the Green Frog Saloon that night. "They don't swell an' stink up like a white man. You's new to these parts, so you likely never saw the skull of that red nigger Luke Mullins kilt a few years back. Luke shot the bastard an' left him just a-sittin' up beneath a live oak to rot. Only the injun's skin just kinda wrinkled up an' peeled back 'round his jaw so'd it looked like he was just a-grinnin' at folks passin' by."

"It's a fact," a fencepost-thin waddie with a brushy, unkempt mustache agreed. "I musta passed by that smilin' prairie nigger oncet a week for nigh on two years. Bet you never seen nothin' like that back in Maryland, eh, lawyerman?"

Ball ignored the two drunken loafers, letting them have their fun at his expense. He killed his shot of what the bartender passed off as Irish whiskey and motioned for a refill. What time was it? Close to midnight? What a day it had been, and from the look inside the Green Frog, whiskey and talk would not subside for hours. He thought of M. J. Shelley, a pleasant girl—unlike most of the ruffians in this wilderness. She had been friends with the wagon boss, Nathan Long, and one of the teamsters, Samuel Elliott. Word had come back from Salt Creek Prairie that seven members of the wagon train had been butchered by the Indians, and by now M. J. Shelley had learned the fate of her friend Elliott. At least the rain had stopped. Ball made a mental note to visit Miss Shelley after court tomorrow morning to offer condolences. Perhaps, maybe the following week, he would see if she needed an escort to church. His prospects in Jack County were beginning to look better.

"I hear tell them savages roasted one of Long's boys alive," the first cowboy said and sipped his beer. "Hear his skull popped open as his brains boiled. Chopped the rest to pieces, cut off their privates an' stuck 'em in their mouths. Scalped 'em, every mother's son."

"Wouldn't surprise me none," the second cowboy said with a grin, bloodshot eyes focused on Ball. "You recollect what they did to Bill Ferguson in Young County, don't you? How they cut out poor Bill's guts and wrapped 'em 'round his throat, strangled him with his own intestines on the prairie." He drained his beer, wiped the foam from his mustache, and elbowed his comrade in the side. "Never seen nothin' like that back in New Hampshire neither, have you there, Lawyer Bull?"

"It's Ball," he answered, tired of their games. "And it's Virginia. Not Maryland, and not New Hampshire." He drained the forty-rod whiskey, set the shot glass on the bar, and turned to face the two grinning idiots. "You boys wear the blue or the gray?" he asked. Jack County had been one of a handful of Texas counties that had voted against secession, so the question wasn't illogical. Some residents had enlisted in the Confederate army after Texas joined the Southern cause, but many remained true to the Union. Ball figured that these boys, however, had stayed home.

"Militia," the second cowboy said. "Kept folks safe from prairie niggers. Hank an' me was stationed at Fort Belknap."

A lie, more than likely, but Ball didn't pursue the matter. "Well, let me tell you what I saw back in Virginia, boys. I saw men in blue and gray blown apart, their guts hanging in pines. I walked across places without touching the ground, the dead were so plentiful. I saw creeks flowing red with blood and drank out of those creeks, not caring, I was so thirsty. I saw hogs rooting in shallow graves, nudging skulls around like balls. There was a rotting arm sticking out of one mound, and we shook that bony, maggot-filled hand for luck as we marched into battle. I saw men decapitated, running twenty more yards before they realized they were dead—like the chicken with its head chopped off. And then there was Point Lookout, after I got captured. Me and about twenty thousand others, living like dogs. Nothing for shelter, no trees, only threadbare tents that acted like sieves when it rained, and boys, that squall we had yesterday and this morning was just a sprinkle compared to what we had to live with on the bay. When it didn't rain, it was a furnace in summer, an icebox in winter. What little ground water we had was filthy—a pig wouldn't even drink out of it—and the guards were promised ten dollars for every Johnny Reb they shot in the line of duty. Murder, it was, plain and simple, and those sons of bitches would just wait for one of us to cross the deadline so they could kill us. The Yankees fed us soup and cornmeal, not enough to feed a rat. So we ate rats. Made a game out of catching the rats—not much else for entertainment, you understand—and then roasted them over a fire. When we were given a candle, we wouldn't use it for light. No, we *ate* the candle. The wax was tasty. Not as good as eating a rat, but it helped keep us alive.

"So, if you think you can make me sick with your childish little stories, you're wasting your time and my time. Good night, gentlemen." He slapped a coin on the bar and looked at the grinning bartender. "Frank," he said, "set these two waddies up with another beer on me. They look a mite pale."

Chapter 3

"With my leg over the saddle, pocket full of
ammunition and my trusty Spencer in my hand, the
world was a good place to live, and life held no
cares, though my body was often tired to exhaustion
and though sometimes when I most hoped for a word
of commendation from General M_____ I received
nothing or if anything a few caustic remarks."
—John B. Charlton

May 19, 1871
Salt Creek Prairie, Texas

"Mother of—" the young trooper began before hunching forward as if he had been gut-shot and spraying his horse's withers with breakfast. *Well,* Corporal John B. Charlton thought, *at least for the horse's sake it's still raining.* He waited for the order, then swung off his blood bay gelding, watching to see if the sick trooper would make it down all right. He did, a bit of a surprise, although he still coughed and spit, wiping his mouth with his shirtsleeve.

Silently, Charlton swallowed down his own bile and followed Sergeant Miles Varily to the charred wagon. A man had been wrapped with trace chains to the tongue, a fire had been built over his head, and he had been burned beyond recognition.

"Scalped him," commented Varily, kneeling beside the grisly carnage.

"Reckon he was dead . . ." Charlton began, but Varily shook his head.

"He was alive when they done it. You can bet your new stripes on that, Corporal. Poor bastard." A trooper sloshed through ankle-deep water and offered the sergeant an arrow for examination.

"Kiowa," Varily announced. "Where'd you get it?"

"Col'nel Mackenzie pulled it from a man 'bout a hunnert yards that way," the private said, pointing to a group of Fourth Cavalry officers and enlisted men. "There's another body out yonder, too."

"Five here," Varily said. "That makes seven." He returned the arrow to the private, who ran back to report to Mackenzie, and repeated, "Poor bastards."

Charlton reached inside his slicker and withdrew his pouch of chewing tobacco. He bit off a substantial amount, hoping it might keep his stomach settled, and offered the quid to Miles Varily, who shook his head while he rose and stretched, cursing the weather.

"Beats nursin' Billy Sherman, huh?" Varily asked.

Busy softening his chaw, Charlton only nodded. He had originally been assigned to escort General Sherman to Fort Sill up in Indian Territory, but those orders had been changed after the Kiowa attack got Sherman's dander up. Instead, Charlton found himself with four troops of horse soldiers, plus sixteen Tonkawa scouts and two civilian guides, chasing these phantom Plains Indians, which left him satisfied. He planned on being a career soldier, and duty in the field certainly held more excitement than drilling back at Fort Richardson or riding along with a four-star general, trying to keep him occupied.

Assistant post surgeon J. H. Patzki walked up, shaking his head at the charred teamster, and Varily ordered a detail to unfasten the corpse so the doctor could examine it and make his report. Charlton was glad when Varily walked away and told the corporal to follow him. His tobacco certainly wouldn't have helped him once Patzki started poking and prodding the remains of what only yesterday had been a human being.

Thousands of corn kernels floated in the water, and mountains of corn had been stacked throughout the massacre site, covered with harnesses, tack, ripped sacks, things the Indians didn't want or need. *A waste,* Charlton thought, then caught himself. The waste had been seven lives, not this litter. Rainwater soaked through his black hat, and his boots sank in the deepening mud. His father had tried to explain to him everything that was expected of a soldier, as if he knew J. B. Charlton would grow up to join the Army, but his father could never have prepared him for this.

Besides, his dad never had the chance. He had died back in Virginia when J. B. was nine years old. In 1865, sixteen-year-old Charlton ran away from home and enlisted in the First Artillery, serving five years in Light Battery K, but manning cannon never had much appeal to him, so he had joined the Fourth Cavalry a year ago and had been sent to Texas.

Varily and Charlton walked to the four other bodies near the wrecked wagons, the sergeant scratching notes in a pad he tried fruitlessly to keep dry. When he pulled an arrow from another corpse, the sickening suction sound made Charlton tremble. A stream of tobacco juice splashed in the puddle beside him, and the sergeant stood up and offered him the bloody arrow. Charlton took it in his gauntleted hands and eyed Varily.

"See them markin's?" Varily asked.

Holding the arrow closer, Charlton made out straight black grooves and spiral red ones on the sides of the weapon. "Yeah," he said. The point was stone, and when he pulled down on the wooden shaft, he found it surprisingly hard. He had spent much of his cavalry career chasing deserters, or assigned special duty as a teamster or stable hand. Taking the field in pursuit of hostiles was new to him and quite exhilarating.

"Another Kiowa arrow?" he asked.

"Un-uh." Varily shook his head. "That one's Comanch, worser than a Kiowa. 'Course all them red sons o' bitches ain't nothin' more than prairie niggers if you ask me. Comanch an' Kiowa been known to ride alongside one another in a raid like this."

Varily took the arrow back and started for another body, but splashing hoofs stopped him, and the two men watched Colonel Mackenzie ride up on his iron-gray single-footer. Mackenzie's salute revealed the two fingers that had been shot off his right hand during the war, and, try as he might, Charlton never could stop himself from staring at the hand. The colonel's icy stare snapped him out of his daze, and he jumped to attention and returned the salute.

"Sergeant," Mackenzie ordered, "I want you to form a burial party, take care of the dead, and report back to Fort Richardson, explain what you've seen here to General Sherman. Corporal Charleston—"

"It's Charlton, sir," Charlton heard himself correcting. He immediately regretted that, for the commander's stare hardened. An eternity of silence passed before Mackenzie looked back at Varily. "The corporal will take over for you and continue with us. Report back that we will remain in pursuit of the hostiles as ordered. Mount up, Corporal."

"Yes, sir," both soldiers shouted and returned to their mounts.

"All right, Corporal," Varily said as the two men waded through the mud, water, and muck. "Keep your eyes open when you're out there, J. B. Watch yourself. Them red niggers is pure devils, slippery, sneaky sons o' bitches, an' I don't wanna be saying 'poor bastard' over your burned body no time soon."

"Thanks," he said and hooked out his tobacco with his finger. "You think we'll find them?"

Varily snorted. "Maybe you'll get lucky," he said, looking at the dark skies. "Maybe they'll drown."

*   *   *

May 21, 1871
Little Wichita River, Texas

"Well?" an irritated Ranald S. Mackenzie asked.

Henry Strong shrugged. "Sorry, Gen'ral," he said, calling Mackenzie by the rank he had been breveted during the late War of the Rebellion. "Rain's washed out the trail. Me and Joe, plus them Tonks, ain't been able to find nothin', and if a Tonk can't find no sign, we're on a forlorn hope. Tonks hate Comanch and Kiowas more'n white folks hereabouts."

Mackenzie sighed, which surprised Henry Strong. He had expected the martinet to blame Strong for losing the trail, blame him for the rain, the mud, the swollen streams, blame him for being born. Ranald Mackenzie was one bona fide son of a bitch.

"All right, Strong," Mackenzie said. "See to your horse and carry on."

Mackenzie spun around in the thick red muck and disappeared inside his mud-stained Sibley tent, where he set up his table and began writing a dispatch to his adjutant back at Fort Richardson. A, B, D, and E Troops had had no luck chasing the Indians responsible for the massacre back at Salt Creek Prairie. If the damnable Texas weather had not been a factor, maybe they would have caught up with the devils, but thunderstorms had turned little creeks into raging rivers, and his men, horses, and wagons could barely manage the mud. High water had forced them to stop on the banks of the Little Wichita, and Mackenzie knew he had no chance of catching the Indians before they disappeared in the Nations, if that's where they were bound. For all he knew, they could be riding for the Llano Estacado, home to plenty of renegade Comanches.

Almost as soon as he had finished his dispatch and started blowing on the ink, an orderly cleared his throat and stuck his head inside the tent. "Colonel, sir?" the pockmarked man said nervously.

"What is it?"

"Lieutenant Boehm just rode up, says he engaged some hostiles near the Big Wichita yesterday."

Swearing angrily, Mackenzie wadded up the paper and hurled it at the surprised soldier. "Damn it, mister, send him in. You're wasting time. Move it, soldier!" The pockmarked face disappeared, almost instantaneously being replaced by an older face with fewer blemishes, a coarser beard, and darker eyes.

Peter Martin Boehm had been in the field for a week and a half now, leading twenty-five men of the Fourth Horse to the Red River and back on what was supposed to have been a thirty-day scout. The A Troop lieutenant looked haggard, and his salute fell far short of military protocol, especially in Ranald S. Mackenzie's army, but the colonel let this slide. Nor did he bother answering the salute.

"You met up with hostiles, Mr. Boehm?" Mackenzie asked.

The lieutenant's head bobbed. "Yesterday afternoon, sir."

"How many?"

When Boehm answered only four or so, Mackenzie's frown stiffened, and he swore underneath his breath. He had hoped to learn that Boehm's force had engaged a strong Indian party and had defeated the hostiles. Then he could report to General Sherman that the murderers of Henry Warren's teamsters had been avenged. That would have satisfied the angry civilians back in Jacksboro. Dejected, he walked to his cot and pulled a bottle of rye from underneath. He opened the liquor with his teeth, stuck the cork inside his blouse pocket, and offered the lieutenant a swig.

"Thank you, sir," Boehm said and drank greedily, returning the bottle to Mackenzie with a smile. Mackenzie wiped the top of the bottle with his sleeve, took a smaller sip, and placed the rye on his desk, leaving the cork pocketed. He had a feeling he wasn't finished with his drinking.

"Go on, Mr. Boehm."

"We ran into them on this side of the river, sir," Boehm reported. "They had killed a few buffalo and were butchering the animals, about a dozen."

"A dozen Indians? I thought you said—"

"A dozen buffalo, sir. Sorry. It was a big herd of buffalo, Colonel, still crossing the river. I have never seen so many buffalo. Must have been at least—"

"Save your nature report for *Scribner's Monthly*, Lieutenant."

"Sorry, sir. We engaged immediately, caught them by surprise. One hostile was killed, but the others mounted and forded the river. We fired, but they shielded themselves with the buffalo, crossed unharmed, and rode away. I ordered a pursuit and search, but our horses were played out, and the hostiles escaped. One of our troopers suffered a flesh wound, as did two horses. Those were the extent of our casualties."

Mackenzie nodded. "Could you tell from whence the hostiles came?"

"Yes, sir. We saw a lot of tracks, Colonel, that had crossed the river, and not buffalo tracks, either. We also found a few boats that had been used to ford the river. Boats made from willow branches and canvas—not the most seaworthy, I warrant, but good construction nonetheless. From surveying the area, I believe a larger party of Indians and stolen livestock crossed the river there. They had come from the south, so I think they raided—"

"They killed seven teamsters on the Salt Creek Prairie a few days ago, Lieutenant. I am in pursuit. Could the tracks you found be followed?"

"No, sir. We lost the trail, else I would still be chasing them, pursuant to my orders. The rains have been heavy, Colonel."

"It doesn't matter, Mr. Boehm." Mackenzie found the bottle and had another drink, a longer pull this time. "The tracks pointed north? I mean, do you think they were bound for the reservation or the Panhandle?"

"The reservation, Colonel, at Fort Sill. I'd bet on that. I suspect they've crossed the Red River by now."

"And so shall I." He passed the bottle to Boehm. "Have a drink, Lieutenant. You will rest your horses tonight at our camp, then ride on to Fort Richardson and make your report. You will also inform Captain Tumlinson that I have given up following the trail and will proceed directly to Fort Sill. Have him wire Colonel Grierson to that effect. I'll find those damned butchers on the reservation."

"Sir? You'll actually follow the hostiles to the agency?" Boehm drank again. He looked like he needed it.

"Those are my orders, Mr. Boehm, from General Sherman himself."

Boehm's eyebrows arched, and he had a final pull before handing the bottle to his commander. "The Quakers will raise holy hell, sir."

"Let them," Mackenzie said.

Chapter 4

"I see much in the Kiowas and all of the other Indians to confirm me that it was right to have them arrested, and I see nothing to make me feel doubtful about it. It has probably saved the lives of many Texas citizens. He whom I endeavor to serve has, I believe, enlightened my understanding in times of need."

—Lawrie Tatum

May 23, 1871
Fort Sill Reserve, Indian Territory

Bowing his head, forty-nine-year-old Lawrie Tatum asked God, in His infinite wisdom, to guide him down the correct path. Tatum's Inner Light was being snuffed out as circumstances propelled him ever farther down the trail of temptation and spiritual error that led to Out of Unity. Beads of sweat formed atop his big bald head as Tatum prayed. He had been tested before, but not like this, and he felt as if he were failing his family, his Elders, the Department of Interior, President Grant, the Army, his Indian charges, and, most importantly, Almighty God.

For not quite two years, Tatum had been in charge of the reservation. The Society of Friends, or Quakers, as they were commonly called, had spoken to Ulysses S. Grant after his inauguration, suggesting that the answer to the Indian Question was God, not the Army. Convert the savages, and the hostilities would end, the Indians would be assimilated into Christian culture, and peace would come to the frontier. Grant thought it made sense, and Tatum had been called to join the Peace Policy, so he had left his Iowa farm for Indian Territory.

"Send Thy humble servant a sign, Lord," Tatum said. "Amen."

When he opened his eyes, he saw a dust-covered, red-bearded soldier with a well-chewed cigar in his mouth and a black porkpie hat in his hand. The visitor was not a Friend—Quakers removed their hats only to honor God—and he did not look much like an Enquirer, or, for that matter, the answer to his prayer.

"I didn't mean to intrude," the soldier said, "but Mr. Leeper sent me in. We didn't know you were in prayer."

Leeper was the agency's interpreter. Tatum stood, wiped his sweaty head with a handkerchief, and held out a meaty hand calloused from years behind the plow. "Thee is most welcome," Tatum said with a smile. "I am Lawrie Tatum."

"I am General William T. Sherman."

"Have a seat. What brings thee to this wilderness?"

They talked about their backgrounds at first. Tatum had been born in New Jersey, then moved to Ohio before settling in Iowa. Sherman said Colonel Grierson at the fort and other officers spoke highly of the Indian agent, even those who disagreed with the Peace Policy. Tatum thanked Grierson, calling the soldier a God-fearing man. He didn't, however, mention his own disillusionment, the tearing of his soul over what he had been taught to believe as a Quaker and what he now felt after living so close to these barbarians. The Kiowas and Comanche had no interest in farming, no interest in accepting Jesus Christ as their savior. All they wanted were free rations and the right to kill, butcher, and rape.

"Mr. Tatum." Sherman tossed his mangled cigar into a spittoon. He had decided to get to the point at last. "A week ago, Indians raided a train in Jack County, Texas, stole forty-odd mules, and slaughtered seven teamsters." Tatum bowed his head in silent prayer. He knew what was coming next. "We have reason to believe that the perpetrators of this barbaric act came from this reservation."

Tatum looked up. His own words surprised him. "Thee likely speaks the truth." Sherman's eyebrows arched, and Tatum went on with his confession. "I have seen many good Indians, but . . ." He sighed. "Such is rare. Kiowas and Comanches come and go on whims. 'Tis not a surprise to hear how these . . . sinners have gone about business as usual. The Indians, Friend, are beyond thee's control, and mine."

The room fell silent briefly. Sherman uncrossed his legs and leaned forward. "Mr. Tatum, here's what I'd like to see happen. I'd like to send these guilty sons of bitches—pardon my bluntness, sir—back to Texas to stand trial for murder."

Tatum's head shook. "Surely thee cannot mean putting a hundred or more savages—"

"No, sir. Not all of them, but the ringleaders, the ones responsible for this raid. Hang them. I know Indians have a fear of dying by the rope. I don't like the Quaker Peace Policy, sir. I'll admit that, but if your plan is to adopt Indians into our culture, then surely they must be subject to our laws."

"The Society of Friends abhors the death penalty," Tatum said sadly.

"And what those butchers did to seven men in Texas?" Sherman snapped. "Does your religion condone that?"

"I must pray on this."

"That's fair. Here's what I'd like you to do, sir. Talk to these Indians. Find out if they indeed committed those depredations. Report back to Colonel Grierson or myself at the fort, and we'll arrest them. If you had to guess . . ."

Tatum was a step ahead of Sherman. "Set-t'ainte is wicked. White Bear it means, but he is known as Satanta."

"Isn't he one of the Kiowas Custer had arrested?"

"Thee remembers well. Custer held Satanta and Lone Wolf in jail a few years ago. Lone Wolf I remember seeing on the sixteenth day of the fifth month, so he could not have taken part in this affair, but Maman-ti is another right arm of

Lucifer, who disappears on the reservation. Maman-ti trusts white men not."

"Anyone else?"

"Ádo-eete. He is called Big Tree. He is a young warrior, yet I find some hope in saving his heathen soul, for he does listen to the word of God." Tatum suddenly snickered. "How could I have forgotten Set-añgya, Sitting Bear, better known as Satank? He is the worst, Friend. He always looks as if he just swallowed raw quinine."

May 25, 1871
Jacksboro, Texas

"Mr. Ball?"

The pleasant-talking Virginian turned around on the warped boardwalk as Samuel W. T. Lanham exited the Jack County courthouse. Lanham was a big man wearing a high-crown black hat, its wide, bound brim curled up slightly on the sides after all the rains. He smoothed his thick mustache before meeting the lawyer.

"Just wanted to thank you for pleading that case out without much of a row. I have bigger fish to fry." He held out his hand and was surprised at Ball's strong grip.

"The sentence was fair, Mr. Lanham."

"Call me Sam."

"All right, Sam. I am Thomas."

As they crossed the street and walked toward the Wichita Hotel, Lanham said, "I hear you wore the gray."

When Ball nodded, Lanham went on. "Me, too. Sergeant in the Third South Carolina Infantry. Took a Yankee ball at Spotsylvania." He had quit school back in '64, when he was eighteen, to enlist in Company K as a private. After the surrender, Lanham was paroled at Greensboro, North Carolina, on May 2, 1865, but the Reconstruction South held no promise for an ambitious man like Sam Lanham. A year later, he married schoolteacher Sarah Meng and moved to Texas, helping his new bride teach school while he started studying law. He passed the bar in 1869 and began practicing in Red River County before Governor Davis appointed him attorney of the "Jumbo" district. Not bad for a backcountry Sandlapper who had to be tutored by his wife. Not bad for a man who would turn twenty-five in July.

"There's a rumor going around that Sherman wants to catch the Indians who killed those teamsters and bring them back here to stand trial," Lanham said.

"I've heard that."

"Do you have an opinion?" Thomas Ball was a taciturn fellow for a lawyer, he thought when the Virginian shrugged. Him? Sam Lanham loved to talk, especially in front of crowds. He hoped to parlay his legal career into a political one. Senator Samuel Lanham had a certain ring to it.

"You're like Joe Woolfolk," Lanham said with a snort.

"How's that?"

"Do you know Woolfolk?"

Ball's head shook.

"He's a counselor," Lanham explained, "though he spends more time on his ranch reading the almanac than in his office reading Blackstone. Peppery bastard. Not much of a talker unless you get him riled. I've tried a few cases against him."

"I haven't had the pleasure," Ball said.

"No matter. Sorry to have gotten off the subject. The reason I was asking you about this rumor is because a few lawyers I've talked too aren't happy with the idea of trying a bunch of Indians for murder in Jack County."

"It would be a first," Ball said without much interest. Maybe pleading his defendant, guilty as the day was long, had rankled him.

"Yeah. It might be a disaster, too. Set us all up for getting scalped." He shrugged. *Then again,* he thought, *it could be the chance of a lifetime.* To prosecute Indians for murdering Texas civilians. A case like that would draw the press from all over.

They stood at the door to Ball's office now, and the two men shook hands again.

"First," Ball said, "they have to catch them."

May 26, 1871
Fort Sill Reserve, Indian Territory

Stone Head wanted to see them, the white man named Lee-Per told Satanta, who grinned. He had arrived a day early for ration day with many of The Principal People, had planned on doing nothing more than watching the *Tehanna* cattle arrive before taking his food and blankets tomorrow, but now he'd get to parley, and Satanta loved to talk, even to the funny-looking man with the enormous, shiny head whose tongue sounded strange even to men who talked white-eye English. Standing straighter, Satanta walked beside Lee-Per to Stone Head's shack, followed by Satank, Eagle Heart, and Fast Bear.

The agent sat behind his desk, dark hat covering his bald head, and Satanta strutted to the front of the desk and waited. "Did thee lead thy warriors across the Red River and attack a wagon train in Texas?" the agent asked. Lee-Per translated, and Satanta announced he wanted to make a speech.

Smiling, Satanta said yes, he indeed had led that raid. He told of the stories going among the people of how Stone Head himself had stolen many goods promised to The Principal People and sent them to the *Tehannas*. He scolded Stone Head for never listening to his talk, never giving The Principal People guns and ammunition. White men planned on sending the iron horse through the country belonging to The Principal People and their friends, the Comanche. So *Gai'gwu* wanted to go live with the Cheyennes on the Antelope Hills. This place stank of *Tehannas*, they were so close to Texas. And if Stone Head and the bluecoats thought they would arrest the great Satanta, well, arresting Satanta had

played out. Yellow Hair had done that once, and Satanta's
wrists would never feel the iron chains again.

He waited for Lee-Per to repeat the words in the foul
white-eye talk before continuing. "I took, a short time ago,
about one hundred of my warriors, with the chiefs Satank,
Eagle Heart, Big Tree, Big Bow, and Fast Bear—"

"Be quiet, you fool!" Satank lashed out.

Frowning, Satanta faced the ancient warrior who had interrupted such a fine speech. "No more names," Satank
added with a scowl. Satanta sought out the other warriors in
the office. Fast Bear nodded in agreement with Satank. Eagle
Heart's face remained a mask, so Satanta turned. He would
not defy Satank. The grandfather had much power among
The Principal People.

"We killed seven men and drove off forty-one mules.
Three of my men were killed," Satanta said, "but we are willing to call it even."

"Did thee lead this raid?" Stone Head asked again, and
Lee-Per repeated the question in words Satanta understood.

He thrust his chin out proudly. "If any other Indian comes
here and claims the honor of leading the party, he will be
lying to you," he said. "I did it myself." He grinned. Maman-
ti had gathered the warriors for the raid, but he wasn't here.
He never showed up when on the reservation, not even for
rations, never learned that the way to more goods, more
power among these white ants, was to talk big. Maman-ti
was a squaw. Satanta spit. He looked into Stone Head's tear-
filled eyes and dared the big man to do something. *He was
Satanta.*

"Thee cannot do such . . ." Stone Head began.

"We don't expect to do any raiding around here this summer," Satanta announced, "but we expect to raid in Texas."
Satank nodded as well.

The agent shook his head sadly and said he had heard
enough. He bowed his head for a moment, then lifted it and
spoke to Lee-Per. "Tell Satanta that a great leader of the bluecoats wishes to talk to him. Tell him that Friend Grierson

shall arrange a meeting, perhaps tomorrow. Tell him that if he speaks to these men, then I will do what I can to see that his people receive guns and ammunition at the next ration day."

Satanta liked that a lot. He would get to make another speech. Stone Head had dismissed him, so he followed Lee-Per outside and walked to the corrals where the rations were being issued. A few minutes later, one of the agent's friends bounded like a deer out of the office, running toward the soldier-fort, clutching a white man's paper in his fist like a war axe. Stone Head left a minute later, head bowed, big hat pulled down low, and briskly walked to the meeting house to pray to his God.

Chapter 5

"You have asked for those men to kill them. But they are my people, and I am not going to let you have them. You and I are going to die right here."
—Kicking Bird

May 27, 1871
Fort Sill, Indian Territory

In ten years of military service, he had run across many commanding officers he disliked, but up until this moment Colonel Benjamin Henry Grierson had never said anything that could have been construed as improper, disrespectful, ungentlemanly—and certainly nothing unchristian—about a general who wore the blue. Now, however, on the creaking veranda of his quarters, he heard himself whisper in a dry voice, thankfully low enough so no one else could hear, "That redheaded son of a bitch is about to get us all killed."

Not quite forty-five years old, Grierson felt a lifetime removed from Jacksonville, Illinois, where he had taught music before the war. In all of his career, he had never sensed his own death this close—not even riding behind Rebel lines during the cavalry raids that made him a national hero. What was he doing here? He should be listening to a piano recital in the parlor of some lovely Morgan County home, not hearing the raving diatribe of an Army officer whom many during the War of the Rebellion—both North and South—had believed to be quite mad.

General William Tecumseh Sherman, dressed in a moth-eaten civilian suit of black broadcloth, chomped on an unlit cigar and paced back and forth across the porch, spouting out vehement sentences and listening to the translations by Horace P. Jones, the post interpreter. High-browed Sherman's red hair was thinning and turning gray, and the stubble of beard on his face, plus his shabby attire, made him resemble a drunk coming off a weeklong fandango with John Barleycorn rather than general-in-chief of the U.S. Army. About twenty Kiowas from the nearby agency had gathered that afternoon to hear Sherman. That was a pretext. Sherman wanted to hear what the Indians had to say, and if they admitted what he thought they would, he would have them in irons before dusk.

Now more and more Kiowas were drawn to the grounds in front of Grierson's house. It was Saturday, and that meant most Indians would be coming to the agency for their rations, and as soon as they found out about the big powwow at Grierson's home, they would hurry to the fort to see what was going on. The colonel could hear them talking among themselves in that impossible-to-understand singsong chatter of theirs, the anger unmistakable. Many wore blankets around their waists or wrapped over their shoulders despite the afternoon heat. Sherman didn't seem to notice this—or he didn't care—but Grierson did. He had been on the frontier long enough to realize that a thick woolen blanket could conveniently conceal a weapon.

"Tell Satanta I want to hear what happened in Texas," Sherman commanded. "Again."

Horace Jones hooked a quid of tobacco from his cheek with a forefinger, spit, and muttered something in Comanche. Both the interpreter and Indian spoke fluent Comanche, but only a Kiowa could understand Kiowa.

Satanta thumped his chest and began a long-winded tale as Sherman marched back and forth, back and forth. The Kiowa was burly for an Indian, his arms so powerful he could likely lift an upright piano and not break a sweat. He appeared to be in his mid-fifties, though Grierson found it hard to tell with an Indian. Long hair the color of a raven, glistening in the afternoon sun, fell to Satanta's left shoulder, a long braid dangling over the front of his major general's jacket, a gift from one of the treaty conferences of years ago, while on his right side the hair was cut short just below the ear. When Satanta finished speaking, he folded his arms and grunted, pleased with himself.

The rawboned interpreter turned to Sherman and drawled, "Ol' Satanta says he led that raid. Says the Kioways are sick to death of not gettin' their annuity goods, so he, Satank, Big Bow, Big Tree, Eagle Heart, Fast Bear, and Maman-ti crossed the Red with about a hundred bucks. Killed seven Texicans and got forty-one mules. Says he lost three men, so he'll call it even if you will."

With a stream of blasphemy, Sherman ripped the cigar from his mouth and whirled around. "That pompous old blackheart," he said and stared at Satanta for half a minute before resuming his pacing.

If he kept up at his current rate, Grierson thought, Sherman's scuffed boots would soon wear through the planks.

The cigar returned to Sherman's mouth. "That's the same story Satanta told that Quaker agent, isn't it, Colonel?"

"Yes, sir," Grierson replied.

They were here because of the Indian agent, Lawrie Tatum, and his troubled conscience. Tatum had heard Satanta boast of leading the raid and had immediately informed Grierson and Sherman. Tatum even said he thought the Indian leaders should be punished—Grierson had no idea how that would sit with the officials at the Indian Bureau and the peace-loving Quakers back East—and Sherman rabidly agreed. He was like a bulldog about that raid. Obsessive. Maybe with good reason. Satanta and his raiding party could very well have killed Sherman and his group down in Texas.

Satanta suddenly frowned hard, suspicious. He began speaking to Jones again, gesturing wildly. Grierson stroked his full beard and studied the crowd of Indians, trying to pick

out the ones Satanta had named, trying to figure out which
one he would have to kill first with his Colt revolver if this
parley deteriorated into a shooting war. He felt certain it
would before long. He didn't know Maman-ti or Fast Bear,
not on sight at least. Big Bow and Eagle Heart were not
around, but they'd show up. The way things looked, the entire Kiowa nation would soon be camped on Fort Sill's parade grounds. Satank sat cross-legged on the ground behind
Satanta, calmly smoking a pipe. He was older than Methuselah but probably the toughest fighter among the Kiowas. He
would be the one to kill first. Kicking Bird was there, talking
to Stumbling Bear. That was good. Kicking Bird was a
peacekeeper and hadn't been on the raid. He might be able to
stop any bloodshed.

And Big Tree? Grierson wet his lips. The young brave had
arrived with Satanta. Where was he now? The colonel
scanned the crowd of Indians again.

"He's changin' his story, Gen'ral," Jones said after Satanta finished his second speech. "Says he was there but
didn't do nothin' but blow his bugle. Says he killed no one.
Says the white men are his friends, but the Kioways need
their rations. He wants you to go back to Washington an' see
what can be done about no more short-changin' your friends
the Kioways."

Sherman stopped long enough to comment, "He's like a
damned politician."

"Yep," Jones agreed. "Ain't called the Orator of the Plains
for nothin'."

Grierson cut in. "Begging the general's pardon, sir, but I
can't find Big Tree in the crowd. He's gone, sir."

The general tore the cigar from his mouth again and
barked out, "Well, Colonel, find him. I want him arrested.
I'm arresting every damned one of these red brigands."

"Yes, sir." He spun around, spotted the two lieutenants
nearest him, and told them to take a company, find Big Tree,
arrest him, and bring him back here. The junior officers
saluted and promptly took off toward the stone corrals, no

doubt eager to get as far away from the colonel's house as quickly as possible.

Grierson didn't blame them.

"All right, Mr. Jones," Sherman said. "I want you to tell Satanta exactly what I think of him. Tell him he is a damned coward. Tell him he is a woman. Those teamsters he killed were not soldiers, but I am. Warriors should fight warriors, not innocent people. Tell him if he is man enough and wants to fight, the United States Army will give him that opportunity. Tell him I would like to kill the gutless bastard right now."

When Jones hesitated, Sherman snapped, "I said tell him."

Satanta straightened at Jones's translation. So did several other Kiowas. Satank stopped puffing on his pipe. Someone in the crowd began singing his death song. Cautiously, Grierson reached to unsnap the flap over his holster, only to realize he already had done so. At that moment, two Kiowa women ducked inside the house. The colonel caught himself swearing again. Sherman and Grierson had a surprise waiting inside that house, and those two women could spoil everything. He heard the scuffling of feet inside his frame home, a muffled shout, the breaking of glass. He hoped they hadn't smashed Alice's china. He stopped in midthought, smiling at the insanity of it all. Here he stood in front of a nation of armed Kiowa warriors who were growing angrier each minute, and he was worried about his wife's favorite dishes.

Outside, a Kiowa roared in anger.

It was Satanta.

Give the general credit, Grierson thought, his smile gone as quickly as it had appeared. *He has nerve.* Unflinching, Sherman stopped his pacing and stared down the Kiowa leader. "Tell him that he is under arrest for murder," Sherman instructed Jones. "Tell him he and those others he named will go back to Texas. Tell him he's going to be hanged for his butchery."

Jones's words sank home again. Satanta ripped off the blanket wrapped around his waist, screamed in Kiowa, not Comanche, and gripped the butt of an old cap-and-ball revolver near his breechcloth.

"What's he saying?" Sherman demanded.

"That he'd rather die here!" Jones said hurriedly, backing away and reaching for his own revolver.

Grierson didn't wait for Sherman's order. "Now!" he shouted, and the wooden shutters behind him sprang open, revealing ten black troopers leveling Springfield and Spencer carbines at the Indians.

Satanta jerked his hand away from the revolver, lifted his arms high, and screamed, this time in the only English he knew. "Don't shoot! Don't shoot!"

Old Satank spit and mumbled something in disgust. Kicking Bird leaped onto the bottom doorstep, between Satanta and Sherman, and sang out. Someone was shouting near the trader's store. That death song seemed louder and louder. Inside the house, the Kiowa women wailed.

"What's he saying?" Sherman asked.

Grierson looked down, saw he held his Colt, saw the hammer had been cocked. He didn't even remember drawing the weapon.

"Kickin' Bird says he's a peace chief. Says you can ask Stone Head or the chief of the buffalo soldiers this. He means Tatum an' the colonel. They'll tell you the same. Says he has done ever'thing he can to stop those raids. Says he will see that those mules are returned. But he says you must not take his brothers to Texas to hang. It is better that they be shot here."

Sherman scoffed. "It's too good for those sons of bitches."

"Release his brothers, Kickin' Bird says. There need not be no more blood spilled."

Suddenly aware that he was holding his breath, Grierson exhaled. Sherman tossed the ruined cigar onto the porch floor and said, "Tell Kicking Bird this: The president has heard of you. We all appreciate what you have done. But this is my day, and what I say will have to go. I want those men. Satanta, Satank, and Big Tree are going to Texas to stand trial."

What about Big Bow, Eagle Heart, Fast Bear, and Maman-ti? Grierson wondered.

Kicking Bird's anger was obvious. He screamed something, pointing his finger at Sherman, then reached for an arrow from his quiver.

"What's he saying?"

Something was going on at the trader's store. Grierson heard more shouts. Glass shattered. Someone—an Indian—ran out the back door, pursued by soldiers. Buffalo soldiers. Lieutenant Pratt's squad. It must be Big Tree.

"You've asked for those men to kill 'em," Jones translated. "But Kickin' Bird says they're his people, an' you can't have 'em. He says, 'You an' I are gonna die right here.' "

A gunshot exploded from near the trader's store. Grierson's heart leaped in his chest. He expected that to start a war, but . . . nothing happened. A few heads turned toward the sound of the shot, but Kicking Bird stared directly at Sherman. Both men's faces hardened.

"Tell him that he and Stumbling Bear won't be hurt," Sherman said. "Unless they try something stupid."

Satank was mumbling something. Kicking Bird had stopped at the gunshot, leaving the arrow in his quiver. Now he spun around, shouting in Kiowa. An Indian on a piebald mare loped toward them. Lone Wolf. Grierson recognized him. The colonel looked back across the grounds. Pratt and his men had caught Big Tree, were escorting him. The warrior looked almost naked, shaken. He was just a boy, Grierson thought, probably still in his teens. A Kiowa woman ran forward and gave the brave a blanket before she was shoved aside by a black sergeant.

Stumbling Bear had walked away from the porch. Raising arrows and bow over his head, he began shrieking at the Kiowas. Haranguing them, Grierson guessed. Firing them up for a massacre. Lone Wolf flew from his horse, landed on the ground, and ran forward. He carried two rifles.

"What's he saying?"

Sherman and Kicking Bird—who was facing the general once more—were still talking. In the crowd, Stumbling Bear whirled and notched an arrow. Lone Wolf pushed his way through the Indians, tossed one of his weapons to a nearby boy. The kid thumbed back the hammer and sang. Two women cheered Stumbling Bear. Old Satank smiled.

"What's he saying?"

Grierson realized then what was about to happen. Lone Wolf or Stumbling Bear would kill Sherman. They'd soon all be dead. "Now!" the colonel commanded as Lone Wolf leveled his carbine. A trumpet blared. Through the corner of his eye, Grierson spotted Troops D and H springing from their hiding places in the stables, weapons raised, blocking any retreat, ready to counterattack if need be. By then, though, Grierson and Sherman would be dead.

The Kiowas shrieked. Grierson forgot about his Colt and ran, leaped, felt himself flying through the air. Lone Wolf hesitated. *Avoid bloodshed,* the colonel told himself. A slim chance remained that no one would be killed. Grierson dropped his revolver just before his lean body slammed into Lone Wolf. He reached up, grabbed for the rifle's breech, felt the case-hardened iron bite into his hand, preventing the hammer from striking the percussion cap.

An arrow sailed harmlessly into the brush in front of the porch. Some Indian had knocked Stumbling Bear astray, spoiled his aim, saved Sherman's life. A trooper rushed forward and shoved Lone Wolf aside. Two more sprang from the house and aimed their weapons at Stumbling Bear, yelling at him not to move an inch. Grierson freed his hand from the rifle Lone Wolf had dropped, tearing the skin. Blood poured freely as he rose to his knees. An orderly stood beside him.

"You all right, Colonel, sir?"

He nodded.

Sherman had stopped pacing again. The yard fell silent. Somehow, some way . . . everyone remained alive.

"All right, interpreter," Sherman said. "Tell Kicking Bird

this. Tell him that we are holding Big Tree, Satanta, and Satank. Tell him those stolen mules must be delivered to me in ten days."

Grierson hardly listened to Kicking Bird's answer or Jones's translation. He stood, wrapped a handkerchief around his bloody hand, and watched in amazement as the Kiowas walked away. All except Satank, Satanta, and Big Tree, now under guard by Grierson's black troopers.

"Very good, Colonel," Sherman said, unbuttoning his coat and withdrawing another cigar from an inside pocket. "You all right?"

Grierson glanced at his hand. "Yes, sir," he said. "What are my orders, General?"

"Have those murdering savages shackled and thrown into whatever serves as a guardhouse."

Grierson gave the order wearily and climbed the steps. The sun had just dipped behind the hills, and the wind had picked up. Refreshing . . . cool. He felt glad, and surprised, to be alive.

Jones carved off another piece of tobacco and shoved it into his mouth. The troopers who had remained inside Grierson's house marched out, releasing the two Kiowa women, who ran to catch up with their retreating people. A gray-bearded sergeant apologized that a window pane had been shattered.

"When you get them mules back, Gen'ral," Jones said, "you gonna release them Kioways then?"

"Hell no," Sherman answered. "I meant what I said. Those red bastards are going to Texas to stand trial for murder. They'll be found guilty and hanged. That's justice."

Grierson cleared his throat. "Are you serious, sir? On what authority can Indians be tried under civil law?"

Sherman bit off the end of the cigar and stuck the stogie in his mouth. "By mine," he said. "Those sons of bitches almost killed me down in Texas."

Chapter 6

"Capts. Warren and DuBose intend erecting a suitable monument to their memory."
—**Dallas Herald,** June 3, 1871

May 28, 1871
Salt Creek Prairie, Texas

"You didn't know Samuel, did you?"

M. J. Shelley didn't look up after asking the question. She busied herself pulling weeds around the rock cairn the Fourth Cavalry boys had piled up to mark the common grave of those unlucky teamsters killed in the Indian raid. Somebody had carved a "7" into the rocks, denoting the number of men buried here, and another had draped a crucifix over the top of the monument.

"I didn't have the pleasure," Thomas Ball answered in his sweetest-sounding Virginia accent. He kept his right hand on the butt of the little Remington in his coat pocket while watching with a mix of amazement and apprehension as the pretty brunette pruned the grave. He certainly wouldn't be sticking his bare hands around that pile of rocks. It looked like the perfect hiding place for scorpions, spiders, and rattlesnakes. Besides, his stomach felt uneasy. Maybe it was because he hadn't quite gotten used to the drinking water out in these parts. Or perhaps because this place still looked like death, and he had seen enough of that during the war. The burned wreckage of the wagons had been piled together in a trash heap. Rain had washed away the blood, while Yankee cavalrymen and sick-headed souvenir seekers had collected most of the arrows, spent bullets, and other plunder, but the wind moaned like something straight out of Washington Irving, and Ball kept scanning the horizon toward Cox Mountain, half-expecting painted warriors to come swarming toward them. He hadn't been in Texas long. Maybe you got used to this after a spell.

He didn't like being here, but M. J. had asked him to take her after church this morning, and Ball wasn't about to tell her no.

"He was sweet." She rose from the blanket Ball had spread to protect her dress while she knelt beside the grave and looked at him with those beautiful yet sad eyes. "You wouldn't expect that from a teamster, but he was a nice man. I mean, he wasn't in love with me or anything, and I only thought of him as a friend, but it hurts when a friend dies. Do you know what I mean?"

"Yes." '

"Mr. Long died, too, and he was a good man as well. He used to tease me that he was jealous of Samuel, of all the attention I gave him. But he was just joking. Samuel was too old for me, and so was Mr. Long."

And just how old are you? Ball wanted to ask, but his father had raised him better than go about asking a woman that question. She could have been eighteen or twenty-eight. He hadn't a clue, but figured she was of marrying age or she wouldn't have let him escort her, unchaperoned, on a buggy ride after church.

He had never seen anyone like M. J. Shelley in Northumberland County.

She stood by his side now. He could smell the fresh soil on her hands, see her brown hair matted on her neck by sweat. M. J. handed him one end of the blanket, and together they folded it up and stuck it behind the seat of the two-spring Phaeton he had rented. She wore a cardinal and navy blue cotton dress trimmed with Hercules braid and anchor, and French kid dress boots that must have taken an hour to button.

He had shed his linen duster and bell crown hat, and wanted to take off that uncomfortable paper collar and black cravat, not to mention his black coat, but he did have an appearance to maintain. M. J. Shelley and the other residents of Jack County thought him to be a Virginia gentleman, so he would sweat in his Sunday best and dream of a nice bath, a nickel cigar, and a shot of Jameson until he got back to town.

They stared at the grave for a few minutes in silence.

"Do you think he suffered?" she asked.

Ball shook his head. "From what I hear, they were killed pretty quick." Brushing away the gnats and mosquitoes, he thought back to his own experiences in battle. "He was scared, no doubt, but I don't think he felt much pain."

That was a lie, though. Maybe the others died quickly, but not Samuel Elliott. Ball had been in the courthouse when a Fourth Cavalry courier told what the troopers had found at the massacre site. Samuel Elliott had been wounded already when the Indians grabbed him, chained him to a wagon tongue, tortured him, and roasted him alive. Two drunken waddies, and many others in the Green Frog, had repeated that story often since the news had arrived.

"Do you think the Army will capture the Indians that did this?" she asked.

Ball decided not to lie this time. From what he had learned about Indian raiders during his two short years in Texas, they usually disappeared into Indian Territory. They reminded him of Mosby's Rangers back in Virginia. Strike fast and hard and disappear before the Yankees knew what hit them.

"It'll be hard, M. J.," he said. "Rains will make tracking them difficult, and if they cross the Red . . . I'm just not optimistic."

She sighed heavily and dabbed her big eyes with the handkerchief Ball had given her earlier that afternoon.

"I hope the Army does find them, even if they're on the Fort Sill reservation," she said and wadded up the handkerchief in a balled fist. "And I pray to God that they strike down those red bastards: women, children, every one of them."

He stared at her with his mouth open. He had never heard a woman use such language, especially on the Sabbath. He recovered from his shock and helped her climb into the buggy. After offering her a drink from his canteen, he pulled on his duster and hat, jumped into the seat beside her, and whipped the mule. It was a long ride back to Jacksboro, and he was in a hurry. He didn't look back, but M. J. did, staring at the rock cairn until it faded from sight because of distance and dust. Only then did she turn around.

She didn't say a thing until they reached the livery in Jacksboro.

M. J. told him she wasn't hungry, so Ball saw her to the door of her home and then walked to his room at the Widow Baggett's boarding house. He changed his clothes, opting for a blue pullover shirt, black ribbon tie, striped britches, suspenders, vest, and gray bowler. He wound his watch, checking the time against the enameled iron Washington clock on the oak sideboard. Rent at the widow's place included supper except on Sundays, and, since he had skipped dinner to take M. J. to the massacre site, he was starving. He walked to the dining room at the Wichita Hotel and found a seat in a corner booth.

Amanda Doniphan waited on him.

"How was your picnic?" she asked.

He looked into her green eyes but couldn't tell if what he saw was amusement or jealousy. She was tall, only two or three inches shorter than himself, with silky blond hair and perfect teeth, the latter a rarity on the frontier. Unlike most Texicans, she had no accent, and while she wasn't as beautiful as M. J. Shelley, Amanda was certainly pretty and carried herself with confidence and independence. Some waitresses would take a lot for a tip, but not Amanda. Tell a joke she didn't appreciate, flirt with her too much or say something inappropriate, and she would make sure the meal was cold or heavy on the pepper. God help you if you slapped her bottom in front of customers. She'd hit back. Ball had been here a few nights when drunken cowboys or soldier boys learned a painful lesson.

"Picnic?" he asked dumbly.

"I saw you and Miss Shelley take off in one of Mr. Winders's fancy buggies after church," she said.

"Oh." Ball looked around. The dining room was quiet this time of evening. When his gaze returned to Amanda, her look hadn't changed, and he still couldn't read her. "It wasn't a picnic. M. J. wanted me to take her to the grave where those teamsters are buried. I think she's pining over Samuel Elliott."

It was Amanda's turn to say "Oh." She waited a moment, finally smiled and said, "You haven't eaten anything?"

"Not since a cup of the widow's coffee for breakfast."

"You must be famished."

"You're right. What's the special tonight?"

She shook her head. "You don't want the special, Tomball." He smiled. Everyone called him Thomas—even his parents—or Mr. Ball or Attorney Ball, but Amanda was different. Tom Ball, only she ran the words together deliberately. He liked the way she said it.

"Well, Amanda Doniphan, what *do* I want?"

The waitress pursed her lips, stared at the ceiling, and suggested, "Fried potatoes, burned steak, two biscuits, peach cobbler, and coffee with the sugar boiled in it. And while you're waiting, a glass of that Irish whiskey you like from the bar."

He smiled. "You've figured me out in six months."

"Five months, and I had you pegged after only three. You're predictable, Tomball. Are all Virginia lawyers as easy to read as you?"

"I don't know, Amanda. One of these nights, I might just surprise you."

She laughed. "How? Order that forty-rod rotgut in the saloon that Ivy calls rye?"

Before he could tell her about the swill poured into an Irish whiskey bottle at the Green Frog he was forced to drink when he didn't feel like splurging at the Wichita, she was heading for the kitchen to place his order. By the time she returned with his glass of whiskey, a few other customers had entered the dining room, so she didn't have time to talk to him. That disappointed him. He liked Amanda Doniphan, her straightforwardness, her humor. There weren't many women like her in Northumberland County, either.

He studied the new customers while sipping his whiskey. One was a drummer of some sort, who wanted the special and milk, and Amanda didn't try to steer him away from the liver and onions. The other was a man and wife who took Amanda's recommendation of fried steak. Ball had seen the man in the Weatherford courthouse, although he couldn't recall his name. Maybe this was the man Samuel Lanham had told him about. He was a lawyer, even if he didn't dress the part. His Johnny Reb cavalry trousers were stuffed in calf-high moccasins, and he wore a dusty bib-front shirt with fancy stitching on the front, similar to ones the irregulars wore in Missouri during the war, and a dirty red bandana. Dust had risen like steam when he flopped his big hat on the table and ran his fingers through wet blond hair.

Recognizing Ball, the man nodded a greeting. Ball held up his glass in acknowledgment. He thought about going over there, offering to buy them a drink, but the man's wife said something, and he turned to talk to her, tugging on the ends of his bushy mustache and answering her in a thick Texas accent. His wife was pretty, too, dressed in a plain dress of blue gingham. Amanda brought them coffee, leaving the pot on their table, then gave the drummer his milk.

She stopped at Ball's table with a smile. "How's your drink, Tomball?"

"Fine."

"Supper'll be out shortly."

He nodded in the couple's direction. "Amanda, I know that man, but not his name. He's an attorney, isn't he?"

"Sure. Y'all haven't banged heads yet in some courtroom?"

"Nope."

"Lucky you, Tomball. That's Joe Woolfolk and his wife, Lizzie. She's sweet as can be, but he's as feisty as they come. No offense, my friend, but if you ever find yourself in a courtroom with that old mule, you had best plead your client guilty, settle before the case goes to a jury, or just give up and skedaddle. And Lord help you if you beat him in a case."

He took a sip of whiskey and asked, smiling, "Why?"

"He don't like to lose, Tomball. Joe Woolfolk's more apt to shoot you than file an appeal."

Chapter 7

*"O sun you remain forever, but we Koiet-senko must
die. O earth you remain forever, but we Koiet-senko
must die."*

—Satank

May 29, 1871
Fort Sill Reserve, Indian Territory

*On the 27th of the 5th month, Satanta and various
other Kiowas came after their rations, when he told
me that he had lately led a party of about one
hundred Indians to Texas, captured a train, killed
seven men, and taken all the mules of the train. I
immediately went to the Post to have Satanta and the
five chiefs who accompanied him in the raid
arrested, which General Sherman, who was at the
Post, and Col. Grierson, the Post Commander, were
more than willing to do. They arrested Satanta,
Satank, and Big Tree. Eagle Heart escaped. Big Bow
and Fast Bear were not here with the others.*

*I know of no reason why Indians should not be
held amenable to the law of the country the same as
other subjects. The treatment they have received of
the Government, however, has caused them to believe
that they are the stronger party, or else they say that
they would not receive presents and annuities for*

*ceasing their wars and depredations. They assert
that when they conquer a neighboring tribe, they
receive of, but never give presents to, the vanquished
party.*

Lawrie Tatum studied what he had so far penned to Enoch
Hoag, superintendent of the Indians, and wondered what his
boss would think. He had a fair inkling. Friend Tatum had
fallen Out of Unity, Elder Hoag and others in Washington
would say. Maybe they would pray for his soul, his Inner
Light. More than likely, however, they would crucify him.
Tatum swallowed down the bile of his own disillusionment,
his sacrilege, and sighed heavily, alone in the confines of his
small office.

Back to Iowa, he figured. Back to the soil, planting corn,
maybe trying alfalfa. He would return home a shamed man,
forced to resign, perhaps even fired, a failure to his Indian
charges, a failure to the Society of Friends. Tatum, the critics
would say, sold his soul to the devil, the blasphemous United
States Army, traded in his children, the filthy Kiowas, and
not even for thirty pieces of silver.

Let them think what they want, Tatum thought, dipped his
pen in the quill, signed his name in an angry scrawl, and
dated the letter. He knew, if no one else did, that he had done
what he thought best. His decision had been just. God knew
that. Didn't He?

After stuffing the report into the envelope and sealing it,
Tatum heard a light rapping on the doorjamb. Although not
in the mood for visitors, he forced himself to say, in an inviting tone, "Enter." William T. Sherman stepped inside the office, and Tatum smiled with relief. Sherman understood
him . . . not that that would mean a thing to Enoch Hoag,
who had never been west of the Ohio River, and those other
sanctimonious bleeding hearts among the Society of Friends
who had never come closer to a real Indian than while turning the pages in some James Fenimore Cooper novel. Such

thoughts made him ashamed, so he silently asked his Savior for forgiveness while directing the general to a wobbly chair.

"I thought thee had left for Fort Gibson," Tatum said once Sherman had settled into his seat and Tatum had closed his silent prayer that he would expound on come bedtime.

"Tomorrow, Mr. Tatum. Wanted to say good-bye."

"I have enjoyed my conversations with thee these past few days. Would to God others could accept our decisions. I pray neither God nor history will condemn us."

Sherman pushed back his small hat. "I care not one whit what history says, sir. We did the right thing. You made a lot of friends in Texas, Mr. Tatum, and at military posts across our nation."

"I have made enemies, as well."

"I think you'll learn, as I have, that it's easy to live with enemies." The general fired up his stogie. "Threatening the Kiowas—and Comanches and other savages—with hanging will cut down the number of raids. Satanta, Big Tree, and . . . that old . . . Methuselah . . ."

"Satank," Tatum said.

"Satank. Right. Thank you. Those three should never go forth again." He paused to bring his cigar to life. "I wrote a letter yesterday to General Townsend. I told him that if your Indian Department objects to a Texas jury, we should try them by military tribunal. If they go free, for any reason in the world, no whites will be safe from Kansas to the Rio Grande. This will be a lawful proceeding. The legal course is the right one, sir. Your Kiowas dread that far greater than a minié ball."

Tatum's head shook sadly. "They are not my Kiowas. And I fear it is not my Indian Department." He gestured at his report to Hoag. "Not once this reaches Elder Hoag."

"I'll do what I can to help you there, Mr. Tatum, but there's one more thing you can do for me."

"What more does thee wish of me?"

"Colonel Mackenzie will arrive in a few days. I don't know what's keeping him. Weather, maybe. Anyway, I have left orders for him to transport these three vermin back to Jack County, Texas, to stand trial. The courts are getting ready for that now. Be a lot of excitement. Anyway, we need witnesses for the prosecution, and you'd make a damn fine one. I can authorize your transportation with Mackenzie's Fourth Cavalry."

The agent bowed his head, finally looked up, and said, "I would make a poor witness." He held up his hand to stop Sherman's objection. "I would provide the defense with a fine target, a Judas, a man likely to have been fired by the Indian superintendent by the time thee's case comes to trial."

Sherman laughed, which surprised Tatum, and flicked cigar ash on the floor. "I see your point, though I don't think that'll have much weight with a Texas jury. Still, it would give the newspaper worms fodder for their presses. How about if we put your interpreter on the stand?"

Tatum nodded vigorously. "Mathew Leeper is a fine, God-fearing man."

"And he heard everything you did?"

"Yes, plus he speaks the languages of Kiowa and Comanche. He would make thee a much stronger witness. And he lived in Texas with the Comanches on the reservation in the late fifties."

"Good. Well, I've kept you long enough, Mr. Tatum." Sherman rose and offered his hand. "Best of luck to you, sir."

"And to thee."

June 8, 1871
Fort Sill, Indian Territory

Big Tree watched.

Bad Hand, the bluecoat chief from Texas, had arrived four days ago, having missed seeing the Great White Leader from Washington, the man who had ordered Big Tree's wrists and ankles locked with iron. Yet this white-eye called Sherman had left word for Bad Hand to take Big Tree, Satank, and Sa-

tanta back to Texas to be hanged. Hanged! That was no way
for one of The Principal People to die. What could a warrior
with an elongated neck do after death? Grandfathers said
they would not be allowed to travel the Great Journey, but
Big Tree was not sure if he believed this. He was not sure
what he believed anymore.

Satank believed it, however, and would never die such a
death. Of this, Big Tree felt certain, so he watched the *Koiet-
senko* as the bluecoats led them out of the dark, dank dun-
geon and into the blinding light of Mother Sun, which Big
Tree had not seen in days.

Sunlight proved painful, but Big Tree kept forcing his
eyes open until the spots vanished and he could see clearly.

Satank held a knife in his shackled hands, hidden from the
bluecoats by the blanket draped over his arms. After today, the
white-eyes would wonder how Satank got such a weapon, but
Big Tree knew. Long before Big Tree was born, Satank had
swallowed an eagle's wing feather. That was his medicine; it
stopped bullets from harming him, with the exception of the
time he was shot in the mouth. Big Tree never understood
how that happened. Perhaps Satank's medicine was not strong
that day, but his power had kept him alive during many raids
against the white-eyes, *Tehannas,* Mexicans, and other enemies of The Principal People. A few nights ago, after the scout
Caddo George Washington visited the prisoners, bringing
them tobacco and word that the stolen mules had been returned to the bluecoats, Satank had coughed up the eagle
feather and used his power to transform it into a knife.

"We will die as *Gai'gwu,*" he told Big Tree and Satanta
after Caddo George had gone.

"Put that away!" Satanta cried. "Did not you hear Caddo
George? The mules have been returned. The bluecoats will
set us free."

Satank grunted. "You are a fool. They will not let us go,
and I do not plan on dying among *Tehannas* with my neck
twisted, dancing with my moccasins not touching the
ground."

Big Tree had remained silent, wondering. It was hard to know who to believe, Satank or Satanta. Both men were wise, much wiser than Big Tree, and both had more experience dealing with the whites. As he spotted two corn-filled wagons surrounded by scores of bluecoats, Big Tree realized that Satank had been right. The prisoners would be returned to Texas. It did not matter that the mules captured during the raid had been returned. The white-eyes demanded revenge. They would go back to Texas for this thing called a trial.

The sight of the soldiers and wagons caused Satanta to stumble. He looked for a friend, his eyes finally lighting on the bluecoat officer Grierson, and broke out of ranks as fast as he could, chains clinking on the ground, crying, "My friend! My friend! My friend!" Two bluecoats ran after Satanta and prodded him with the knives attached to their rifles, but Grierson waved them off. When Satank saw this, he moved toward Grierson as well, only Big Tree knew that Satank was not about to plead for his life. Unlike Satanta, he had not lost his nerve, did not plan on making some fine speech and crying. Begging was not the way of a *Koiet-senko*.

Still, if Satank killed Grierson, the bluecoats would surely cut down his murderer, along with Satanta and Big Tree, and Big Tree did not want to die. He had barely seen twenty winters, and his death would be of his own choosing. He would not be shot down like a dog because a bitter, feebleminded *Koiet-senko* wanted to travel the Great Journey to join his dead son.

He must act quickly. Lunging forward, Big Tree grasped Satank with his own manacled hands. Satanta heard Satank's cry and spun, forgetting Grierson, knowing what was happening, hurrying back to help Big Tree prevent the assassination. Bluecoats surrounded them, and Grierson walked away to talk to the other soldier-leader, Bad Hand, perhaps never to know how close he came to death.

Big Tree's grip was strong, for he was young, and Satank was old. "Why have you done this?" Satank cried out, tears streaming down his face, and Big Tree could not look the old

warrior in his eyes. "Must I die among women?" More bluecoats forced the prisoners toward the wagons, helping Big
Tree and Satanta into the back of one and half-dragging Satank to the second wagon. A bluecoat with two stripes on his
sleeves climbed into the back of Big Tree and Satanta's
wagon and sat on a mound of corn, cradling a shoots-a-heap
Spencer rifle in his arms.

"Up, you damned red nigger!" someone shouted, but Satank said nothing, simply turned his body into a piece of petrified wood. The soldiers lifted him and tossed him into the
back of the wagon, and Satank threw the blanket over his
head and began singing.

His words haunted Big Tree.

> *Iha hyo oya iya o iha yaya yoyo*
> *Aheyo aheyo waheyo ya eya heyo e heyo*
> *Koiet-senko ana obahema haa ipai degi o ba ika*
> *Koiet-senko ana oba hemo hadamagagi o ba ika.*

The next voice belonged to the white man who spoke the
language of The Principal People and the Comanches. Hor-
Ace-Jones. *A good man,* Big Tree thought. "You best watch
that old injun," Hor-Ace-Jones shouted to a bluecoat officer.
"He means trouble." Big Tree could not understand the
white-eye language, but he could guess that Hor-Ace-Jones
was warning the soldiers.

Satank was singing his death song.

The wagons began rolling.

Satanta hung his head, but Big Tree could not look away
from the wagon behind him. Two bluecoats, including another one with two stripes, sat up front. The driver ignored
Satank, but the other two-striped bluecoat began laughing
and mimicking the *Koiet-senko*'s death song.

Satank stopped just long enough to lower his blanket and
stare at the soldier. "You will die, too," he said before covering his head again and resuming the haunting chant.

Bluecoats are stupid. Big Tree did not quite understand

how a tribe this dumb could have put three of The Principal People's greatest warriors in chains. They did not notice the blood dripping from Satank's lips when he spoke to the mocking soldier. They did not understand that, hidden by the blanket, he was tearing his flesh with his teeth and the secret knife, cutting away skin so he would soon be able to slip his hands free from the iron bracelets.

"Get ready, my son," Satank cried out from underneath his blanket. "Fill your pipe, for we shall smoke together today. Make room for me. I am coming."

When the wagons and horse soldiers had reached Cache Creek, less than a mile from the post, Satank dropped the blanket. He spotted Caddo George riding alongside the wagons and said, "Take this message to my people. Tell them I died beside the road. My bones will be found there. Tell my people to gather them up and carry them away." A moment later, Satank nodded at a pecan tree. "See that tree? When I reach that tree, I will be dead." Next, his eyes found a Tonkawa scout accompanying the bluecoats. "You may have my scalp," he said. "The hair is poor. It isn't worth much, but you may have it."

Still, the bluecoats paid no attention.

Big Tree held his breath. It was coming.

Satank leaped forward, slashed the mocking bluecoat's leg with the knife and grabbed the fast-shooting Spencer from the stunned man's arms. The soldier driving the wagon leaped to the ground with a scream, leaving his bleeding companion to the mercy of Satank. Satank, however, ignored the wounded man, dropping the knife and working the lever of the soldier's gun. The carbine jammed.

"Fire," a bluecoat officer shouted.

The soldier in front of Big Tree chambered a cartridge, aimed, and pulled the trigger. Even Satanta looked up after the explosion. Other bluecoats joined the shooting. Satank staggered back and dropped to his knees as a bullet buzzed past Big Tree's ear and struck the white-eye driving the wagon, who shrieked like a squaw and dropped over the side, clutching his arm, accidentally hit by his own men.

"Criminy!" yelled the bluecoat near Big Tree, the one who had fired first. "Watch who you're shootin' at, you dumb sumbitches!" He jacked another round into the carbine and spit out a mouthful of brown juice.

Fearing he would be shot himself, Satanta began crying out that he was doing nothing, and Big Tree's shame grew. Suddenly, he wished the bluecoats would turn their guns on him, kill him, put him out of his misery. He had no honor this day. All honor belonged to Satank, who, to the surprise of Satanta, Big Tree, and the bluecoats, pulled himself to his feet and worked on the jammed Spencer.

"Shit," a white man said. "That bastard ain't dead."

"Fire! Kill that son of a bitch!"

When the closest bluecoat, whom he had heard called Corp-Ral-Charl-Ton, brought up the Spencer, Big Tree reached up and touched the soldier's arms. Satank was finished, his weapon useless. Big Tree pleaded, *"No bueno,"* but Corp-Ral-Charl-Ton flung Big Tree's chained wrists aside and took aim again. Big Tree could not watch. He closed his eyes as more bullets ripped through the old warrior. A horse squealed. Men cursed, cried, shouted. Silence. An eternity passed, but no more rifles barked, and no bullets struck Big Tree. Only when Satanta mumbled something did Big Tree dare to look.

Bad Hand and other soldiers had galloped to the scene, and the bluecoats ran around like The Principal People on ration day. The soldier who had mocked Satank looked pale, clutching a red-stained thigh with both hands, sweat peppering his brow, crying to Sweet Jesus that he was going to die. Someone told the whining man to shut up. Big Tree's eyes dropped, and he felt tears, of respect and of shame, roll down his cheeks.

Satank, the greatest of The Principal People's warriors, lay on the side of the road, blood pouring from his mouth. As the light faded from his hard eyes, he was still trying to sing his death song.

Chapter 8

"Old fellow, war is hell, and you're a bloodthirsty savage, but, by criminy, I'm not, and I'll be damned if those mosquitoes shall bite you while you are helpless."

—John B. Charlton

June 8, 1871
Cache Creek, Indian Territory

"Damn it, damn it, damn it!" screamed the officer of the day, Lieutenant George K. Thurston, holding an emptied Remington revolver in his gauntleted right hand while trying to steady his nervous blue roan.

Corporal John B. Charlton stared at the smoking Spencer carbine in his hands, cleared his throat, slid off the wagon's open tailgate, spilling corn as he dropped to the ground, and looked back at Big Tree and Satanta, who sat unmoving in the back of the wagon, both apparently surprised to still be alive. Colonel Mackenzie and others loped forward. *Oh hell,* Charlton thought.

"Who kilt Satank?" a voice called out, and Charlton turned to face the trumpeter named Oxford, who had been riding at the column's point and had missed the excitement.

Excitement? That was an understatement.

"I did," he answered tentatively, "and I'm afeared I'll catch hell for doin' it."

Oxford shook his head and rode toward Mackenzie,

Thurston, and the other soldiers, while Charlton covered the distance between the lead wagon and the second one, now stopped beside the ditch on the side of the road. Caddo George Washington looked down at Satank, shook his head, and turned his horse around, only to stop when Satanta shouted something.

"What'd he say?" Charlton asked the scout.

"Him say tell Kiowas he might never see 'em again. Say tell 'em to be at peace with whites." Caddo George Washington kicked his horse into a gallop and headed back to Fort Sill, scared. *Of what?* Charlton wondered. The danger had passed.

"Corporal," Trooper A. J. Hogan said. "Lookee yonder."

A dozen or more Indians had gathered several rods away, near the trees, watching suspiciously, silently. Sunlight reflected off a rifle, and Charlton began sweating, suddenly wishing he had ridden off with Caddo George Washington.

"They ain't botherin' us, Hogan," Charlton said with more confidence than he felt. "Don't do nothin' stupid. Let 'em watch."

Charlton knelt beside Satank, pulled the blood-soaked blanket over the old man's dead eyes, and shuddered. He had never killed anyone before, not even a savage Indian, and it didn't sit well in his stomach. He leaned his weapon against the wagon and picked up the carbine Satank had taken after stabbing Corporal Robinson. Spencers weren't always reliable. *Lucky for us,* Charlton thought. Robinson had already chambered a round, so when Satank cocked the lever, it jammed the mechanism. He tossed the weapon aside, picked up his own, and emptied his mouth of more tobacco juice.

"Ain't never seen such bravery," he told the dead Indian.

A Tonkawa Indian appeared at his side, mumbling something, pointing at the dead prisoner and holding out his knife.

"Get out of here!" Charlton snapped, pushing the Indian toward his horse. "You ain't takin' his scalp."

"Him say!" the Indian fired back. "Him say!" He kept pointing at Satank.

"I don't give a damn what he said. Here!" He reached down and jerked off the blanket. "Take this as your bloody trophy, you son of a bitch!" He hooked out his tobacco and tossed the old rag to the scout, who caught it, studied it, then draped it over his shoulders, sheathing his scalping knife as he grabbed the hackamore and mounted his horse. Charlton's mouth felt dry, and he started for the creek for a drink or maybe just to splash some water on his face before he threw up.

"Who killed Satank?" he heard Mackenzie ask, and immediately afterward came Oxford's reply. "Corporal Charlton."

Charlton hadn't been the only one who fired, but at least he was certain his bullets struck Satank, not one of his own men. He straightened, delaying his drink of water. Turning around, Charlton watched some soldiers work on the wounded wagon driver, while another told the wailing Corporal Robinson of D Troop to shut up, that his knife wound wouldn't kill him. He chanced another glance at the gathering Kiowas, who still kept their distance.

"Corporal Charlton!" Mackenzie barked.

"Sir?" He snapped to attention.

"Where did Satank get that knife?"

"We don't know, sir. Someone must have slipped it to him. Caddo George visited him last night, sir."

"Where is he?"

"Rode back to the fort, sir."

"All right. We'll deal with this later. Corporal, search those other two savages. Mr. Thurston!"

The lieutenant holstered his revolver and spurred his horse forward. "Sir?"

"Get the hell out of here as fast as you can."

"Sir?"

"Are you blind, Lieutenant? See those Indians by the trees? I don't want them to think we're murdering their chiefs and have the whole Kiowa nation upon us."

"Yes, sir. What about Satank, sir?"

"The hell with him. Let Grierson's niggers bury him. Let's move, Lieutenant. We're sitting ducks out here. Corporal!"

Standing in the back of the wagon, Charlton whirled while two troopers finished patting down Satanta and Big Tree. "No weapons, sir," he said. He had expected that.

"Very good, Corporal. Mr. Thurston, you have your orders. I'll catch up with you after I make my report to Colonel Grierson."

June 12, 1871
Wichita River, Texas

The bluecoats were afraid.

Since leaving the soldier-fort near Cache Creek, they had doubled the guards watching the horse herd every night and kept a close eye on Satanta and Big Tree, forcing the prisoners to lay on their backs after attending to nature's call, next lashing their hands to a stake driven into the ground above their heads, then binding their feet to another stake. Two guards sat between them, rifles in their arms, and, unlike most soldier sentries Satanta had seen, these bluecoats never fell asleep.

Perhaps the soldiers feared The Principal People would rise up and swarm upon the patrol, counting coup and lifting scalps, freeing Satanta and Big Tree and showing the white-eyes who had the greatest power. For the first few days, Satanta waited, but warriors never came—not Big Bow, not Maman-ti, not even Eagle Heart or Lone Wolf. He spit, cursing Kicking Bird's name. That Quaker-loving, peace-talking pig must have persuaded The Principal People to let the bluecoats take Big Tree and Satanta to Texas. It figured. With Satanta out of the way, Kicking Bird would wield much power. The Principal People would listen to his words and believe it when he said they should follow the white man's road. Look what the white man's road had meant to Kicking Bird: More flour, more money, a home like those the white-eyes lived in, horses, calico for his wives, cigars, trips to Washington to see the Great White Father. And what had been Satanta's reward for choosing the warrior road?

Shackled in irons and carted off to face the angry *Tehannas*.

Satanta could speak seven languages, but the white man's words felt heavy on his tongue. One could not make sense of such gibberish, and he had a hard time understanding what the *Tehannas* meant by this trial. He had been held prisoner before—he and Lone Wolf by the yellow-haired bluecoat called Custer—but there had been no speeches made. Yellow Hair had simply ordered the two chiefs manacled and thrown into a sweatbox.

Killing the white traders was a crime, the *Tehannas*, Quakers, and bluecoats said, but Satanta could not see it that way. The Principal People had been making war long before the white-eyes invaded their land, and had not the white-eyes made war on *Gai'gwu?* Didn't the bluecoats even make war upon themselves back East not that many summers ago? There was nothing wrong with war, and attacking the *Tehannas* had been war. War was good. It gave young braves a chance to prove their bravery. It provided The Principal People with horses, robes, and slaves. Perhaps this trial was a sham, another lie for Kicking Bird to believe. So far, Bad Hand's bluecoats had done nothing but stake Satanta and Big Tree to the ground at night and keep their hands and feet chained as they rode to the white settlement called Jacksboro during the day. Already the bracelets rubbed Satanta's skin raw. It itched horribly.

This, Satanta figured, wasn't much better than being thrown into the hot darkness by Yellow Hair. It did not befit a warrior of his stature, especially here in the *Tehanna* swamps, where mosquitoes, some of them almost as large as ravens, swarmed and attacked without mercy, landing on Satanta's face, covering his arms and legs, drawing his blood.

The bluecoats suffered as well, but they had built fires by their small canvas tepees and bedrolls, using green wood to make a thick smoke that kept the tormentors away. Satanta and Big Tree, however, had no such luxury.

Sweat dampened his face, and Satanta tugged at the rawhide and iron bindings. The *Tehanna* mosquitoes hurt. A shadow crossed his face, and he opened his eyes to see the two-striped bluecoat named Corp-Ral-Charl-Ton staring down at him. He said something, speaking to Satanta in the ugly white-man words as if Satanta could understand. Satanta said nothing, simply watched in the twilight, trying to figure out this strange bluecoat.

"Hogan," Corp-Ral-Charl-Ton spoke, and another bluecoat answered, "Corporal?"

"I want you and Valdez to go to the riverbank, cut a couple of leafy branches, and bring 'em back here. Then fan them two prisoners to keep the skeeters off 'em."

"You joshin' us, Corporal?"

"No, I ain't. We ain't savages, Hogan. I ain't gonna let them skeeters suck the blood out of 'em while they's helpless. You got a problem with that order, Trooper?"

"I reckon not. C'mon, Valdez."

When the two bluecoats disappeared, Corp-Ral-Charl-Ton squatted beside Satanta, spit a river of brown juice to the side, and pulled a ring of keys off his belt. "This be for humanity's sake, injun," he said, and leaned forward. Satanta could not believe this. The bluecoat unfastened the iron manacles clamped against his wrists, cut through the rawhide that strapped his hands to the stake, then moved over to Big Tree and began freeing his hands.

Satanta sat up, grunted, and slapped his cheeks. He looked at his bloody hand, wiped it on his breechcloth and swatted the mosquitoes biting his thighs. Beside him, Big Tree sat up suddenly and attacked the bloodsuckers torturing him. Corp-Ral-Charl-Ton backed up, dropped the iron cuffs beside the stake holding Satanta's feet, and nodded in self-approval.

"Corporal, what the Sam Hill are you doin'?"

The bluecoats Corp-Ral-Charl-Ton had sent away had returned, to Satanta's surprise, with branches from the riverbank. Corp-Ral-Charl-Ton spit again, wiped his mouth with the back of his hand, and answered in the white-eye tongue. One of the bluecoats started to protest, but Corp-Ral-Charl-Ton barked something else, harsher in his tone, and the first bluecoat nudged the second one, who decided not to speak anymore. Instead, the two soldiers approached the prisoners tentatively. They lifted the tree branches and began fanning Satanta and Big Tree, occasionally even brushing the mosquitoes off their legs and arms.

Satanta grunted in approval as Corp-Ral-Charl-Ton walked back to the soldier houses. This was much more like it. This was how the Orator of the Plains should be treated.

June 14, 1871
Jack County, Texas

Back during the War for the Suppression of the Rebellion, Colonel Ranald S. Mackenzie remembered, myriad politicians, journalists, and even Army brass believed William T. Sherman to be quite mad. Mackenzie had never believed it, however. General Sherman was temperamental, certainly, set in his ways and void of diplomacy, one who would speak his mind and damn the consequences. But insane? Not hardly. A genius? Quite.

Then again, Mackenzie had often overheard junior officers and sergeants voicing similar concerns about a brash young commander named Ranald Slidell Mackenzie during the late Rebellion, and on more than a few nights Mackenzie would have agreed with them. War is Hell, Sherman had said, but it also played hell with the faculties of the best leaders of men.

A few Fourth Cavalry troopers now expressed their thoughts about Uncle Billy Sherman's state of mind. What kind of imbecile would order two Kiowas to stand trial in civilian court for seven murders committed during an Indian raid? And what chance would a detail of federal soldiers have of getting those Indians to the county seat alive?

Whether Sherman was insane was a matter Mackenzie would leave to the historians of another century, but the other question troubled him.

"Suggestions?" he asked in his Sibley tent.

"I wonder if we're not being overly cautious, General," Lieutenant Robert G. Carter said, addressing Mackenzie by the rank breveted him during the War of the Rebellion. "Unionists comprised most of Jack County during the late war, sir. Surely they would not fire on federal soldiers. March them in, sir, heavily guarded, of course. Have the band greet us. Make a show of it all."

"If that had been my brother on Salt Creek Prairie," Lieutenant Thurston argued, "with his fingers and pecker chopped off and stuck in his mouth, I wouldn't give a damn if I voted for secession or the Union. I'd want to shoot the bastards myself, and anyone who got in my way—no matter if he wore the blue. And I damn sure wouldn't want a *show.*"

Lieutenant Carter shrugged. "It could be moot, sir. Folks might not know where we are."

"I don't think so, Mr. Carter," Mackenzie said. "I daresay they've been waiting for our arrival since we left Fort Sill. I think you might be right, Mr. Thurston. Personally, I wouldn't care if Satanta and Big Tree were shot to pieces on the parade ground of Fort Richardson—if someone else were in command. But we're under orders from General Sherman himself, and I won't have my record tarnished by some trigger-happy Texas peckerwood. I want Satanta and Big Tree in the post guardhouse an hour before the people of Jack County know we have them. So, how do we accomplish that?"

That stumped his officers, so Mackenzie found his bottle and emptied its contents into three glasses. Maybe bourbon would make a good brain tonic.

"Help yourselves, gentlemen," said Mackenzie, raising his own glass in a toast.

Whiskey finished, Lieutenant Carter wiped his lips and cleared his throat. "Perhaps we could use a decoy, General."

Mackenzie arched his eyebrows. The bourbon had helped. "Go on, Mr. Carter."

"Well, sir, we ride in down Jacksboro's main street and head to the fort, greeted by the regimental band. We surround the two prisoners under heavy guard, only the prisoners aren't Satanta and Big Tree. They're two Tonkawa scouts. We're the decoy, General."

"And where are Satanta and Big Tree?"

"Already in the post guardhouse, sir. We send them out tonight with Corporal Charlton. He's treated the prisoners decently, sir, better than I would have, and Horace Jones says Satanta trusts him—Charlton, that is. Give him an escort of ten troopers and Jones. If the Texans start shooting, well, General Sherman still gets to have his trial."

Mackenzie set his empty glass on the table. He liked the idea. If the Texicans opened fire, well, maybe two Tonk scouts would be killed. Hell, the Eastern papers might even call Ranald Mackenzie a hero for protecting those two murdering sons of bitches. Even Lieutenant Thurston nodded his approval.

"See to it, Mr. Carter," Mackenzie said.

"We'll still have to bring the prisoners to the courthouse for trial," Thurston interjected.

"Under heavy guard," Mackenzie said. "These are dangerous times." He laughed suddenly. "It would be ironic, wouldn't it, gentlemen, if we got killed defending those red niggers?"

Thurston slid his glass on the table and smiled. "Speaking of that, General," he said, "I'd hate to be the poor bastard who has to defend those two."

Chapter 9

"I well remember the excitement in the community when we heard about the famous wagon train murder. . . . I was there at the trial, and will say that the excitement was running plenty high. There were over a thousand people there, besides a lot of Indians."

—H. P. Cook

June 15, 1871
Jacksboro, Texas

"Did you all have a nice time last night?" the Widow Baggett asked while passing a tray to Thomas Ball, who picked up two sugar cubes and dropped them in his cup of coffee.

Mrs. Prudence Baggett reminded Ball of the blue-haired old ladies back in Northumberland County: delicate, chatty, proud of their heritage and their china, with nothing better to do than conduct harmless interviews over coffee or tea and then gossip about what they had learned. Only Prudence Baggett's hair was graying red, her good china was tin, and her accent was Texas, not Virginia. A tiny woman who'd be carried away by a strong norther, the widow made stout coffee and biscuits every morning and engaged her boarders in polite conversation. She never scolded Ball, always late for breakfast, always apologizing that he had been reading law and making notes and time had gotten away from him, never guessing, or at least never showing any sign of guessing, that

the real reason he strolled in after eight-thirty for cold biscuits and potent Arbuckles' coffee was that he loathed the
drunken drummer, preachy cobbler, and icy seamstress who
also roomed in the humid stone house a block from Main
Street.

"Yes, ma'am." Ball noticed the widow's green eyes
sparkle. "Hope I didn't wake anyone up when I came in."

"Not at all. I was reading the Bible. Always do till ten
o'clock. You've been out much later. So has"—she
frowned—"Mr. Perkins." Ed Perkins was the drummer, who
spent more time drinking his wares in the Green Frog than
selling them. "M. J. is a nice girl. I'm glad you two are seeing so much of each other."

Ball felt himself blushing. Actually, he had seen M. J.
Shelley only a handful of times. Last night he had taken her
to the Wichita Hotel for supper, where he found his waitress,
the usually perky Amanda Doniphan, a bit testy. Jealous?
Ball wasn't sure, but figured he had made an error in judgment and would do well to stay out of the Wichita for a few
nights. Amanda had no reason to be jealous—well, not yet,
anyway—and the widow was a bit premature if she had
planned on making a wedding announcement over supper
tonight. Ball wasn't quite certain what to make of M. J. Shelley—or Amanda Doniphan, Prudence Baggett, or just about
anyone in this windblown little burg of three hundred souls.

"Any cases coming up of interest?" she asked and passed
him a plate of cold biscuits. She should be a reporter for *The
Flea,* Jacksboro's newspaper, which came out whenever the
editor figured he had enough news worth printing, occasionally twice a month but more often once every two months.

"I have to go to Weatherford the first of next week," he
said, accepting one thick, floured biscuit. "To take a deposi-
tion. Nothing important."

"I suspect the Kiowas will be here before then." She
sipped her coffee. "Ed Perkins heard it from Peter Lynn that
General Mackenzie passed through Postoak. Half the town's
getting ready."

That kind of news traveled fast on the frontier. Sherman had managed to capture the ringleaders and had ordered them back to Jack County to stand trial for murder. Three Indians. Or, rather, two—the third had been killed near Fort Sill. That was all anyone wanted to talk about these days.

"Be a lot of excitement, I imagine," he said casually.

The tin cup clinked on the table, and the widow frowned. "Thomas," she said, "you stay clear of them prairie niggers. Trial." She snorted. "What a bunch of hogwash."

Ball's eyes widened. He had never heard his landlady employ such language, and he quickly began reevaluating his assessment of sweet Prudence Baggett. She and M. J. Shelley could be full of surprises when discussing Indians.

"Sherman should have shot all of them savages," the woman railed. "That's a damnyankee for you. A trial! Like there's any doubt they're guilty. Trials cost money, Thomas, taxpayers' money, and I don't like it one bit that I have to pay for it. I have four rooms rented out and six rooms empty. Money's tight, and . . ." She smiled again. "Oh, there I go just a-ranting away. Forgive me, Thomas. You're the nicest tenant I have. I shouldn't be taking things out on you."

Ball had just left the boarding house when the shouts came from Main Street. "It's Mackenzie!" someone yelled. "Mackenzie's back, and he's got the Kiowas!" Heralds went out as in some Shakespearean play, and men and women—the widow Baggett included—rushed from their homes and businesses, lining Main Street as if watching a parade. Ball hadn't seen such a turnout since the war, when the boys of the Forty-seventh Virginia Infantry stood shivering in a February rain to catch a glimpse of Robert E. Lee. But these onlookers had little interest in Ranald Mackenzie. They wanted a glimpse of his two prisoners.

Some cursed, but most just watched in silence as the soldiers rode slowly down the street. Men and women craned their necks and stood on tiptoe for a better look, but the Union soldiers surrounded the two Kiowas like a coyote fence. Ball caught a glimpse of raven black hair but nothing else. Saddle leather creaked and wagon chains jingled.

Cowhand Peter Lynn scratched his right palm against the hammer of an old Navy Colt stuck in his waistband. Ball had heard all about Lynn's troubles with the Indians. Ed Perkins whispered something in the waddie's ear, and Lynn's frown hardened. His hand swallowed the revolver's butt.

Ball frowned. Next to Perkins and Lynn stood M. J. Shelley, tears streaming down her face. He weaved through the crowd until he stood next to the threesome. As Lynn started to pull the revolver, Ball reached out and grabbed his arm.

"Don't be a fool," he said.

Lynn pivoted and pulled away, still gripping the walnut butt but leaving the weapon in his waistband. Ball had seen that look before, the crazed look of a killer, but Lynn froze, his eyes lost their glassiness, and his Adam's apple bobbed. The danger passed. The cowhand released the grip on his pistol, spun around, and vanished down the crowded boardwalk. To Ball's surprise, M. J. Shelley gave him a scowl before whirling to follow Lynn. Ed Perkins merely clucked his tongue and turned his attention to the passing military column.

June 16, 1871
Fort Richardson, Texas

Lieutenant Robert G. Carter, post adjutant, met the committee from town in his long office on the southeastern corner of the parade grounds. He knew most of these men—merchant W. M. McConnell, Sheriff Michael McMillan, County Clerk J. R. Robinson, newspaperman Roy Scott, popular Charley Jordan, and lawyer Samuel Lanham—and felt prepared. Major J. K. Mizner, who had been left in command of the post during Mackenzie's absence, had filled Carter in.

Ever since word reached town that Sherman wanted the Kiowa leaders to stand trial in Jacksboro, protests and pleas had been flooding the fort. Even Austin and distant Washington were inundated. Major Mizner had sided with the citizens, writing to Governor Davis that, in his view, a trial and execution would lead all Indians on the reservation to the warpath. McConnell and others had begged the Army to supply the men of Jack County with rifles, powder, and shot. They had a right to defend themselves. The Kiowas were coming—sure as Judgment Day.

"Good morning, gentlemen," said Carter, expecting more of the same complaints and unattainable requests.

Apparently the spokesman for the people of Jack County, Sam Lanham stepped forward. He wore a bib-front shirt of royal blue twill, the collar, cuffs, and bib trimmed in yellow, with fifteen buttons featuring Texas stars attaching the bib. It seemed a tad warm for the shirt, but it caught one's eye, which is why, Carter figured, Lanham had picked it from his wardrobe. The lawyer liked to make speeches, and, more so, liked to look good while making them. That's why he had won so many cases.

But he would lose this one.

"Lieutenant, the good people of Jacksboro have asked me to make our case. We don't want a trial here in town. It's too risky. We don't want more blood spilled on our roads, and that is what we fear will happen if the government and military proceed on this immoral course."

"It's a military matter!" Roy Scott snapped. "Y'all should have killed them Kiowas back at Fort Sill and been done with it."

Lanham frowned, not pleased with the interruption, and Carter took the opportunity to head off the protest.

"My hands are tied, gentlemen," Carter said from his desk chair. "General Sherman's orders are specific. Satanta and Big Tree must be tried for murder and as many other crimes as you"—he nodded at Lanham, the district prosecutor—"can approve. Our job is to protect the two prisoners from being mobbed or lynched."

"Certainly, you can see the reason for a change of venue," Lanham said.

"That's a matter for the judge. My job is simple: Hold the prisoners until trial, then make sure they reach the court-house safely."

"Why don't you just turn them over to Mike now?" Roy Scott said. "And we'll take care of them."

"Hush up, Roy," muttered Sheriff McMillan, not happy in the spotlight.

"The hell I will," Scott shot back. "You seen how many Indians are around town? I got no desire to see my wife and kids killed. The Army's gotta do something about that."

"Those Indians," Carter said calmly, "are Tonkawa scouts, not Kiowas, and no harm better come to them. Tonks hate Kiowas and Comanches more than you do. We've increased patrols. So have Colonel Wood at Fort Griffin and Colonel Grierson at Fort Sill. I think your fears of a Kiowa attack are unfounded. Kicking Bird is keeping his warriors on the reservation. Rest assured, gentlemen, that the people of Jack County will be protected during the course of the trial. And so will Satanta and Big Tree."

Mumbling, the townsmen began filing out of the picket building, but Carter cleared his throat. "A word with you, Sam?"

Lanham waited till the rest of his friends had stepped out-side, then closed the door, hooked his thumbs in his waist-band, and waited.

"You don't think the Kiowas would really attack Jacks-boro, do you?" Carter asked.

"I love my wife, Robert. In that regard, I'm like Roy Scott. I'd kill myself if her scalp became some buck's tro-phy."

Carter respected that answer, but Sam Lanham seemed to be missing the larger picture of what this murder trial would mean to Jacksboro and to the "Jumbo" district's solicitor. "I understand, but if I were you I'd start preparing a case against Satanta and Big Tree. I'd start writing an opening statement and closing argument. I'd make sure they were the very best."

"I've thought about that," Lanham said. "Long and hard. Sarah's even mentioned it to me. But I keep coming back to her. My wife comes first. A bunch of lawyers have asked me to get a petition to Judge Soward," Lanham said. "We're going to petition him not to hold next month's term. Maybe you're right, Robert, maybe the Kiowas won't attack, but that's a mighty big risk."

"I've always found you to be a mighty big risk-taker, Sam, and not just at a poker table. This is an open-and-shut case. You know that. I know that. Hell, everyone knows it. But this is the kind of case that can make your career, make Sam Lanham a name known all across not only Texas, but the nation."

"What do you mean?"

Carter cackled and opened a box of cigars, picking one up and tossing it to his friend. Sometimes Sam Lanham brimmed with confidence and power, but other times the backward, self-educated South Carolinian acted like a naive schoolboy.

"Sam, have you looked around town lately?" Carter asked.

June 19, 1871
Jacksboro, Texas

Climbing out of the stagecoach unsteadily, Joe Woolfolk stretched his legs, brushed off his linen duster, and checked his pockets for a plug of tobacco. No luck. Must have left it on top of the chest of drawers back home, along with his pocketwatch, change purse, and the locket with Liz's photo inside. Criminy, he had caught the stage at Belknap only by the grace of God. It's a wonder he had remembered to bring along his grip containing affidavits and a change of clothes.

He had spent all night with a mare in foal, which finally delivered a sharp-looking colt too late for breakfast.

Woolfolk started to take off his duster but spotted the bloodstains on his shirtsleeve and realized he hadn't even had time to wash his hands or change his shirt. Liz would have a fit over that, but she was back home and he was on his way to Weatherford.

"I got time to run over the Harry's and buy me a plug, Kurt?" Woolfolk called out to the jehu.

"If you hurry," the driver replied.

He looked up, surprised to see Jacksboro's streets bustling. There must be a person standing in every door; a line had formed outside both Carroll's Café and the Wichita Hotel for dinner, and a sign on the side of the stagecoach station said the company would increase its runs to and from Weatherford to three times a week until further notice. "Golly," he said aloud. Jacksboro looked like San Antonio today. He took a long step toward the mercantile, then muttered a curse underneath his breath. His change purse. Son of a gun, Woolfolk had left home without any money.

"Problem?"

Woolfolk looked up to see a familiar face, a gent holding a carpetbag in one hand and a book by Charles Dickens in the other. He had seen this fellow around—in courthouses here in Jacksboro and in Weatherford, and only a couple of weeks ago eating supper at the Wichita Hotel—but he couldn't fathom the name. The man was a contrast to Joe Woolfolk. He wore a gray frock coat of broadcloth, a matching double-breasted vest with ribbon trim, a blue tie, striped britches tucked inside shiny stovepipe boots, and a bell crown hat, making Woolfolk keenly aware of his blood-and-manure-stained muslin shirt, duck trousers, scuffed boots, battered spurs, frayed bandana, and sweat-stained gray slouch hat.

Even the copy of *Hard Times* made Woolfolk uncomfortable. About the only reading material a body could find around his house, other than Liz's Bible, were a few broken-spine law books and battered almanacs. One of these days,

Woolfolk figured, he wouldn't have to be taking stage-coaches to Weatherford, wouldn't have to be pleading cases in front of pettifogging judges and better (paid, talented, and dressed) lawyers. One of these days, Woolfolk would quit the bar and concentrate on land, cattle, horses, and good Brazos River bottomland. One of these days.

"Nothin'," he answered.

"Didn't mean to intrude," the man said.

The driver yelled, "You goin' to get yer 'baccy, Joe, or ain't you?"

"I ain't, Kurt," Woolfolk shot back, walked around the well-dressed lawyer, and stuck his hands in the water trough. He scrubbed as much blood and dirt off his cuffs as possible without soap and splashed tepid water over his face, drying off with his bandana. By the time he had finished, Kurt was yelling to board up or get left behind, so Woolfolk climbed back inside the coach. The smartly attired lawyer sat across from him.

"Just you and me?" Woolfolk asked. Usually, the Monday run from Jacksboro to Weatherford had passengers crammed inside and riding up top with Kurt.

"No one's leaving town," the man said. "Newspaper reporters are arriving every day, from Dallas, Austin, even New York. Even the Widow Baggett's boarding house is full up. Getting ready for the trial."

"The Kiowa trial." Woolfolk nodded, at last understanding, and stared out the window as Kurt whipped the mules and sent the Concord swaying.

"You're Joseph A. Woolfolk, aren't you?"

He looked back, eying the man suspiciously. You didn't ask a man's name on the frontier. Downright rude, it was. If a fellow wanted you to know his name, he'd tell you. Woolfolk's head bobbed in a reluctant reply. He hoped this gent would stick his nose in *Hard Times* and forget conversation. Woolfolk wanted some sleep before Weatherford, if Kurt could manage to miss a few potholes.

"I thought so. I'm Thomas Ball." He offered his hand,

which Woolfolk begrudgingly accepted. The gent did have a strong grip, and he reached inside his frock coat after the handshake and pulled out a pouch.

Joe Woolfolk took back every bad thought and suspicion he had held about this Thomas Ball.

"Hope you don't mind Star Navy," Ball said and passed the chewing tobacco to Woolfolk.

Chapter 10

"It is a well-known and indisputable fact that the County of Jack . . . is to an unusual and very dangerous extent infested with large bands of hostile Indians, and that . . . owing to the great number of Indians in this country, we do not think it would be humane and just to force litigants and jurors of Jack County to leave their families and attend court. . . ."
— Petition to Judge Charles Soward

June 21, 1871
Weatherford, Texas

This was a pleasant surprise. Well, at least it had been for a while. M. J. Shelley had met Thomas Ball at the Parker County Inn and invited him out to breakfast. Of course, Ball accepted. She was in Weatherford to visit Charles Soward, she told him, to plead with the judge not to try those murdering savages in Jacksboro. Peter Lynn had accompanied her. The pleasantness started fading once she mentioned the cowboy's name. Thomas Ball found his jealousy surprising.

"Mr. Lanham, Mr. McConnell, and others tried to talk some sense into General Mackenzie's adjutant but got nowhere. So now we hope Charles listens to reason." She batted tear-filled eyes while sipping coffee. *Listens to reason,* Ball thought. *More like, listens to me.* Charles Soward would have to be a tough customer, much tougher than Thomas

Ball, to ignore M. J. Shelley's exquisite lips and tormented eyes.

"Where is Peter Lynn?" asked Ball, halfheartedly carving his slice of greasy ham.

"Talking to a fellow about a horse," M. J. replied and laughed. "Can you believe that?"

His appetite returned until a man in a plaid sack suit and brown bowler rushed to their corner table and sat down uninvited. "Howdy, Miss Shelley," he said. "Pardon my intrusion, but you're Thomas Ball, right?"

"I am." Ball set his cup of coffee down and studied the sweating man with a nervous facial tic and tight-fitting wire spectacles that almost sawed through the bridge of his nose.

"Thought so. I'm A. J. Hood. Practice law here in Weatherford. Anyway, I asked Sam Lanham to write this petition." He slid a legal document across the table. "I'm no hero, Tommy. I don't fancy getting scalped on the road to try two savages everyone knows are guilty as hell."

A pen followed the paper, and Ball stared at the writing utensil and the pockmarked, rheumy-eyed jackass sitting at his table uninvited.

"Well, sign it," Hood demanded.

Ball ignored the proffered pen and lifted the papers, written on Parker County letterhead, and ignored the cold stares from both Hood and M. J. Shelley. Bar members were asking Judge Soward to cancel the July term of court, citing hostile Indians in the area and dangerous traveling conditions, calling the idea of a trial inhumane for litigants and jurors. Samuel W. T. Lanham had signed first, followed by Hood and other names, some of which Ball recognized, some of which he didn't. One name was conspicuously absent.

"I don't see Joe Woolfolk's name," Ball said.

Hood snorted. "Criminy, Tommy, I doubt if that rapscallion knows how to write. Sign it, will you! I need to get this over to Lanham, and I'm already late for a meeting with a client."

Frowning, Ball picked up his coffee mug instead of the

pen. Where did A. J. Hood get off calling him *Tommy?* No one called him that, not even his parents. Who did this pompous Texican think he was, barging in on him during breakfast? And what kind of lawyer made a client wait?

"I'd like to think this over," Ball began.

"What's there to think over?" The explosion came from M. J. Shelley, who looked horrified at her breakfast companion. "My God, Tom, you exasperate me. Stop acting like a hero. Stop trying Mr. Hood's nerves and mine. Do you want to be killed by Indians? Do you want to wind up like Samuel or Nathan . . ." She gasped, shuddered, and fetched a hanky from her purse, dabbing her eyes.

Reluctantly, Thomas Ball took Hood's pen. He felt like a louse for making M. J. cry, but he felt even worse, like a coward, as he signed his name to a document he didn't believe in.

June 22, 1871
Weatherford, Texas

"To the Honorable Charles Soward, Judge of the Thirteenth Judicial District of the State of Texas," the paper began in the flowery penmanship of Samuel W. T. Lanham. "We, the undersigned members of the bar, practicing attorneys, most respectfully request and petition Your Honor not to hold the next ensuing term of District Court at Jacksboro, Jack County, Texas."

Charles Soward had been expecting this. First came the letters from respectable men in Jack County like W. M. McConnell and Charley Jordan. Yesterday, sweet M. J. Shelley and waddie Peter Lynn had paid him a visit and spilled their guts. Now, here were the barristers, those gutless wonders. Sitting in his office, headquarters for the sprawling Thirteenth District, he skimmed over the rest of Lanham's pompous prose and looked at the signed names. Lanham . . .

A. J. Hood . . . J. L. L. McCall . . . R. J. Mackenzie . . . O. W. Bolls . . . J. C. Stone . . . H. F. Hensley . . . Thomas Ball.

"Joe Woolfolk did not sign?" asked Soward, smoothing his mustache and beard to hide his smile. He enjoyed the hot-around-the-collar look Woolfolk's name caused Sam Lanham. "He's here in Weatherford," Soward continued. "Couldn't you find him?"

"N-no, Your Honor," Lanham stuttered. He sighed and loosened his cravat. "I mean, we found him, but Woolfolk refused to sign."

The judge didn't bother to hide his smile now. He had wondered if Lanham would lie, say Woolfolk hadn't been located, but the "Jumbo" district's district attorney had passed this test. Joseph A. Woolfolk didn't cotton to petitions and would have wiped his ass with this one sooner than putting his John Henry on it. Soward had never thought much of Woolfolk as a lawyer. Some attorneys considered him a fighter, but the only thing that hard case would fight for was his land. Come to think of it, word was that Joe Woolfolk had done his share of fighting Indians before the war.

"I'm going to deny your petition, Sam," Soward said, tossing the paperwork on his desk. Lanham nodded slightly. "I believe it is paramount this court be convened and a grand jury impaneled. This was a terrible murder, and I want those Indians tried and, if proved guilty, executed. That's why I'm turning you down. You knew that before you brought this in, didn't you?"

"Yes, Your Honor."

He thought about asking the young prosecutor why he had written and signed the document, why he had let his colleagues talk him into such nonsense, but Soward decided he had a good idea already. Sam Lanham wasn't just a lawyer; he was a politician and had been straddling the fence, trying to make everyone happy. Deep down, Lanham undoubtedly wanted the trial to proceed in Jacksboro. His wife, even more ambitious than this backwoods lawyer, would have seen to that. Sarah Lanham was quite a woman.

"The July term will proceed, Sam," Soward said. "I will, however, not require any litigant party to appear at the term unless by consent of all parties. You'll be chief prosecutor. You can find your second chairs in Jacksboro, if you think you'll need them. Court will convene Saturday, July first. Tell Sheriff McMillan to prepare to issue a *venire facias* for a grand jury. This is all informal, Sam. I'm just giving you a little advance notice. We'll make everything formal in Jacksboro." He paused. "Something troubling you, Sam?"

Lanham shuffled his feet. "I hope you're right, Judge," he said a moment later. "You and the Army. I hope we don't have anything to fear from the Kiowas."

"This is an important trial, Sam. The whole nation will be looking at Jack County, Texas. Your name will be in every newspaper in the country." *And so will mine,* Soward thought with a grin.

"So I've been told. I pray everything works out. Who'll be defending those two Indians, Your Honor?"

Soward picked up the petition. "I seriously doubt if anyone will come barging in, demanding to represent Satanta and Big Tree," he said absently before returning his attention to Lanham. "Don't worry about your adversaries, Sam. I'll pick a couple." He needed to find two men who wouldn't be a bother, who wouldn't get in the way of Soward's ambition, not to mention Lanham's . . . or Lanham's wife's. "If I were you, I'd skedaddle back to Jack County and start preparing an ironclad prosecution. Lose this case, my friend, and it won't be Kiowas you have to fear, but every white man west of the Trinity River."

June 28, 1871
Jacksboro, Texas

Ten in the morning seemed a little early for a whiskey, so Joe Woolfolk wondered what Charles Soward wanted to see him about on this hot Wednesday. A problem with that affidavit he had handed the judge back in Weatherford? No, that could wait. Had to be important, making him ride all the way from his ranch. And why meet in a saloon and not the courthouse or the judge's room at the Wichita Hotel? Soward wasn't rumored to have bottle fever. Woolfolk suddenly felt like a lawyer. Too many questions. Not enough answers. Woolfolk pushed through the Green Frog's batwing doors and spotted the Kentuckian sipping coffee at a table, making small talk with Thomas Ball. The two were the only patrons in the saloon. Even the barkeep was missing.

"Come on in, Joe," Soward called out real friendly, motioning toward an unoccupied chair.

Hesitantly, like a man walking to the gallows, Woolfolk headed to the table, pushed back his hat, and nodded at Ball before sitting down.

"Glad you could make it," Soward said. "How's the wife and kids?"

"Fine."

"And that new foal?"

"Fine."

Enough pleasantries. Soward didn't like Woolfolk. Never had. "Do you have any cases to be heard during the upcoming term of court here in Jack County?"

"No, sir."

"Neither does Thomas Ball. You do know Tom, don't you, Joe?"

"We've met." His head bobbed in a second salutation to the well-dressed Virginian.

Soward paused to finish his coffee before resuming the small talk. "Town's packed. More people coming in every day. This should be some trial, don't you think?"

"More like a circus," Ball said, which surprised Woolfolk. "How's that?"

"No offense, Your Honor," Ball said. "I did not mean to slander your reputation, but I don't see how two Indians can get a fair trial in Texas. They don't even have representation."

That prompted a chuckle from Soward and a whispered curse from Joe Woolfolk. He knew what was coming.

"On the contrary, Mr. Ball, Mr. Woolfolk, those two Kiowas have just been appointed defense attorneys."

Ball's eyes lifted from his coffee mug. He stared at Woolfolk, not Soward, and mouthed, "Shit."

He might be a greenhorn on the frontier, but Thomas Ball was no simpleton. Woolfolk's head bobbed in satisfaction.

"That's right, gentlemen," Soward said. He left them alone at the table, went behind the bar, and fetched another mug and a coffee pot. He returned and filled all three mugs. "That's why I chose to meet with you two here, alone, not in the courthouse. Satanta and Big Tree need representation. I'm appointing you two to lead the defense. Joe, I'm sure your past experiences with the savages won't influence your defense of the accused."

Condescending, arrogant, lying bastard, Woolfolk thought and was about to tell Soward so when Ball started talking. "Your Honor, Joe Woolfolk has a wife and family. I think it would be in the best interest, for humanity's sake, to spare—"

"I don't need your pity, Ball," Woolfolk shot out, turning his anger to the Virginian. "I ain't beggin'." Woolfolk glared at Soward. "You want me to defend them two bucks, Judge? Fine. Hell, you might be doing me a favor. After this case, if I ain't killed, I won't have any clients to speak of and can quit this bull and concentrate on ranchin'. But Ball here, he deserves a fightin' chance. You was the one who suggested he hang his shingle in this miserable town. Now you want to get him killed?"

"Back up, Woolfolk," Ball said. "I'm a member of the bar and can defend myself."

Soward chuckled, satisfied. "Then, seeing how neither of you has any objections, I'll leave you to your own devices. Half past eight Saturday at the courthouse, gentlemen, to impanel a grand jury. I'll send word to Fort Richardson that you two need access to the prisoners. See you in court. Good day." He tipped his hat, took three steps, and turned. "Oh, there was probably no need for these precautions. I just wanted to be safe, keep the newspapermen from gossiping just yet. If people raise Cain, tell them you were appointed. You're not defending those Indians of your own volition. Be smart, gentlemen." He left, downright chipper for such a mealymouthed son of a bitch.

Neither lawyer said anything for two minutes. They just sat there letting their coffee grow cold until finally Ball pushed back his hat and said, "Well, I guess we'll get our names in some newspapers."

"Might be our obituaries."

Ball laughed and lifted his coffee mug as the somber mood inside the dark saloon disappeared. "What did Soward mean about your 'past experiences with the savages'?"

"Nothin'."

Ball let the answer slide. "I wonder why Soward picked us," he said. "To ruin our careers? I thought he liked me."

"Your career won't be ruined," Woolfolk said. "I was just joshin' 'bout the obituary thing. Plead 'em guilty and be done with it. That's what Soward's thinkin'. He figgers you're too green to put up a fight, and I ain't interested in practicin' law anymore."

"What happens if we plead them guilty?"

"Same as if we plead 'em innocent. They hang. Hell, Ball, you know that. You were right. It's a circus. If you're lookin' for justice, you best ride back to Virginia. It ain't to be found in Jack County—at least, not in this term of court." Ball seemed to be wavering, so Woolfolk continued. "Make a fine speech, plead for mercy, give them inkspillers somethin' to get excited 'bout. Just don't start thinkin' you can win this case, can save them two bucks. Then they might just be writin' your obituary after all."

Ball started to nod, then shook his head. "I can't do that, Woolfolk. I signed that damned petition against my better judgment. Hell, those two Indians deserve a chance, and if

I'm their attorney, I have to fight for them. That's the way I practice law, the way I live with myself."

"Ball, you ain't been in Texas that long. You don't know a damn thing 'bout injuns. I've fought them bastards. Don't believe that 'noble red man' garbage them Eastern papers print. Injuns are savages, merciless, and Kiowas and Comanch are the worst. Start pleadin' their case for real, you won't have to worry 'bout livin' with yourself. You'll get planted."

When their eyes met, Woolfolk realized he had underestimated Thomas Ball. So had Judge Soward. "I'll handle this alone," Ball said. "The worst that can happen is Soward holds you in contempt. I don't think you'll get disbarred by not showing up. Go back to your ranch, Woolfolk. Don't worry about me. I can take care of myself."

Woolfolk shrugged. "It's your funeral, Ball," he said, drained his coffee, and headed outside. Ball sat alone, listening as the batwing doors stopped swinging, before he sighed, rose, and walked into the morning sunlight.

"W-o-o-l-f-o-l-k."

He turned to find Joe Woolfolk leaning against the stone building, biting off a chaw of tobacco and passing the plug to Ball. "How's that?" Ball said, slightly stunned, as he accepted the chewing tobacco.

"That's how to spell my name," Woolfolk said. "Might need to know that. For my obituary."

Chapter 11

*"Satanta and Big Tree . . . willfully, unlawfully,
feloniously, and by their malice aforethought did kill
and murder contrary to the form of the statute on
such case made and provided, and against the peace
and dignity of the State of Texas."*

—Grand Jury Indictment

June 29, 1871
Weatherford, Texas

"Are you sure you want to pack that shirt?"

Knowing better than to protest or even answer, Sam Lanham simply glanced at the blue-and-white-striped boiled shirt and hung it back in the armoire. He reached for a gray corduroy shirt with pewter buttons, waiting for his wife to clear her throat. When she did, following that with a comment about how hot it was to be wearing cords, Lanham chuckled.

"I knew you'd say that," he said. "I know it's too hot for that shirt."

"It was too hot to wear that fancy bib shirt you wore to Jacksboro two weeks ago, but you did anyway."

"You weren't here to oversee my wardrobe." He looked at her then, smiling, holding out an ivory pullover shirt for inspection. She always said he looked good in white or ivory. Of course, Sam Lanham preferred something a little more colorful, fancy, and realized colleagues and friends would label him henpecked if they knew how often his wife picked out his clothes. Then again, Sarah was usually right, and he didn't mind having her around to dress him properly for each occasion.

"Paper collar?" Sarah asked.

"Already packed."

"What kind?"

"Stand-up."

She shrugged. "Tie?"

"Black stripes to match my pants. With the stick pin you got me for Christmas last. Black coat, too. That's for the trial, if it comes to that. I have my brown suit packed for the grand jury."

"You'll need extra shirts and ties."

"Done. White shirts." A lie by omission. He had also packed his favorite bib shirt.

"How long will you be gone?" she asked as he took his approved ivory shirt and two more pullovers, which he folded carefully and laid in his luggage, expertly hiding the bib-front shirt in case Sarah inspected his clothing.

"Not long. Preliminary stuff, pretrial motions on Saturday, impanel the grand jury, probably get a bill of indictment by Tuesday. Should be back by the end of the week. Maybe sooner. With luck, those two red niggers'll plead guilty."

"Don't call them that, Sam. You know I loathe that word."

"Sorry."

"You sure you don't want me there?"

After closing the suitcase, he looked back at his wife. Sarah was a small woman with blue eyes and long auburn hair kept in a bun. She wore a plain prairie dress of gray, which figured. Ever conservative, Sarah didn't like flash in her clothes—nor in her husband's. Lanham frowned at the worry in his wife's face. She had been a beautiful woman when he met her, but five years in Texas had aged her, dried out her skin, turned her hands to leather, though she still remained pretty, hadn't lost her Carolina accent, and those eyes could melt most men, especially a backwoods bumpkin like Sam Lanham. Often he regretted the move west, but it had been her idea, and even after too many hard labors, one tornado, incurable asthma, and God knew how many Indian scares, she never once complained. Not even after losing two children in infancy.

Texas was a hard life.

Some folks called his wife ambitious, pious, straight-laced, but Lanham found her to be gracious, romantic, hard-working. To be sure, she believed every word of the Bible and didn't allow liquor, not even wine or cooking sherry, in her home, frowning whenever her husband came home with John Barleycorn on his breath. But it wasn't Sarah Lanham who was zealous; it was her husband. She just wanted to help. She always wanted to help. Without her, he'd probably still be picking cotton and cropping tobacco.

Back in South Carolina, he had barely been able to believe that a Meng would be willing to accompany him to a dance and a few months later even marry him. Him? Barely able to write his name when he had enlisted in Kershaw's Brigade. His friends back home couldn't believe it, either. The daughter of Garland Meng, a big planter from Pacolet, fell in love with this dumb oaf from Spartanburg. Stood before family and friends and took Samuel Willis Tucker Lanham till death do us part on September 4, 1866.

Almost a year older than her new husband, Sarah Beona Meng Lanham had suggested they pack their wagon and go west—only a month after their marriage—and forget South Carolina and its passel of Yankee soldiers, Reconstruction government, and thieving carpetbaggers. They left South Carolina with nineteen other Southerners wanting a new life. Lanham could remember every backbreaking mile of that journey, so long and arduous. *Arduous.* Sarah had taught him that word. The newlyweds settled for a year in Old Boston in East Texas, making do in a two-room log cabin where they both taught school. Well, to be honest, she did most of the teaching, but Sam Lanham learned quickly. He had always been a fast learner, probably would have made it through his *Readers* himself if there had been time. Farm work interrupted most of his studies, though, and then came the war.

And afterward came Sarah, and everything changed.

One year he had been a struggling farmer-turned-school-teacher who couldn't multiply or divide or even read Washington Irving without stumbling, and the next Sarah was telling him he should be a lawyer. She became his tutor, and they moved from Old Boston to Bowie County for another year, another school, and in 1869, a year after they had settled in Weatherford for another teaching job, he became an attorney. Now he stood before judges and juries as prosecutor of one of the state's biggest and wildest districts, and he never stuttered or let his meager education show while arguing law or making impassioned statements.

Gazing at his wife, though, he suddenly thought they should have stayed in East Texas. The climate was similar to what they had grown up with along the Carolina border, with thick pine trees that whistled in the wind, good water, and the sun tolerable. Out here, the wind wailed like a banshee, the water was hard, and the sun roared like the fires of Hades.

Prosecutors didn't make much money. He often found himself away from home, wondering how Sarah managed to care for their son and teach at the conscription school set up in the front of their home.

"I want you there," Lanham said sadly, and a forced smile appeared under his thick mustache, "but we don't want Weatherford's younguns to grow up to be as dumb as I used to be." He didn't want her there just in case the Kiowas did take the warpath. "Besides." He pointed at her stomach, already showing. "You need to stay off your feet." He hoped this one lived. Little Claude, only three years old, could use a brother or a sister.

"I'll be staying at the Wichita Hotel," he said. "And . . ." He couldn't think of anything to add. Stress still showed in her face. What was the distance between Weatherford and Jacksboro? Forty miles maybe? A bumpy stagecoach ride separating the civilization, relatively speaking, of Weatherford and the raw frontier of Jack County. She'd be safe here, and he hadn't lied about the schooling.

"I'll fix some dinner before you go," she said. "What time does the stage leave?"

"Couple of hours." Lanham returned to his armoire, opened a drawer, and began pulling out a few pairs of socks. He shook his head with a smirk when Sarah called from the back door, "You aren't taking that bib-front shirt, are you, Sam?"

June 30, 1871
Fort Richardson, Texas

The corporal of the guard sprayed a beetle with tobacco juice while marching across the parade grounds—pretty good aim, Thomas Ball considered—past the barracks, turning right, and continuing on to the stone guardhouse. Always a slow walker, Ball had trouble matching the bowlegged gaits of the soldier, Joe Woolfolk, and interpreter Horace Jones. The smell coming from the bakery reminded Ball again that he had even missed the Widow Baggett's cold biscuits this morning.

"Them injuns been actin' up any?" Woolfolk asked.

"Nah," Corporal John B. Charlton replied. "Tame as kittens, almost. Like to hear the regimental band play. That entertains the old one. Younger one don't say much. Y'all ain't got no reason to be scairt. Them bucks won't harm you."

Horace Jones spat. "You forgettin' Satank, Corp'ral?"

"Nope. But Satanta and Big Tree ain't no Satank."

They arrived at the guardhouse. The United States Fourth Cavalry took no chances with those two tame-as-kittens Kiowas inside. Two troopers stood in front of the doorway, another sat in a wobbly chair on the roof, carbine cradled across his lap, and a marksman rested on top of the magazine, which also had two guards positioned at the door. Other troopers stood at each corner of the cavalry stables, more than a handful watched from the post trader's store, and there seemed to be a lot of policing going on near the thickets along the banks of Lost Creek.

The guards at the door stepped aside without comment

while Corporal Charlton found the right key on his chain and
unlocked the door. He pulled open the heavy door and stepped
aside, allowing Woolfolk, Jones, and Ball through first. Ball
took a step into the darkness and stopped, the smell over-
whelming him. Dark. Piss. Sweat. Rot. He felt transplanted
more than a thousand miles east and more than five years back
in time. Point Lookout. He had stepped through the Hell's gate.

"You all right there, sir?"

The corporal's voice snapped Ball out of the nightmarish
illusion, and he nodded, muttering an apology, and maneuvered down the steps. Charlton walked around him and
ahead of the others until he came to the last cell. He unlocked
that barred door before motioning the three visitors inside.

"I gotta lock you gents in," Charlton said. "Colonel's orders.
We'll leave the outer door open, though, so just holler when
you're done. Give you some sunlight, anyway. And them."

It was only when the trooper tilted his head toward the
cell's corner that Thomas Ball spotted the two Kiowas. Horace Jones began speaking a guttural language, and the Indians stepped into the light, heavy chains rattling as they
moved. Locked in a cramped, stifling, malodorous cell void
of most light, the two prisoners still had their hands and legs
shackled.

Ball studied his two clients and realized at the same time
that the two Kiowas were sizing up the attorneys. Satanta
was tall, maybe even six feet, slightly chubby but muscular,
with broad shoulders and a barrel chest, his shoulder-length
hair and clothes caked in dust. His embroidered moccasins
would have been beautiful if not for having been soiled with
excrement and mud, and a giant round presidential medal-
lion, tarnished, hung over his heart. Even in the dim light,
Ball could see Satanta's face clearly. His black eyes shone
hard, anger masked his face, and he spoke back at Horace
Jones in a belligerent tone. Big Tree was shorter, slimmer, his
skin not quite as coppery, his nose not as flat. He wore only
plain moccasins and breechcloth, with a lone eagle feather in

his braided hair. It dawned upon Ball that he had never been this close to an Indian.

Jones spoke again in the harsh tongue, and Satanta answered less harshly. The great Orator of the Plains stepped closer, still studying Ball and Woolfolk, as the interpreter from Fort Sill made the introductions. Big Tree remained silent. After a few more exchanges between Jones and Satanta, the Kiowa chief nodded, and Jones, in English, told Woolfolk and Ball to be seated.

There were no chairs, and Ball struggled to sit cross-legged on the hard floor, finally giving up and sticking his legs out to his side. Woolfolk had no problem with the posture. Nor did Jones. Satanta said something and pointed at Ball, and even Big Tree joined in the laughter.

"Satanta says you sit like a woman," Jones said.

"Tell him it's an old war wound," Ball replied. "Prevents me from sitting like that."

"I ain't tellin' him no lie."

"It's no lie," Ball said. "Tell him the wound was given to me by the bluecoats."

After Jones's translation, Satanta nodded approvingly and began a long speech about the mistreatment of the Kiowas, culminating with his wrongful imprisonment. Ball watched in amazement as the Kiowa and Jones conversed in rapid-fire talk and hand gestures. After Jones ended the translation, he explained to the two attorneys. "I'm speakin' to him in Comanch. 'Tain't quite as hard on one's ears as Kio-way. Satanta an' Big Tree both speak it good. My Kio-way ain't as strong as my Comanch, an' I don't savvy all the languages this ol' buck can talk."

"What other languages does he speak?" Woolfolk asked curiously.

Jones asked the question in Comanche, and Satanta answered proudly. "In addition to Kio-way an' Comanch," Jones translated, "he says he speaks the tongue of the Cheyenne, Arapaho, Apache, an' Mexicans—"

"You can't talk to him in Spanish?" Woolfolk asked again.

"My Mex ain't that good. His ain't neither, if you wanna know the truth. Satanta also can speak the tongue of the black robe."

"Black robe?" Ball asked, which led to another speech, which Satanta ended with: *"Quid agitur."*

Ball blinked, tried to place the saying. He remembered his years at The College of William and Mary. No, even further back.

"Latin?" Joe Woolfolk had solved the mystery first.

"Uh-huh," Jones said and spit, missing the slop bucket in the opposite corner, not that it mattered.

"Latin." Ball looked at Satanta and said, *"Cedo tuam mihi dexteram, agedum."*

The Kiowa responded, *"Em debatur, tene."*

"Latin ain't one of my lingoes either, gents," Jones said. "The black robes was the priests, come out here to educate these heathens, save their souls. Lot of good they done. Catholic priests. Now Quakers. Injuns ain't Christians an' don't wanna be. Hell, I ain't neither an' don't wanna be."

Satanta spoke again, in Comanche, and Jones translated. "He says he has seen your face in battle, Mr. Woolfolk, says he knows you to be a warrior. He says Mr. Ball is a thinker, but also your wound proves you to be brave. Satanta trusts fighters. He will trust you with his life and the life of Big Tree. He asks you to explain this trial, though."

Ball stretched out his already stiffening right leg and began to reply to his client's request.

July 1, 1871
Jacksboro, Texas

The *venire facias* had been issued, calling for "fifty good and lawful men" to show up at the Jack County courthouse at eight-thirty Wednesday morning. Charles Soward thanked the sheriff, the county clerk, the district solicitor, and the two appointed defense attorneys.

"Is there any other matter that merits this court's attention on a Saturday morning?" he asked without feeling. "If not, I'm in the mood for breakfast. All I had was a cup of coffee this morning."

"Your Honor?" The table legs scratched the second-story floor as Joseph A. Woolfolk stood.

Sam Lanham and clerk J. R. Robinson looked surprised. Soward frowned his annoyance. "Yeah?" The judge's eyes darkened.

"If the grand jury bills our clients for murder, Your Honor," Woolfolk said, "I want you and the esteemed prosecutor of the Thirteenth District to know that we intend to file for a change of venue."

"That's outrageous!" Lanham snapped.

"Shucks, Sam," Woolfolk drawled. "I seem to recall hearin' that you wanted to change the venue last month. Said it wasn't safe to hold trial here in Jack County with all them injuns runnin' 'bout the countryside." Woolfolk grinned before returning his stare to the judge's bench. "Judge, you know for a fact that it's impossible to seat an impartial jury against two injuns in this town."

Soward's gaze left Woolfolk and landed on Thomas Ball, still seated. "Do you agree with this, counselor?"

"We're just informing Your Honor of our intent to file a pretrial motion for a change of venue, in the fairness of justice," Ball said. He must have been practicing the speech. "We wouldn't want a trial verdict overturned on appeal because of an error by Your Honor."

Son of a bitch. At least the gallery was closed to reporters this morning. The newspapermen hadn't expected anything big to come out of today's proceedings. Neither had Soward. "I remember telling you two to be smart," Soward said sternly. Ball and Woolfolk did not answer.

"If you file such a motion, gentlemen, it will be denied," Soward said.

"Fine," Woolfolk said. "Then, should we lose the case, we'll appeal."

"And you'll lose there, too," Soward said testily. "Where would you have us try Satanta and Big Tree—if they are indicted? You say two Kiowas couldn't get an impartial jury in Jacksboro. Well, could you seat twelve disinterested men in Parker County? Tarrant County? Travis County? I say, and the appellate courts in this state will back me up, that you stand as good of a chance in Jack County as you would anywhere else in Texas." The gavel banged. "Court is adjourned until the grand jury convenes here Wednesday."

Soward swore under his breath as he shed his robe and retreated to his quarters. He fetched his bottle of bourbon from a drawer and splashed three fingers, then another two, into a glass. Immediately, he drank. The whiskey burned, and he coughed, unlike a good Kentuckian, but he was edgy. Damn Woolfolk and Ball to hell. It had seemed smart appointing those two as defense counselors. Not only did Joe Woolfolk hate practicing law, he hated Indians—or so Soward had thought. Hell, Woolfolk certainly had fought them enough. And Thomas Ball? A nice man, a good lawyer, but green as they came. He expected those two to plead their clients guilty, maybe make an impassioned speech pleading for mercy to get their names in the national press. But to press for a change of venue? Well, maybe they just wanted to strut a little. They had better act smarter, however, after Satanta and Big Tree were indicted.

He took another swallow. This time, he did not cough.

July 4, 1871
Jacksboro, Texas

It felt good to hear Amanda Doniphan's friendly greeting. "What you been doing, Tomball?" she asked upon arriving at the table in the Wichita Hotel's dining room. It was probably the first time Ball had smiled in days.

"I thought you were mad at me." He caught Joe Woolfolk,

sitting across from him, staring at the cracked ceiling, trying not to listen to the conversation.

"I got over it. So, what you been doing?"

"Speaking Latin to a Kiowa chief, reciting T. Maccii Plauti. And preparing for trial. I'm actually surprised you or anyone else is speaking to us."

She shook her head. "Most folks ain't mad at you two because y'all got hoodwinked into taking the case. Least, that's what I hear. Somebody had to defend 'em. They ain't gonna shoot you for that. 'Sides, folks here like a good speech. I hear they indicted them two this morning."

"They did," Ball said. "Big surprise."

"What y'all two eating today?"

"What do you recommend?"

Well, some things had not changed in Jacksboro, although, after Amanda left to place their orders, Ball wondered what M. J. Shelley thought of him. He had not seen her since her surprise visit to Weatherford. He heard a Texas drawl and looked up. "You say something, Joe?"

His colleague shook his head. "I said I hear Lanham plans on makin' a speech after supper." He stuck out his jaw toward the opposite end of the restaurant, and Ball followed the gaze. "Celebratin' Independence Day."

Samuel W. T. Lanham stood in the corner, flanked by reporters furiously scratching on their note pads. Outside, Ball and Woolfolk had passed another pack of journalists interviewing slow-talking Sheriff Michael McMillan.

"You want to go hear him?"

"Nah."

Like the rest of Jacksboro, the dining room was packed. Jack County's seat had suddenly become the place to be. The stageline had upped its run to and from Weatherford daily, while the Widow Baggett had started putting two guests in each room, although Ball, so far, had been spared a roommate—perhaps because he remained her nicest tenant, even though he had been forced to defend those two Kiowas.

"Funny," Ball said softly.

"How's that?" Woolfolk looked up while stirring his coffee.

"Mackenzie's hounded by writers. So are McMillan, Soward, Lanham. Everyone, it seems, but us, the defense attorneys. You'd figure the press would be interested in what our clients have to say."

"Them scribes don't know us yet, Tom," Woolfolk said, calling his partner something other than Ball for the first time since they had met. "But they will. Come tomorry."

Chapter 12

"Mistaken sympathy for these vile creatures has kindled the flames around the cabin of the pioneer and despoiled him of his hard earnings, murdered and scalped our people, and carried off our women into captivity worse than death."

—Samuel W. T. Lanham

July 4, 1871
Jacksboro, Texas

Torches and lanterns outside the Wichita Hotel attracted scores of june bugs and every other pesky insect that called Texas home, but also brought perhaps five hundred people to gather in front of the frame building, churning up thick dust while they talked excitedly, waiting for Jack County's man of honor to finish his supper, step outside, and regale the throng with a speech.

M. J. Shelley stood across the street in front of McConnell's Jacksboro Mercantile, leaning against the stone building between two windows displaying bone cutters, corn shellers and grinders, stubble plows, and other necessities available for purchase. She wanted to hear this lawyer Lanham reassure the people of Jack County—but mostly herself—that the Kiowas who butchered her good friends Samuel Elliott and Nathan Long would pay for their barbarism, would hang by the neck until dead.

Unseemly thoughts for a lady? What had become of

Christian charity? Forgiveness? She couldn't answer those questions. Or could she? She was human, suffered human foibles, and she was Texican. Maybe the latter explained why she wanted not only justice, but revenge. In fact, she didn't want Satanta and Big Tree to hang. She wanted them to be tortured, like those fiends had brutalized poor Samuel Elliott.

The din rose as the Wichita Hotel's front door swung open but died just as suddenly when two men—neither of them Samuel W. T. Lanham—walked outside. M. J. joined the gathering with a sigh until she recognized one of the men leaving the hotel as Thomas Ball.

Most folks in Jack and Parker counties spoke highly of the young Virginian. Prudence Baggett had cornered her after church one Sunday, saying how a man like Thomas Ball would be a fine catch to land, good-looking and a lawyer to boot. M. J. had simply smiled pleasantly and excused herself without making any comment the slim widow could spread across the county faster than a telegraph wire. She hadn't even kissed Thomas Ball and likely never would. He was a greenhorn, no doubt about that, and had the misfortune to have been appointed to defend those two savages locked up at Fort Richardson. She pitied him, but not his appointed partner. She had never cared much for Joseph A. Woolfolk.

Sliding into the shadows, M. J. prayed that neither lawyer would see her. The precaution proved unnecessary, as Ball and Woolfolk walked down the opposite boardwalk, never glancing in her direction. For days she had been avoiding Thomas Ball, although she wasn't quite sure why. Mainly, she didn't know what to say to him, forced to defend the two Kiowas she loathed. Forced to plead for the lives of those two butchers. Maybe he would say they were guilty, throw them on the mercy of a sure-to-be-merciless judge and jury. That's what everyone expected the defense attorneys to do. She prayed Joe Woolfolk wouldn't talk him into doing something stupid.

Everyone in Texas knew Satanta and Big Tree were guilty. Mayor McConnell and Sheriff McMillan were already planning the gallows, trying to figure out the best place where the most people could attend, and haggling with Roy Scott over the cost of printing and delivering the invitations to the executions. Funny, she thought, how the people of Jacksboro had been adamant against holding this trial in their town. Fear had made way for excitement. Earlier today, she had heard one townsman comment, "Who needs fireworks on this Fourth of July?" No one had expected this. Visitors from across the state, journalists from around the country, arriving daily because Indians were to be tried under white law for the first time in the United States. Little old Jacksboro would be written about in history books.

Several men, and a few women, including Mrs. Prudence Baggett, walked down the street, joining the throng, except for two cowboys who made a beeline for the Green Frog. Suddenly, they spotted M. J. One nudged the other, and the two lanky, pigeon-toed waddies with greasy hair and thick mustaches ambled over to the mercantile.

"Evenin'," one said, crushing out his cigarette on the boardwalk with a boot heel.

"You look divine, ma'am," said the other, sweeping off his dust-covered, sweat-stained Boss of the Plains.

Both men reeked of sweat, tobacco, and whiskey.

The first cowhand glared at his bunky, not pleased at being upstaged, before turning back toward M. J., smiling and adding, "Yes'm, divine. Yer the purtiest thing ever I laid eyes on." He looked up at the brim and quickly remembered his manners, or so he probably thought, and snatched off his slouch hat. M. J. simply stared at the torches in front of the hotel. The two simpletons moved closer, flanking her, leaning against the two windows.

"My name's Rex," said one man.

"I'm Danny," said the other.

First drunk: "Come up from McLellan County to see the show."

Second drunk: "Guess we wasn't the only ones. You live hereabouts?"

First drunk: "She's deaf, Danny. Must be dumb, too."

Second drunk: "Pity. I like my gals to make noise." He laughed, and M. J. shuddered and closed her eyes.

First drunk, snickering: "Well, least she's moving. That means she's alive."

New voice: "Why don't you two boys move along?"

M. J. forced her eyes open. Peter Lynn stood on the boardwalk in front of her, backed by a handful of men, some of whom she knew. Lynn kept his thumbs hooked around the Navy Colt shoved in his waistband. The first cowboy donned his hat, spun around, and hurried toward the Green Frog, never saying a word. The second one, however, took a challenging step toward Peter Lynn.

"Go ahead," Lynn said evenly.

The cowboy dropped his right hand near a holstered revolver. M. J. held her breath.

"Come on, Danny!" the first drunk called. "Let's finish gettin' roostered."

She felt the tension lift as the second cowboy swung off the boardwalk and joined his companion.

Peter Lynn approached her, removing his hat while the rest of her rescuers left them alone to find a better place to view the speech. "You shouldn't be out here all alone, Miss Shelley," Lynn said.

Miss Shelley! When would he ever call her M. J.? When she didn't answer—she had yet to recover her voice—Lynn cast a hard look at the two weaving cowhands. "You say the word, ma'am, and me and the boys'll run them two walking whiskey vats out of town on a rail. You just say the word, Miss Shelley. I don't like it one bit. Used to have us a nice town here. Now it's full of tinhorns and newspapermen and all sorts of rapscallions. Be glad when this trial is over." He was looking at her again. "Yes, ma'am, you give the word, and I guaran-damn-tee you—pardon my language, Miss Shelley—but you tell me, and I'll make sure that them two waddies won't be no bother to you no more."

Smiling with relief, and maybe something even stronger,

she stepped toward her friend. She felt like collapsing in his long arms but stopped abruptly when someone cried out from down the street, "We catched them Kio-ways! The Kio-ways escaped, but we got 'em! Fetch a coupla ropes!"

She had never seen a stampede before. Naturally, living in Jacksboro, she had heard cowboys and ranchers describe them, but she never could really picture what one must look and feel like until now—until she watched five hundred men, women, and children storm down Main Street toward the voice, crying, shouting, jerking free the torches for light, leaving M. J. and Peter Lynn in darkness.

"Christ A'mighty," Peter Lynn swore.

M. J. stepped around him. "Let's go see," she said but felt his right hand clamp her wrist and pull her back.

"No, ma'am," Lynn said forcefully. "That ain't no place for a lady, Miss Shelley. I'm taking you home."

Gagging on the tobacco juice he had swallowed, head pounding, lungs burning, Corporal John B. Charlton crawled on his knees through the thick dirt, reached out with his left hand, and grasped the top of an empty hitching rail. When he vomited, the strangest thought passed through his mind: *"Serves you right,"* he could hear his mother telling him. *"I tol' you an' your pa that chewin' baccer's a nasty habit."*

He waited for the dizziness to pass and his vision to clear, then wiped his mouth on his shirtsleeve before gripping the rail with his right hand. Somewhere behind him came the sound of shouts and curses, and he shook his head, coughed, and pulled himself to his feet.

Charlton wobbled a moment, searching the ground for his Remington revolver. No luck. Damn Texicans had stolen it, which meant a replacement would come out of next month's pay. Probably two months, even more if that martinet Mackenzie tore off Charlton's stripes and busted him down to private. Another wave of nausea came, and he shuddered, knowing he had already puked his guts out and hating the feeling of dry heaves.

Well, it was his own darn fault. Lieutenant Carter had asked if he wanted a detachment to accompany him to the sheriff's office, and Charlton had declined. All he was doing was delivering a letter to Sheriff McMillan detailing Colonel Mackenzie's plans for the transfer of the two Kiowa prisoners to the courthouse. He had personally placed the envelope in the sheriff's hands, then decided to stick around outside the Wichita Hotel to hear the speech prosecutor Lanham was supposed to make. Shucks, it was Independence Day, and hearing a good speech certainly beat listening to the regimental band toot its horns back at the post.

A Texican pointed at Charlton's uniform and started jawing with Charlton real friendly-like, describing the campaigns with Hood and Cleburne and the slaughter at Franklin, telling him how, yes, sir, the Yanks had earned his respect that day—not grasping the fact that, in 1864, John B. Charlton hadn't yet run away from home to enlist, that he hadn't joined up until after the surrender and had never even been to Tennessee. One minute Charlton had been listening to this gent, and the next thing he knew, somebody was airing his lungs, saying Satanta and Big Tree had escaped but had been captured here in town, and Charlton was running with the crowd to keep from being trampled.

When he had seen the two Indians a handful of cowboys held, hands tied behind their backs, Charlton had fought his way through the howling mob, protesting, cursing, battering one of the dumb peckerwoods with his revolver's butt before he himself went down, punched, clubbed, kicked.

The crowd had moved on. After the nausea passed, Charlton reached out and tested the knot on the back of his skull, the cut above his right eye, his bloodied nose and busted lips. Probably had a few bruised ribs, too, maybe even broken. Sergeant Varily would say Charlton deserved another promotion, but he kept thinking how if he didn't stop those

dumb Texicans, he'd probably land in the guardhouse next
door to Satanta and Big Tree.

He left the safety of the hitching post and staggered after
the mob, which had assembled now in front of Waggoner's
Livery Stable, painted with eerie shadows from the flicker-
ing torches in the crowd. Summoning strength he didn't
know he possessed, Charlton decided the best course of action would be to flank the mob. He had learned the follies of
a frontal assault the hard way, like the Texican fighting with
Patrick Cleburne and John Bell Hood. Since the waddies had
stolen his revolver, Charlton made his way to the side of the
livery and lifted a singletree. The iron bar didn't give him the
comfort of a .44, but he'd lay some mighty bad headaches on
them clods before they lynched anybody.

"You hold on there!" yelled Charlton, braining the first
man who turned around. He clubbed another, shouting that
those two men were innocent, that the Kiowas were locked
up at Fort Richardson under heavy guard. Another Texican
went down. Someone fired a pistol, and Charlton gasped,
eventually understanding that the shot hadn't been at him. He
jabbed one man in the stomach, spotted his stolen Remington, and cursed.

Then he went down.

"Stop it! Stop it! Stop this criminal act!"

Yelling in protest, Sam Lanham pushed Roy Scott aside,
punched one cowboy in the stomach, and fired his .31-caliber
Manhattan over his head repeatedly until he stood in front of
two bloodied Indians who stank of whiskey and vomit. Ever
taciturn, the Indians just stared, either too drunk to realize
what was about to happen to them or simply resigned to their
fate. Two ropes dangled from the rafters of the livery, but the
saddle tramps who had caught these two unfortunate
Tonkawa scouts had yet to put the nooses over their heads.
Lanham whirled around, turning his back to the cowboy
ringleaders, and faced the crowd, surprised to recognize
many faces. Faces of good men. Faces of some of Jack

County's leading citizens, several who had served on the grand jury that had handed down the bill of indictment earlier today. It shamed him. Off to his right, two men parted and let a battered and bruised corporal off the ground. The soldier, panting, bleeding, half-dead, still gripped a singletree as if it were Excalibur.

"Gentlemen," Lanham said. He blinked in shock and corrected himself. "Ladies and gentlemen, please, I beg of you. Stop this and go home before you make a horrible mistake."

"Them ain't even Kiowa!" the corporal shouted. "They's two Tonk scouts from the fort!"

"He's a Yankee liar," said one of the cowboys behind Lanham, who turned to face the man, a weather-beaten waddie with broad shoulders and an old horse pistol in his right hand.

"Is he?" Lanham asked. His voice remained surprisingly calm. "Do you want to risk the wrath of General Mackenzie and the Fourth Cavalry? These men . . ." He motioned to the prisoners and faced the mob. "These men are your protectors as much as the federal soldiers. These men hate the Kiowa and Comanche as passionately as many of you. Don't commit murder. Don't make me try you for a horrible crime. Don't make me send you to Huntsville or the gallows."

Sheriff McMillan, Charley Jordan, W. M. McConnell, and a handful of other men, armed with shotguns, pushed their way through the crowd, and Lanham knew the danger had passed. The corporal and the Tonks would soon be free to return to the post and nurse their injuries and hangovers. Behind him, he heard the leader of the cowboys holster the massive horse pistol.

A dry voice whispered, "Let'm go, Jed. We'll kill them two bucks tomorrow morn before they reach the courthouse."

"I know most of you men," continued Lanham, addressing the crowd. He had wanted to make a speech tonight, had been expected to, and he wouldn't disappoint—not that this was the speech he had written. "I understand your pain. But mob rule is not justice. Hang these innocent Tonkawas or gun down the two Kiowas on the streets tomorrow, and everyone fails. Me. Sheriff McMillan. General Mackenzie. Judge Soward. General Sherman. And you. You've seen the newspaper reporters around town. Do you want them to write in their Eastern papers that Jacksboro, Texas, is home to seditionists and murderers? Do you want them to say that you—no, we—are no better than the savages we are attempting to assimilate into our culture?"

He shook his head, pleased that he hadn't stumbled over *assimilate*. Sarah would be proud of him.

"Wasn't it only a few weeks ago that we cried out how this trial would bring the Kiowas down upon us? We were wrong. Tonight proves that it is not the Indians we have to fear, but ourselves, our friends, our neighbors. We brutally attack a soldier who has fought the Indians we loathe. We threaten to lynch two wards of the federal government, two scouts who risk their lives to defend our farms, ranches, stores, and families."

His head shook again, this time for effect.

"I'm not one for speeches, friends. I have no political aspirations." Sarah would laugh when she heard about that bald-faced lie. "I just want to do my duty, to please my Creator, to honor my wife and son. Five years ago, I left a state ravaged by war. I came west for a new life. I settled in Texas and grew to love her almost as much as I love my wife, my parents. But tonight my heart is heavy, for I don't feel that love. I feel shame. I feel disgrace. Help me, ladies and gentlemen. Help me, and these journalists from New York, from Boston, from all over our land, help us all see that Texas, and especially Jack County, believes in God . . . believes in justice . . . believes that your humble servant can ease your pain by seeing two guilty Indians hanged." His voice roared as he pointed to the still-bound Tonks behind him. "But not these two innocent creatures!"

He realized he still held the pocket revolver, which he shoved into his shoulder holster. "Go home, friends. I promise you that tomorrow you will see justice prevail, and you will have your revenge."

When the crowd started to disperse, Lanham spun around, pulled a pocketknife from his trouser pocket, and began to saw through the ropes binding the Tonk scouts' hands. The Army corporal laid the singletree aside, pulled a revolver from one cowhand's mule-ear pocket with a curse, slid the weapon into his empty holster, and stepped forward to help Lanham free the Indians. Sheriff McMillan jabbed the barrels of his shotgun into the cowboy leader's stomach and instructed him to light a shuck out of Jack County tonight, and the would-be lynch party left without another word.

"Reckon you can make it back to the fort safe, Corporal?" McMillan asked once the streets were relatively empty and the Tonkawas were freed.

"Yeah. Thanks, Mr. Lanham." He offered his hand, which Lanham accepted, then spoke to the two scouts. "Come on, you two. Let's mosey on back before Bad Hand lifts our hair."

The Indians started to follow, but the shorter of the two paused, wiped his bloody nose, and looked back at Lanham.

"Good speech," he said in a throaty voice.

Only then did Samuel Willis Tucker Lanham remember the significance of the date, Independence Day, 1871. Today he turned twenty-five years old.

Chapter 13

"The Adjutant-General of the Army has forwarded to the Commissioner of Indian Affairs, for his information, a copy of a telegram received at the War Department from Gen. J. J. Reynolds, dated San Antonio, Texas, which states that the trial of the Indian chiefs, Kiowas, is progressing at Jacksboro. . . ."

—*New York Times,* July 16, 1871

July 4, 1871
Fort Richardson, Texas

Post Adjutant Robert G. Carter leaped from his chair, almost spilling the contents of his tumbler over his blouse. He immediately recognized the man who had just entered the office, even though the only military-issue clothing worn by the Army commander was a dark blue vest and a pair of shining cavalry boots. He wore a black porkpie hat, white shirt, no coat, broadcloth britches, and carried a Winchester Yellow Boy repeating rifle. "Sir!" he shouted before looking dumbly at the glass, recovering to slam it on the desktop and stand at attention.

"At ease, Lieutenant," William Sherman said mildly. "Happy Fourth of July."

Carter became vaguely aware of the metallic notes from the regimental band conducting a concert in front of the post hospital. Colonel Mackenzie would raise hell, privately, at

General Sherman's unexpected arrival, taking out his frustrations on the post adjutant and any other junior officer—after Sherman had left. The commanding general had foiled the colonel's plans once already, sneaking into Fort Richardson back in May when Bad Hand Mackenzie wanted to put on a show. Now he had done it again, although this time, if only by coincidence of the holiday, at least the band was playing.

"We didn't expect the general, sir," Carter apologized, still at attention despite the at-ease order. Smiling, Sherman walked forward and picked up the glass, lifted it to his nose, then swirled the amber contents around.

"Brandy?"

"Yes, sir." Carter swallowed. "If the general will allow me to explain . . ."

"Hogwash," Sherman said. "Relax, Mr. . . . Carter, isn't it?"

"Yes, sir."

"Well, Carter, let me remind you that I served with Ulysses S. Grant in the late war, and neither as a general nor as our supreme commander has the president ever been known to preach temperance. Nor has Colonel Mackenzie, though, if memory serves, he favors bourbon." He handed the glass to the lieutenant, who took it hesitantly. "I'm traveling quietly, Mr. Carter. Want to observe the Kiowa trial. You'll be a witness, isn't that right?"

"Yes, sir." He quickly gulped down the brandy and slid the empty glass across the desk. "If the attorneys plead Satanta and Big Tree innocent."

"They will," Sherman said matter-of-factly.

He studied the four-star general briefly. "Perhaps," he said after an uncomfortable pause, "but most people around here believe those two will plead guilty and ask for clemency."

Sherman reached inside his vest and withdrew a cigar. He clipped it, found a match, and fired up the smoke, thought of something else, and fetched another long nine from the pocket and tossed it to Carter. "Would you?" he asked Carter after flicking the match into a spittoon.

"Sir?" Uncomfortably, Carter allowed William Tecumseh Sherman to clip his cigar and light it.

"Would you plead those two guilty if you were a defense attorney?" Sherman asked after Carter exhaled a plume of blue smoke.

"Well, sir, it's hard to say. Satanta and Big Tree are obviously guilty. Woolfolk and Ball live around here. If they defend them, they'd be called Indian lovers. Their lives might be threatened. On the other hand . . ."

"On the other hand, they are members of the Texas bar and duly sworn to fight for their clients. I don't know Mr. Ball or Mr. Woolfolk, but I imagine they desire glory. This case could promise them that. At least, I hope they defend their clients. With zeal, too. If they don't, the savage-loving Eastern papers will call this trial a farce, and I don't want the sentence Satanta and Big Tree deserve overturned."

"Yes, sir." Carter wasn't about to argue with a four-star general, even if he'd bet his annual salary that neither Joe Woolfolk nor Thomas Ball sought any glory.

"Who else from the Army does Lanham want to testify for the state?"

Carter cleared his throat before replying. "Colonel Mackenzie and Sergeant Varily, along with the post's assistant surgeon, Captain Patzki."

"I'm thinking I might throw in my two cents' worth during the trial myself," Sherman said and removed the cigar. "If you would, Lieutenant, I desire to talk to Colonel Mackenzie."

"Yes, sir," Carter said, fired off a salute, and raced into the darkness to fetch his commanding officer.

"General," Ranald Mackenzie protested. "Lieutenant Carter here informs me that you traveled from Indian Territory without the benefit of a military escort. Sir, you are too valuable—"

"Balderdash," Sherman said. "I told Mr. Carter I was traveling quietly. Besides"—grinning, he picked up the .44 rifle he had leaned in a corner and patted the stock—"I have sixteen shots here myself."

The two men chatted briefly about the upcoming trial, about the testimony from Army personnel, until Sherman, seemingly satisfied, suggested that they retire to Mackenzie's quarters. It certainly beat listening to the dreadful regimental band. Before they could leave the adjutant's office, however, a pale, bruised, and bloodied corporal walked through the doors, letting in the miserable strains from the band attempting Bach, and saluted. Two equally misused Tonkawa scouts followed him.

"Corporal Charlton!" Lieutenant Carter exclaimed. "What in blazes happened to you?" His gaze carried past the soldier to the Tonks. "And them?"

"Had a little row in town, Lieutenant," Charlton said in a drawl. "Dumb oafs saw these two scouts and thought they was Big Tree and Satanta. Came close to lynchin' 'em. Figgered I'd best report to you, sir."

"Did you deliver my letter to Sheriff McMillan?" Mackenzie asked.

"Yes, sir," said the corporal, apparently noticing the other two officers for the first time. His eyes widened when he recognized William T. Sherman, who just stood there, jaws working, shredding his cigar like a McCormick Reaper.

"Texans," Sherman said at last, spitting his ruined cigar into the spittoon. "The whole lot of them lack the brains of one tiny cockroach."

"That's the God's honest truth, Gen'ral," the corporal agreed before continuing his report to Mackenzie. "Sir, the district attorney calmed them down, and the sheriff ran the leaders of the lynch mob out of town, but I think we should double the guards tomorrow." The glare from Mackenzie's face stopped Charlton cold. "Pardon me for blurtin' out my feelin's out of turn," the buffoon mumbled apologetically. "I ain't no officer."

Mackenzie was about to tell Corporal Charlton that he was absolutely right, that no noncommissioned officer started telling him what the United States Fourth Cavalry should do, but before he could form his rebuke, Sherman stepped in front of Charlton, placing a hand on the man's torn blouse at the shoulder, and said, "That's all right, Corporal."

"Indeed," Mackenzie added, recovering quickly and spinning to face Lieutenant Carter. "Mr. Carter, you will hand-pick the guard detail for tomorrow morning, and you will command it. Put sentries tonight along the banks of Lost Creek. Those brambles would make a fine spot for a sharp-shooter. I want enough soldiers surrounding Big Tree and Satanta that a flea couldn't jump off one of those red niggers."

"Very good, sir," Carter barked out.

"Report to Doctor Patzki, Corporal Charlton," Sherman told the corporal, to Mackenzie's surprise. "You look like you need stitches. And tell the captain to give you a shot of whiskey. Tell him I said so."

July 4, 1871
Jacksboro, Texas

Clear but potent liquid splashed from Joe Woolfolk's flask into two shot glasses Thomas Ball had fetched from the chest of drawers. The Widow Baggett ran a nice boarding house, Woolfolk had heard, so what would she say if she learned her favorite guest kept the evil tools of scamper juice in his room? Likely, Ball also had a bottle stashed somewhere, too, but Woolfolk figured his personal stock was better than anything this dandy kept on hand. After passing one glass to his host, Woolfolk lifted his own in toast. "Salute," he said and threw down the corn liquor.

"Here's how," Ball said, lifting his glass, and downed the forty-rod without flinching. Ball gestured to a chair and sat on the edge of his bed. Woolfolk took the proffered seat and thumbed idly through a law book on the table.

"Any ideas in here?" he asked.

"Many great ideas," replied Ball, the liquor thickening his

Virginia accent, "many great laws, but none pertaining to our case. You sure you want to go through with this?"

He shrugged. "Folks call me a fighter. Can't disappoint 'em even if they don't know nothin'."

"You fought the Indians," Ball said. "Satanta even remembers you. He said so."

Another shrug. Apparently Ball didn't notice Woolfolk roll his eyes at the comment.

"Were you born here?"

"Nah," Woolfolk answered. "Meade County, Kentucky." He found the flask, refilled his glass, and leaned forward to give Ball another drink. They both downed the shots easily, and Woolfolk stretched back. The corn liquor, from his own still, loosened his tongue. "Didn't arrive here till 'fifty-eight, when I was twenty-two."

"As a lawyer?"

His head shook. "Actually, I come here as a surveyor. Oh, I had a law degree. Went to St. Mary's College, University of Missouri, and the University of Louisville's law school. You'd figger a man with so much education could speak English a mite better than I do." He smiled. "Comes from too many years out here on the frontier, I reckon. Anyhow, I settled in Young County, surveyed, even got elected county clerk before the war."

"When did you fight Indians?"

He snorted, shaking his head. "My reputation as an injun fighter is mostly nothin' more than a bunch of big windies."

"Big windies?"

"Tall tales, fishin' stories. Bunch of ol' Texicans makin' up lies, stretchin' the truth. Oh, when I first got here I chased them red devils almost before I had my horse unsaddled and threw many a shoe on many a horse durin' the war tryin' to catch 'em. Got elected second lieutenant of the rangers out at Fort Belknap. Most of the menfolk went off to fight the Yanks, and the Comanch and Kiowa took advantage. Lifted many scalps. Burned out many a homestead. Weren't pretty. But to be honest, I chased the savages more'n I ever fit 'em.

Sent a few balls after 'em, but they were out of range. No, sir, Ball, I never once heard a war whoop up close. Don't recollect seein' Satanta neither. More'n likely, that ol' liar was just tryin' to butter me up with a Kiowa compliment. Wish I had had him in my sights, though. Wish I had shot that bastard dead many years ago."

"So you spent the war out here?"

"Nope. Got sick of that. No pay. Nothin' but saddle sores, headaches, and the trots from bad water. Anyway, I schemed me a commission in the regular army, and they sent me back East." He made a mock salute. "General John Hunt Morgan. Joined him up in Tennessee."

Ball arched his eyebrows. "Really. You served with Morgan?"

Woolfolk couldn't figure that one out. Ball was impressed that he had ridden alongside John Hunt Morgan, that crazy but brilliant Alabaman whom many considered to be no better than a horse thief. Hell, Ball had fought with Robert E. Lee, an honest-to-God hero respected by Yanks and Rebs, priests and paupers. He answered, "Till the Yanks invited me up north as their guest."

"I know that feeling," Ball said somberly. "Point Lookout."

"I was at Camp Chase. Morgan led us across the Ohio to bring back some Yankee horseflesh. That's when Morgan got captured, sent to the Ohio pen."

"But he escaped?"

"He did, then got killed in Tennessee. Quite a character. Anyway, I wound up a prisoner, too, long before the Yanks caught Gen'ral Morgan. Me and three others got catched by Virginia militia around Point Pleasant. Those dumb Yanks, though, only sent two guards with us four prisoners, so it wasn't long before we jumped them, tied them to a tree, and took off south. Didn't make it far, though—us being afoot— before we got captured again, and they shipped us, with a few more guards this time, to Camp Chase. That was an eye-opener. Stinkin' mud and shit. Smell alone would gag a turkey vulture. Smallpox. Dysentery. Seven thousand of us Rebs crammed in a calaboose built for half that many. Damn near killed me." He shook his head sadly at the memory, sighed, and continued. "I got paroled, but the war was all but over then, for me and the Confederacy. Camp Chase ruined my health, took me three, four years before I completely re-covered. Went back to Kentucky, met up with Lizzie again, and tied the knot, then came back to Texas in 'sixty-seven. That was Lizzie's idea. She figgered the climate would do me good after Camp Chase. What about you?"

"Not much to tell." But Woolfolk knew Ball would talk. The corn liquor would see to that, coupled with the fact that Ball was a lawyer. The Virginian motioned at the flask, and Woolfolk filled the shot glasses again. "I was admitted to the Virginia bar in 1858 after four years at the College of William and Mary," Ball began. "I practiced in Northumber-land County—that's where I grew up—till the war. I was elected lieutenant in the Forty-seventh Virginia Infantry."

"Reckon you saw more action than I did."

Ball showed his sad smile again. "More than I ever wanted to. Seven Pines. Manassas. Sharpsburg. Fredericksburg. Chancellorsville. Gettysburg. Anyway, I took a ball in my leg during the Wilderness fight, got captured and sent to Point Lookout. That was my living hell." He shivered, though the room remained a furnace. "Still is, I think. But I survived somehow, made it back home after the surrender, tried my practice again, but, oh, Virginia just wasn't the same anymore, so I moved here. New state, new future. Texas held promise. That's what everyone was saying back in 'sixty-nine."

"Promise." Woolfolk scoffed, and, flask empty, reached inside his pocket for a plug of tobacco. He bit off a mouthful and tossed the quid to Ball. "Only thing Texas promised any-body is an early grave, Ball. You got hoodwinked, same as a ton of tenderfeet."

Ball took a substantial chaw himself before returning the plug to Woolfolk, who ran long fingers through his unkempt mane, still shaking his head at the naivete of Thomas Ball and many other settlers.

"Why did you take this case, Joe?" Ball asked suddenly.

Woolfolk leaned to his side and spit, and Ball relaxed at the reassuring ping of the juice hitting the brass spittoon underneath the wash basin. After wiping his mouth with the back of his hand, Woolfolk stared at Ball and answered, "No reason."

"I told you you didn't have to."

"You did."

"You don't really hate those Indians, do you?" Ball's voice, while steady, held a challenge to it.

He spit again, hitting his target, and leaned forward, pointing a long, calloused finger at Ball. "Now, you don't know what the Sam Hill you're talkin' 'bout. There ain't no such thing as the 'noble red man.' I done told you that before. I ain't a newcomer like you, Ball. I seen what those braves can do. Buried many a friend, includin' some of 'em killed at Salt Creek Prairie."

Ball smiled pleasantly, which really irritated Woolfolk. The Virginian fired a stream of juice into the spittoon and said, "You respect them, Satanta and Big Tree. So do I."

Damn that arrogant Virginian, speaking so smoothly, not acting mad, just talking like a gentleman. "I respect what they can do," Woolfolk snapped. "I respected the Yanks I fit in the war, too. Don't mean I like 'em none."

He sighed and realized at last he had been enjoying this . . . debate . . . as much as his counterpart. Neither man once raised his voice, although perhaps because they feared they would wake up the neighbors and incur Prudence Baggett's wrath. They weren't angry, merely debating. Good practice, Woolfolk decided, for tomorrow's shindig.

"Do you believe those two Indians should hang?" Ball asked as he stood, opened the armoire, and—Woolfolk grinned with the knowledge his earlier suspicions were correct—withdrew a bottle of Irish whiskey, which he used to fill the two shot glasses.

"It's better'n rottin' in Huntsville," Woolfolk answered and shot down the whiskey, careful not to swallow any tobacco juice. "I do know a little 'bout injuns, Ball. They're a lot like you and me in that regard. Point Lookout. Camp Chase. Put a Kiowa in a place like that, the state prison, and it'll kill 'em, only long and slow. That ain't right. A hangin's merciful."

Ball also managed to down his whiskey but not his tobacco juice, which took a careful man. Woolfolk had seen many a ranger and Reb lose his supper trying that maneuver. "But not lawful," Ball said. "That's why you took the case, isn't it?"

This debate left him tired. "Maybe it's 'cause I fit for the Confederacy, Ball, just like you. Maybe I believe in lost causes."

He rose then, gingerly, the corn liquor and Jameson making his legs unsteady, as if he had been riding a horse all day and had just swung down from the saddle. He spit a final time, found his flask, slipped it into a back pocket, and grabbed his hat, jamming it on his narrow head. "Best turn in," he drawled. "We got us a big row tomorrow. We'd better come up with some strategy before breakfast."

"I'll meet you at the Wichita Hotel at six. Where are you staying?"

Woolfolk hooked his thumb. "Out yonder somewhere. I'll make a camp."

"A camp?" Ball rose, perplexed. "Surely you can't be sleeping in a bedroll with the trial of the century about to start . . ."

"Can and will," Woolfolk said as he pulled open the door to Ball's room. "I ain't sleepin' three or four to a bed at the hotel or bunkin' with you, and it's too far for me to be travelin' to and from my ranch. 'Sides, one thing I did learn chasin' injuns. It's hard to shoot a body who don't stay in one place. Be hard for any of Nathan Long's friends to gun me down, but you . . . You'll make an invitin' target cooped up here." He grinned as he left. "I'm joshin', Ball. Leastways, I hope I am."

"I hope so, too," Ball said to the closed door.

Part II

Part II

Chapter 14

"Col. McKinzie, when called upon, proudly delivered the prisoners to Sheriff McMillan, who guarded them in the Court House, where a large crowd had already congregated."

—Dallas Herald, *July 22, 1871*

July 5, 1871
Fort Richardson, Texas

"Watch your head," Big Tree heard Hor-Ace-Jones say in Comanche and felt a strong hand on his shoulder as the blue-coats led Satanta and him from the guardhouse into the blinding sunlight. He thought back to the day at the soldier-fort called Sill, how his eyes had been burned by the sun on that morning, too, after being held captive in the darkness for so long. The memory saddened him. That's when the great warrior—Big Tree was respectful not to think the dead brave's name—had been killed in a final act of resistance.

Satanta stumbled, but the long knives did not kick him when he was down. Instead, they helped him to his feet. One even brushed the dirt off his red blanket. This seemed out of character for bluecoats. Only twice had the prisoners been allowed outside since arriving at this foul-smelling *Tehanna* soldier-fort. The first time they had been examined by the white doctor, a wretched man with wooden and metal weapons that he used to pound on Big Tree and Satanta's joints and teeth. The only enjoyable moment about that day had been hearing the bluecoats make their music. Satanta, ever partial to the bugle he often carried into battle, had nodded in approval. The music had been playing the second time, too, three suns ago when the bluecoats and Hor-Ace-Jones escorted the two chained prisoners to a little creek in the woods behind the soldier-fort and told them to wash, that they must be clean for the trial.

Today the blindness lasted only briefly, as a cloud blocked out the sun. Lifting his chained hands to protect his eyes once the sun reappeared, Big Tree stared at the strange sight in front of him. Twenty bluecoats lined the pathway from the guardhouse to the awaiting wagon, which itself was flanked by many long knives mounted on fine dun ponies. Yet few of these white-eyes bothered to watch Big Tree or Satanta. This, too, struck him as odd. Chains rattling, the two prisoners made their way to the wagon, and Big Tree understood at last that these white-eyes were not here to prevent their escape but to prevent any white-eye from killing them. He mentioned this to Satanta, who at first laughed at such a notion but a moment later nodded and praised Big Tree's keen observations.

Hor-Ace-Jones and old Stone Head's interpreter, Lee-Per, assisted first Satanta, then Big Tree, into a wagon much like the one that had brought the two warriors to this place. The bluecoat Corp-Ral-Charl-Ton, his nose bandaged, left eye swollen shut, and face and hands bruised, climbed into the seat beside a redheaded driver, spit his brown juice at the closest mule's tail, and mumbled something while resting a carbine—cocked, Big Tree noticed—on his lap.

Before the wagon started moving, two men on foot maneuvered through the tight line of horsemen. Big Tree recognized the bluecoat leader Bad Hand immediately. The second man he did not know. This white-eye was no bluecoat, though. A duster covered his clothes, but Big Tree could tell that the man's pants were black striped and his shoes were neither those worn by the long knives nor the walkabout soldiers. They shined so brightly that Big Tree thought surely shoes such as these would be worth many ponies, although personally he favored the moccasins his wife made. A high-crown black hat topped the man's head, and he tugged on the ends of a bushy mustache while studying the bluecoat arrangement.

"Very good, Lieutenant," this strange man told the long knife called Car-Ter. "I'll meet you at the courthouse in a few minutes."

Big Tree did not understand the meaning of these words. Bad Hand and Big Mustache disappeared behind the horses, Car-Ter shouted an order, and the wagon lurched forward. Hor-Ace-Jones, sitting in the back of the wagon beside Lee-Per and between two other bluecoat guards, swatted a fly and spoke in Comanche.

"The man with the big hat and mustache is called Lanham. This is the man who will speak against you in the trial, like Ball—He Who Speaks The Black Robe Tongue, as you call him—explained to you the other day."

"He must have much power with his people," Satanta said.

"Sometimes yes, sometimes no. Usually yes, though, from what I hear tell. His words are strong."

"As strong as Satanta's?" the chief asked.

"We'll see," Hor-Ace-Jones replied.

Satanta grunted and folded his arms as best as he could with the heavy irons. Big Tree stared at his wrists, which, like his ankles, had been rubbed raw by the iron bracelets. He did not understand this kind of fighting, no matter how many times He Who Speaks The Black Robe Tongue or his friend, Wolf Heart, tried to teach him. Fighting with words instead of arrows? The white-eyes were a strange tribe, with many strange customs. He chanced a glance at Satanta, who had not spoken much since their captivity. Satanta's words carried power with The Principal People. His words had once carried power with the white-eyes as well. If Satanta, He Who Speaks The Black Robe Tongue, and Wolf Heart did not speak well in this trial, Big Tree would hang.

*   *   *

July 5, 1871
Jacksboro, Texas

Two boys raced around the corner of the courthouse and al-most knocked M. J. Shelley into the dust. Grabbing her bon-net, she staggered back into Peter Lynn's arms while the boys jerked to attention and swept off their hats, begging forgive-ness and looking at Lynn with abject fear—with good reason. The cowhand's eyes showed murder. "I ought to peel your hides, the both of you," Lynn said, and, once satisfied that M. J. was out of danger, he took a threatening step toward the boys, frozen in fright, only to be stopped by the touch of M. J.'s hand.

"It's all right," she said softly, then glared at the culprits and hardened her voice. "Jehu, H. P.! The two of you should be in school. Playing hooky! Why, Wesley Call-away will—"

"No, ma'am," sixteen-year-old Jehu Atkinson blurted out. "Mr. Callaway ain't holdin' school today."

"*Isn't.* Don't say *ain't.*"

"Yes'm. He turned all us out to see the trial. Said this'd be better'n anything he could learn us at school."

"Is that true?" she asked the petrified H. P. Cook.

"Answer her, *pronto,*" Lynn snapped when the boy didn't respond immediately. "Where's your manners?"

"Yes, ma'am," he said, staring at his dusty brogans.

"Swear to it?" Lynn demanded.

"Uh-huh. No school today. We ain't lyin'."

Jehu's voice rose as he picked up the plea. "Can we go now, Miss Shelley? We're plumb sorry we scared you so, but we want to get us a seat up close so we can see them two Kio-ways."

Indignant, M. J. shook her head in disapproval. Free of school, Jehu Atkinson and H. P. Cook should be off fishing or swimming in Lost Creek or, better yet, helping their folks with chores. Besides, the trial would likely bring out some ghastly details that a teenager and little H. P., maybe ten years old, had no business hearing. "Well, all right," she relented. "But no running. Court is like church. And keep those hats off once you're inside." The two children nodded enthusiastically, jammed on their hats, and sprinted for the door, ducking behind Michael McMillan and his waiting deputies. The annoyed sheriff turned after them, muttering a curse, but, sighing, told an eager deputy to let the two kids go.

"We best hurry, too," Lynn told her, "since they want me to serve on the jury."

"I hope you're not picked, Peter," M. J. lied to him.

"Me, too," Peter Lynn lied back.

They fell into an ever-growing line and waited. The line didn't move. Sheriff McMillan wasn't letting anyone into the courthouse yet—with the exception of the two fast-running boys and the officers of the court—not until the prisoners were safely inside.

"They should let you in," M. J. told her companion. "You've been summoned for jury duty."

Uncertain, Peter Lynn shrugged, but, coaxed by M. J., asked one of the deputies if jurors were allowed inside yet. The deputy stared blankly and asked the sheriff, who stepped off the boardwalk. Cradling a shotgun underneath his left armpit, McMillan consulted a note pad in his right hand as he approached M. J. and Lynn. "You're on the jury list, ain't you, Peter?" the sheriff asked, then answered his own question. "Yeah, there you are."

"Can I go in now?"

"Not yet, Peter. Sorry. Nobody goes inside before Satanta and Big Tree."

"It's all right," Lynn said.

"Hot day," McMillan said absently.

"Yep," Lynn replied. "Gonna get hotter."

"Yep."

"Peter?"

"Yeah, Mike?" Lynn looked up, saw the sheriff had shoved the pad into a coat pocket and was holding out his right hand, palm up, in front of the cowboy.

"I'll take that Navy Colt of yours. No weapons allowed in the courthouse. Not today."

Having whipped the gray mare into a lather, Sam Lanham had to pull hard on the reins as the buggy rounded the corner and he saw the courthouse. Actually, he could see only the second story. A crowd obliterated the ground floor and the entire block.

Once he had the horse under control, he began to doubt himself. Had he and Lieutenant Carter designated enough soldiers to get the two prisoners to town safely? Did Sheriff McMillan have enough deputies? He knew Jacksboro was packed, but until he saw this throng, he hadn't realized how many people had come to the little frontier town. Math had never been his strongest subject—well, he hadn't really had a strong subject. His father used to tell him his only gift was gab. It had taken Sarah to parlay that gift into an education and law career. He prayed he wouldn't disappoint her today.

He stopped his rig in front of the Wichita Hotel, paid a boy there two bits to take the horses and buggy to the livery, picked up his grip, and hurried to the courthouse, unbuttoning his duster as he walked, answering howdies and good mornings with polite nods, shaking a few proffered hands along the way. He hadn't expected this, either. Talking to newspapermen, certainly—in fact, he looked forward to those interviews—but these folks treated him as if he were by-gawd Sam Houston or John Bell Hood. Shucks, he was just doing his job.

"You make sure you hang them sumbitches, Lanham!" came an unfriendly voice from the crowd. "Or it's your scalp."

So, not everyone treated him like deity. Yes, he surely hoped he didn't fail Sarah today.

He draped the duster over his grip and shook hands with Sheriff McMillan in front of the courthouse. From an open window in the courtroom upstairs came a few boyish taunts. Lanham's eyes became suspicious, but McMillan simply shrugged.

"Coupla kids, Sam," the sheriff drawled. "Got inside before I could stop 'em. Ain't harmin' nobody."

"Why didn't you haul them back down and tan their hides?" he asked. The threat from the faceless voice a moment earlier had hardened him this hot morning.

"I ain't sendin' a deputy chasin' after two boys not old enough to shave, Sam," McMillan replied just as testily. "Not when I need ever' shotgun I got out here." He craned his head toward a pair of wheelbarrows stationed underneath the courthouse's awning. Two guards stood next to them, shotguns on their shoulders. One wheelbarrow was already full of revolvers, gunbelts, knives, and two or three old muskets. The other looked only half full.

"Sorry, Mike," Lanham said. "Nerves."

The sheriff's head bobbed in acceptance of the apology.

Voices from the crowd grew animated, and Lanham heard trace chains jingling and horses snorting as the cavalry detail brought the prisoners down the road. He found himself scanning rooftops and facades, searching for an assassin's rifle barrel, but saw nothing out of the ordinary.

"All right, boys," McMillan called out. He stepped away from Lanham, jabbed his shotgun in an overeager black man's stomach, and warned, "Back in line, Bertram." Then he raised his voice. "Ever'body keep still. Give the Army some room. Come on now, step back. Step back. Remember, it's too hot a mornin' for buryin'. Don't y'all be foolish."

The crowded street parted like the Red Sea, making room for wagon and outriders to pass. Lieutenant Carter removed his gauntlets as he sat in the saddle and, speaking formally, asked Sheriff McMillan if he would take charge of the prisoners. Once McMillan nodded, the cut and bruised corporal jumped from the driver's box and ordered the tailgate lowered. The civilian interpreters helped Satanta and Big Tree to the ground.

No one in the crowd spoke. Even the two kids upstairs fell silent.

McMillan's deputies quickly surrounded the Kiowas and

rushed them inside the courthouse, slamming the door behind them. The transfer had gone off without a hitch. Military precision. Not bad for Carter's damnyankees and McMillan's frontiersmen. A murmur began rising from the crowd as Carter barked orders to the corporal, telling him to get the reliefs back to Fort Richardson on the double. As the soldiers started moving, Carter and Sergeant Varily dismounted, tethering their horses to the hitching rail in front of the courthouse.

"All right to leave 'em here, Sheriff?" the sergeant asked McMillan, who looked to Lanham for an answer.

"I think so." Lanham, feeling the tension lift, barely heard his own voice.

"Lieutenant," McMillan said. "I'll have to ask you and the sergeant to surrender your weapons."

The soldiers began unbuckling their rigs. "Let's get inside," Lanham said.

"Case Number Two-twenty-four, the State of Texas versus Satanta and Big Tree," clerk J. R. Robinson read. "Indictment for murder."

M. J. Shelley held her breath as the door to the second-story courtroom opened and in walked those two red devils, chains rattling, making her think of the spirits Charles Dickens had written about in *A Christmas Carol.* Thomas Ball and Joe Woolfolk followed them down the center aisle to the defense table. Sam Lanham, accompanied by W. M. McConnell and Captain C. L. "Charley" Jordan, came in next. After Judge Soward entered and motioned for the spectators to sit down, M. J. collapsed onto the uncomfortable bench, her heart pounding.

"The defendants will rise," Soward ordered.

More chains. They wore on M. J.'s nerves like fingernails on a chalkboard.

"What say you: guilty or not guilty?" Soward's voice boomed.

"Not guilty," answered Thomas Ball, and a cry went up

from the spectators, stamped out at once by Soward's sharp call for order. Only then did M. J. realize that she had been the one to yell out in shock.

She recovered quickly, telling the Widow Baggett, sitting next to her, that she was all right. She didn't like all this attention, but it soon passed. The people had crammed into the stifling thirty-by-thirty-foot room to see two murdering Kiowa renegades, not an overwrought young woman.

"Your Honor," Joe Woolfolk said once the crowd's whispers and the judge's gavel died down, "if I may." He leaned against the rickety table in front of him. "We object to this trial on the grounds that the State of Texas has no jurisdiction in this matter."

Sam Lanham jumped to his feet instantly. "Your Honor," he protested, "the crime was committed in Jack County, and, according to the map hanging in my office, Jack County is still in the great State of Texas. This most certainly is a matter for this court."

"Maybe so," Woolfolk said, "but the two men standin' before you as the accused are not citizens of Texas. Fact is, they ain't citizens at all. They's injuns, and that means they be wards of the federal government. May it please the court, we move that these proceedings be stopped and the case be transferred to the federal court that has authority in this matter."

A man sitting to M. J.'s left bolted out of his chair.

"Damn your injun-lovin' hide, Joe Woolfolk! I'll kill you for—"

Judge Soward's gavel thundered, and two fast-moving deputies grasped the enraged man. M. J. gasped. She knew him. Fred Stinson. Sang in the choir at church. Hardly ever raised his voice to anyone.

"Sheriff," the judge was ordering, pointing the handle of his gavel at Stinson, still struggling. "Remove this man and hold him in jail. Fred Stinson, you are charged with contempt of court and fined ten—"

"Contempt's exactly what I got, Charles," the man roared.

He was like an animal. "Contempt for that sumbitch Joe Woolfolk!"

"Twenty dollars and twenty days!" Soward shouted. "Get that man out of my sight."

As two deputies led the writhing, cursing Stinson away, Soward pounded on his gavel to stop the rising voices. "This is a courtroom, ladies and gentlemen. One more outburst like that, and I'll have the court cleared."

Two or three minutes passed before the mood settled. Only then did Joe Woolfolk continue his argument. When he sat down, Sam Lanham shook his head, staying in his seat, and said, "Mr. Woolfolk makes a nice speech, but I didn't hear him cite one case, one precedent."

"I agree," Soward said, and M. J. exhaled her relief. "Your motion is denied, counselor."

"Exception." This came from Thomas Ball. M. J. stared at the back of his head. What was he doing? She could expect this recalcitrance from a flagrant sort such as Joe Woolfolk, but Ball? Why was he fighting for those two . . . fiends?

"Noted. Is the state ready to proceed?"

"Yes, Your Honor."

"Is the defense ready?"

Ball answered. "Yes, Your Honor, but we request a severance. Big Tree and Satanta should be tried separately."

Soward tugged on his beard before facing Lanham. "Any objections, Mr. Lanham?"

"Well," Lanham said slowly, "I guess not, but I've only written one closing argument."

The crowd chuckled, and, after such a tense morning, Soward let the laughter die down on its own. "The severance is granted," he then ruled. "Big Tree will be tried first. Any objections?"

"None," the attorneys said.

"Then let's get a jury seated, shall we?"

This was *voir dire?*

Thomas Ball sat down at the bench after questioning the

prospective juror and huddled with Joe Woolfolk. "We have to strike him," he whispered.

Woolfolk spit into the brass cuspidor and shook his head. "You gonna use up all your challenges, Ball."

Ball was incredulous. "We have cause. His sister was killed by Indians!"

"Peter Lynn's honest, Ball. Hell, you start challengin' ever'body who's had a set-to with an injun, and you won't have a jury to seat."

"Which postpones our clients climbing the gallows."

It was too hot to be arguing, even though Judge Soward had ordered every window in the courtroom opened. Most of the men had already shed their coats, and the ladies fanned themselves, trying but failing to get a decent breeze going. Satanta and Big Tree, still chained, sat on the bench next to the two lawyers, staring blankly at the Texas and United States flags hanging limply behind Judge Soward. Sweat drenched their faces and clothes, but the two Indians never moved, barely breathed, and seldom blinked.

"You get a mistrial, Ball, and those injuns'll be yanked out of the post guardhouse tonight. Be a lot of Yanks and Texicans kilt over it, too. You want that on your conscience?"

He paused, but only briefly. "I don't want the execution of these two Indians on my conscience, either."

"Then you best seat Peter Lynn on that jury, Ball. I'm tellin' you, he's honest as the day is long. You make a good case, and he'll vote to acquit. Only takes one to hang a jury."

Ball shook his head. "You just said a mistrial would lead to insurrection."

"That's a fact. But the town would be puttin' a noose over Peter's head, not Satanta's or Big Tree's, if he hangs the jury." He spit again and softened his tone. "Trust me, Ball. I know the people in this county better'n you. I—"

Judge Soward's command ended the debate, and Ball rose.

"We have no objections to this juror, Your Honor," he said reluctantly, and Judge Soward ordered Peter Lynn to the jury box. As the bailiff called the next potential juror, Ball leaned over and whispered to Horace Jones.

"Tell them that Peter Lynn's sister was killed by Indians but that Woolfolk thinks he's honest. Tell them that we must put eleven more men in that box, and they will decide on a guilty or innocent verdict, if it comes to that. We will endeavor to put twelve honest, impartial men to hear the case." He found that impossible, not here, not in Case Number 224. "This is the way the system works."

Or didn't work.

Jones began the translation, and Ball turned back to face the new prospective juror, catching a glance of M. J. Shelley. Her fan wasn't moving. She was simply sitting there five rows back, her pretty eyes, now malevolent, locked on the two defendants—or maybe Thomas Ball.

Chapter 15

*"They were ably defended by Mssrs Thos. Ball and
W. Woolfolk, . . . who had been appointed by the
court for that purpose. The former gentleman's
speeches were at some points most eloquent. . . ."*
                                        —*Dallas Herald*, July 22, 1871

July 5, 1871
Jacksboro, Texas

Stroking his beard, Charles Soward studied the twelve jurors
once again as they settled onto two long, rough-hewn
benches. He liked what he saw. Thomas W. Williams, a fire-
breathing Unionist. Town merchants Daniel Brown, Little
Evert Johnson, and Stanley Cooper. All good men, well respected. John H. Brown, L. P. Bunch, John Cameron, James
Cooley, Peter Hart, William Hensley, Peter Lynn, and H. B.
Verner. He didn't know all of them personally, but he knew
their reputations. The Indian-loving papers shouldn't be able
to find many faults with such a jury. These were twelve honest men, good men, not riffraff, many of them pillars of
whatever kind of society flourished in Jack County.

His eyes next landed on the prisoners, unaffected, staring
blankly, wrapped tightly in dusty blankets despite the un-
bearable heat. How would they be able to stand that thick
wool by midafternoon? Finally, Soward shot an icy look at
those two damned uppity troublemakers, the lawyers he had
assigned to the defense. He had warned them to play this

smart, but they wanted their glory. His favorite Bible quotation came to him. "For though I would desire to glory, I shall not be a fool. . . ." He had used that text from Second Corinthians, chapter twelve, verse six often, a little out of context perhaps, when sentencing some fool who had tried to hold up a stagecoach, rustle cattle, or steal a horse. Well, Thomas Ball and Joseph A. Woolfolk were fools. If they didn't watch their backs, Charles Soward would likely be trying some unfortunate Texican for their murder—provided a grand jury didn't no-bill the killer.

The bailiff swore in the jury and read the indictment. Taking notice of the newspapermen seated behind the prosecution table, Soward realized that he should have prepared a better opening, but he had been preoccupied writing his sentence for those two damned Kiowas. His wife suggested he was being a bit premature, but he belittled that notion. Acquittal? Not a chance in hell, and this courtroom certainly felt like hell. Well, maybe he didn't need to set the ground rules for the trial. He had pretty much done that anyway after Fred Stinson's outburst. Soward started to say something, but a bird slammed into a window, and the loud thump startled everyone.

They must have thought the Kiowas had launched an attack.

"It's just a bird!" came a cry from below, and little H. P. Cook leaned out the open window and agreed with the report before Prudence Baggett yanked him by his suspenders back into his seat.

"Looks like everybody's trying to get in for this show," Sam Lanham quipped, and Soward enjoyed the spontaneous laughter.

"Six inches lower and he woulda been in here," Sheriff McMillan said. "Stupid bird. Hit the glass instead when the window's open."

"Suicide," someone muttered, and Soward decided it was time for the gavel.

"Ladies and gentlemen," he said, "this is no laughing matter. This is a murder trial. Two men's lives are at stake." That should please the Eastern newspaper readers. "I know it's hot, I know it's uncomfortable, but I will not sacrifice the dignity of this court. No outbursts of any kind will be tolerated. And may I remind you that if a weapon is discovered on anyone's person, that person shall feel a wrath ten times hotter than this courtroom. Is the state ready to proceed?"

"We are, Your Honor."

"And the defense?"

"Yes," said Ball, "we are."

Soward pushed back from the bench. "Very well, counselors. You may make your opening statements."

Sam Lanham should have listened to his wife. The blue bib-front shirt was soaked, sticking to his skin as he stood to make his opening statement. He could shuck his coat, but then everyone would see how much he was sweating, and some idiot inkspiller would attribute the perspiration to fear of the defense rather than a heavy cotton shirt meant to be worn in fall or winter. He decided he'd cut his speech short. Judge Soward would likely recess for lunch after opening statements, and he could hurry to the hotel and change into a nice, thin white shirt.

"Gentlemen of the jury, this is a trial for murder, and the law is clear. If you find that Satanta and Big Tree willfully and feloniously participated in the brutal massacre at Salt Creek Prairie—and the state will prove this beyond a reasonable doubt—then you must reach a verdict of guilty.

"I don't want you to think about the defendants' race." He kept focusing on the jurors, making eye contact with each man, driving his point home. "I want you to think about Mr. Long, Mr. Baxter, Mr. Williams, Mr. Mullins, Mr. Bowman, and James Elliott. And I want you to think especially about Samuel Elliott. The defense will claim the accused were defending their homes. Defending their homes? They have a home north of the Red River where the federal government feeds and provides for these Indians. And this is how they repay us? The defense will claim that this was open warfare. Balderdash! What happened on Salt Creek Prairie was not warfare, it was butchery, it was savagery, it was murder in the first degree."

He turned to the gallery. "Ladies, I beg of you to close your ears, as what I say now is not delicate. Please forgive me." Back looking at the jury. "Picture those poor seven men, stripped naked, lying on the cold, wet ground, pounded by torrential rain. Can you see Samuel Elliott? Can you see him chained to a wagon tongue and roasted alive? Can you see the makeshift shelter the Kiowas built to keep the rain from putting out that horrible fire? Can you hear him screaming, begging for mercy, begging for death?" His voice rose as he whirled to face the Kiowas, pointing a defiant finger at them. "Can you hear these two butchers laughing?"

He shook his head and walked back to his seat. He had probably sweated out ten pounds this morning. *Morning! God help us this afternoon.* Except for the post interpreter's translations, the courtroom remained silent. Even with the windows open, no sound came from outside, despite several hundred people waiting below, listening, trying to discern what was happening upstairs. "You have a duty," Lanham said as he sank into his chair. "That duty is to find the defendants guilty. Of course, you can set them free. Only if you do that, the next scalp lifted may be yours."

Oddly enough, Thomas Ball felt no butterflies in his stomach as he stood, rounded the table and looked at Satanta and Big Tree. "It's easy to think of these two Kiowas as savages," he said, and turned to face the jury while Horace P. Jones translated his words for the defendants. "We call them savages, but are they? The Chinese and Japanese call us barbarians. Are we? These men are Kiowas. We are Americans. Kiowa, American, Chinese, Japanese, English, German, Scottish, Comanche, Apache, Tonkawa, Lipan, Aztec, Inca, African, Prussian, Canadian. We are simply from different cultures, and what one culture descries as barbaric or savage, another sees as glorious and dignified. When I look at Satanta and Big Tree, I see my brothers."

Well, no one had shot him yet.

He walked across the warped plank floor and leaned against the wooden rail in front of the two jury benches. Most of the men stared at him impassively, although one, James Cooley, spit a stream of tobacco through a crack in the floor. Ball thought about pointing to the spittoons at the end of the benches but didn't want to break the rhythm of his speech.

"I look at my brothers," Ball said, "and think of what they have had to endure, endured since the late fifteenth century. Spanish conquistadors burned villages, enslaved my brothers, wiped out cultures with disease and sword. I think of the words of Montaigne: 'So many goodly cities ransacked and razed; so many nations destroyed or made desolate; so infinite millions of harmless people of all sexes, status, and ages, massacred, ravaged, and put to the sword; and the richest, the fairest, the best part of the world turned upside down, ruined, and defaced for the traffic of pearls and peppers! Oh, mechanic victories, oh, base conquest!'

"Conquest. Isn't that what our culture is about? I think of the times of the Aztecs, of Cortez and Montezuma. I shed a tear when I picture Cuauhtemoc, tortured by the Spaniards, his feet burned with hot coals. The Spanish weren't alone in their cruelty. We learned from the Spanish—oh, how we learned. I think of how the great Apache leader Magnas Coloradas was tortured, his feet prodded with hot bayonets, until he jumped and was gunned down—murdered I tell you!—in Arizona Territory in 1863."

By now, he had become used to the Comanche translations from Horace Jones. He no longer heard the molasses-slow drawl forming the guttural exchanges of the Comanche. Phlegmatic faces, dampened with sweat, stared back at him in the jury box and in the gallery. Reporters worked their pencils furiously trying to keep pace with his smooth accent, much faster than Woolfolk's, Lanham's or Soward's drawls.

Ladies fanned themselves while holding onto his every word, but he dared not make eye contact with M. J. Shelley.

"I hail from Virginia, and her history flows with the blood of the wronged. Sir Thomas Gates, the governor in 1611, ordered all Indian priests put to death. . . . Poor Nemattanow, executed—wrongly, even John Smith said so . . . eleven years later. To Virginia's south, in 1713 in North Carolina, Colonel James Moore massacred hundreds of Tuscaroras and sold hundreds more, captured, into slavery to pay for his expedition. To her north, in Connecticut, they slaughtered the Pequots in 1637 near the Mystic River. Tell me, how many of you have heard of the Pequots?" He let out a mirthless laugh while shaking his head. "It brings to mind the wise words of Chief Tecumseh of the noble Shawnee. 'Where today are the Pequot?' he asked. 'Where are the Narragansett, the Mohican, the Pakanoket . . . ?' Where are they? Destroyed by our peaceful nation. And where today are the Shawnee? We have reduced a once mighty tribe to a mere handful. Where are the Cherokees? Driven from their homeland, and these 'savages' were among the most civilized we know. The Choctaws, the Seminoles, the Creeks, the Chickasaws. All forced to endure their own forced removal, to our country's everlasting shame."

Bowing his head, Ball walked back to the defense table, his limp slightly more pronounced, and shed his coat. He removed a handkerchief to mop the sweat off his brow, draped the coat over his chair and approached the Indians. "We moved west. Greed drove us west. Greed for gold, greed for land. So we invaded the homeland of my brothers. Perhaps the Orientals are correct. We are barbarians. We cheated these people. We took their land."

He pointed to the two Kiowas. "I ask you: Can you blame my noble brothers for defending their homeland, their families. Isn't that what many of you did when you enlisted, like me, in the Confederate Army? Isn't that what many of you did when you joined the Union Army? Aren't we brought up to believe that there are things worth fighting for? Isn't that honorable?

"You know for a fact that the bloody history our Indians have had to live through is not just from previous centuries. I point to the Washita River in Indian Territory. I remind you that Sand Creek in Colorado Territory still runs red. Less than a decade ago, we slaughtered the innocent. We still do. Yet we have the gall to call them savages. The Cheyenne at Sand Creek and the Washita were not warring Dog Soldiers but innocent people, most of them women and children. Can we blame Satanta and Big Tree for fighting to avoid a similar fate? No. We cannot. We would have done no less had we been the persecuted, the wronged."

He walked to the American flag hanging limp in the heat and pointed to the staff. "When I think of the United States, and when I think of my brothers that I am defending, I have a vision." He lifted his index finger to the top of the staff, gesturing to the brass eagle affixed there. "The eagle has long been a symbol of our freedom. This majestic raptor is also idolized by the Kiowa. I ask you, I beg of you, to think of the eagle, think of yourselves, put yourselves in the place of the two defendants. Do this, and I know that you will let these great leaders fly away as free and unhampered as the eagle. Thank you."

He didn't bother looking at the jury as he returned to his seat. That was always a mistake. It was the second chair's job to surreptitiously read the faces and guess the opening's effect. As Horace Jones finished the interpretation, Satanta suddenly grunted in approval and nodded vigorously. Even taciturn Big Tree muttered something while bobbing his own head.

Well, at least two people here found credence in my words, Ball thought.

Judge Soward glanced at his pocketwatch. "You may call your first witness, Mr. Lanham," the judge said, and Lan-

ham frowned. No break. He might die here. Now *that* would
be a story.

"Thank you, Your Honor," he said without feeling and
turned to consort with W. M. McConnell. McConnell and
Charley Jordan had volunteered to assist him. McConnell
would, for all intent and purpose, be his second chair for the
trial against Big Tree, and Jordan would take over in the second trial. Not that Lanham needed any help. McConnell
passed him a note pad, and Lanham glanced at it.

"The state calls General Ranald S. Mackenzie."

"Objection," Joe Woolfolk said.

Incredulous, Lanham spun around in his seat and cried
out, "On what grounds? I have a right to call this witness."

Woolfolk answered with the ping of tobacco juice hitting
the cuspidor beside the defense table. "You can call him,
Sam," Woolfolk said, "but call him by his correct rank.
Mackenzie's paid the wages of a colonel." He turned to
Judge Soward. "Promotin' Mackenzie to general is a blatant
attempt to prejudice the jury, to make his testimony seem that
much more respectable."

"Your Honor," Lanham said, "Colonel Mackenzie was
breveted major general during the late war. It is military
courtesy to call him by that rank."

Charles Soward sighed. "Aren't you splitting hairs, Mr.
Woolfolk?"

"Fine, Judge," Woolfolk said. "If we're gonna start pullin'
rank, so to speak, then I suggest that we all receive the same
courtesy. Address ever'one of us by our rank durin' the war.
I am Lieutenant Woolfolk, and my esteemed colleague is
Lieutenant Ball. So go ahead and call Gen'ral Mackenzie,
Sergeant Lanham."

The reporters and a few other onlookers laughed at Sam
Lanham's expense, but nervous comments and oaths rapidly
replaced the cackles once Satanta started grumbling.
Mackenzie, halfway to the witness chair, stopped in his
tracks, reaching for his holster only to realize he had left his
rig and revolver in a wheelbarrow out front. Satanta, talking

excitedly, stood up. Mike McMillan and two deputies immediately trained their shotguns on the Kiowa chief while Soward's gavel banged like musketry. Jones whispered urgently to Ball, who stood up and requested a recess.

"Control your client!" Soward ordered.

"A brief recess, please, so Satanta—"

The chief lifted his manacled hands, barked something, and dropped them. His blanket fell at his chained feet.

"What is he saying?" Soward demanded.

"Well," Horace Jones drawled, "it's kinda delicate with ladies present."

"A recess, please?" Ball begged.

The gavel rang again, abruptly stopping as Satanta lifted his breechcloth and . . .

A woman gasped. Several men swore. Lanham rolled his eyes as Satanta began pissing on the hardwood floor. It had all happened so fast, but now things slowed down. Surreal. Like a dream. Mike McMillan took three steps toward the Kiowa but stopped, and Lanham couldn't blame him. Probably didn't want Kiowa piss spraying his spit-and-polished boots. After all, it certainly stank up the courtroom. He could smell it across the aisle.

"That's how I feel about the whole affair, Satanta," said Woolfolk, lifting his boots as the river of yellow urine began flowing down the uneven floor, draining through the cracks a few inches from the defense table, dripping onto whatever was unfortunate enough to be directly below. Thomas Ball just stared, mouth agape.

Finished, the Indian sat down as if nothing had happened and picked up his blanket. Women and men began fanning themselves ferociously, while a few bolted outside. Judge Soward glared at the yellow pool, and Lanham's dreamlike state ended. After a long moment, Soward's gavel crashed again and the judge pointed at the two defense lawyers. "Counselors, you will instruct your client that this is not a privy. This is a courtroom. I would not . . ." Soward struggled for the right word, remembering the presence of women

and reporters, regaining his composure. "I would not relieve
myself in his lodge. If he . . . answers nature's call again like
that he will spend the rest of this trial in the post guardhouse.
Mr. Jones, make sure he understands this in your translation.
What Satanta did is disgraceful. Tell him that. And Mr. Wool-
folk, the court fines you ten dollars for contempt of court.
Watch your mouth, counselor. Sheriff, clean up this mess.
Court is in recess until two o'clock this afternoon."

Chapter 16

"This is a novel and important trial, and has, perhaps, no precedent in the history of American criminal jurisprudence."

—Samuel W. T. Lanham

July 5, 1871
Jacksboro, Texas

A half-dozen waddies appeared in the alley he usually took that ran between the Wichita Hotel and Glazner's Apothecary, making Thomas Ball realize he should not have taken his shortcut this afternoon. He showed no fear, though, just kept walking toward the cowhands. One cracked his knuckles. Two others hefted their gunbelts.

"Good afternoon," said Ball, tipping his hat as he tried to squeeze through the men, but a raw-boned gent with bushy Dundrearies moved closer to block him in. Another man said, "Nice speech this morn." Ball became aware of the smell of sweat, tobacco, horses, and, most prominently, whiskey.

Stepping back, Ball considered the six men. He wanted to look behind him to see if someone might be watching from the main road but dared not for two reasons. He didn't want these ne'er-do-wells to think they had him buffaloed, and he dared not turn his back on these sons of bitches.

"Can I help you gentlemen?" he asked mildly.

Dundrearies pushed back his sweat-stained slouch hat and

smiled. "We thought we might critique your opening statement, counselor," the man said in a New England accent that
didn't match his chaps and big rowel spurs. This man had an
education, and Ball thought he might make it back to the
boarding house alive after all.

"I'm listening," he said.

"Well, sir," Dundrearies began while the other cowhands
circled around Ball. "If memory serves, you mentioned how
Indians were slaughtered by the Spanish and other civilized
races. The torturing of Cuauhtemoc and Magnas. Nemattanow's execution. The massacre of the Tuscaroras and Pequots. Custer's charge on the Washita a few years back and
Chivington's attack of the Cheyennes at Sand Creek in
'sixty-four."

"That's pretty good," Ball said, "considering I don't recall
seeing you in the courtroom this morning."

"We were standing outside along with more than half the
town. Mighty good acoustics. May I proceed?"

Ball bowed slightly, and Dundrearies smiled before continuing.

"Well, counselor, allow me to point out that you over-
looked a few battles, massacres, incidents, whatever you
choose to call it. Are you familiar with Jean de Brébeuf?"

"No."

"He was a Jesuit missionary to the Hurons. The Iroquois
captured him, tortured him, and finally murdered him in
1649. And you didn't mention the Natchez attack against the
French at Fort Rosalie in 1729. They slaughtered two hundred and fifty men, and took three hundred women and kids
prisoner. The Yamassees killed a hundred or more men,
women, and children in South Carolina in 1715. On Good
Friday, I believe. But like you said, that's all ancient history.
Let's talk about some more recent events that you failed to
include in your speech."

The men behind him moved closer, and sweat burned
Ball's eyes. He might not be so lucky after all. A fight was

coming. Six against one. The only question Ball could think of was: Would they kill him or just beat him senseless?

Dundrearies spoke. "Let's keep our facts to Texas. In the winter of 'thirty-eight, a few girls and men left their homes to gather pecans when Comanches jumped them. One of the girls was barely in her teens. Matilda Lockhart. I guess you never heard of her, Mr. Ball. The Comanches held her captive for a year or more. Squaws burned every part of her body with hot brands, made her a slave. Bucks raped her. She died just a couple of years after she was returned to her relatives. Broken heart, my uncle used to say. Oh, and what about the Harvey Massacre back in 'thirty-six? Old man Harvey was killed running for his cabin. Bucks pulled his wife screaming out of the house and murdered her. Not just murdered her, counselor, but cut out her heart and left it on her body. These are your *brothers* I'm talking about, sir. Shot the boy twenty or thirty times and took a little girl captive, sold her to the Mexicans some time later. Why didn't you mention that, counselor? Or the Parker Massacre? I won't bore you with all the details.

"What else? The School House Massacre four years ago in Hamilton County. And here in Jack County back in 'sixty-six when the red bastards killed the entire McKinney clan— husband, wife, and three kids. The McKinneys never hurt no one, counselor. Am I missing anything, fellows?"

"What about Salt Creek Prairie?" came a voice so close that Ball could feel the man's hot breath on his neck.

"Oh, yeah," Dundrearies said, "the Salt Creek Prairie Massacre. That's quite recent. Nathan Long. N. J. Baxter. James Bowman. James Williams. Samuel and Jimmy Elliott. John Mullen. These men weren't warriors, sir, they were just honest teamsters trying to make a living on twenty dollars a month, freighting corn and grain. Never harmed a soul. They weren't trying to take your *brothers'* land. They weren't threatening to build a railroad through Kiowa land. You forgot to mention that little affair, counselor. What else can I say? Oh, yeah, I should mention this: Those men were friends of ours."

Dundrearies buried his fist in Ball's stomach.

* * *

Sam Lanham hurried up the steps to the top floor of the Wichita, found his key, turned the lock, pulled the door open, stepped into his room, and stopped, dropping his carpetbag on the floor and trying to form a sentence.

His wife, ironing one of his white shirts, formed one first.

"I told you not to wear that blue shirt, Sam."

Recovering, he laughed and pulled the door shut. He should never underestimate Sarah. He loosened his ribbon tie, removed his coat, and began working the myriad buttons it took to remove the sour-smelling bib-front shirt. "What are you doing here?" he asked. Instead of waiting for an answer, he walked to her and kissed her. She lowered the iron and held up the pressed shirt for his inspection.

"That'll do," he said.

"You better clean up first. A clean shirt won't hide that smell." She giggled and stepped away from him. "You stink, Mr. Solicitor."

"It's hot," he said. "Too hot for school?"

"Mr. Philips is substituting for me the rest of the week. And looking after Claude."

"So you came to wish me luck."

"And a belated happy birthday. I didn't think about that until you were gone."

He found a washcloth and soaked it in the basin of water, sponging his chest and underarms, trying to get as clean as possible. "How do you feel?" he asked.

"Great. I saw Miss Kinder before I left Weatherford, and she said I'm in fine health." Miss Kinder was Parker County's best midwife. "Everything's all right." He felt her behind him now.

"I missed you, Sam." She wrapped her thin arms around his waist.

Lanham replaced the washcloth with a towel and began to dry himself off. Sarah squeezed tighter. Someone had once told him that women felt a little more romantic, downright frisky, when pregnant, yet he had scoffed at that idea. She hadn't acted like that during her pregnancy with Claude or the others that didn't survive. He felt attracted to her but remained a bit nervous. He didn't want anything to go wrong with this pregnancy. Still, if Sarah kept this up, he would soon forget his uneasiness. Hell, he had forgotten it already.

"How was your opening statement?" she asked.

"Effective. But so was Ball's."

"Anything happen?"

Well, he wasn't going to tell her about Satanta's decision to pee. Her hands began to massage his stomach. "I'm sorry I missed your birthday," she whispered.

Yes, he thought, this was the woman he had married, the woman who made his blood boil, the schoolmarm people said was a prude, pious, stiff-necked. What did anybody know?

"When does court reconvene?" Sarah asked.

"Two o'clock." He barely found his voice.

"Good," Sarah said, slipping a tiny right hand inside his trousers.

"What the Sam Hill happened to you?" Woolfolk asked his colleague.

"Some locals gave me a history lesson," Ball answered as he sat down in the courtroom and removed the handkerchief pressed against his nose. It had stopped bleeding, at least, and he shoved the bloody rag into his coat pocket. "I'm all right," he said, feeling Woolfolk's stare.

"Any broken bones?"

"No."

"How many were there?"

"Six. Felt like sixty."

Woolfolk laughed. "You file a complaint with McMillan?"

"He has enough problems." Ball snickered. "I ought to be mad at you. You wrote most of my opening. Those six clowns took exception, wanted to correct my oversights, and they made a pretty good case before they started kicking the bitter hell out of me. Anyway, I've lost fights before. No harm done."

"You might start packin' a gun."

"I've got a pocket Remington. Didn't do me any good this afternoon."

"I mean a gun, Ball, not some toy. And don't hide your pistol in a coat pocket. Strap on a gunbelt, counselor. This be Texas. You fit in the war. I'm damn sure you know how to use a six-shooter, and you're likely to run 'cross genuine sumbitches before this deal's finished. Them boys you had a row with today ain't nothin' compared to what you and me are likely to meet before this thing's finished. I got an extry Army Colt in my saddlebags. I'll fetch it for you tonight."

Ball shrugged and noticed Woolfolk for the first time since he had returned to the courthouse. "And what happened to you?" he asked, gazing at the red indentations on his cheek.

"Your gal, M. J.," he answered and hooked out his chaw of tobacco. "Told me I was an injun lover. I ain't. Said I was leadin' you astray. I told her it was your idea. She popped me and took off a-runnin'. Women." He pulled a twist of tobacco from his coat pocket, tore off a mouthful, and offered it to Ball, who politely declined.

Whistling caught Ball's attention, and he turned in his chair to see Samuel W. T. Lanham stroll down the aisle, arms swinging at his sides, and glide into his seat at the prosecution table. He had replaced his gaudy bib shirt with a clean white one and was wearing a black cravat instead of the ribbon tie he had worn this morning. What was he trying to do, change clothes like a dance-hall girl at a fancy establishment?

"Kinda chipper for such a hot day," Woolfolk commented. "Hope he don't think he's got this won yet. He's got another think comin', unless them six pugilists convinced you to see the error of your ways."

"Persuaded," Ball said.

"Huh?"

"The correct word is *persuaded,* not *convinced.* And, no, counselor, all those sumbitches did was persuade me to do my damnedest to win this case."

"General Mackenzie," Lanham said after the first witness had been sworn in. He shot a glance across the room at Joe Woolfolk to see if the lawyer would object to the rank again, but Woolfolk seemed preoccupied with his fingernails, cleaning them with a pocketknife while his jaws worked vehemently on the tobacco in his cheeks. "Can you relate the event that occurred at Fort Richardson and afterward on the evening of the eighteenth of May?"

"Yes, sir," the colonel answered. "I was at my home that night when the officer of the day reported that two teamsters had stumbled onto the post and were at the hospital. I dressed and went there immediately, and sent a trooper to bring General William Sherman to the hospital. General Sherman was at the fort that night on his tour of the frontier establishments in Texas and Indian Territory."

"Go on," Lanham coaxed.

"I met two men, one of them in tremendous pain from wounds to his foot."

"What kind of wounds?"

"Bullet and arrow."

"Continue, please, General."

"The men were Thomas Brazeal and Hobbs Carey. Mr. Brazeal had the serious wounds. They worked on Henry Warren's wagon train. They said they had been attacked by Indians earlier that day at Salt Creek Prairie. I immediately ordered the trumpeter to sound 'boots and saddles,' and after General Sherman heard the story of the teamsters, he ordered me to go to Salt Creek Prairie at once."

"Did you?"

"Yes, sir."

"What did you find at Salt Creek Prairie?"

Mackenzie sighed and ran his fingers, those remaining on

his mangled hand, through thinning hair. "We found the wagon train looted, seven men killed and scalped, one of those tortured most gruesomely." He paused, blinked, and added, "I need to correct myself, sir. I said seven men had been killed and scalped, but one was not scalped. He was bald."

"Thank you, sir." Lanham walked back to his table, where McConnell handed him a leather-bound journal. He returned to Mackenzie and handed him the book. "Do you recognize this?"

"It is the report of Doctor Patzki, our assistant surgeon at Fort Richardson."

"May it please the court, the state wishes to enter this as Exhibit A."

"Noted," Judge Soward said, and Lanham went on.

"Would you read Doctor Patzki's report?"

Mackenzie nodded, found his spectacles in his blouse, pinned them on his nose, and opened the book. " 'All the bodies were riddled with bullets, covered with gashes, and the skulls crushed, evidently with a bloody axe found there.' " He stopped when a woman began whimpering.

"Go on," said Lanham eagerly, blocking out the soft sobs and Horace Jones's Comanche translations.

"Umm." Mackenzie found his place. " 'Some of the bodies exhibited also signs of having been stabbed with arrows. One of the bodies was even more mutilated than the others, it having been found fastened with a chain to the pole of a wagon lying over a fire with the face to the ground, the tongue being cut out. Owing to the charred condition of the soft parts, it was impossible to determine whether the man was burned before or after his death.' "

"Thank you." Lanham collected the ledger and handed it to the clerk. "Did you pursue the hostiles?"

"I did, pursuant to General Sherman's orders." Mackenzie summarized the chase, and Lanham leaned back and tried to contain his glee. Neither Woolfolk nor Ball objected. Woolfolk kept cleaning his fingernails while Ball took notes faster than any reporter, hardly paying attention to Mackenzie's testimony. Lanham found the colonel's tone, however, to be monotonous, and he thought of Sarah and their tryst in the hotel just a short time earlier. He'd take her out to supper tonight, show her off to the people of Jacksboro and the newspaper correspondents.

Mackenzie had finished, he realized, so he asked, "Describe the incidents with Satanta and the other Kiowas and General Sherman and General—"

"Objection." This came from Ball, still scribbling away, not even looking up. Surprised, Lanham turned to look at the until-now silent defense lawyers. What had happened to Ball's nose? Lanham wondered as he asked, "On what grounds?"

"Your Honor," replied Ball as he lowered his pencil and looked at Judge Soward, "Colonel Mackenzie did not arrive at Fort Sill until several days after General Sherman left. He wasn't there, so he cannot testify to what he did not see or hear personally. It's hearsay."

"So it is, counselor," Judge Soward said. "The objection is sustained. Find another tack, Mr. Lanham."

It didn't matter. "Did General Sherman leave behind any Indians under arrest?"

"He did, sir. Three Kiowas. Satanta, Big Tree, and Satank."

"Why were they in jail?"

"They were charged with the murder of the seven teamsters at Salt Creek Prairie. I was ordered to transport them back to Jack County to stand trial."

"And you followed those orders."

"Yes, sir, although Satank was killed trying to escape shortly after we left Fort Sill."

"And the two remaining murderers—"

"Objection!"

"Sustained."

He had known Ball would object to that, but, again, it didn't matter. "The two surviving Kiowas arrested and charged with the murders of those seven men. Do you see them in this courtroom today?"

"I do, sir. They are the defendants, Satanta and Big Tree."

"Thank you, General. I have no more questions."

Judge Soward faced the defense table. "Cross-examination, gentlemen?"

"We have no questions of this witness, Your Honor," Ball said, and Lanham smiled as he sat down, twisting the ends of his mustache. Maybe those two cock-of-the-walk attorneys had conceded the case already. They should have. They didn't stand a chance of winning.

"How long have you been fighting Indians?" Lanham asked the next witness, Sergeant Miles Varily.

"Since I j'ined the cavalry shortly after the War of the Rebellion," the noncommissioned officer answered and spit into a cuspidor.

"Do you consider yourself an expert on the warfare of the Plains Indians, such as the Kiowa?"

"Reckon I know more'n some folks. Recruits look to me for help. Officers, too. You learn fast in the field, 'specially in Texas."

Lanham picked an arrow off the tabletop, stood, and walked to the witness's chair, handing the arrow to the soldier for inspection. "Do you recognize this, Sergeant?"

"Yep. It's an arrow. We pulled it out of a body at the Salt Creek Prairie Massacre." Still no objections from the defense. Lanham thanked the sergeant and passed the arrow to the bailiff.

"May it please the court, we offer this into evidence as Exhibit B." Again, no objections. He moved back to the witness.

"What kind of arrow is that, Sergeant?"

"Kio-way."

"Are you absolutely certain?"

"Yep. I know a Kio-way arrow when I see it. God knows, I seen enough of 'em the past five years."

"It's not Comanche? Not Cheyenne? Not Lipan?"

"Kio-way," Varily said firmly, shaking his head. "I swear to it."

"So is it safe to say that, in your expert opinion, that arrow was fired by a Kiowa brave?"

"Yep."

"Where did you find that arrow, Sergeant?"

"It was pulled out of N. J. Baxter's cadaver."

"So that arrow killed Mr. Baxter?"

"It helped. No way of tellin' if that's the death wound, though. He had a handful of other arrows in him, too. All Kio-way arrows. Plus his head was bashed in, an' his pecker had been chopped off an' stuck in his mouth."

Another gasp from the gallery. Lanham thanked the witness and sat down. The defense table remained deathly quiet.

"Cross?" Soward asked, and this time Joe Woolfolk rose.

"Only Kiowa arrows were found in Baxter's body?" Woolfolk asked.

"That's what I said."

"How 'bout the other bodies. All of 'em full of Kiowa arrows?"

Varily spat. Lanham frowned. "Not exactly," the sergeant said reluctantly.

"What kind of arrows were also found on the battlefield?"

"Comanch."

"I see. Tell me, Sergeant, in your expert opinion from years of service in the field, if a Comanche brave comes across a Kiowa arrow, either by barter or in a battlefield, will he take it?"

"He might."

"To use it later?"

"Reckon so."

"Were any Kiowas found dead at the battlefield?"

Lanham shot out of his chair. "Objection, Your Honor. I object to counselor Woolfolk using the term 'battlefield.' This was no battlefield. It was a massacre."

Soward's gavel slammed once. "Gentlemen, don't foul up my court with picayune objections. Proceed, Mr. Woolfolk."

Lanham sank into his chair. He couldn't believe Charles Soward refused to sustain his objection. Well, maybe he could. Soward had to play to the newspaper reporters, but Lanham couldn't believe Joe Woolfolk was raising excellent questions on cross. Woolfolk repeated the question, and Varily replied that no Indians of any tribe were found.

"So for all you know, Sergeant, the raid could have been staged by Comanches—or any tribe, for that matter—and they could have been using Kiowa arrows they traded for, found, or stole? Isn't that true, Sergeant?"

"Reckon so."

"In your expert opinion, Sergeant, can you tell if this arrow was shot from Satanta's bow?"

"Nope."

"Big Tree's bow?"

"Nope."

"So, based on your discovery at the site, you can't say in absolute certainty that Kiowas was there at all, let alone the two defendants, can you?"

"Nope."

Chapter 17

*"We have tried the white man's road and found it
hard; we find nothing on it but a little corn, which
hurts our teeth; no sugar; no coffee. But we want to
walk in the white man's road. We want to have guns,
breech-loading carbines, ammunition and caps.
These are a part of the white man's road. . . ."*

—Satanta

July 5, 1871
Jacksboro, Texas

A nice-looking middle-aged man in a plaid sack suit pledged
to tell the truth, the whole truth, and nothing but the truth, his
graying hair slicked back, his face freshly shaven. He seemed
out of place in this furnace where women and merchants
were outnumbered by cowboys and mule skinners. In fact,
Sarah Beona Meng Lanham decided, this Mathew Leeper
about to testify was probably the second most handsome man
in the Jack County Courthouse, behind her husband—although
the defense lawyer Ball and Judge Soward were certainly
pleasant to look at, and Joe Woolfolk might be nice-looking
if he'd take time to shave, get a haircut, and wear decent
clothes.

Sarah leaned forward in the uncomfortable bench and
gazed at her husband. She had not been in a courtroom since
his first case, and she wanted to hear his every word in this,

what would surely be his crowning moment, the trial of the century.

"Mr. Leeper," Sam began, "would you please tell the jury your current occupation?"

"I'm interpreter for Lawrie Tatum." Mathew Leeper had a soft voice, unlike her husband's, and much easier on one's ears than the throaty syllables the bushy-mustached man in a plaid sack suit kept saying, translating for the two Kiowas. She found herself looking away from Sam, and the nice-looking Leeper, and caught herself staring at the profiles of the defendants, coppery men, faces already damp with sweat, dark eyes seldom blinking despite an army of gnats assaulting them, bodies wrapped snugly with woolen blankets, chained like bears, iron bracelets clamped so tightly around their ankles the skin had been rubbed raw.

"By Mr. Tatum, you refer to the Indian agent at the reservation near Fort Sill in Indian Territory? Is that correct, sir?"

"Yes, sir."

"So that means you must speak the language of Mr. Tatum's wards, the Comanche and the Kiowa?"

"I do, sir."

"Where did you learn those languages, sir?"

"I lived with the Penateka Comanche a while back on the Texas reservation. I was agent over on the Upper Reserve on the Brazos. The Kiowa came a little later. It's harder to learn."

"But you mastered it, right? You can carry on a conversation with a Kiowa?"

"Yes, sir. I'm pretty fluent in the language now."

Sarah turned back to find that her husband, sharp looking in his white shirt and black cravat, had approached Judge Soward's bench. "Your Honor, if the court would indulge me, I'd like to prove how well Mr. Leeper understands the Kiowa tongue. What I propose is to have the court's interpreter, Horace Jones, ask Satanta a question, then have the witness translate both question and answer. Mr. Jones can grade his efforts."

The judge shrugged and asked if the defense had any objections.

"It's unnecessary," Thomas Ball said. "The defense will stipulate that Mathew Leeper speaks perfect Kiowa."

"Very good," Soward said. "Forget your show, Mr. Lanham, and proceed with your examination of the witness."

Sam bowed graciously and walked back in front of Leeper.

"Mr. Leeper, where were you on the twenty-sixth of May of this year?"

"At the agency, sir. Agent Tatum asked me to bring some Kiowas to his office for questioning."

"Are those Indians present today?"

"One is, sir. Satanta. Big Tree was not there."

"Did Mr. Tatum interview the Kiowas?"

"He did. I was there to translate for him and the Indians."

"Summarize the conversation, please."

"Agent Tatum asked him immediately if he had led the attack against a wagon train down here."

"By 'down here,' you mean Texas? In fact, the incident Mr. Tatum was referring to—"

"Objection," Thomas Ball said. "He's leading the witness."

"Sustained. Rephrase your question, Mr. Lanham."

"Of course, Your Honor. Mr. Leeper, what attack was the Indian agent referring to?"

"The one at Salt Creek Prairie where those seven men were killed."

"Thank you. What did Satanta say?"

"He said he led the raid."

Sam arched his eyebrows in mock surprise. "He admitted this?"

"Yes, sir. He's cocky as a bantam rooster. He said they killed seven men and stole forty-one mules." Leeper shook his head. "I remember his words exactly. 'Three of my men were killed, but we are willing to call it even.'"

"Cocky bantam rooster indeed," Sam said, which brought

out an objection that Judge Soward quickly sustained, admonishing the prosecutor with his standard, "Save the commentary for your closing argument, counselor."

Sam simply smiled and asked the witness to continue.

"Well, sir, Agent Tatum asked Satanta again if he led the raid, and Satanta said he did, said don't believe it if someone else takes credit. He told us that the Kiowas wouldn't raid around Fort Sill—probably wouldn't, anyway—but he expected to be allowed to raid in Texas."

"That was it?"

"For the most part. Agent Tatum told Satanta he would arrange a meeting with General Sherman and Colonel Grierson. Satanta liked that. After that, they left to get ready for ration day the next morning."

"Thank you, Mr. Leeper. Thank you very much." Sam sat down, satisfied with the testimony, and he had reason to be pleased. He had done well. Sarah wondered what kind of lawyer Thomas Ball would prove to be as he stood to begin the cross-examination.

"You said Big Tree was not at this meeting?" Ball asked in a pleasant accent.

"That's right, sir."

"Do you know Big Tree?"

"Slightly."

"What do you think about him?"

"He's a decent sort. Quiet. Doesn't get drunk. Treats his wives well. Even goes to church once in a while. Good with horses. The Kiowas say he's a great warrior, too. Very brave. Very brave."

The next question shocked Sarah. "If he were white, would you like him?"

It shocked Mathew Leeper, too. He blinked, leaned back, and said after a moment, "Well, sir, I kind of like him now."

"But he's not your friend?"

"I wouldn't call him that, sir."

"What about Satanta? Is he your friend?"

"No, sir. Not even if he were white."

"Why? Because he's a cocky bantam rooster?"

"That's one reason. I don't dislike Satanta, Mr. Ball. I just . . ." He shrugged.

"That's all right," Ball said. "Is Satanta truthful?"

Now Leeper laughed, and Sarah knew Ball was an excellent attorney. Her husband had a strong opponent. She hoped he realized this.

"Not always. He can tell a lie better than most Texicans."

Laughter filled the gallery, silenced only by Soward's trusty gavel, although she detected a thin grin behind the judge's thick beard.

"So, was he telling the truth when he said he led the raid, or was he lying?"

"I think he was telling the truth, sir."

"You *think. You think.*" Clucking his tongue, Ball returned to his chair. "No more questions, Your Honor."

"Redirect?" Soward asked, and Sam shot out of his chair.

"Big Tree wasn't at the meeting, but did his name come up?"

Good job, Sarah thought, and beamed, recalling how far her husband had come since they burned coal oil at night going over law books, her tutoring him. She had always known there was something more to Samuel Willis Tucker Lanham than her friends or father ever saw. They had found him to be a bumpkin, an uncouth backcountry plowboy. What would they think of him now? She could just picture her father reading Sam Lanham's name in *The New York Times* and *Harper's Weekly.*

"Yes, sir," Leeper answered. "When Agent Tatum asked Satanta if he led the raid, he said he took about a hundred warriors along with Satank, Big Tree, and a few others. Satank told him to shut up."

"But he did mention Big Tree's name?"

"Yes, sir."

"Thank you. One final question, sir. What is it that makes you think that Satanta was telling the truth when he admitted to leading the raid?"

"He knew seven men had been killed, and he knew forty-one mules were stolen. Those mules—all forty-one—were later returned after Satanta's arrest."

Perfect. Sarah had taught her husband well. He had shot down the holes the defense had pointed out, but now Ball was asking for his own redirect.

"Why were the mules returned?" the lawyer asked.

"The Kiowas thought if they returned the mules, the Army would release Satanta, Big Tree, and Satank."

"So the Army lied to the Kiowas?"

"I don't know, sir. I don't know exactly what the Kiowas were told by Colonel Grierson or General Sherman."

"Did Satanta say why he led the raid?"

"Yes, sir."

"Tell us, Mr. Leeper. We'd all like to know."

Leeper paused to wipe his sweaty brow, stuck the hanky in his coat pocket, and said, "It was a long speech, the kind Satanta likes to make. He said Stone, uh, Agent Tatum, had stolen goods from the Kiowas and sent them to Texas. He wanted guns, bullets, and powder. Said he had heard talk that the whites would send a railroad through their country, and he didn't want that. He also said he'd never be arrested again. That's pretty much the gist of it, sir."

"Thank you. So, let me see if I got all of this right, sir. Satanta thought the government was stealing annuities belonging to the Kiowas and sending them to Texas?"

"Yes, sir. I don't think that's true—"

"'Yes' or 'no' will suffice, Mr. Leeper. Tell me, sir, if your family was starving, if the government kept lying to you, taking your land, cheating you, sending your property to Texas, would that make you want to raid Texas to get—"

"Objection!" Sam barked.

"Withdrawn," Ball said. "I'm finished with this witness, Your Honor."

The law of the *Tehannas* got stranger.

Hor-Ace-Jones had been informing Satanta of the words

being said, but now Hor-Ace-Jones had to speak for the
white-eyes, so old Stone Head's voice, Lee-Per, was trading
places with Hor-Ace-Jones, placing his right hand on the
book the white-eyes worshipped, lifting his left hand, and
promising to do his best. Satanta did not care what Hor-Ace-
Jones had to say. He tried not listen to Lee-Per once the
mouthpiece of the foolish, weak Quaker sat beside him.
What Satanta wanted to do was to scratch his back. It
itched—worse than his wrists and ankles—but the white-
eyes kept his hands chained, and he could not reach it. He
dared not try, either. He had made the dark-bearded judge-
chief angry earlier today when he had relieved himself. What
did the white-eyes expect of him? To wet his breechcloth?
He had tried to tell these fools, but they had acted too slowly.

Hor-Ace-Jones sat in the seat where all the white-eyes
tried to condemn Satanta and Big Tree to die by hanging. The
chair must have some sort of power with the white-eyes,
more powerful than their Bible. Still, it did not look like
much of a chair. One leg was shorter than the other, or maybe
it was the crooked floor the white-eyes had laid. And the
chair had no arms. Nor did it rock. Kicking Bird had a much
better one in the white-eye house the Quakers and bluecoats
had built for him, but Satanta did not like it, either. For sitting, nothing felt better than a buffalo robe.

"Were you at Colonel Grierson's house on the day General Sherman ordered the defendants to be placed under arrest?" Lee-Per translated the words of the powerful
white-eye Lan-Ham, and Hor-Ace-Jones began talking his
slow talk, spitting his brown juice every so often into a shiny
brass white-man-container beside the crooked chair. Satanta
did not want to hear this story again. It made him sad, and he
did not want to hear any words spoken by Lee-Per. How
could he know if Lee-Per were telling him the truth?

Lee-Per had lied to him, lied to him through Stone Head's
bidding. Told Satanta if he met with the bluecoats, Stone
Head would try to get The Principal People weapons and
ammunition. They could hunt buffalo and antelope with the

white-eye guns. With such guns, The Principal People could raid the stupid Mexicans and bring back slaves, scalps, and horses—as long as that fool Kicking Bird didn't tell the bluecoats or the Quaker what the true warriors were doing. But there were no guns to be given. The bluecoats had merely wanted to put Satanta in chains as Yellow Hair had done.

He felt himself growing angrier as Hor-Ace-Jones talked and talked, and Lee-Per explained, even though he wanted to stop up his ears to Lee-Per's words. Words? Lies. He tried to think of something else and turned to look at He Who Speaks The Black Robe Tongue. His nose was swollen, dried blood still in his nostrils. Perhaps Satanta had misnamed this lawyer. He was a fighter like Wolf Heart beside him.

If he lived through this, if Wolf Heart and He Who Speaks The Black Robe Tongue stopped the *Tehannas* from hanging him, Satanta would invite these two white-eyes to the homeland of The Principal People. He would teach them the ways of *Gai'gwu*. These men could perhaps one day make treaties with the white-eyes and The Principal People, treaties that the white-eyes would not break.

He sighed as Lee-Per's voice told him what Hor-Ace-Jones was saying. Wolf Heart and He Who Speaks The Black Robe Tongue could not save him. They could not save Big Tree.

Satanta would die here in Texas, die with his neck stretched, die away from his people. Die for some reason he could not understand. If the *Tehannas* and bluecoats wanted him dead, fine. This he understood. It was the way of a warrior. Kill him in battle. So be it. All warriors must die, and to die in battle was honorable. But to die by the coiled rope, with one's neck tilted like a broken green branch? No honor could be found in such a parting.

Perhaps that was why the white-eyes wished to kill Satanta and Big Tree in such a manner.

Doctor Patzki from the fort followed for the prosecution, describing in lurid detail the wounds inflicted on the deceased, although his thick accent made the testimony hard to understand. No wonder Lanham had asked Mackenzie, and not the surgeon, to read his field report. Thomas Ball didn't ask him any questions on cross. Then Sam Lanham called Thomas Brazeal to the stand. Swearing under his breath, Ball rolled his pencil across the tabletop as the witness walked down the center aisle, his crutch thumping against the hardwood floor. Of all the survivors of the Warren Wagon Train massacre, Samuel W. T. Lanham had the gumption to call this man. It was grandstanding, nothing more, an attempt to prejudice an already prejudiced jury, but, hell, Thomas Ball would have done the exact same thing.

"Do you swear to tell the truth, the whole truth, and nothing but the truth, so help you God?" the bailiff asked.

"I do."

"Please take the stand."

Thomas Brazeal leaned his crutch against the judge's desk and sank into the unstable chair. Ball's eyes fell on the witness's missing right foot.

"State your name, occupation, and place of residence for the record," Brazeal was instructed. He did so, and Samuel Lanham rose.

"You worked for Henry Warren?" Lanham asked.

"I did. Drove wagons."

"Is that how you lost your foot?"

"Well, I was working for Captain Henry. We were delivering a train of corn to Fort Griffin when we were attacked by Indians. I caught a bullet in my foot. Then an arrow hit me in almost the exact same place. I made it to Fort Richardson as fast as I could and saw the post surgeon. The doc did his best, but infection set in a week or two later, and he had to saw it off."

"I'm sorry, sir. When was this Indian attack?"

"This past May. The eighteenth. I remember it well."

"Could you tell us, Mr. Brazeal, in your own words, exactly what happened that day?"

Chapter 18

"These poor men made a short but desperate fight, feeling that a horrible death was imminent. None attempted to leave till all hope of resistance was at an end."

—*Dallas Herald*, June 3, 1871

May 18, 1871
Salt Creek Prairie, Texas

"It's about to come a turd float," Jimmy Elliott said. Pardon my language. It just stuck in my mind, is all, that sentence. If you knew Jimmy, you knew he was a good man, happy-go-lucky, never had a care in the world. I mean, he's the kind of fellow who'd lose a month's wages playing keno and shrug it off as just a bad run of luck, yet he'd fight the dealer if he found him cheating a friend. Yes, sir, Jimmy would give the shirt off his back for a pal. Anyway, it's just not right that a man like that, a good man, his last words had to be "It's about to come a turd float."

But that's what he said.

We were a few miles past Rock Station near Cox Mountain, taking the road to Fort Griffin with a load of corn. Captain Henry, he has a government contract to haul supplies to the frontier posts. Who all was with us, you ask? Well, Boss Long—Nathan Long, I mean—was our wagonmaster. Jimmy's brother, Samuel, was the night watchman. We had ten wagons and ten teamsters. I was one of the teamsters, driving the third wagon. Jimmy's wagon was right in front of me.

Now, I'd been working for Captain Henry since I got home from the war. The captain is a good man, for a Yank, always treated us right. Anyway, I'd been hauling corn and freight to Fort Griffin since the post was established back in 'sixty-seven and never once had any trouble with Indians. Oh, sometimes you might see a few in the distance, but they never done us any trouble.

It was about three o'clock that afternoon, and the wind had picked up. I could smell the rain coming. Thought it'd be a blessing, hot as it had gotten that day. Seemed like we were heading straight for those black clouds, so I was looking for my poncho—likely most of the other teamsters were doing the same thing—and that's why we never saw the Indians.

That's when Jimmy yelled back to me, joking, about the . . . well, I've told you what he said.

Then the Indians hit us.

Give me a moment, will you?

Thanks. Sorry. It's just that every time I talk about . . . well . . .

I don't know how many there were. I guess I told General Sherman there had been three hundred, but everyone says there wasn't but half that many. Maybe so. Sure seemed like three hundred, though. I remember one was blowing a bugle. Others sounded bone whistles. But most of them were just screaming, and every mother's son of them rode like they had been born a-horseback. Coupled with the howling wind, it was like nothing I'd ever seen before. I pray to Jesus Christ in heaven that I never see anything like it again. I pray that none of you will ever see it.

I apologize, Your Honor. I'll try to keep to the facts.

Boss Long, he was on a blood bay gelding, having a whale of a time controlling that horse, but he shouted for us to get the wagons off the road, and we tried to circle them. For a good defense. That's the way it's done, you know. It's not just some story them hack writers put in those half-dime

novels. Nobody shirked his duty on our part, neither. I'd
guess that every last man among us had worn either the blue
or the gray during the war, so we knew how to handle ourselves in a fight. But the Indians were so close. They got inside our circle before we could close the gap.

That's when I saw Jimmy killed.

He had just hopped down from the wagon, trying to cock
his musket, when a buck rode by and slapped him with the
end of his bow. Another lowered a six-shooter—they had
guns, Mr. Lanham, Judge Soward. Pistols, rifles, maybe even
a shotgun or two. Plus arrows and lances. Soon it felt like the
air was full of arrows and lead. I was sweating something
fierce. Anyway, this one buck was riding right behind the one
that slapped Jimmy with the bow. Counting coup, I hear the
Indians call it. The second one fired that pistol right in
Jimmy's face. He was dead before he hit the ground.

I shot the one who killed my friend. Not sure if I killed
him or not, 'cause I was reloading, and when I looked up two
Indians rode by, swooped up the one I shot, and galloped for
the trees away from Cox Mountain. I made out a few other
Indians that way. First I thought they'd be the second wave,
but they never moved, and later Hobbs Carey told me they
were squaws, just cheering on their men in the fight.

All of us teamsters had only single-shot rifles and muskets. None of us had a pistol except Boss Long. None of us
carried a repeating rifle, but I swear to God that those Indians had a few repeaters.

I didn't see Boss Long fall. I just remember looking up
after I had charged my Enfield again and saw him down, his
horse galloping off, and there must have been ten or twelve
braves over his body, just a-hacking away.

Well, I shot again, then a bullet took off my hat. Hobbs
Carey was at my side long about then, shouting above the
wind and bullets, saying we had to get out of there or else
we'd all get killed. James Bowman was running to us. He
threw his rifle down and screamed, but it didn't matter to
those Indians. One of them knocked James down with his

horse, leaped off the ground, and fell on his back. There was nothing I could do. I swear to it. I hadn't had time to reload my Enfield. The murdering son of Satan just lifted James's head by his hair, James screaming the entire time, and slit his throat like he was butchering a hog in the fall. I turned away before James was scalped.

N. J. Baxter ran to us, too. Seems like most of the survivors were gathering right beside my wagon. "We gotta make for the trees!" he said. "We gotta have some cover, else we're dead."

I nodded my agreement and charged the Enfield again. John Mullen started to say something. I don't know what it was 'cause he never finished. A bullet slammed into his forehead, blew his brains out on the wagon tarp beside me, and he just sank into the tall grass like he was taking a nap.

So we ran.

Folks, everyone here has got to believe me. I swear to God I didn't know we were leaving Jimmy's brother, Samuel, back in the wagons, back with those butchers. If I had known that . . .

I didn't make it fifty yards before an arrow hit my right foot and knocked me to the ground. Don't know how that Indian managed to hit me there with me running. Lucky shot, I guess. It tore through my brogans. Hobbs Carey knelt beside me. He could have run on, but he didn't, and quick as you could blink, he broke the shaft and jerked the arrow out. Then he and N. J. Baxter helped me up. It felt like we were running through musketry and grapeshot, like we did so often in the war. Only in the war, if we were retreating, the Yanks wouldn't shoot us down like dogs. But those yellow-livered sons—

I apologize again, Your Honor. I know. Stick to the facts. The Indians must have opened up, because just then N. J. went down, and so did Hobbs. Hobbs jumped back up immediately, an arrow sticking out of his shoulder. Then I saw N. J.

Blood poured from his mouth. He had two bullet holes in

him, and three arrows. "Go on," he told us. "Go on. I am killed."

James Williams came back, helped pull me to my feet. That's when a bullet hit my foot, practically where the arrow had gone through. I thought I might die then. Sometimes I wish I had. Anyhow, we staggered on. I don't know how we made it to the tree line. I guess the Indians were more interested in the wagons than us. Most of them, anyway. A few were still chasing us, but the clouds opened up and sheets of cold, cold rain started falling. Right about the time we made cover, James Williams fell dead. Bullet went right through his heart, Hobbs told me. I didn't know Williams that well. He had just hired on with Captain Henry, but I won't forget him. He came back, helped me and Hobbs make it to the trees. I guess I owe him my life. Without him, I'd be buried on that godforsaken prairie.

Anyway, five of us reached the trees at the mountain base alive, but every last one of us was hurting, especially me. Hobbs had the arrow in his shoulder I done told you about. Richard Davis had an arrow wound through his hand. Freddie Montague's left ear had been shot off. And Sean Cruickshank had a couple of ribs busted by some buck swinging a war axe. He also had a gash on his cheek.

Thunder cracked, and it started hailing a bit, just for half a minute or so, and then the rain really came down harder. We couldn't even see the wagons anymore.

"We need to get out of here," Davis said.

"Hell, no," Cruickshank argued. "We'll be out in the open. Here we got cover."

"Here we don't have a chance," Davis said, and he was right. Criminy, we all knew it. "If those Indians come back looking for us, we'll be deader than those back yonder." He motioned toward the wagon train, but nobody looked that way. Nobody dared to look there, not after all we'd seen, after all we'd just been through. "Now's our chance," Davis said, "while they're ransacking the wagons and the rain's coming down in buckets."

So we headed back toward Jacksboro, afoot. It never stopped raining. Hardly slacked off for the first two or three hours. We were miserable, but we didn't dare stop. Not because we didn't want to.

"We gotta get back to Richardson," Hobbs Carey kept saying. "We gotta tell General Sherman what just happened."

You see, that was the first time the rest of us heard that General Sherman was coming to Fort Richardson, was going to listen to the settlers tell him the way things were—are—out here on the frontier. That's what pushed us. That's how I kept going despite my foot. I pulled off my brogan at one point and wrapped the foot with my bandana, using my Enfield as a crutch. Hobbs, he helped me some. So did the other fellows. We kept walking. When it got dark, we still walked.

I had never been so tired in my life when we hit the Mahan Ranch. That was some twenty miles from Cox Mountain. Nobody was there, though. Old Man Mahan had ridden in—we learned this later—the day before to talk to General Sherman, and he had stayed in town. We could only find two horses in the corral, so we talked it over. I was bad hurt. Couldn't walk anymore. In fact, Hobbs and Cruickshank had to carry me the last three miles, but I knew I could sit a saddle on one of Old Man Mahan's gentle mares as long as I kept my bad foot out of the stirrup. They decided I needed to go because I was hurt the worst. Hobbs went along because of his shoulder wound and the fact that he knew his way around the area better than Cruickshank, Freddie, or Davis.

So we rode on, reached Fort Richardson late that night, and told the first officer we saw what had happened. The soldiers took us straight to the hospital on the post. A short time later, Colonel Mackenzie arrived, and Hobbs told him what had happened. Then General Sherman came in, and I told him the Indians had hit us, killed those poor boys. He sent a rider to Weatherford to tell Captain Henry what had happened and ordered the colonel to go after those renegades.

I guess that's all.

Chapter 19

*"They are both hideous and loathsome in
appearance, and we look in vain to see, in them,
anything to be admired or endured."*
—Samuel W. T. Lanham

July 5, 1871
Jacksboro, Texas

"Do you recall seeing either of the two defendants on the battlefield that afternoon, Mr. Brazeal?" Thomas Ball asked
from his seat after Lanham finished his interrogation.

The teamster fell silent, but Thomas Brazeal had no poker
face. Ball knew exactly what Brazeal thought of him.

"You must answer the question," Judge Soward prodded
him gently.

"No," Brazeal mumbled.

"So you don't know for certain if Big Tree took part in the
attack, do you?"

Brazeal leaned forward and spit, suddenly as animated as
a cornered badger. "I know he's a damned Kiowa, mister, and
that's all I have to know about that prairie nigger." For the
most part, Brazeal had been reserved during his testimony
for the state, although Judge Soward had admonished him a
few times. Now the teamster looked on the verge of leaping
from the chair after Ball.

Soward's gavel slammed, and he instructed the jury to
disregard Brazeal's outburst, then sternly warned the team-

ster that he was on the verge of being held in contempt. Brazeal wiped his mouth and found his crutch, obviously done answering anymore questions from the defense table.

Ball let him go. He was finished with him anyway.

"Call your next witness, Mr. Lanham," Soward said.

"Your Honor," Lanham said, "at this time the state rests."

So be it. Well, Ball conceded, the prosecution had made a good case, but never once had anyone admitted that Big Tree had been in the battle, except for Mathew Leeper's translation of Satanta's dialogue with Agent Lawrie Tatum. If a white man had been on trial, Ball felt absolutely certain he would have been acquitted. Criminy, in his relatively short legal career on the frontier, he had already witnessed criminal cases end with an acquittal or hung jury because no one had seen the defendant fire his weapon or because the victim had been wearing a gun—even if he had been shot in the back.

"Counselors." Soward addressed Woolfolk and Ball. "You may start the ball."

"Your Honor," Ball said hesitantly, "the defense also rests."

An excited murmur began rising in the gallery, and reporters stopped taking notes to stare at the defense attorneys. Woolfolk and Ball had talked over this strategy, and although Ball didn't feel totally comfortable with it, his partner had brought up a good point. "Who would you put on the stand?" Woolfolk had asked over breakfast. "One of them injuns? That would get 'em hung. Ain't no character witnesses to be found. Hell, it's a lost case anyway. So it'll come down to the close. We gotta win over that jury . . . somehow."

After glancing at the Regulator clock on the wall, Judge Soward stroked his beard. "Court will recess for thirty minutes, at which time summations will begin."

She didn't know how much longer she could take this, cooped up in the dense courtroom, surrounded by sour-smelling men and women with nary a breath of air, and her own clothes beginning to feel soaked with sweat, unseemly for a woman. Twice M. J. Shelley had fought off dizziness by fanning herself. Earlier in the afternoon, someone had quipped that the fires of hell would be ten thousand times hotter, so they had better get religion after the trial, but few people had laughed. Even if the lamentable circumstances had warranted such a joke, it was too hot for humor.

After peering outside in a fruitless attempt to find thunderheads in the clear blue sky, M. J. Shelley craned her neck and looked at the wall clock ticking away monotonously during the half-hour recess. No one had left the courtroom for a breath of fresh air. No one had even walked to the open windows. No one dared to lose his or her seat.

Four o'clock. She sighed. The sun had a ways to go before it disappeared, and even then, she knew from experience, the heat would never completely die. That was Texas, this was July, and the summer would only get worse.

Joe Woolfolk also felt the heat. He shed his filthy coat and loosened his tie after Charles Soward asked the defense to begin its closing argument. He walked to the jury box and spit enough tobacco juice into the cuspidor to fill a canteen. Disgusting. M. J. was glad Peter Lynn didn't have the tobacco habit.

"Y'all know me pretty good," the scoundrel told the jurors, and M. J.'s eyes immediately fell on Peter Lynn, who looked downright miserable in his Sunday-go-to-meetings, his hair wet and his face shining with perspiration. "Unlike my distinguished colleague, I ain't got no fanciful visions of the noble red man. Noble." He snorted and spit again.

"You show me somethin' noble about burned-out homesteads, all that's left from years of sweat and blood from tryin' to make a livin' in this godforsaken country. Noble? Is it noble to butcher your enemy, to commit rapine, to plunder, steal livestock and take kids hostage to turn 'em into slaves? Is it noble to bash a screamin' infant's head against a blackjack limb to shut her up? Noble, my arse. There ain't one

damned thing noble about these two defendants. I guaran-
damn-tee you that."

M. J. leaned back in her seat and saw others had done the
same. She stared at the recalcitrant Joe Woolfolk, perplexed.
Even Judge Soward stopped stroking his beard and considered the attorney with a mix of apprehension and befuddle-
ment. This was the closing summation for the defense? What
was he attempting? To get a mistrial? M. J. knew it certainly
couldn't be that their little row during the dinner recess had
convinced him of his errors, made him change sides. Nor
would anyone ever accuse that pigheaded fool of being a
coward. So why? Had he simply become fed up with Thomas
Ball's ideals? She found herself looking at the back of Ball's
head and felt herself fuming. That overzealous Virginian was
an Indian lover. Well, M. J. was glad to have seen the man's
true nature before he started courting her seriously.

"I've served as pallbearer," Woolfolk went on, now shedding his sleeve garters, stuffing them inside his trousers'
mule-ear pockets and rolling up his shirtsleeves, "at many a
friend's funeral since I got here in the late fifties. Closed cas-
kets, most of 'em. That's noble for you. No, sir, gents, I don't
reckon there's a body in this courtroom that hates them red
vermin more'n me. And that includes you, Peter Lynn. God
knows, you got reason to shoot Satanta and Big Tree dead
today, got reason to hate the whole Kiowa nation. And I ain't
forgettin' you, James Cooley. Remember when we rode after
them bucks that run off your best stock back in, what was
that, the spring of 'sixty? Boss Verner. Me and you lost many
a horseshoe chasin' Comanch and Kiowa when we was
rangerin'. Hell, all of you men know what it's like livin' out
here." He gave a dismissive gesture at the reporters busily
jotting down Woolfolk's words. "More'n them boys."

He spit again, wiped his mouth with the palm of his hand
and his hand on his trouser leg. "Yup, I could talk to you all
afternoon and half the night about injuns, depredations, and
the like. But that ain't why I'm here." He shook his head and

waved a bony finger in Peter Lynn's face. "I'm here to talk to you about the law."

Suddenly, Woolfolk whirled, stretching his arm out toward the defendants, shouting so that everyone jumped back in their seats, and causing a mule to bray outside. "Hate them murderin', thievin' sons of bitches till Judgment Day! Hate 'em for what they be! Loathe 'em, every mother's son of 'em, and forget what the Good Book says, 'cause Jesus Christ never met no Kiowa buck—we ain't Mormons here— and he damn sure wouldn'ta turned his cheek on a loud-mouthed rapscallion like Satanta or an evil-eyed miscreant like Big Tree and lived to preach about it.

"But don't forget the law!"

As soon as the Fort Sill interpreter finished translating for the Indians, Woolfolk faced the jury again, still waving his finger like a Methodist circuit rider. "You men know for a fact that the law don't apply to injuns. It can't. They ain't got no concept of law, no matter how well Mr. Horace P. Jones tries to explain it. What Big Tree was doin'—if he was even there—was not homicide. It was warfare. Heck, we all know about warfare. Was any Texicans tried for murder for what happened at Dove Creek durin' the war? Them was peace-able injuns, Kickapoos, not Comanch, that got attacked, but no white man was indicted. And I reckon just about ever' last one of you has at least heard the story of that Comanch buck that got shot dead and staked up underneath that tree till he rotted away. Some of y'all probably even seen his skeleton. That poor injun was roostered on forty-rod whiskey when he was shot dead, and that's murder, gents, if you go by the law books. Y'all know it as well as I do. But we didn't put no-body on trial." He shook his head and spit again before continuing.

"Now, y'all know I ain't much of a lawyer. Don't like the palaver, the affidavits, nothin' like that. Don't like much about this job, 'cept for one thing. When the law works, when I take a case where I know I'm in the right, and more'n that, I know with all certainty that my clients are in the right, well, that's why I ain't flung my shingle and degree into the fireplace just yet."

His voice had softened as he leaned on the rail in front of the jury, blocking M. J.'s view of Peter Lynn. He seemed to be addressing him personally. "Forget the fact that no one proved beyond a reasonable doubt that Big Tree took part in this battle. No eyewitnesses placed him there. We only have a secondhand comment from Satanta, and ever' witness for the prosecution that knowed Satanta says he ain't known for his truthfulness. That means acquittal, folks. Nothin' else it could be. But like I say, just forget that. Even if Big Tree was at Salt Creek Prairie, it don't mean a hill of beans. My client was in the right, folks. Not the way we look at it, for sure. Not the way God looks at it, I guess. But they were in the right accordin' to Kiowa law, and that's the law they go by. They committed no crime, unless it's a crime to be a defeated nation." He was walking back to his chair as he finished. "Most of y'all know what that's like. And the Yanks didn't hold us accountable for murder after our surrender."

Sarah Lanham wet her lips as Woolfolk sat down. He had done well. In fact, Sarah would have to call his summation brilliant. He had addressed the jurors' prejudices as well as his own, had cited the law without boring them, had appealed to their sentiments as Johnny Rebs, although she knew the jury foreman, Thomas Williams, was a diehard Yank whose brother was a bigwig politician up in one of the Northern states like Indiana or Illinois. She studied each juror as her husband gathered his papers and walked toward the box. Her husband had kept his closing summation short, saving his artillery for the rebuttal he was about to deliver. Sarah couldn't read the sweaty faces, but she understood that Sam would have to do well.

Oh, she wasn't worried about an acquittal. If a Texas jury brought in a not-guilty verdict in this case, she'd stop believing in God and start teaching her students at Weatherford all about being an atheist till the good folks of Parker County burned her as a witch. No, Satanta and Big Tree would be found guilty and sentenced to death, but the journalists would make Joseph Woolfolk's words shine like a beacon in all the Eastern newspapers unless her backcountry husband could astound them with his rebuttal.

She pressed her fingertips together in a makeshift prayer formation and listened as her husband started explaining the trial's importance before painting a rather gruesome picture of the two poor Kiowas and the seven victims.

"This vast collection of our border people," Sam Lanham went on, "this sea of faces, including distinguished gentlemen, civic and military, who have come hither to witness the triumph of law and justice over barbarity and assassination; the matron and the maiden, the gray-haired sire and the immature lad, who have been attracted to this tribunal by this unusual occasion, all conspire to surround this case with thrilling and extraordinary interest. Though we were to pause in silence, the cause I represent would exclaim with trumpet-tongue."

He sounded more like a man stumping for Congress than a solicitor, but that's how Texicans liked their speeches. Yes, Sam had learned well. Bowed head shaking, he took a position in front of the two defendants. " 'Satanta, the veteran council chief of the Kiowas—the orator, the diplomat, the counselor of his tribe—the pulse of his race. . . . Big Tree, the young war chief, who leads in the thickest of the fight and follows no one in the chase—the mighty warrior athlete, with the speed of the deer and the eye of the eagle, are before this bar, in the charge of the law.' " He let out an empty laugh. "So they would be described by Indian admirers"—he was looking at Ball now—"who live in more secure and favored lands, remote from the frontier, 'where distance lends enchantment' to the imagination, where the story of Pocahontas and the speech of Logan, the Mingo, are read and the dread sound of the war whoop is not heard."

He raised his voice steadily as he walked back to the jury. "We who see them today, disrobed of all their fancied graces, exposed in the light of reality, behold them through far different lenses!

"We recognize in Satanta the archfiend of treachery and blood, the cunning Cataline, the promoter of strife, the breaker of treaties signed by his own hand, the inciter of his fellows to rapine and murder, the artful dealer in bravado while in the powwow and the most abject coward in the field, as well as the most canting and double-tongued hypocrite when detected and overcome.

"In Big Tree we perceive the tiger-demon who has tasted blood and loves it as his food, who stops at no crime, how black soever, who is swift at every species of ferocity and pities not at any sight of agony or death—he can scalp, burn, torture, mangle, and deface his victims with all the superlatives of cruelty and have no feeling of sympathy or remorse."

Sarah found herself staring at the Indians as Sam continued his assault. He had come far in his speechmaking. Four years ago, he would have stuttered and stammered before completing three sentences, but now, even in this furnace, everyone listened to him. Yet as he began pointing and lambasting those two "vile creatures," Sarah couldn't help but think of Joseph A. Woolfolk's summation and Thomas Ball's fine opening statement, though she hadn't heard the latter firsthand, and, despite her better judgment, she began hoping that the jury would see that the defense must be right, that those two "marauders" should not be found guilty, that this trial—no matter how far it propelled Samuel Willis Tucker Lanham—was a mockery.

No, *mockery* wasn't right.

A *tragedy*.

"It speaks well for the humanity of our laws and the tolerance of this people," Sam was saying, "that the prisoners are permitted to be tried in this Christian land and by this Christian tribunal." That's right. Preach to their religion. Make it a sin not to hang them. Sam Lanham knew all the tricks, and it made his wife sad. His speech would win over the reporters. They would forget the words of Woolfolk and

Ball. "The learned court has, in all things, required the ob-
servance of the same rules of procedure—the same princi-
ples of evidence, the same judicial methods, from the
presentment of the indictment down to the charge soon to be
given by His Honor—that are enforced in the trial of a white
man. You, gentlemen of the jury, have sworn that you can
and will render a fair and impartial verdict. Were we to practice *lex talionis,* no right of trial by jury would be allowed
these monsters; on the contrary, as they have treated their
victims, so it would be measured unto them."

A few rows behind Sarah, someone shouted his vehement
agreement, and Judge Soward's gavel cannonaded until a
deputy escorted the rowdy outside and on to jail.

The interruption didn't faze Sam Lanham. He waited until
the door closed, bowed slightly in thanks to Judge Soward,
and picked up where he left off. "The definition of murder is
so familiar to the court, and has been so frequently discussed
before the country, that any technical or elaborate investigation of the subject, under the facts of this case, would seem
unnecessary." Still, he went over the statute first before getting to the case before the jury.

"The testimony discloses these salient features: that
about the time indicated by the charge, the defendants, with
other chiefs, and a band of more than a hundred warriors,
were absent from their reservation at Fort Sill; that they were
away a sufficient length of time to make this incursion and return; that upon their return, they brought back their booty—
the forty mules, guns and camp supplies of the deceased; that
Satanta made a speech in the presence of the interpreters,
Lawrie Tatum, the Indian agent at Fort Sill, and General Sherman, in which he boasted of having been down to Texas and
had a big fight, killing seven *Tehannas* and capturing forty
mules, guns, ammunition, sugar, coffee, and other supplies of
the train; that he said if any other chief claimed the credit of
the victory, he was a liar and that he, Satanta, together with
Big Tree and Satank, were entitled to all the glory. Here we

have his own admission, voluntarily and arrogantly made, describing minutely this whole tragic affair."

Now he had to pause to wipe his brow with a handkerchief and smooth his mustache before summing up the other testimony.

"Then we have the testimony of the orderly sergeant, who, himself, is an old Indian fighter and familiar with the modes of attack and general conduct of the savages. He, with a detachment of soldiers, went out from Fort Richardson to the scene of blood, to bury the dead. He describes how they were scalped, mutilated with tomahawks, shot with arrows; how Mr. Samuel Long was chained to the wagon tongue and burned, evidently while still living. He tells of the revolting and horrible manner in which the dead bodies were mangled and disfigured, and how everything betokened the work and presence of Indians. He further describes the arrows as those of the Kiowas.

"The same amount and character of testimony were sufficient to convict any white men. 'By their own words let them be condemned.' Their conviction and punishment cannot repair the loss nor avenge the blood of the good men they have slain; still, it is due to law, justice, and humanity that they should receive the highest punishment." He faced the Kiowas again. "This is even too mild and humane for them."

He walked back to his chair. "Pillage and bloodthirstiness were the motors of this diabolical deed. Fondness for torture and intoxication of delight at human agony impelled its perpetration. All the elements of murder in the first degree are found in the case. The jurisdiction of the court is complete, and the State of Texas expects from you a verdict and judgment in accordance with the law and the evidence."

After Sam sat down, Judge Soward began instructing the jury, but Sarah didn't listen. She kept staring at the Kiowas and found her hands were now really clasped in prayer and that she was praying for those two poor souls, praying for a mercy she knew would not be found in this courtroom.

Chapter 20

SATANTA, SATANK, AND BIG TREE'S RAID.
"There is no act of savage cruelty recorded in the history of our Indian warfare more barbarous and inhuman than the unwarranted attack by one hundred and fifty warriors under the leadership of the three above-named Kiowa chiefs upon Henry Warren's wagon train on the eighteenth day of May, 1871."
—J. W. Wilbarger, *Indian Depredations in Texas*, 1889

July 5, 1871
Jacksboro, Texas

The jury room looked no bigger than a closet and, as it lacked any windows, felt like a furnace. Peter Lynn followed the example of his fellow jurors by shedding his coat and loosening his tie before finding a seat around the wobbly round table. They had elected Thomas W. Williams foreman, mainly because he scared the hell out of the remaining eleven. A pious man with a booming voice and a dour, narrow face chiseled out of marble, Williams spoke his mind and never considered consequences or diplomacy. Everyone knew the story that in 1861, when Jack County held its secession convention, Mr. Williams had voted against joining the Confederacy, signing his name and beside it writing, "The Union Forever." His politicking persuaded a lot of residents to follow his example, and when the ballots were all tabulated, Jack County had voted to remain loyal to the United States, although few other counties followed suit. In fact, most of the jurors sitting beside Lynn now had likely voted against secession only to join the Confederate Army when Texas withdrew from the Union.

"We should deliberate," Williams said in his Yankee snarl, "unless you want to vote right away."

"Ain't nothin' to talk about," said James Cooley as he carved a chaw of tobacco with his pocketknife and shoved the brown square, knife blade and all, into his big mouth.

"Cooley's right," H. B. Verner agreed. "Just sign the verdict, Tom, and let's get out of this hellhole. I done lost about fifty pounds just listenin' to that horseshit out yonder. I ain't gonna lose another fifty listenin' to more of the same in here."

Williams nodded deliberately. "Are we all agreed?"

"Well," Peter heard himself saying, "maybe we ought to talk it out a mite. I mean, I sorta thought Woolfolk made sense."

"Woolfolk!" Daniel Brown shouted. "He's a horse's ass, Pete."

L. P. Bunch joined in. "You believe that nonsense, Peter? Those red niggers are guilty, and you know it."

"We figger 'em guilty, Peter," Cooley added. "Ain't that right, boys?"

Ten heads around the table bobbed slightly. Williams didn't join in, but his blazing stare told Lynn what he thought of further debate. "I just want to do what's right," Lynn said softly, which prompted a curse from L. P. Bunch.

"Gentlemen," Williams said, "we will remain civilized. Peter, do you believe Satanta and Big Tree took part—"

"Only Big Tree's on trial today, Tom," Stanley Cooper said. "We get to hang Satanta tomorrow."

"Be that as it may," Williams said, obviously annoyed at Cooper's interruption, "do you think, beyond a reasonable doubt, that Big Tree took part in the massacre at Salt Creek Prairie?"

"Well, yeah, I reckon so."

James Cooley shook his head in disgust. "Then what's your problem?"

Evert Johnson Junior piped in. "You think M. J. Shelley's gonna let you steal a kiss if you hang this jury, you—"

Williams slammed his fist against the table. "There will be none of that, sir!" he snapped, his face red with fury. "We will conduct ourselves as gentlemen, and if you insult the honor of a woman of our fair county again, sir, we shall meet on the field of honor."

Humbled, Johnson sank back in his chair and searched for the makings to roll a smoke.

"Peter," Williams said, his voice softer now, "the good judge's instructions are clear. If you think Big Tree took part in the raid, then you must vote guilty, and, as such, for the death penalty. It doesn't matter what Woolfolk and Ball argued. All that matters is this: Did Big Tree butcher those poor seven men?"

Cooley spit through another crack in the floor. "All that matters, Peter, is your conscience, too."

"Some of them seven was friends of yourn," Verner piped in.

"Think of your sister, son," Stanley Cooper said. "Think of Mary. For all we know, those two damned Kiowas took part in that raid, too." Lynn knew that was a stretch. His sister had been killed in '58, and Big Tree couldn't have been more than ten years old then. But Cooper went on. "Think of Tom. Think of Bill Cambren and what those vermin did to his family before . . ." He shuddered, and Lynn knew that hadn't been faked.

"You know what I think, Lynn?" L. P. Bunch said. "I think if little Mary Cambren could talk now, she'd tell you that this is your chance to avenge the Cambrens and your family."

"The only way we can make this frontier safe, Lynn," Daniel Brown said, "is to hang them two bastards, to send the rest of those savages a message. You got to vote to convict, son. It's the only way."

*　　*　　*

"Has the jury reached a verdict?"

Thomas Williams stood. "We have, Your Honor."

"The defendants will rise." Horace Jones finished his translation, and Ball and Woolfolk helped the manacled Indians to their feet. "Look at the judge," Ball told them, which Jones repeated in Comanche. Ball filled his lungs and turned to face the bench himself, holding his breath, nervous, as if this were his first capital murder trial.

With a nod from Judge Soward, Sheriff McMillan walked from his position, shotgun snug underneath his left armpit, and took the slip of paper from Williams's fingers, then handed it to Soward, who unfolded the verdict and read silently without visible emotion. Charles Soward could play some mighty fine poker. Thomas Ball knew that from personal experience. The judge looked up at the defendants and read aloud, " 'We the jury find the defendant Big Tree guilty of murder in the first degree and assess his punishment as death. Signed Thomas Williams, jury foreman.' " Turning to the jurors, Soward asked, "Is this verdict unanimous?"

"It is, Your Honor," Williams answered, and eleven silent heads confirmed his statement.

A stunned silence fell over the courtroom, although Ball couldn't understand why. Everyone had expected this verdict. Someone sniffled—now, that did surprise Ball—and then the room erupted behind the defendants, and Judge Soward's pounding gavel could not stop the uproar. Little H. P. Cook ran to the nearest window and yelled at the spectators below.

"Guilty! Guilty! Big Tree's gonna hang!"

Applause and cheers answered the herald.

Ball couldn't look Big Tree in the eye, couldn't even glance over at Satanta. He felt Woolfolk's hand on his shoulder, heard his partner mutter something, though with the banging gavel and cheers around him, Ball couldn't understand a word Woolfolk said.

The hammering gavel and shouts of order from Soward and McMillan silenced the courtroom at last, although the cheers continued outside. Someone had started firing his pistol in the air, a belated Independence Day celebration, and a deputy leaned out of a window, risking getting his head blown off, and yelled at the swarm below to shut up.

"If there are no objections, I will defer sentencing until after Satanta is tried," Soward said. "Gentlemen of the jury, you are dismissed until tomorrow morning, at which time you will hear the trial of Satanta on a charge of murder in the first degree. Court is adjourned."

"You look like you're the one facin' the gallows, Ball," Woolfolk said at Ball's small office. "I told you we couldn't win this case. Satanta'll get his due in the morn."

Ball shrugged, opened a drawer, and pulled out a bottle of Jameson. He looked briefly for a clean pair of tumblers, found none, so tossed the bottle at Woolfolk, who caught it, uncorked it, and took a long pull.

"There's been one good thing from all this," said Woolfolk, tossing the bottle back after corking it. "I got some mighty good whiskey out of this deal."

In no mood for humor, Ball didn't even crack a smile. He kept replaying the trial through his mind, trying to figure out what he had done wrong. Should he have put Big Tree on the stand? No. Woolfolk had been right about that. Big Tree, unfamiliar with the proceedings, would have botched his testimony, would likely have admitted to taking part in the raid. Joe Woolfolk's closing summation had been good. More than that, the summation had been right. Soward had charged the jury fairly, and Ball couldn't fault Sam Lanham's long-winded but fine closing argument for the state.

"You want to help me file an appeal?" Ball asked.

Cackling, Woolfolk grabbed the bottle and took a longer drink. "You're plumb loco, Ball. You done your job. Let some other fool take up the cause. 'Sides, we gotta figger how to get Satanta off the gallows tomorrow." He set the bottle on the desktop. "I'm gonna saddle up and find a comfortable campin' place. You wanna join me?"

He looked up, curious.

"You might not be safe, Ball," Woolfolk explained. "Whiskey's flowin', tempers flarin', and it's hotter'n hell in August. Yeah, Big Tree's gonna hang, but I figger some folks ain't gonna forget your openin' statement or my closin' one. They'll do their best to run you out on a rail. So I'm takin' to the prairie like I been doin'. Don't plan on killin' no friend of mine over this. Don't plan on gettin' kilt, neither."

That wasn't cowardice, Ball knew. Not Joe Woolfolk. More like common sense. But still he shook his head. "I'll lock myself in my room at the Widow Baggett's, Woolfolk. Thanks for the concern, though." He had a final sip of Irish, slammed the cork back inside the neck, and stuck the bottle into the drawer. "Meet for breakfast again at the Wichita?"

"Fine," agreed Woolfolk, pulling open the door. "See you in the mornin', Ball. Try not to get kilt."

They met him in front of the Widow Baggett's boarding house.

Ten men, as far as Ball could tell from the dim lantern on a corner post, none of them the cowboys who had thrashed him during the lunch recess. Ball thought about ignoring them, trying to make it into the house without some stupid confrontation, but stopped when he saw two hurriedly packed trunks and two carpetbags in front of the doorsteps.

His luggage. His clothes. His law books.

The screen door opened, and Prudence Baggett stepped into the light, standing proudly, so fine and proper. "I'll have my key," she said icily, "you miserable Indian lover."

He considered some response, but one of Mrs. Baggett's eviction squad thumbed back the hammer of a battered single-shot shotgun. Ball reached inside his vest pocket, found the key, and tossed it in the dirt beside his pathetic accumulations of thirty-four years. "I've already paid my rent for July," he said.

She didn't respond. Another cowhand scooped up the key, wiped off the dirt, and placed it in the landlady's hand. The screen door slammed behind her, as did the front door. Sweet little Prudence Baggett had thrown him out, left him to the wolves.

He slipped his hand inside his coat pocket, finding the feel of the pocket Remington uncomfortable instead of reassuring. Woolfolk had been right. He should have strapped on a heavier weapon, not some concealed hideaway gun. No one moved, and Ball didn't know what he should do. Draw the Remington? Walk away? Take one of his grips and sleep in his office? One of the men answered his question.

"We'll send your traps, Ball."

Another added, "To Indian Territory. Reckon that's where an injun lover belongs."

He shook his head with contempt and stepped forward, picked up a grip with his left hand, keeping his right hand on the Remington's butt, and said, "You won the case. Big Tree will hang. Why don't you go celebrate with Lanham and Mackenzie?"

"Why don't you go to hell," the nearest man answered, and they swarmed him.

He managed to get the revolver out, swinging the grip with his left hand and caving in one man's nose, but someone slammed the stock of a rifle or shotgun against his bad leg, and he fell, writhing in pain. A calloused vise clamped onto his hand, and he felt the Remington being wrestled out of his grasp as boots nailed his ribs, head, and legs. He pulled the trigger, satisfied at a man's yelp. The gun didn't go off, but the hammer must have pinched some waddie's finger or fleshy palm. A spur raked across his forehead, and he wished again that he had taken Joe Woolfolk up on his offer. Virginia pride had kept him in town, and for the second time today, he was paying the price.

Only this time, these men might just kill him.

"No!" M. J. Shelley screamed and pulled frantically on Peter Lynn's coat sleeve.

He pivoted, gently pried her fingers from his arm, and

said, his voice firm but reassuring, "You stay here, Miss Shelley." Then he disappeared down the alley, drawing his revolver as he ran.

The scene in front of the Widow Baggett's boarding house shocked him. He half expected to be breaking up some fight between drunken cowhands, buffaloing them if they needed it, and chastising them for causing a disturbance in front of a God-fearing woman's home. Immediately, however, he recognized the prostrate form of Thomas Ball, attorney-at-law. He stopped, frozen, but this lasted only momentarily.

"Get off him!" Lynn shouted and brained the closest man. Another waddie looked up, and Lynn busted his nose with the revolver's barrel, then fired a round into the air. The report got everyone's attention. "I said get off him!" Lynn yelled, thumbing back the hammer.

One of the assailants, Homer Jericho, snorted and swung the barrel of his shotgun toward Lynn's midsection. "You got a lot of nerve, Lynn."

"Shut up, Homer," Lynn snapped, "and put that damned shotgun up before somebody gets hurt. All of you. Get out of here!" He lowered the hammer, stuck the pistol in his waistband, and knelt down.

Ball rolled over. Blood dripped down his forehead and flowed freely from his nose and a busted lip. "You all right, sir?" Lynn asked. The attorney shook his head, not to answer Lynn's question but to clear his brain, then pulled himself to a seated position in the dirt and spit out a mouthful of blood and sand. He blinked dully, recognition coming slowly.

"Lynn?"

"Yes, sir. Come on, counselor, I'll get you to Doc Patzki over at the fort."

"I'm all right," Ball said stubbornly. "Help me up, will you?"

A woman gasped, and Lynn spun around. "I told you to stay put, Miss Shelley." He swung back toward the cowhands. "All of you boys, clear out. I know practically every last one of you. If you don't light a shuck now, I'll

fetch Mike McMillan, and you can sweat it out in his calaboose."

Slowly, they ambled away, and Lynn pulled Ball to his
feet. He stood unsteadily, tested his legs, and asked Lynn to
pick up his Remington and hat. Lynn obliged, dusting off the
ruined hat.

"What happened?" M. J. asked.

Ball answered with a laugh. "I got evicted."

"By Prudence Baggett?" Lynn couldn't believe it. "She's
a good woman."

Ball shrugged, jutting his jaw toward the disappearing
cowboys. "Those are pretty good men, I warrant," he said
and staggered down the path. "In normal times."

·He was gone, leaving Lynn staring at the trunks of clothes
and books, wondering where he should take them.

July 5, 1871
Fort Richardson, Texas

Lieutenant Robert G. Carter had just filed a report when the
door to the adjutant's office opened and Corporal John Charlton showed a battered young man, his clothes dirty, bloody,
and torn, inside. At first Carter feared the Kiowas had attacked another wagon train, that the whole affair would repeat itself, but as Charlton introduced the man, Carter
recognized defense counselor Thomas Ball.

"Good God, sir!" he exclaimed. "What happened to you?"

"Same thing that happened to me a while back," Charlton
answered for the attorney, who was busy dabbing a handkerchief to his busted lip. "Damned Texicans."

"Twice today," said Ball after stuffing the handkerchief
into a pocket. "There won't be a third time." Carter could
read men, and he knew Ball meant that. Those stupid yokels
in town had pushed this man too far.

"Sir," Charlton said, "the counselor desires to talk to the
prisoners, his clients."

Carter checked his pocketwatch. "It is rather late, Mr. Ball," he said, weighing his options. What would General Sherman want him to do?

"I know, Lieutenant," Ball said, "and I won't be long. I ask for your indulgence, sir. At least one of my clients is bound for the gallows."

Probably both, Carter thought, *and good riddance.* "All right," Carter said. He'd send Charlton and the Virginian on to the guardhouse, then inform Colonel Mackenzie and General Sherman of the lawyer's presence. If they didn't like it, they could always order Ball off the post. "Corporal, is an interpreter around?"

"Jones is waitin' by the guardhouse, sir."

"Very well, but keep your interview short, counselor."

Satanta greeted He Who Speaks The Black Robe Tongue in the strange language of the old Jesus men, which momentarily stopped the lawyer. Big Tree sat in the corner of the stinking cell, watching the three men greet Satanta warmly before finding a spot on the cell floor. They carried only lanterns, which made Big Tree happy. He feared they might bring ropes to hang him by the neck till he was traveling the Great Journey. The white-eyes sometimes carried out their justice quickly.

Big Tree did not listen much as Hor-Ace-Jones began his introduction. Instead he thought of his wife, wondering who would take care of her after the *Tehannas* made his neck crooked and long. The white-eyes likely had come to see Satanta. White-eyes always came to greet Satanta, to bring him gifts and listen to his speeches, to ask him to sign treaties or trade horses. No one ever came to see Big Tree.

Yet Hor-Ace-Jones called out his name, and Big Tree found He Who Speaks The Black Robe Tongue staring at him. For the first time, Big Tree noticed He Who Speaks The Black Robe Tongue. This lawyer had been in a big fight, it seemed. Was this, Big Tree wondered, his punishment for losing the trial? If so, no wonder he and Wolf Heart had fought so hard with their words, trying to save Big Tree.

"He Who Speaks The Black Robe Tongue asks Big Tree if he needs anything," Hor-Ace-Jones said in Comanche.

"No," Big Tree answered timidly. He didn't know what he could ask for, although he hungered for buffalo liver, but surely the white-eye lawyer could not give him that.

The man the white-eyes called Ball said something else, and Big Tree waited for Hor-Ace-Jones to turn the words into something softer on Big Tree's ears.

"He says you must not lose hope," Hor-Ace-Jones said. "He says he will take your case to a bigger court after Satanta's trial. This is the way things are done in the *Tehanna* courts. If anyone is found guilty and faces a death sentence, he can ask more important judges to look at the trial again. This is called an 'appeal.' Sometimes the bigger judges say, 'This verdict was wrong. You must have a new trial.' Sometimes they say the lower judge made a bad mistake. 'You may go free,' they might say, 'because you are not guilty.' This is the way of not only the *Tehannas,* but all Americans."

This he had not considered. He wet his lips, uncrossed his legs, and asked, "Do these bigger judge-chiefs always do this?" He would like to see the bigger judge-chiefs. The man with the wooden hammer who constantly played with his dark beard stood taller than most *Tehannas*. A white-eye bigger than him would be something to see, something to tell The Principal People about back home.

He read the answer in He Who Speaks The Black Robe Tongue's face before Hor-Ace-Jones finished explaining Big Tree's question. Sometimes, Hor-Ace-Jones said a moment later, the bigger judge-chief says the court was right, that the man should hang.

"I understand," Big Tree told him and stared at the dark ceiling, knowing the bigger judge-chiefs would not set him, a *Gai'gwu* warrior, free. He was doomed, no matter how hard He Who Speaks The Black Robe Tongue fought.

The white-eyes then spoke to Satanta, who had turned a

little grumpy once he realized the visitors had come to talk to Big Tree and not the great Orator, placating him, explaining the trial to be held in the morning. Satanta asked if he would get a chance to make a big speech, and He Who Speaks The Black Robe Tongue shrugged and said, "We'll see."

They left a few minutes later, and Satanta began telling Big Tree the great speech he would make, one that would save them both from the *Tehannas*. Big Tree did not listen to him. He thought back . . .

Chapter 21

"I claim this wagon, and all in it, as mine!"

—Hau-Tau

May 24, 1871
Saddle Mountain, Indian Territory

Weathered but nimble fingers tapped the *kinnininnick* into the calumet pipe with the precision of a younger but experienced man. Big Tree's eyes wandered from the old warrior to items in the rear of the lodge, held on pedestals: the yellow shield, painted with green birds, that proclaimed his host's membership in the Eagle Shield Society, and the long red sash and warbonnet that said he fought with the Crazy Dogs. Only Satank had been invited to join both societies, but his biggest honor rested in a tepee behind this one. It held no buffalo robe, no warbonnets, flutes, or lances. It was home only to the ten sacred bundles known as "The Ten Grandmothers," the holiest of all of *Gai'gwu's* possessions, entrusted to Satank's guard.

As Satank lit the pipe, Big Tree studied the warrior briefly before dropping his gaze to the red and blue blanket lying on a buffalo robe beside the fire.

"My son welcomes Big Tree to his lodge," said Satank, offering the pipe to the four directions and passing it to the guest.

Hesitantly, Big Tree took the pipe and puffed, still focused on the robe containing the bones of Satank's favorite son. He returned the pipe to Satank, who smoked a long time.

"You are silent, my son."

Big Tree looked up, uncertain if Satank had been addressing him or the blanket of bones. "You have never been much of a talker," Satank said with a laugh, and Big Tree relaxed. "An-pay-kau-te, my oldest son, who has raided with you into Mexico, did not say a word until he was seven years old. Then an Osage brought him a bottle of white-eyes whiskey, and An-pay-kau-te drank it. He said a few words, and when I came home from a raid and heard him talk, I sent for more whiskey from this Osage. Each day, I sampled the whiskey before letting An-pay-kau-te drink, but he drank a little each day and soon was talking and talking, cured by whiskey." Satank sighed. "Sometimes, though, I wish I had not discovered this cure, for An-pay-kau-te talks more than Satanta." The great warrior's voice lowered. "You are troubled, Big Tree."

His head bobbed slightly.

"This I knew. I knew you would come to see me and my son. I know many things, Big Tree. The fight with the *Tehannas* troubles you."

Satank had been given The Ten Grandmothers for a reason. As a warrior, he had no equal. As a healer, he had been honored with more horses than anyone else owned. As an oracle, few saw things clearer or truer. "It is so, grandfather," Big Tree answered.

"Smoke some more, my son."

Big Tree accepted the pipe and listened to Satank's words while studying the old man's face, his graying mustache, the scarred lip, the crevasses and scars, the black eyes that burned with hate yet also shined with wisdom.

"You have been on many raids. When The Principal People say the name of Big Tree, it is a name of respect. Big Tree, I have heard them sing, is a great warrior, fearless, owner of many fine horses, a young man taking the true road of The Principle People but willing to listen to the talk of the white-eyes. There is nothing wrong with that. You can even pray to the white-eyes' *Daw-ki* or *Paygya-Daw-Ki*. You can learn from the white-eyes, but do not make the mistake of Kicking Bird and others. Do not believe them.

"The white-eyes are inferior, yet they are many, and that is their only strength, except for their coffee and shoots-a-heap weapons. And the whiskey I got from the Osage that cured An-pay-kau-te of his tied tongue." Big Tree matched Satank's brief smile. "The white-eyes beat their young ones, which is something The Principal People never do. They eat birds, fish and even bear, which we, the true People, know is taboo. They take, but they do not ask, and when they do ask, they lie. They shoot hundreds of *pau-mah* for only the hides, leaving the meat to rot on the plains that the true god, the god of *Gai'gwu,* gave to us."

He expected Satank to make a wide circle with his words, eventually getting to the matter troubling Big Tree. That is the way Satanta would have spoken, or Lone Wolf or Kicking Bird, but he had forgotten that Satank spoke only when he had something to say.

"I did not believe Maman-ti's vision, but I smoked the pipe and joined his raid because it was right. It is right to make war against the *Tehannas,* against all white-eyes. We brought home forty-one mules for our families. We lifted six scalps and would have had one more, except the white-eye was afflicted with the same disease that has shed that fool Stone Head of his hair. Guns and corn and coffee and weapons. We returned home victorious. This is what I remember from the raid, Big Tree. Now tell me your memories."

It is true what you say, grandfather. I shared Maman-ti's pipe because I am a warrior, even if I do listen to Stone Head and these Christians. But Stone Head and the Great Father in Washington cannot feed my wife and children enough. Maman-ti is smart, I believe, and he is kind to all of *Gai'gwu.* It would be an honor to follow him into battle, especially once you accepted his pipe, grandfather.

More than one hundred of us joined Maman-ti. The great warriors of The Principal People, plus the Comanche and Kiowa-Apache. We were strong. After crossing the big river, we camped at Skunk Headquarters in the land of the *Tehannas,* leaving four boys too young to raid there to look after our extra horses and gear. Maman-ti told us to leave some horses behind, as we would be bringing many, many back, so several of us rode double. I let Hau-Tau ride behind me. My stallion was strong enough to carry us both. Soon we reached the old road the *Tehanna* wagons that carried people and mail once traveled. A good site for a raid it was, because although the white-eye wagons did not run as often as before, many *Tehannas* still traveled this road, as it connected the soldier-forts. I had raided along that road many times before I had seen my sixteenth winter.

That night, Maman-ti walked to the far side of the hill with his talisman to seek his vision. I waited to hear the voice of my grandfather or some other long-departed warrior, as did many of us on the raid. An owl hooted, wings flapped, and quiet resumed. That is when Maman-ti returned to us and told of his vision.

"Tomorrow," he said, "two parties of *Tehannas* will pass our way. The first will be small. It would be easy for us to attack, but we must let it pass. My medicine commands this. Later, another party will come by us, and we shall attack it. We shall be successful."

So we went to sleep and waited, although I was too excited to sleep. The next day we saw the white-eyes on the trail, heading toward the rising sun. We saw long knives and a bluecoat wagon. Many warriors wanted to attack, but Maman-ti reminded us of his vision, of his medicine, so we let the bluecoats ride away without doing them any harm. Nothing else traveled down the road that day, and some of the men became angry with Maman-ti, saying his vision was no good, but he told us to be patient. You and Satanta said we should remember Maman-ti's vision, his foretelling of a successful attack. So we waited. The sun baked us all the next day, and we grumbled when still no travelers appeared. That afternoon, clouds began rumbling in the west, and the wind began blowing hard. Yet just when some of the warriors had become so frustrated they wanted to ride or walk back home, ten covered wagons appeared, plodding along from the east, and we grew excited again. As I tied up my pony's tail for battle, I told Hau-Tau that he would have to run instead of ride with me. He was disappointed, but he understood how foolish it would be to ride double into battle. He said he would run as fast as he could. Perhaps, he told me, he would outrun my horse and count first coup. I did not see him again until after the white-eyes had fled.

We waited until Maman-ti raised his lance and Satanta blew a note on his bugle. Maman-ti's women made music on their bone whistles, and we attacked, galloping furiously down the hill. I wanted the honor of first coup, but Yellow Wolf's horse was too fast for mine. The *Tehannas* tried to turn their wagons into a circle, but we rode swiftly and had surprised them. Yellow Wolf cut off the last wagon, and I struck a white-eye with the tip of my bow and felt proud. I counted coup first. I believed Maman-ti's vision.

But everything changed. Or-dlee, the Comanche, had no horse. He had left his behind at Skunk Headquarters. He ran to a *Tehanna* to count coup or kill him, I do not know which. Brave was Or-dlee, but the *Tehanna* shot Or-dlee dead. Red Warbonnet then fell with a bullet in his thigh, and lead buzzed over my head. The white-eyes shot dangerously. They were not fools. They were very brave.

We fought on as the wind blew and the clouds swallowed the sun. Tson-to-goodle, the Kiowa-Apache, was shot in the knee, but two warriors rode by and lifted him off the ground. You know that story is true, grandfather, because I saw it with my own eyes. You were one of the men who saved Tson-to-goodle.

The white-eyes had had enough, and they ran to the mountain. Yellow Wolf and others rode after them but let them go. The *Tehannas* had fought bravely, and rain began pelting us. We did not need any more scalps. We had all we needed. The wagons and mules were ours.

That is when Hau-Tau ran to a wagon. He was brave, grandfather, but foolish. I heard you shout, "Keep back! It is dangerous!" Satanta agreed, yelling that we should attack the wagons from behind, but Hau-Tau kept running. White Horse and Set-maunte were unfastening the mules and tried to stop him, but he was too slippery. Like a snake. He climbed onto a wagon and yelled, "I claim this wagon, and all in it, as mine!"

Suddenly a *Tehanna,* hiding in the back of the wagon, opened the canvas with his rifle barrel and shot Hau-Tau in the head. He fell. White Horse and Set-maunte dragged him away.

This made us very angry. Yellow Wolf had ridden back just in time to see Hau-Tau fall. He charged the wagon, followed by me and ten other braves, and we dragged the *Tehanna* out before he could reload his musket, screaming. I kicked him in the head until he shut up. White Horse found a bucket of white-eye burning water with the pine odor and shouted his idea, and we all agreed. We gathered dry wood and *Tehanna* papers and placed it near the long stick of the wagon. White Horse poured the burning water over this pile as others, including me, lifted a wagon canvas to protect it from the wind and rain. You were there, grandfather, telling us to tie the *Tehanna* to the wagon pole, facedown, and we obeyed. He soon woke up, screaming, but Yellow Wolf cut out his tongue. Then Maman-ti struck a white-eye flame stick and tossed it on the burning water. Our women cheered as the *Tehanna* burned and cried.

"He is trying to pray to *Paygya-Daw-Ki,*" White Horse said, "but he chokes because he has no tongue."

White Horse found this funny, but I grew tired of the *Tehanna*'s screaming, so I found the axe and smashed his head. He cried no more. Yellow Wolf took the axe and, howling, ran to the other *Tehannas* we had killed and split their

heads. Then we tore down the canvas, and the rain pounded
out the burning water.

We took the mules and many possessions home with us,
but we did not talk much. Hau-Tau was alive, but you could
see his brains, and we knew he would not live long. A short
while later, when we thought the white-eyes would not chase
us, we buried Or-dlee so the *Tehannas* and bluecoats could
not find him.

After we crossed the river near the Medicine Mounds,
Quitan and Tomasi spotted a herd of *pau-mah* and asked if
they could stay behind and hunt. Maman-ti called this foolish, but let them. White Horse and Set-maunte, longing for
liver and roast of *pau-mah,* stayed with Quitan and Tomasi.
Long knives found them later, though, and killed Tomasi and
his horse, but the others escaped.

By the time we reached our village, the screw worms
had infected Hau-Tau's head. He died two days later. It was
a sad day.

That is the fight as I remember it.

Forgive me, grandfather, for mentioning the names of
those no longer walking our earth, but it is the only way I
could tell the story. Since I have been home, Hau-Tau has
visited me in my lodge at night. That is what troubles me.

Satank's eyebrows arched. "Does he speak to you?" he
asked.

"I try not to listen," Big Tree answered. "I look away from
him, for the screw worms are larger, and his face is rotting.
The bloody worms crawl out of his nose and ears. I do not
like his visits, grandfather." He shuddered, took a deep
breath, and continued. "I close my ears, but I hear him anyway. He says we made a mistake by not attacking the long
knives that traveled the path first. He says The Principal People will pay a terrible price. He says we must live at peace
with the white-eyes, but that it might be too late for Satanta,
Maman-ti, and . . ." He lowered his eyes. "And you, grandfather."

"Not you?" Satank asked.

Big Tree shook his head, and Satank refilled the pipe bowl, lighting it with a brand from the fire. "He laughs and leaves when my wife asks him what is to become of me." After this, Big Tree said nothing. Nor did Satank, and they smoked in silence. After they finished, Satank put away the pipe and spoke briefly to the blanket of bones before facing Big Tree again.

"The spirit who speaks to you has often spoken to me, Big Tree." He paused, finding the right words, staring at the opening in the top of the tepee. "These are words I will not say to anyone but you, my son, so listen well." His hard eyes lowered until they bore through Big Tree.

"The Principal People cannot defeat the white-eyes. Yes, they are inferior, as I told you earlier. They have no honor, and they do not respect us or our allies, the Comanche and the Kiowa-Apache, nor the Cheyenne, the Lakota, the Arapaho, the Apache. They do not even respect and honor the Caddos and Wichitas and Cherokees and Choctaws and other lesser people. Yet they are too many. If they cannot kill us with their guns, they kill us with their sicknesses: the spotted death, the coughing disease, and many more. Or they kill us with their whiskey. The copulate with our women and kill us with their offspring. It is a sad day for *Gai'gwu*. It has been a sad day since the white-eyes first arrived."

Shaking his head, Satank continued. "Do not believe the white-eyes. Kicking Bird says I am old, and I am old. I knew your father's grandfather as a young man, but—despite what Kicking Bird or Satanta might say about me—the evil spirits have not invaded my body yet." He tapped his temple lightly. "I am not mad, but I will not be thrown out. This is the way of *Gai'gwu*, to leave the ancient ones behind, and it is the right way. Spirits do take over the minds of the old, so they must be abandoned. They must also be mourned. Stone Head, the Quaker, and the other Jesus Christ talkers, do not like this. They think we are harsh, but they do not know anything. I tell you this because you must know that the man

who speaks to you"—unlike Big Tree, Satank took care not
to mention the dead brave's name—"does not include your
name for a reason. You will take a journey, one that will not
be easy for you or your family—or The Principal People who
remain behind. You will discover the path you must take on
this journey. Perhaps it shall be the way of The Principal
People. Perhaps you will take the white man's road. I do not
know. The white man's road is not the path for me, my son.
I hope it is not the path for you, for I see in you a warrior to
be entrusted with The Ten Grandmothers when I am gone.
But you must choose your own path. That is the way of
Gai'gwu. So be it."

A long silence followed, and Big Tree sat there uncomfortably, uncertain if Satank had finished. An eagle cried far
overhead, and Satank nodded as if the great bird had spoken
to him, and perhaps it had. Satank's magic had been the eagle
feather.

"You will not fear the white-eyes," Satank said, "but they
will soon come for Satanta and me. So the man who speaks
to you also speaks to me. It is a good thing for an old man
like me to be able to see my son as he used to be." He patted
the bundle at his side gently. "I look forward to that day. But
as I say, I will not be thrown out, my son. I will die *Koiet-
senko.*"

His eyes turned vacant as he stared at the fire.

"Soon," he said. "Very soon."

Chapter 22

"He is the personification of robbery, arson, and murder, and should never be allowed to escape alive."

—William T. Sherman

July 6, 1871
Jacksboro, Texas

Men, and a few women, crowded the hallway on the second story of the Wichita Hotel, talking in hushed but excited tones, sharing whiskey flasks, repeating every bit of the testimony and speeches from the trial. They ignored Sam Lanham, for the first time this night, as he fumbled with the lock. It was like this everywhere in town. No one could sleep, and he couldn't imagine how wild things would become after Satanta's trial. Once the door opened with skin-crawling squeaks, Lanham ducked into his room and pulled the door shut as quickly as possible. After turning up the wall lamp just high enough so he could see, he tossed his big hat on the dresser, removed his already loosened cravat, and emptied his pockets of change, cigar case, and money clip, trying not to wake Sarah, whose figure he detected underneath the covers.

"You're up late," she said softly, and Lanham sighed, removed his coat, ducked out of the suspenders, and sat on the bed while he pulled off his boots, tossing them tiredly beside his satchel.

"I didn't mean to wake you," he said, hoping the cigar

smoke would hide the whiskey on his breath. "Been givin' speeches aplenty." His accent escaped, as it did when he drank, and he felt condemned.

"What time is it?" Sarah asked sleepily, apparently not noticing his slight intoxication or simply deciding to hold off on introducing it into evidence until a later time.

"One-thirty. Go back to sleep, honey." He unbuttoned his shirt, listening to the murmur of voices still in the hallway. Who could sleep?

She sat up instead. "No. I wanted to talk to you."

He removed his shirt, pants, and socks and hurried across the hardwood floor to the wash basin. "What about?" he said, found a peppermint and popped it in his mouth, then toweled off his face and came back to bed, sliding underneath the covers despite the warmth.

That would be another giveaway, he realized too late. Sam Lanham's blood ran hotter than anyone Sarah had ever known. He would sleep on top of blankets and sheets unless the temperature dipped below forty degrees. He adjusted the pillow, rolled over and faced his wife, smiling, recalling the love they had made earlier that day. Time to confess.

"I've had a few drinks."

"I know. That's not what I want to talk about."

"What's on your mind?"

"What will happen to Big Tree?" she asked.

He let out a sarcastic snicker without thinking. "He'll hang," he said triumphantly. "Thanks to me."

Sarah's sigh surprised him, and he pulled himself into a seated position on the bed, wrapping his right arm around her delicate body. He remembered the sniffle he had heard after the verdict had been announced and wondered, though he couldn't comprehend why, if it had been his wife.

"You don't think," she began, "that Judge Soward would commute the sentence despite the jury?"

"They'd hang him," he said honestly. "They deliberated only seven minutes, dear." About five minutes longer than he had expected.

Sarah's tone confused him, but she had confounded him all day. She hadn't talked much during supper—perhaps because he didn't let her get a word in, so thrilled had he been with the guilty verdict. Strangers and friends kept coming to their table to shake his hand and tell Sarah what a great man of law she had married. When she retired to their room early, he just figured she was run-down after a long, blistering afternoon in the courthouse. So he celebrated alone. Well, not quite alone. All night, Samuel W. T. Lanham had been the biggest man in Jack County, probably all of Texas. He had been treated to a dozen cigars and half that many drinks, far more than he was accustomed to smoking or drinking. He had endured bone-crunching and joint-popping handshakes, bruising pats on the back, flirtatious winks from courtesans, and countless questions from nosy reporters. Plus, he had been forced to make three or four speeches, till his voice became hoarse. The whiskey and tobacco hadn't helped his throat, either.

Sam Lanham felt certain he could be elected governor if the good people of Texas would open the polls this night. He could probably stage a *coup*—he forgot the French phrase, needed Sarah's help there—kick Governor Davis out of office and take over the capital on this night. When he convicted Satanta today or tomorrow, Texas would withdraw from the Union, become a Republic again, and elect Sam Lanham president.

He wet his lips and studied his wife, who seemed on the verge of tears, a fact that dumbfounded the man celebrating the greatest victory of his career.

"Honey, Big Tree deserved what he got. He butchered seven men not a day's ride from here. White men. And Satanta's worse. This country won't be safe till—"

"Don't, Sam Lanham!" she said, sitting up. "Don't make speeches to me. I am your wife." She flew out of bed, pulled on her robe, and Lanham knew a fight was coming, although he couldn't figure out what had set her off. He let out a heavy sigh and sank deeper into his pillow.

"Do you remember anything from all the law you've read?" she asked, not giving him time to answer before cutting him with: "And what do you mean coming in here reeking of whiskey? You know I do not abide intoxication." Only a moment ago, she had said his drinking hadn't been troubling. Something else angered her. She was just using that to pick a fight.

"Lower your voice, Sarah. People are tryin' to—"

That was the wrong tack, not to mention a lie. He just didn't want any reporters in the hallway to hear their little ruction. "Don't tell me what to do, sir. By God, I will not allow that. If it weren't for me, you'd still be cropping tobacco in South Carolina. You could barely read before you married me."

"That's unfair," he said, stunned, hurt by those stinging words, and turned away. "If you want to fight, let's fight when we get home. I have a case to try in the morning." Dismissing her. Let her stew or come to bed. As her demeaning words sank in, he grew angrier but held his tongue. He needed to sleep, to be well-rested to face Satanta and his slippery lawyers.

He heard footsteps as she paced back and forth, kicking his dirty clothes across the room, whispering to herself, finally shedding her robe and crawling into bed. "We're not finished," she said. Oddly enough, that made him feel better.

"I know." His eyelids felt like lead.

"Big Tree doesn't deserve to die," she said softly. "Nor does Satanta. On a battlefield, maybe. Killed by settlers or the Army, sure. But not in a courtroom, Sam. They don't understand our law. Mr. Woolfolk was right in his closing summation. Hanging's wrong. That's not justice. It's murder. And you know it."

He didn't see it that way but knew better than to argue. She carried another child, and, like her other pregnancies, this one had not been easy. Sarah needed rest, should have stayed in Weatherford. He ground his teeth and stared into the darkness, not hearing her soft snores, trying to understand her reasoning. He had expected her to greet him warmly, proudly, almost busting her seams with joy at his triumph. This was the kind of case that could take the Lanhams places, take them far away from the hardscrabble life on the frontier, teaching other couples' children the three R's through subscription, or settling dreary cases at Watts, Lanham and Roach for a handful of greenbacks or a farrier's service on trade.

He had done his job, and he would do it again tomorrow, only better. Big Tree was a young buck, known only to Indian agents and a handful of soldiers before the trial. But Satanta? He was Cochise, Red Cloud, Tecumseh, Ridge, and Osceola wrapped into one miserable, haughty Kiowa. He had been profiled by journalist Henry Morton Stanley and been featured in newspapers from London to San Francisco. Maybe today or tomorrow, after the newspapers and telegrams began arriving, Sarah would come around.

July 6, 1871
Fort Richardson, Texas

The general and Colonel Mackenzie certainly were burning the midnight oil, Lieutenant Robert G. Carter thought as he knocked timidly on the commanding officer's front door. A muffled voice told him to come in, and Carter obeyed, finding William T. Sherman and Ranald Mackenzie in the smoke-filled parlor, a half-empty bottle of rye and two tumblers resting on a table.

"Pardon the intrusion, Colonel, General, but I wanted to inform you that counselor Ball has left the post," Carter reported after firing off an unanswered salute. They probably couldn't see through all the cigar smoke, he figured, and, after seeing Mackenzie's bloodshot eyes, he decided the colonel couldn't see much of anything tonight.

"Do you know what they talked about?" Sherman asked.
"Jones says nothing much," Carter answered. "Asked if

Big Tree needed something." That resulted in a harrumph from Sherman. "He told Satanta the trial tomorrow, er, today, would follow along the same lines as Big Tree's did."

"With the same results, by Jehovah!" shouted Mackenzie, slurring his words.

"Thank you, Lieutenant," Sherman said and crushed out a stub in an overflowing ashtray. "You should turn in."

Carter saluted again and turned to go, but Sherman stopped him at the door.

"Sir?" Carter said, spinning around.

"Did you talk to Mr. Lanham about tomorrow's proceedings?"

"I did, General. We will follow the same routine to escort the prisoners to the courthouse—"

"Prisoners? You mean only Satanta, don't you?"

"No, sir. Mr. Jones thinks it would be more comfortable for Satanta if Big Tree were there, too. Judge Soward agreed. Besides, Mr. Lanham said that way Big Tree can be in court to be sentenced after Satanta is found guilty."

"Very good, Lieutenant. Did Lanham talk about his strategy?"

"Same witnesses, he said. It should be a repeat of today's testimony. Or rather yesterday's testimony. It's after midnight."

Sherman scratched his beard and stifled a yawn. " 'Should be.' I dislike that. I don't want any excuses, Lieutenant. I want to make sure Satanta is found guilty and is sentenced to death."

"I wouldn't worry, sir," Mackenzie shot in. "It's the same jury—"

"I know. I know." The general had started pacing around Mackenzie's sofa. "But you two have never heard that long-winded Satanta make a speech."

"I doubt if Woolfolk or Ball will put him on the stand," Carter said. "Mr. Lanham doesn't think they will."

"Lanham has never heard Satanta, either," Sherman fired back and fell silent as he paced and fumed, fumed and paced.

Carter stood uneasily at the door, waiting for his dismissal. Mackenzie flopped in the parlor chair and crossed his legs.

"Send word to Mr. Lanham, Lieutenant," Sherman said once he stopped walking. He looked at the mantel clock and added, "First thing tomorrow morning. Tell him he needs to add a witness to the state's list."

"You, sir?" Carter asked incredulously.

"You're damned right, Mr. Carter," Sherman snapped. "I'll make sure that son of a bitch hangs."

July 6, 1871
Jacksboro, Texas

Someone had been kind enough to drag his trunks and items from his former residence to underneath the awning over his office window, so Thomas Ball found his key and went inside, hauling trunks heavier than a buffalo and poorly packed carpetbags inside. Straining, he dragged the largest trunk, a wooden one painted green, last, opened it quickly, and began tossing out shirts, coats, and journals thrown in unceremoniously by his eviction squad until he reached a Confederate Army gunbelt and holster with the brass buckle of the Forty-seventh Virginia Infantry. He unfastened the flap and pulled out the revolver, well-oiled but unloaded. He'd take care of that.

Ball struck a lucifer and lit a coal oil lamp, then went back to the trunk and found a copper powder flask, a leather bag of lead balls, and an unopened package of percussion caps. He smiled at the pistol, a Georgia-made .36-caliber Leech & Rigdon, basically a Confederate copy of the Navy Colt, which he had carried since Chancellorsville, although he had not worn a sidearm when he was captured. That's why he, and not some faceless damnyankee, had the revolver today. It, along with the gunbelt and holster, as well as other personal belongings, had been sent home to his parents by his commanding officer after Ball had been captured. The weapon felt good in his hand as he began the cumbersome loading process. The gunbelt, however, wouldn't fit that well. He hadn't been able to put his weight back on since rotting away at Point Lookout.

The hinges on the office door squeaked, and Ball pushed back in his chair, bringing up the half-loaded revolver—though he had not had time to place percussion caps on the nipples, so the gun remained useless if anyone called his bluff—and thumbing back the hammer.

"You're touchy, Tomball," Amanda Doniphan said in the doorway, and Ball sighed as she stepped into the light.

"And you're up late, Amanda," he said, returning to reloading the pistol. "What time is it anyway, two?"

"Two-thirty. Supper was busy tonight. I just got off work. Don't you have a case to try in the morning?"

He nodded, concentrating on ramming down the last ball, then placing the caps on the nipples for firing. Amanda didn't say anything until he lowered the hammer and laid the .36 on his desk.

"You put on six caps," she said.

"I did."

"That's not safe." He noticed her eyes, filled with concern, locked on the weapon he had just loaded. Ball rose, found the gunbelt, and strapped it on. Too loose, as he expected. He'd have to punch another hole or two in the belt. "Most folks around here keep only five beans in the wheel," Amanda told him. "To keep from shooting off their toes."

"I keep running into more than five men," he said, "who want to kick in my face and run me out of Jack County. So I'll keep six beans in the wheel."

She looked lovely. Tired, of course, with a straw hat poised back on her head, but the light caught her perfectly, illustrating the contours of her face, her bright eyes. She had to notice his bruises and cuts, but she said nothing.

"Would you allow me to escort you home?" he asked.

A grin lighted her face then, and Ball smiled with her. "Well, you're well-armed," she said, offering her arm.

He walked her outside, locked the door behind him, and led her down the boardwalk before he realized he had no idea where she lived. She took the lead, however, and he suddenly liked the idea that she was on his arm. His bad leg didn't hurt so much. Boisterous music and laughter echoed from the saloons, and more than a handful of drunken revelers staggered down the streets, but no one accosted the defense attorney or Wichita Hotel waitress. He wondered where they'd all sleep. Then again, where would he?

"This is it," she told him, and Ball looked up at a small adobe jacal several blocks south of the courthouse. "It ain't much, but it's home. Thank you, Mr. Ball."

"My pleasure, Miss Doniphan," he said and turned to go. He didn't plan on looking back, but stopped after several yards and tried to think of his most pressing concern.

"Where you going, Tomball?" Amanda called out from her door. He shuffled his feet, sighed, and walked back to her. She had heard about his eviction. He detected that in her voice, and it came as no surprise. Everyone in Jack County by now knew how the Widow Baggett had thrown him out with help from a gang of ruffians.

"I figured I'd rent a horse," he told her, "and find Woolfolk. He's camping someplace nearby."

Amanda laughed. "You're crazy, Tomball. You'd never find Joe Woolfolk. You'd get lost and scalped."

She regretted the last word immediately, but he let it pass. A sudden gust of warm wind caused her to reach out to hold on to her straw hat. She pushed open the door, pulled off her hat, and tossed it inside. Her long locks fell to her shoulders. "I'll sleep in the office, ma'am," he said. "Good night."

"You'll do no such thing, Tomball." She grabbed his hand and led him into the jacal. Darkness swallowed them until she found a match and lit a lantern. "If someone came gunning for you, Tomball, the first place he'd look is your office. I wouldn't be surprised if someone torched the place tonight. And that would burn down the Wichita Hotel and my place of employment. You can stay here." When he hesitated, she put her arms on her hips and said in mock anger, "I don't bite."

He still refused to budge. "You're a single woman, Amanda, and I won't put you in a compromising position."

She laughed at this, grabbed his hand, and pulled him closer, kicking shut the door. He'd be the first to admit that he had not offered that much resistance. She kissed him lightly and ran her fingers over the spur cut across his fore-head.

"I can't believe them idiots did this to you," she said softly after she broke off their kiss. "Does it hurt?"

"Not anymore," he said, wanting to kiss her again, but re-membering he was the Virginia gentleman.

His eyes swept the room, and he realized the jacal was just one room. It held a stove, two chairs, one table, a few odds and ends, and a small straw mattress in the far corner.

"You sleep on the floor, Tomball," she said. "I'll find you a blanket."

Chapter 23

*"Big-tree was tried and sentenced to death today.
Satanta . . . will be tried tomorrow, and as the
evidence is much stronger in his case than in Big-
tree's, the result is not doubtful."*
—Colonel Ranald S. Mackenzie

July 6, 1871
Jacksboro, Texas

Clouds teased a man out here.

Back in the Carolinas, or while traipsing around Virginia
with Kershaw's Brigade, or even when living in East Texas,
if Sam Lanham saw dark clouds gathering in the west, he
knew to break out his india rubber poncho. But in Jack and
Parker counties, only fools predicted rain.

Dark and low, the gathering thunderheads promised a del-
uge and cooler temperatures, but he knew better than to believe them. Perhaps thermometers proclaimed it a little cooler
this morning, but it felt five times more humid—stinking, miserable humidity that turned a man into a walking sponge—as
he hurried to meet Charley Jordan and W. M. McConnell for
breakfast, shunning the overcrowded Wichita Hotel for flap-
jacks and bacon at Ignacio's Café. He passed a few residents
on the boardwalk, including one man who studied the clouds
in quiet irritation, as if he knew they'd move on without
dropping a hundredth of an inch of rain. No farmer or
rancher, Lanham stopped thinking about the weather and

tried to polish his strategy for today's trial, but he couldn't get Sarah out of his mind. He had kissed his sleeping wife good-bye a few minutes ago, whispering that he'd look for her in the courthouse gallery while wondering, after their unsettled spat last night, if she'd actually show up.

Ignacio's was a small establishment on the south side of town, known for the cook's *atolé piñon* hot cakes and *huevos rancheros*. Popular with cowboys and Mexicans, it lacked the charm, service, and liquor to be found in the Wichita Hotel, so Lanham and his assistants figured it would be less crowded. Carrying his satchel, he slipped inside the front door and looked around. Sitting at a corner table, Charley Jordan flagged him over, yelling—as if Lanham could somehow have missed seeing the sweat-stained Stetson he had been waving—that they had saved him a place.

Lanham sank into the uncomfortable chair and ordered coffee and hot cakes, shaking his head when Jordan handed him a sack of Bull Durham and papers. His mouth felt as if he had breathed in smoke from a forest fire; his throat remained raw, and he wondered if his hoarse voice would fail him during the trial.

"Reckon it'll rain?" McConnell asked.

Jordan shook his head. "Wouldn't dare bet on it."

Would he have to turn over interrogations to the likes of McConnell and Jordan? Good men, well-liked, but hayseeds without a clue as to what it took to make a persuasive speech or understand the nuances of law and courtroom shenanigans, no match for accomplished orators such as Woolfolk and Ball. Lanham suddenly laughed. He had just described himself only a few short years ago.

McConnell and Jordan looked up at him with blank stares.

The waitress saved him by bringing their plates, butter, and a pitcher of syrup, and they ate in silence, but not for long.

"I was talking to a fellow last night," Jordan said after swallowing a mouthful of pancakes. "A reporter from

Omaha. And he says the Satanta trial will be anti . . . anti-cli . . . "

"Anticlimactic," Lanham said.

"Yeah. Says we'll just rehash Big Tree's trial. The evidence is certainly stronger against that old rapscallion Satanta than it was against Big Tree."

Lanham considered Post Adjutant Robert G. Carter's note in his breast pocket, delivered to his hotel room less than an hour ago from Fort Richardson by Corporal Charlton. "I'm hoping Ball and Woolfolk think the same thing," he said, "because I plan on throwing them a surprise later this morning."

Sheriff Mike McMillan greeted Woolfolk and Ball with a smirk. "You did make sure your client took his mornin' piss before he left Fort Richardson, didn't you, counselors?" he chided, hitching up his gunbelt and waiting for a response.

Ball walked on through the courtroom's doors without a word, but Woolfolk stopped, pulled out his quid of tobacco, and bit off a mouthful. "You musta been up all night practicin' that one, Mike," he said, shoved the plug into his mouth, and followed his colleague.

Cocky sumbitch, he thought. Acting like he had convicted Big Tree yesterday all by himself. Working the tobacco furiously, he settled into his chair and looked around the courtroom, empty except for McMillan and a deputy busy opening windows.

"Why in Hades didn't you boys leave 'em open last night?" Woolfolk said. "Then it wouldn't feel like St. Louis in here."

"Judge thought it might rain," the deputy replied.

"Wishful thinkin'."

Ball pulled out his papers and placed them on the long bench in front of him. He hadn't said much over breakfast, and Woolfolk hadn't broached the subject of the nasty cut across his noggin or the new bruises and swollen lip. Nor had he made any pithy comment about the Johnny Reb–issue

gunbelt he wore. Sheriff McMillan had simply stared at it
when they walked inside, letting Ball proceed because, as an
officer of the court, maybe he was exempt from the firearm
ban. Woolfolk certainly hoped so. He carried a Navy Colt in
his boot top and had been carrying it since the trial began.
The darn thing was leaving a blister on his calf, but Woolfolk
would tolerate such discomfort for protection.

"Satanta wants to testify," Ball whispered, and Woolfolk
almost swallowed his tobacco juice. He spit quickly and
stared at his partner.

"I spoke to him last night," Ball continued. "And Big
Tree."

"You can't put him on the stand," Woolfolk whispered urgently. "Lanham—"

"I know," Ball said. "I didn't mention it over breakfast because the dining room was packed with reporters and half the
town. But I thought—"

A cry from outside silenced him. The Army was bringing
in Satanta and Big Tree under heavy guard, and the two
lawyers quickly followed Mike McMillan downstairs.

"All rise."

Charles Soward immediately noticed the gunbelt partially
hidden by Thomas Ball's coat, and his face hardened beneath
his handsome beard. Ball, however, refused to give way to
Soward's penetrating stare, and as the judge took in the rest
of the lawyer's battered face, he decided to drop his gaze and
the subject. Everyone knew what had happened to Ball last
night—Peter Lynn had told him at the Lost Creek Saloon—
and momentarily Soward had felt as if he were to blame for
the attorney's plight. But, he had decided after two whiskeys
and several newspaper interviews, he had warned Ball and
Woolfolk not to play stupid games. They had only themselves to blame.

Still, he wondered where Ball had slept last night. He
looked better than Woolfolk, no surprise, for Joe Woolfolk
always appeared like a man fresh off a three-day drunk or

three days in a barn. His hair and clothes sported more dirt, dust, and grime than those of the two prisoners.

"Bring in the jury," said Soward, settling into his chair.

The Indians grunted, about the only sound they ever made, and their chains rattled as they lowered themselves onto the bench.

"Objection!"

Soward's eyes shot up angrily at the feisty defense table. Ball had remained standing.

"What is it this time, counselor?" Soward already felt grumpy. The courtroom felt like an oven, and those clouds overhead merely trapped the heat, turning up the sogginess. His shirt beneath the black robe already stuck to his wet skin, and his forehead felt slimy. He was in no mood for Ball and Woolfolk's mischief.

"The defense objects to the jury," Ball said. "This jury was sworn in for the trial of Big Tree. It cannot be impartial in the matter of Satanta. That is the reason we asked for a severance, Your Honor."

Do you think I can find twelve more men to hear this ridiculous case? he considered asking but merely shook his head and leaned back. He'd let the state fight this one out, but Sam Lanham blinked stupidly, his mind far from Jack County. The prosecutor confounded him even more when he craned his neck to peer into the gallery. Soward turned his wrath in that direction.

"Mr. Lanham, are you preoccupied?"

"No, Your Honor," Lanham answered but turned back to face the court a tad too slow to suit Charles Soward.

"Because, sir, I see no reason we can't adjourn for an hour or a week." Soward folded his arms. "I'm sure whatever's on your mind is far more important than this capital murder case. Do you think these reporters and citizens have nothing better to do than sweat and wait? Or our two esteemed guests from Indian Territory?" He planned on going on, but Lanham was standing, pressing his fingertips on the desk before him.

"My apologies, Your Honor." The prosecutor recovered

quickly. Soward liked that about him. "The objection by the defense is absurd. These men were sworn in for Case Number Two Hundred Twenty-four, the State of Texas versus Satanta and Big Tree. When the court granted the severance of the trial, no motion was made to disregard the cause, nor was any made regarding the indictment, which billed both defendants to stand trial for murder. This is the second part of that trial. The jurors remain under oath, like a grand jury impaneled to hear various cases."

That argument even astounded Soward, who quickly forgot his minor annoyance with Lanham's lack of attention.

"I know of no precedent allowing one criminal jury to hear two cases," Ball shot back.

Lanham just smiled. "Well," he said smugly, thickening his accent, "this is Texas, and we Texicans have been known for makin' our own precedents."

Soward had to bring out his trusty gavel to squelch the guffaws and applause, then overruled the defense's objection.

"Exception," Ball said.

"Noted. Bailiff, bring in the jury at this time."

Ball settled into his chair, looking fairly pleased despite the ruling. Or maybe he had expected and desired such a ruling. Yes, that was it. Thomas Ball figured he had great grounds for appeal once Satanta was convicted and sentenced to hang. *Fine,* Soward thought.

Let him think that.

It turned her stomach again, listening to the Army doctor describe the wounds suffered by Samuel Elliott, Nathan Long, and the others for the second time in two days. The stifling heat and humidity didn't help matters, either. M. J. Shelley glanced out the window, praying for rain, just a few drops, a bit of relief.

No one seemed eager today. Reporters yawned and barely took notes, and M. J. couldn't blame them. Everything being said had been said a day earlier. The two annoying little boys,

H. P. Cook and Jehu Atkinson, were back in school, or should be. Even Wesley Callaway had seen no reason to give his young students two days off to observe this unique trial, and Prudence Baggett had remained home. So had the nice-looking woman sitting near her yesterday who had let out an unexpected whimper when the verdict dooming Big Tree had been announced. The courtroom, however, remained packed, and hundreds gathered outside just as they had done a day earlier. The testimony, however, remained the same. Poor Thomas Brazeal had been called to the stand first, relating the callous Indian attack till a lone tear rolled down his cheek. Colonel Mackenzie followed with his monotonous drone, and now Doctor Patzki described the carnage the Kiowas had left behind.

M. J. looked at the sweating jurors. Peter Lynn looked miserable, bored like everyone . . . excluding foreman Thomas Williams, the fire-breathing Yankee sympathizer, who stared relentlessly at the witness. James Cooley continued to work on a disgusting bulge of tobacco in his cheek, and H. B. Verner bit his fingernails. She tried to block out the horrific testimony, even though she had heard it all before, and listened to the Army interpreter repeat the words in that somnolent Comanche grunting.

Finally, the doctor finished. The defense attorneys didn't bother asking him any questions—perhaps they realized the folly of their ways and knew Satanta would be found guilty no matter what they argued—and the state called Horace P. Jones to the stand. This meant another boring courtroom procedure, the same as yesterday, when the other Indian-man, Mathew Leeper, had to be sworn in to translate for the defendants. Jones took his oath and settled into the chair, spitting out tobacco juice and wiping his mouth with his a hankderchief. After stating his full name—Horace Pope Jones—for the record, he waited for Lanham's first question.

"Where were you born, Mr. Jones?"

"Jefferson City, Missouri. But I've lived in Texas and the Nations since I was seventeen."

"When were you born?"

"Twenty-ninth of March in 'twenty-nine."

She hadn't really studied Horace Jones much, just listened to him reciting that indecent language of heathens or spitting tobacco juice, but she stared at him this morning with a bit of wonder. Neither he nor Mathew Leeper looked anything like she, or the cover artists for those half-dime novels, would have imagined. Oh, he spoke with a drawl and had picked up several ungentlemanly habits along the frontier, but he looked, well, like a gentleman. He was in his early forties and wore striped blue pants, a boiled shirt with a paper collar, a narrow tie, and a black sack coat. He didn't even wear boots, but well-shined shoes. No fringed buckskins, no wide-brimmed, high-crown hats or beaded gloves. He looked more like a businessman. Mathew Leeper had been attired in similarly fashionable clothing.

"So you've been in Texas and Indian Territory since 'forty-six. Have you had any dealings with savages?"

"Objection."

Lanham smiled. Obviously, he had expected this. Judge Soward sustained the objection—though M. J. thought he was wrong in doing so. Confound it, they *were* savages.

"With the Indians?" Lanham corrected.

"Yes, sir."

"And you know the defendant, Satanta?"

"Yes, sir."

"May it please the court, I'd like some latitude here, to show the witness's qualifications and experience with the sav—with the Indians."

Lanham had not done this yesterday. Probably wanted to leave nothing to chance in the trial against the bigger chief. Woolfolk and Ball simply shrugged, and Soward gave an approving nod in the prosecutor's direction.

"Tell us," Lanham told the witness, "your experience with these Indians my distinguished colleagues keep painting as noble heroes incapable of committing wrong while blaming the white race for all of their, and our, troubles."

Chapter 24

"*Satanta wanted it understood that while Satank and Big Tree had accompanied him on the raid, he alone had commanded. He was the Big Wind, the Terror of the White Man, the Admiration of the Braves, etc. And he called upon the sun, the moon and the stars to witness that if any other Indian claimed part of the glory such a one was a liar and lower than a white man.*"

—Paul Soward Leeper, *Frontier Times*, April 1930

July 6, 1871
Jacksboro, Texas

After I left Jefferson, Texas, my first dealin's with Indians come about in 'fifty-five, when Texas an' the U.S. created a couple of reservations on the Brazos. Most of y'all rightly recollect that. The Lower Reserve was at the Forks of the Brazos, an' the gov'ment put the Caddo, Waco, an' other smaller tribes on that one. The Upper Reserve was where I got hired on as a farmer. That's the one they put on the Clear Fork of the Brazos. The Penateka Comanch was moved there, an' that's where I learned Comanch. Also met Mr. Leeper yonder durin' that time. He was a Comanch agent back then.

The Comanch liked me, an' I liked them. They was the Honey-Eaters. Nothin' like the Kwahadis, the most warlike of the tribes, or other bands of Comanch. Nope, the Penateka was a lot more peaceful. Anyway, after a spell, they adopted me into their tribe. So when the Comanch was sent up to Indian Territory, I tagged along. Durin' the War Between the States, Mr. Leeper was appointed Commissioner of Indian Affairs for the Confederacy, an' he settled at Fort Cobb an' got me a job as interpreter at the Washita Agency. I done that, also scouted an' interpreted for the Rangers an' the likes whenever needed.

No, sir, you're right, Mr. Lanham. Wasn't always peaceful livin' with Indians. In the fall of 'sixty-two, October I think it was, the Yankees sent the Osages to attack the Tonkawas, who was livin' on the Wichita Agency, 'cause the Tonks had sided with us Rebs. Well, it's a long story, but I got out alive, barely, an' come back to find the Osages had massacred the poor Tonks there. Almost wiped 'em out. Kilt all the whites who hadn't escaped, too.

Yes, sir, all them bodies was mutilated.

Anyway, that left me without a job, so I started up to Fort Arbuckle. I did odds an' ends, picked up some other languages there, like the Kioway, though I don't speak it as good as I do Comanch, an' after the war I got hired on as scout an' interpreter at Fort Arbuckle. Stayed there till they founded Fort Sill an' been there since.

"Regarding this massacre you described," Lanham began, "do the Indian tribes you know usually conduct themselves with such barbarity?"

"Objection," Ball said from his seat. "Latitude was given to show Mr. Jones's qualifications. He has done that, Your Honor. The only Indian attack that matters is the one at Salt Creek Prairie."

Soward sustained the objection.

"Very well," continued Lanham, unfazed. "Let us get to the matter at hand. How long have you known the defendant, Satanta?"

Before Jones could answer, the crowd outside began whistling, echoed by a cacophony of euphoric voices. In the courtroom, a farmer in dirty homespun and soiled suspenders started to stand up and see what the commotion was about, but Soward stopped him by pounding his gavel, telling him to stay seated or be thrown out, then instructed Sheriff McMillan to inform the rabble standing on the courthouse lawn that if they did not lower their voices, they would be removed forthwith. *So far, so good,* Lanham thought, guessing what had excited the citizens below. His surprise remained a mystery. Once the sheriff had quieted the gathering, Lanham repeated his question.

"I met him in passin' while workin' at the Wichita Agency durin' the war, but come to know him pretty good after the Kioways signed the treaty at Medicine Lodge in 'sixty-seven an' Fort Sill was established a coupla years later."

"Do you recall what happened on the twenty-seventh of May this year?"

"I do."

"Please tell the court what happened, sir."

May 27, 1871
Fort Sill, Indian Territory

Col'nel Grierson's bluebellies had planned ever'thing pretty good. He had 'em hidin' in the corrals an' inside his home. Mr. Tatum had tol' Satanta that Gen'ral Sherman wanted to meet him an' talk to him 'bout things an' such, an' Satanta, he was always hankerin' to make a big speech. So he showed up, along with just about ever' big brave the tribe had. 'Bout twenty, all tol'. At first. That's when I walked over with Satank, Satanta, an' all the others. I made the introductions, then climbed up the steps to the col'nel's porch an' translated for Gen'ral Sherman.

Well, sir, it got kinda ticklish real quicklike. I hadn't been that nervous since the Osages attacked the Washita Agency. Satanta, he started complain' that he wasn't bein' treated right, an' Gen'ral Sherman, he said to never mind that, to tell him 'bout the raid in Texas.

Well, Satanta, he likes to brag in his speechifyin'. He harangued some young bucks tryin' to talk first, then he puffs out his chest an' tells the gen'ral, "Let no chief claim the credit of killin' those seven men in Texas; I am the big chief that did that killin'."

He talked some more 'bout the raid. Bellyachin' 'bout not gettin' enough goods. Then he says that he, Satank, Big Tree, Big Bow, Eagle Heart, Fast Bear, an' Maman-ti were on the raid. Says he lost three men, but he was willin' to call it even if Gen'ral Sherman was. 'Course, the gen'ral didn't have that notion. I guarantee you that.

Well, Satanta kept talkin', but then he started growin' suspicious, started realizin' his mistake by talkin' so much. Ol' Satank, he had warned Satanta before not to name any names. So he, Satanta I mean, changed his story in midstream, said he had been there, but he hadn't done nothin' more than toot his bugle. Says Maman-ti was the real leader. Satank tol' him to shut up again, an' Satanta did.

Gen'ral Sherman, he called Satanta a woman. Said he was lower than a beetle to fight teamsters instead of bluecoats an' threatened to oblige the Kioways with a fight right then an' there if they taken the notion. That got their dander up, sure as shootin'. I figured blood would run for sure, an' it came mighty close. The gen'ral, he arrested Satanta, an' things got prickly. Satanta started to draw a pistol. Said he'd rather die here, but Grierson sprang his trap, an' them buffalo soldiers came out of the woodwork, throwin' open shutters, levelin' carbines at them Indians.

Satanta knew enough English to beg 'em not to shoot.

Kickin' Bird started talkin' then. He's always been real good to the whites, an' I reckon we've been good to him. He spoke to the gen'ral, tol' him that he couldn't let'm take away his men, even Satanta—Kickin' Bird never cared too much for that ol' bird, an' vicey versy. It got touchy again, but the bluecoats hidin' in the corral shot out, springin' another trap, and the Kioways knew it was over. Anyhow, Gen'ral Sherman did some more smooth-talkin', then things got quiet. The gen'ral, he took Big Tree, Satank, an' Satanta into custody.

That's 'bout all there was to it.

July 6, 1871
Jacksboro, Texas

"Let me get this straight, Mr. Jones," Lanham said. "Satanta admitted at first that he had led the raid that left seven God-fearing men slain on the Texas prairie? He said this on his own volition?"

"Yes, sir."

"He wasn't under arrest at the time of his statement?"

"Well, not technic'ly, sir. I don't reckon Gen'ral Sherman woulda let him go, though."

"But Satanta did not know this?"

"No—"

Ball shot out an objection. "Unless the witness is a mind reader, he has no idea what Satanta thought at that time."

"Sustained," Soward ruled. "The jury will disregard Mr. Lanham's last question and the witness's answer."

"Sir, did you believe Satanta when he said he led that raid?"

"Well . . ." Lanham realized his mistake. He had asked Mathew Leeper the question yesterday and gotten the answer he wanted, but the first rule of prosecuting was to know the witness's answer before you asked the question. He had assumed Jones would have the same reply, only the interpreter's timid response told him otherwise, so he quickly rephrased the question. "I mean, sir, do you believe Satanta took part in the raid?"

"Yes, sir. I do."

Lanham dared not glance at the defense table. That would give away his fear that they would pounce upon his mistake.

At least he had one strong final question. "Why should we believe your testimony, sir?" he asked.

Nonplussed, Jones spit and answered. "I never held truck with liars. What I done tol' you is the gospel, sir."

"In fact, the Comanches have given you an Indian name, have they not?"

"Yes, sir. They call me The Man Who Never Tells A Lie."

"Thank you. I pass this witness."

Yesterday, Thomas Ball had directed a brief cross-examination of Jones, but Joe Woolfolk had asked for the opportunity in the Satanta trial, and Ball had relented without protest. After all, Woolfolk and Jones spoke the same language, and both had been on the frontier far longer than Ball. Woolfolk removed his tobacco, tossed it in the spittoon, rinsed out his mouth with a glass of water on the table and spit out the water as well before walking to the witness.

"Horace, you talked 'bout the Comanch reservation down here. Peaceful, you say?"

"Yes, sir. Penateka Comanch was mighty peaceful."

"Why was the reservation moved?"

Lanham shot out an objection, but Woolfolk had anticipated that. "He opened the door, Your Honor, by bringin' in the witness's past experiences."

"So he did," Soward said easily. "Answer the question, Mr. Jones."

"Well," Jones drawled, "folks nearby didn't cotton to Indians livin' that close to 'em."

"You mean, the white settlers livin' contiguous to the two Texas reservations." He wondered if Horace P. Jones knew the meaning of *contiguous*. Laughing to himself, he wondered if Samuel W. T. Lanham did.

"Not only them," said Jones, whose accent belied his education. "Practic'ly ever' county in the region."

"Includin' Jack County?"

"I reckon so."

"So, are you tellin' us that these peaceful Indians were expelled from their reservation in 'fifty-nine to the Washita Agency in Indian Territory?"

"Yes, sir, that's what happened."

"In addition to Mathew Leeper, you worked under Robert Neighbors, did you not, sir?"

"I did."

"Robert Neighbors was another Indian agent?"

"Yes, sir. Major Neighbors had been workin' with the tribes in Texas since the days of the Republic."

"What happened to Major Neighbors and the Penateka Comanch?"

"Well, a no-account fella named John Baylor got himself fired from the agency an' started stirrin' up trouble. Blamed the Penateka for some raids goin' on. A day or two after Christmas back in 'fifty-eight, a bunch of white devils kilt three squaws an' four braves—not even Penateka, but Caddo and Anadarko, 'bout as harmless as an Indian comes. They had been shot while sleepin'. A judge ordered some suspects brought in, but Rip Ford, he was rangerin' here at that time, said he wouldn't do no such thing. Well, things got hot. Major Neighbors, me, an' some Indians had to fight off white settlers on the reserve. So in June of 'fifty-nine, the State of Texas an' the U.S. government moved the Indians to the Territory—for their own safety, I guess. That's what they said. Most of the folks hereabouts just said good riddance an' started filin' on what had been the reserve. Me an' Mr. Leeper, we tol' Major Neighbors not to go back to Texas, but he did. Had some matters to settle. He was at Fort Belknap, talkin' to a friend, when a ne'er-do-well named Ed Cornett shot him in the back. Kilt him."

Lanham stood again as Woolfolk stepped aside. "Your Honor, the state moves that this whole line of testimony be stricken from the record. Ed Cornett was killed by Rip Ford's Rangers after murdering Major Neighbors, and these events happened a dozen years ago. They have no bearing on this case, sir. The Penateka Comanche are not on trial. The Kiowas are."

Tugging on his beard, Soward faced Woolfolk for his response.

"Wasn't there an Indian at Fort Belknap who witnessed the murder?" Woolfolk asked Jones, hoping Soward would let the witness answer before ruling on Lanham's objection.

"Yes, sir. A half-breed we called Danny Cimarron."

"What tribe?"

"Kioway."

Soward had stopped tugging on his beard, but Lanham reminded the court of his objection. The judge silenced him with a wave of his hand.

"And what was his reaction to the murder of Major Neighbors?"

"He wailed all that day an' all the next night."

Woolfolk felt pleased. He craved taking a break to bite off another mouthful of tobacco, only didn't want to interrupt his rhythm. "Let's move forward, sir," he said. "Durin' the events you have described that took place at Fort Sill this past May, did General Sherman ask you to explain to Kickin' Bird why Satanta, Big Tree, and Satank were bein' held?"

"Yes, sir. The gen'ral tol' me to tell Kickin' Bird, 'Those stolen mules must be delivered to me in ten days.'"

"You explained this?"

"Yes, sir. I did."

"Was it your understandin' that those three chiefs would be released after the mules were returned?"

"Well, I asked the gen'ral 'bout that, but he tol' me no."

"What was his exact words?"

Jones spit. "He said, 'Those red bastards are goin' to Texas to stand trial for murder.' He said they'd be hanged."

Satisfied but far from finished, Woolfolk returned to his chair, timing his question to irk Sam Lanham. "The distinguished prosecutor asked if you thought Satanta led the raid, then changed his mind and asked you somethin' else. So, why don't you answer his first question. Do you think Satanta led the raid?"

"No, sir. I reckon not."

"Did Big Tree lead it?"

"No. Big Tree's too young to lead a raidin' party that size."

"So who was the leader?"

"Well, from what I hear tell, it was Maman-ti."

Lanham started to object but settled into his chair. That surprised Woolfolk, but he kept his pace. "Do you believe Maman-ti is capable of leadin' such a war party?"

"Sure as shootin'."

"So why isn't Maman-ti standin' trial?"

"Well, he wasn't there when Gen'ral Sherman had the chiefs arrested. An' he ain't the easiest rabbit to catch on or off the reserve. Takes to hidin' like a chameleon. I ain't seen him since before the chiefs got arrested."

Shaking his head, Woolfolk said, "So this is justice for you. The state and federal government that conspires to kick peaceful Indians off their reservation also conspires to arrest three Indians for a crime because they showed up to hear William Sherman's lies while the ringleader—"

Now Lanham did object, and this time Judge Soward sustained the motion and reminded Woolfolk he was interrogating witnesses, not making his summation. Woolfolk bowed slightly and pulled a tobacco plug from his pocket.

"Redirect?" Soward asked.

Lanham shot out of his chair. "A half-breed Kiowa named Danny Cimarron cried over the foul murder of Robert Neighbors?"

"Yes, sir."

"You were there with Neighbors and this Danny Cimarron?"

"No, sir. I was up at the Washita Agency."

"And you just heard that Maman-ti led the raid on Salt Creek Prairie?"

"Yes, sir."

"From whom?"

"Mostly Comanch. The Kioways been too scairt to talk 'bout it any. They fear they all might get sent down to Texas an' hung."

Lanham had to raise his voice slightly to be heard over the whispered responses in the gallery to Jones's last sentence. "But you did hear with your own ears the defendant, Satanta, the great Orator of the Plains, confess to leading the raid?"

"Yes, sir."

Lanham whirled to face the judge. "Your Honor, I submit to you once more that Mr. Woolfolk's entire cross-examination consists of nothing more than hearsay, and I respectfully suggest that the court has no choice but to throw out this entire line of questioning."

"Agreed, counselor," said Soward, tapping his gavel. "The jury will disregard everything—"

"Whoa!" Woolfolk sprang to his feet, spitting out a few small chopped tobacco leaves. "Under the state's direct examination, the witness said, under oath, that he heard Satanta say Maman-ti led the raid."

The gavel slammed harder. "Sit down, Mr. Woolfolk. I've made my ruling."

"But it ain't right, Judge."

"Sit down, sir, or I'll hold you in contempt . . . again."

He felt like pulling that Navy hogleg from his boot and shooting Charles Soward where he sat. "You can disregard the testimony about Major Neighbors, Danny Cimarron, and the whole damn Penateka reservation, Judge, but you can't throw out what Jones says he heard Satanta say."

"Not only can I," Soward boomed, "but I have already done so! Your cross-examination was totally out of line, Mr. Woolfolk, and if you do not sit down, I shall fine you ten dollars."

"But—"

The gavel rapped. "Twenty dollars, sir!" Soward shouted. "You've been fined ten already for your outburst yesterday. Keep it up, and I'll own your ranch."

Thomas Ball gently tugged on Woolfolk's jacket, and, fuming, the lawyer sat down, staring at Soward with malevolent eyes as Mathew Leeper finished his Comanche translation.

Chapter 25

"The only good Indians I ever saw were dead."
                                    —General Philip Sheridan

July 6, 1871
Jacksboro, Texas

That exchange snapped the reporters out of their stupefied daze, but Sam Lanham would best Joe Woolfolk. He waited until the defense lawyer settled down and Judge Soward silenced the murmurs in the gallery, letting a lengthy quietness settle over the courtroom until he knew everyone was staring at him, waiting. Only then did Sam Lanham stand.

"At this time, the state calls General William Tecumseh Sherman."

The audience's roar followed instantaneously, and heads rotated as two deputies opened the double doors. Clamping an unlit, soggy, chewed-up cigar in his jaw and squeezing a black porkpie hat in his right hand, Sherman made a beeline down the aisle. He wore scuffed cavalry boots sans spurs; black wool trousers, civilian-issue; a boiled white shirt, the sleeves rolled up, with a dirty paper collar; a regulation Army vest, unbuttoned; and a stained black cravat—an unseemly outfit that made Joe Woolfolk look like an advertisement for a Philadelphia tailor. There was nothing military about Sherman except his weathered countenance and purpose in manner.

Lanham took a moment to sweep the gallery, sighing as

Sherman passed him toward the witness chair. Sarah wasn't here. Maybe she had decided to stay in the hotel to rest. He hoped she wasn't still angry at him. He prayed she understood and had finally realized he stood in the right. As Sherman was sworn in, Lanham slowly turned around and remained standing, ready to fend off any objections from Woolfolk and Ball.

The state had not put Sherman on the witness list—no time, really; the general had demanded that he take the stand this morning—so the defense had grounds to object. That's probably what the two defense attorneys were discussing in grave whispers as they huddled across the aisle. Lanham folded his arms, waiting.

"Is there an objection, gentlemen?" Judge Soward finally asked, which broke up the debate.

"No, Your Honor," Ball answered, flipped his note pad to a new page, and began scribbling notes.

Lanham's eyebrows arched, and he pursed his lips. Were he the defense attorney, he would have raised an objection. Probably wouldn't have won, but he would certainly have made an argument just on principle.

"Proceed, Mr. Lanham," Soward instructed.

"General, you are based in Washington, D.C., so could you explain to the court why you were in Texas this past spring?"

Sherman pitched his cigar into the spittoon. Usually, before he gave testimony or dictated an affidavit, he rehearsed what he was supposed to say with some team of highfalutin attorneys, but he hadn't given Lanham that chance. Well, he figured Lanham was pretty capable, a smart man for a Southerner, ambitious, too, and likely wouldn't steer him down the wrong path. Besides, Sherman considered his take on things fairly straightforward.

"The inspector general and I were touring the frontier," he said dryly, "visiting the various military outposts in Texas and Indian Territory and letting citizens address their concerns and express what they wanted from the Army."

Lanham made him specify that the inspector general's name was Randolph Marcy before asking the next question. Details. Lawyers bogged down every legal proceeding with minutiae. "So, you talked to settlers across Texas?"

"Yes, sir. At most of the posts established on your frontier."

"Sir, why were these military posts established?"

Lanham might be a frontier barrister with Southern leanings, but he could be just as irritating as some big-city attorney back East with his stupid questions. "To protect settlers from Indian war parties," he said dully.

"And what sort of comments did you hear from the good people of our state?"

"That we, the Army, that is, weren't doing enough. Just about every place we stopped, people cited various depredations carried out by the savages."

"By savages, to what tribes were they referring?"

"Mostly Comanche and Kiowa." He wasn't sure Lanham would follow through, so he went on. "The farther north we traveled, the more we heard that many of these raids were believed to have been conducted by Indians living, at the government's expense, on the federal reserves in Indian Territory."

"Did you believe these reports?"

He didn't like that question but answered truthfully. "Inspector General Marcy did. As we rode from Fort Griffin to Fort Richardson, General Marcy pointed out several burned-out homesteads, and he remarked to me how there weren't as many whites living out here as he had seen during a previous expedition eighteen years ago. I had doubts about the number of raids these Indians had allegedly perpetrated."

"Did the inspector general say more?"

"He did, sir. He said, 'If the marauders are not punished, the whole country might quickly become totally depopulated.'"

" 'Totally depopulated.' " Lanham whistled. "I see. You crossed Salt Creek Prairie on your way from Griffin to Richardson, did you not?"

"I did, via Fort Belknap, taking the old Butterfield stage route."

"Did you see any Indians?"

"I didn't see a damn thing but dust, vultures, and starving coyotes."

That prompted a few chuckles from the gallery, and Lanham asked when the general's party arrived at Fort Richardson.

"We left Fort Griffin on the sixteenth of May, made it to Belknap that day, where we made camp. The following morning, the seventeenth, we departed Belknap and arrived at Fort Richardson late in the day. On the eighteenth, I listened to various citizens tell horrifying accounts of Indian depredations in Jack County alone." He almost singled out the juror Lynn, saying he remembered his story well, but quickly realized how stupid that would have been. The last thing he wanted was to give the defense adequate reason to force Charles Soward to declare a mistrial.

Lanham expertly guided Sherman through his other observations: the first meeting with the settlers, his talks with Colonel Mackenzie, and his interview, complete with his feelings of shock and disgust, with the badly wounded teamster and his colleague in the post hospital on the night of the eighteenth. Sherman also addressed his orders to Colonel Mackenzie at Fort Richardson and Colonel Wood at Fort Griffin, how and why he had given them permission to pursue the hostiles into Indian Territory, including the Fort Sill Reserve.

"On the following day, did you have another meeting with the citizens of this county?"

"Yes, sir. They were furious, and I couldn't blame them—"

Lanham cut him off to drive home a point. "You mean, General, that you now believed the stories you had heard regarding Indian butchery were not exaggerations?"

"That is correct, Mr. Lanham."

"What did you tell the citizens in this second interview?"

"I told them I believed that all, or almost all, of the Indian attacks were coming from Indians living on the Fort Sill Reserve, but my powers were limited. Reservation Indians are the responsibility of the Indian Department, not the United States Army. I invited them to travel with me to Fort Sill, where we could meet with the Indian agent. They declined—not wanting to leave their homes, I suspect—but presented me with another affidavit regarding the attacks, which I forwarded to the War Department."

"Why couldn't the Indian Department control its wards?"

"I talked to Agent Tatum—Lawrie Tatum—shortly after my arrival at Fort Sill. He's a good, honest man, and he frankly admitted the Kiowa and Comanche were beyond his control. They came and went as they pleased, but he was bound by the rules of the Indian Department, so he had to continue the distribution of provisions and supplies to the Indians."

"You told the agent about the massacre at Salt Creek Prairie?"

"I did. He was frustrated—I could not blame him—although the news did not surprise him. In my report to Washington, I suggested that Agent Tatum be instructed to issue rations only to Indians present on the proper day and that he should withhold supplies from them when there is proof of murder and robbery."

Damn him, Lanham didn't follow up on that point, didn't give Sherman a chance to blast the witless Indian Department or President Grant's foolish Quaker Peace Policy. Instead, the prosecutor asked, "Agent Tatum met with the defendant during your stay at Fort Sill, correct?"

"Yes, sir. He questioned Satanta in his office and reported to me that Satanta had admitted to leading the raid. The Indian's statement included details only those responsible for the crime would know, so Agent Tatum sent word to Colonel Grierson and myself of Satanta's confession, and on the twenty-seventh of May, I met with the Indian leaders in front of Colonel Grierson's house on the post."

Sherman recalled the events, Satanta's confession, the bloodshed that had been avoided, and the subsequent arrest of Satanta, Big Tree, and Satank perfectly. *That should hang the red bastard,* he thought.

"You mentioned you filed a report to Washington. In addition to your suggestion regarding the issue of rations, what else did you say regarding the three chiefs you had arrested?"

He had known that question would come at some point during Lanham's examination. In the note he sent this morning, Sherman had directed Lanham to ask that question. "I recall exactly what I said. 'These three Indians should never go forth again. If the Indian Department objects to their being surrendered to a Texas jury, we had better try them by a military tribunal, for if they go back to their tribes free—for any reason—no life will be safe from Kansas to the Rio Grande.'"

Smiling, Lanham returned to his seat, thanking Sherman for his testimony, praising him because the Indians would still be rampaging were it not for Sherman's boldness.

That brought about an objection, which Soward sustained. Sherman crossed his legs and waited for one of the defense attorneys to begin the cross-examination. He expected Woolfolk to handle this assault, but Thomas Ball rose. Lieutenant Carter had informed Sherman that the defense attorney had been engaged in a round or two of fisticuffs, but Sherman hadn't expected the lawyer to be that badly used: a narrow cut across his forehead, a black left eye, a swollen, split lip and chafed knuckles. The lawyer wore a gunbelt, too, and Sherman didn't blame him. Damned Texans. Sherman didn't care much for Ball or Woolfolk—they kept putting up too much of a fight in this, what Sherman had expected to be an open-and-shut case. But the man didn't deserve to be pummeled during every recess for doing his job.

Despite his injuries, Ball didn't have any trouble getting out of his chair or walking, although he still favored one leg.

He fired out a quick question as he approached the witness chair—"What did you think of Satank, General?"—and was standing in front of him before Sherman finished his answer.

"I thought he should have been shot dead a long time ago."

Someone cheered, and Soward slammed his gavel, ordering Sheriff McMillan to throw the man in jail and fining him twenty dollars. The judge had grown tired of these outbursts. His previous fines for contempt of court had been only ten dollars.

"And Satanta? Didn't the Kiowa peace chiefs beg you to release him? Isn't that why they returned the stolen mules?"

"Kicking Bird and Lone Wolf did beg hard, but it was time to end Satanta's career. He is impudent. And Big Tree's a bloody demon."

"The fact is, General, you don't care much for any of the Kiowas, do you?"

"Kicking Bird's all right, I guess."

"What about Lone Wolf?"

"I would have hanged him if I could."

"The only good Indian is dead. Something like that, sir?"

"Phil Sheridan said that, or something like it. Not me."

"But you agree with it, don't you?"

"No, sir. I cannot say that I do. I've met many good Indians in Washington. And like I said, Kicking Bird tries hard to keep those bloodthirsty Kiowas in check. But in Texas, I suspect there is some truth to that statement. If you don't believe me, turn around and ask anyone sitting behind you."

He expected that to elicit a few whispers, or maybe even another shout, but Judge Soward's recent remonstration must have remained on the crowd's mind, because nobody even nodded.

Ball shrugged and walked away, and Sherman guessed that the examination had ended, but Ball didn't sit down after all. He veered until he stood in front of Satanta, pointing to the damned savage and saying, "This man speaks several languages, sir, and he lies in none of them. But you, and the government you represent, have lied to him and his people time and time again. Isn't that true?"

Horace P. Jones's translation prompted both Indians to nod.

Bristling, Sherman snapped, "It's not true! Satanta is as big a liar as any man I've ever met. And I did not lie to him or any of them."

"You lied by omission, sir. You led the Kiowas to believe that Satanta, Big Tree, and Satank would be released upon the return of the mules."

"The mules were the property of Henry Warren, sir. The Kiowas did not deserve them. There were no lies said, Mr. Ball, except for the lies from that man's tongue." He jabbed his finger in Satanta's direction. "He said he led the raid, then lied and blamed some other savage." Sherman had changed his mind. Thomas Ball deserved to get his butt whipped, and if he didn't watch his mouth, Sherman would be standing in line, his boots ready to kick that cock-of-the-walk little se-cesh back to Virginia.

"Treaties have been broken—" Ball began, but Sherman cut him off.

"Broken by him!" he fired out. "The treaties do not give Satanta and his people the right to wage war on white settlers."

"Thank you, General," said Ball, rounding the desk and sitting in his chair. "That's what I wanted to hear."

Bewilderment masking his face, Sherman stared at Ball. He clenched the brim of the hat in his lap tighter, wondering what the defense counselor meant.

" 'To wage war.' That's what the Kiowas were doing, isn't it? War. You are familiar with war, General, are you not? Loyal soldiers of the Confederacy were not charged with murder during the recent unpleasantness, were they? I mean, as far as I know, there are no warrants for my arrest. Or Mr. Woolfolk's. Or Mr. Lanham's?"

"The Articles of War guarantee the humane treatment of prisoners of war," Sherman answered readily, "for recog-

nized soldiers. You also took the oath of allegiance and were
paroled. You might recall, counselor, that the late war also
saw irregulars who were no more than banditti, white trash,
on both sides, too, North and South. Those men, once captured, were summarily executed—as they deserved, I might
add. So were spies and saboteurs."

Ball nodded as if he had expected that answer. "If that's
what you thought, why didn't you have Satanta executed?"
He didn't wait for an answer. "I submit to you, General, that
this case is not a civil matter. If anything, the Indians should
be tried by military tribunal."

Lanham objected, but Sherman shook his head and
smiled, saying he wanted to answer. "Someone agreed with
me, counselor," he said after Lanham sat down with a shrug.
"We're here, not at Fort Sill, with a civilian jury and not an
Army board."

Ball fired another round, and Sherman began to begrudgingly admire the man's persistence. Probably had been a
good officer with the Johnny Rebs. With more men like him
under his command, Sherman probably could have ended the
war sooner. "You and Mr. Jones have testified that, on the
twenty-seventh of May, you criticized the defendant, called
him a coward, said only a coward waged war on civilians instead of soldiers. Is that true?"

"Those were my words. We do not carry out a war against
civilians."

Ball laughed, causing Sherman to straighten in his seat.
"General," the lawyer said, "then how do you explain your
actions in Georgia and the Carolinas?"

He answered with a malevolent glare. Trying to formulate
a reply, he cleared his throat, about to explain that the march
across Georgia was necessary and that none of his troops
ever fired knowingly at civilian parties, but before he could
open his mouth, Ball had waved him off, saying, "He doesn't
have to answer, Your Honor," and Soward dismissed him.

Ball had set him up, but it wouldn't mean a damn thing in
the long run. Satanta and Big Tree would hang. Still, it irked

him. Sherman leaped to his feet and stormed out of the court-room, jamming his hat on his head and patting his vest pockets for cigar and match. He was followed by at least a half-dozen reporters, peppering him with questions.

Chapter 26

"The good Indian, he that listens to the white man, got nothing. The independent Indian was the only one that was rewarded."

—Satanta

July 6, 1871
Parker County, Texas

Like an improperly moored skiff in a gale, the Concord rocked savagely as it bounced from one hole to another along the bone-jarring road from Jacksboro to Weatherford. Sarah Lanham's fingers dug into the dusty wood as she leaned out the window and vomited again. Finished, she pulled her head back inside and found a handkerchief in her purse, dabbed her mouth, and ran a clammy hand across her forehead. She felt feverish but didn't want to yell at the driver to stop, didn't want anyone to see her in this condition. She sank back into the hard-as-iron seat, trying to find a comfortable position, breathing heavily, glad she had the stagecoach to herself this morning.

"Not many folks leavin' town, Miz Lanham," the driver had told her before departing Jacksboro. "Been comin' here faster than locusts, but I ain't had nothin' but my own comp'ny on the return trips. You sure you wanna travel by your lonesome?"

"I'm sure, Mr. Regan." Kurt Regan had been one of Sam's first clients after he became a partner at Watts, Lanham and

Roach. Regan had been driving stagecoaches between
Weatherford and Belknap since the Butterfield days before
the War Between the States. When a stagecoach accident left
one man crippled and another dead, the families of both passengers filed a civil suit against Roach, charging him with
drunkenness and irresponsibility. Sam Lanham had argued in
court that no one was responsible for the wreck, least of all a
temperance man like Kurt Roach, who knew that trail better
than anyone. The jury had agreed.

That had been the young lawyer still connected to his poor
Southern roots. The old Sam Lanham had been a strapping,
swaying, ruggedly handsome plowboy who would get
tongue-tied asking a girl to dance. Sarah had met Sam at such
a dance in Pacolet; he hadn't been able to choke out an invi-
tation to waltz with him. Later, when he came calling at the
Meng mansion four miles out of town, her father told her the
boy wasn't fit to be his daughter's manservant, but she had
pleaded with him, and he begrudgingly came to accept that
Sarah would see Sam Lanham one way or the other.

No one could see the fire burning in the young man except Sarah. Yes, he was barely literate, but he had an im-
mense hunger to learn, and when his tongue was loosened, he
could articulate his feelings better than the sons of lawyers,
doctors, planters, and merchants who had being trying to
woo her since she turned sixteen. She tutored him, first in
South Carolina and later in Texas, watching him advance
from *McGuffey's Readers* to half-dime novels to Shake-
speare, Tennyson, Longfellow, Dickens, and, finally, the
Commentaries of jurist William Blackstone.

She had pushed him. She had changed him.

In Weatherford, Sarah still heard the busybodies remark
that Samuel W. T. Lanham was nothing but a glory hunter.
Being given the job as prosecutor for the "Jumbo" district
just tossed coal oil on those flames. It's a wonder the parents
let such an ambitious young zealot teach their children history and arithmetic. Why, he wouldn't settle for anything less
than the governor's mansion in Austin. Others blamed her for

his meteoric rise. It wasn't Sam Lanham chasing power and prestige, it was his prudish little wife, a woman of means back in South Carolina but nothing but a poor schoolmarm out on the frontier. You couldn't blame her for wanting to wear fancy clothes and go to fancy balls again, but she knew no bounds. She'd drive her husband to glory or an early grave.

Maybe they were right.

The old Sam Lanham would not have been so intent on sending two Indians to the gallows. He would have been fighting alongside Joseph Woolfolk and Thomas Ball, screaming for justice, not vengeance, arguing that the Indian question must be settled on the prairie or by treaties, not in a courtroom by a jury that could not possibly be impartial. This new man, though, saw only his name in headlines, envisioned himself as the Lone Star State's incarnation of Abe Lincoln. Sam Lanham had become the lawyer with blind ambition that many people said he was.

He had also become a stranger.

She pressed her right hand against her stomach. Sam had been right about one thing. The trip had been too hard on her. What had she been thinking, leaving her students with only two weeks left before summer break, traipsing across the district like a healthy woman, not a pregnant girl with a history of a miscarriage and one baby who didn't survive to see its first birthday? She had put another son—at least, she prayed she could give Sam another boy—in jeopardy.

July 6, 1871
Jacksboro, Texas

Dear Sam:

I'm not feeling well, so I have gone back home to Weatherford. Don't fret. I'll see you after the trial.

Sarah

He had found the note in the hotel room during the noon recess, and it remained burned into his memory as he sat in the Jack County courthouse that afternoon listening to Thomas Ball's cross-examination of Mathew Leeper.

I'm not feeling well. Back in late winter, Miss Kinder, their midwife, had also told him not to worry, said he had been blessed with one son and God made no promises to any couples. What did she know? Sam Lanham loved little Claude more than anything in the world—except his wife. He couldn't believe the midwife. That old hag had been telling him to prepare for another bad pregnancy that would likely end in a miscarriage or sickly infant who wouldn't survive long, so just be glad you have one healthy child. *Don't fret.* No chance of that. He had been worried about Sarah and the baby since he learned she was expecting.

I have gone back home ... He had panicked, fearing "home" meant Pacolet and her father, until he saw "to Weatherford." She must have known how he would react, or she wouldn't have added the prepositional phrase. *I'll see you after the trial.* She remained angry with him, for she had not wished him luck. Had not even signed the note "Love" or "Fondly," just her name. He wouldn't let her mood compromise his prosecution, though. He had to make sure that Big Tree didn't stand on the gallows alone. Satanta must die.

He felt confident the Indian would, too. Ball's cross-examination put no dents in Leeper's testimony.

Lanham had rearranged the witnesses for Satanta's trial. Charley Jordan said it would keep the journalists from becoming too bored, but Lanham had more judicial reasons.

Putting the crippled teamster, Thomas Brazeal, on the stand set the mood. Then Colonel Mackenzie and Doctor Patzki drove home the point about the savagery of the murder scene. Horace Jones's testimony would do damage, Sherman would give the reporters plenty of fodder, and now Leeper could convict Satanta because he had heard the blasted fool admit to leading the raid. To chisel that fact into the minds of the jurors, Sergeant Varily would testify last, identifying the arrows at the massacre site as Kiowa.

"You're overly cautious, Sam," Charley Jordan had told him over dinner. "You think that jury's gonna even consider acquittin' that old warhorse? That red nigger's damned no matter what order you bring on the witnesses."

Maybe so, Lanham thought, *but I'll take no chances.* He would make no mistakes here, give the higher courts and governor no reason to set the verdicts aside or commute the sentences.

A cheer erupted outside, and everyone turned toward the windows. Lanham felt the fresh air, cooler, carrying with it the scent of moisture, and realized it had started raining. The courtroom immediately turned cooler.

Judge Soward let the cheers from the gallery die down on their own.

Rain never brought anything good when dealing with the white-eyes, not as long as Satanta could remember. He brushed the gnats away from his nose and eyes and briefly checked the thunderstorm outside. Big Tree simply stared at his moccasins. Without hope was this young warrior, but Satanta would save him—and himself.

At least, he had thought he would, until the rains came. Rain showers when in the presence of the white-eyes made bad medicine to The Principal People. Such had always been the case.

Maman-ti, Satank, and Satanta had scored an impressive victory over the *Tehanna* wagon drivers not far from here less than two moons ago. Perhaps Hau-Tau and Tomasi would still be alive if the storm had not blown up, but not Ordlee. He would have died anyway, and it did not matter, for he was not of The Principal People, but of the Comanche. The rains, however, had changed everything, had washed away Maman-ti's power, had sent the bluecoats chasing them back to their country. If the sun had remained shining that day, Satanta felt sure he would have been dining on *Tehanna* mule meat in his lodge, listening to The Principal People sing songs about his bravery, instead of sitting here, smelling the stink of the white-eyes, breathing in gnats, and listening to bad medicine raindrops pound the roof, perhaps washing away the power of the words he wanted to speak, the words that, had it not rained, might have saved his life.

It had been raining that afternoon during The Summer of the *Koiet-senko* Sun Dance when Satanta had met with the bluecoat chief Han-Cock near the soldier-fort called Dodge. Satanta had admired Han-Cock, especially now, because this white-eye did not lie. He had not put Satanta in the dark, hot hole as Yellow Hair had done. He had not put chains on his feet and hands and sent him to Texas as Sher-Man and Bad Hand had done. Hancock had only spoken the truth.

"You know very well that in a few more years the game will go away," Han-Cock had said. "What will you do then? You will have to depend upon the white man to assist you and upon the Great Father to feed you when you are hungry. The white men are coming out here so fast that nothing can stop them—coming from the east and coming from the west, like a prairie on fire in a high wind."

Satanta had not believed it at the time, and would not admit it to The Principal People even now, but Han-Cock had been right. One could not stop the white-eyes. They had pushed The Principal People—and all of the other tribes— off their land. They had shot down Satank. Yet the white-eyes remained fearful of *Gai'gwu*. They had the power to hang Big Tree and him; they were many, but they were weak. That much he had learned from the Comanche words spoken by Hor-Ace-Jones. The *Tehannas* must know that The Principle People would not stand by and let them hang great warriors like Big Tree and Satanta. The Principal People were not women. Even Kicking Bird could not keep the warriors from riding for vengeance. The white-eyes were not the only ones like "a prairie on fire in a high wind." The Principal People would turn Texas into a pile of ash. Big Bow, Lone Wolf, Maman-ti, and others would see to that.

Satanta had to make the *Tehannas* know this.

As Stone Head's Voice, Lee-Per, left the powerful chair, Satanta turned to He Who Speaks The Black Robe Tongue and told him in the tongue of the strange Jesus men, "I must give them a great speech."

The bruised and cut white-eye blinked stupidly and said, "Huh?"

Satanta repeated his words in the Black Robe tongue and then in Comanche, letting Hor-Ace-Jones translate into English, only Hor-Ace-Jones did not finish because the Black Robe words finally registered with the lawyer.

"Does your client have to answer nature's call?" Judge Soward asked.

Thomas Ball spun around, flustered. "No, Your Honor," he said. "Satanta was telling me something."

"Remind your client that he does not speak unless he's on the stand."

What was Soward going to do? Fine Satanta twenty dollars for contempt? Ball whispered to Satanta in Latin, "Do not fear. You will have your chance to speak soon." Satanta's eyes registered delight, and Ball faced the judge and jury as Lanham called Sergeant Miles Varily to the stand.

"You ain't gonna put Satanta on the stand," Joe Woolfolk whispered. Ball had forgotten that aspiring lawyers studied Latin at the University of Missouri and Louisville's law school, not only at the College of William and Mary.

"He'll hang anyway," Ball shot back.

Soward glared at them while Varily was sworn in, and Ball let his eyes apologize for the conversations.

Ball only half-listened to the sergeant's testimony. After all, no one had contradicted any statements made during Big Tree's trial. The only surprise had been Sherman's appearance, and Ball felt he had done pretty well during his cross-examination. Not enough to get an acquittal, of course, but he had pissed off the great Billy Sherman, had even likely caused a few former Confederates in the gallery and jury to smile in spite of themselves, no matter what they thought of Thomas Ball. The rain stopped as Lanham questioned the soldier, but the clouds hid the sun, keeping the temperatures down while threatening to open up again soon.

Lanham introduced the Kiowa arrows into evidence, got a few more descriptions of the battle site, and passed the witness. Joe Woolfolk handled the cross, keeping his questions short. "What other kind of arrows were found there, Sergeant?" And, "Can you tell if Satanta fired those arrows?" Varily shot back with equally curt answers. Woolfolk had asked more questions yesterday, but he apparently didn't want to bore the jury, spectators, and reporters—or perhaps he was resigned to Satanta's fate. He thanked the witness and sat down. Lanham had no redirect, and the state rested its case. Ball checked the clock.

One forty-three. Even with the additional witness, Satanta's trial had been much shorter than Big Tree's.

"Mr. Ball, does the defense also rest?" Soward asked. He seemed as bored as everyone else in the courtroom. They'd likely all be asleep had it not been for Sherman's morning testimony and the brief afternoon rainstorm.

Well, they were in for another surprise.

"Your Honor," Ball said, "the defense has no witnesses to call, but the defendant wishes to make a statement for the record. This is against counsel's advice."

Whispers rose behind him, but Soward refrained from using the gavel. Instead, the judge asked Lanham if he objected.

"No, Your Honor," Lanham replied. "I'd like to hear what he has to say myself, as does, I'm sure, everyone else in this room."

"He understands he does not have to say anything, doesn't he?" Soward asked. "He's aware of his Fifth Amendment rights?"

What rights? Ball thought bitterly but answered with a pleasant, "Yes, sir."

"You've explained to him thoroughly?"

"Yes, sir."

"Very well. Mr. Jones, will you translate for the court?"

"Yes, Judge."

Soward shrugged. "Let him talk."

Chapter 27

"It must be remembered that in cunning or native diplomacy SATANTA has no equal. In worth and influence RED CLOUD is his rival; but in boldness, daring, and merciless cruelty SATANTA is far superior, and yet there are some good points in this dusky chieftain which command admiration."
—*New York Times*, October 30, 1867

July 6, 1871
Jacksboro, Texas

The little man with odd-looking pieces of glass that made his eyes look bigger did not make Satanta raise his hand and speak to his god as the other speakers had been told to do. Maybe, Big Tree thought, because Satanta did not care much for the white-eye god or his squaw of a son, although Big Tree himself liked the stories of that Jesus man. More than likely, however, the white-eyes simply did not want to unlock the iron bracelets clamping Satanta's wrists to accomplish this ritual, fearing Satanta would attack them all. They had not forgotten the stories of the no-longer-living great *Koiet-senko*'s challenge near the soldier-fort called Sill, but Satanta was not *Koiet-senko,* and to attack the many enemies in this foul-smelling room would have been foolish. Too many *Tehannas* had their shotguns trained on the great chief's stomach, waiting, and likely wanting, to send him on the Great Journey.

Satanta held up his arms, rattling the chains. "I cannot speak with these things upon my wrists," he said in the tongue of the Comanche, which Hor-Ace-Jones repeated in words the *Tehannas* could understand. He spoke to the great gathering, not to the powerful judge-chief with the dark beard and robe, and not to the twelve men in the little corner that most of the other speakers had talked to. Big Tree wondered if Satanta was making a mistake by not looking at these *Tehannas* when he talked. They seemed to be more important than the others, but Satanta believed in the power of numbers, and hundreds of white-eyes sat quietly in their seats, listening to the Orator of the Plains, their eyes wide, drops of sweat rolling down their foreheads despite the cooler weather.

When Satanta realized no one would release him from his shackles, he lowered his hands and said gruffly, "I am a squaw."

Satanta uncharacteristically paused, and he seemed to grow fearful. "Has anything been heard from the Great Father?" he asked, and when no one replied, he grunted and continued. "I have never been so near the *Tehannas* before. I look around me and see your braves, squaws, and papooses, and I have said in my heart that if I ever get back to my people, I will never make war upon you."

His words flowed easier now, like the great Orator Big Tree had so often heard. "I have always been the friend of the white man, ever since I was so high." He brought his clamped right hand level with his thigh. "My tribe has taunted me and called me a squaw because I have been the friend of the *Tehannas*. I am suffering now for the crimes of bad Indians—of the ancient *Koiet-senko* whom the bluecoats shot dead"—he respectfully did not say the dead warrior's name—"and Lone Wolf and Kicking Bird and Big Bow and Fast Bear and Eagle Heart, and if you will let me go, I will kill the latter three with my own hand."

He did not mention Maman-ti, but this did not surprise Big Tree, for Maman-ti wielded much power. Some whis-

pered that Maman-ti practiced sorcery, that he could wish
death upon anyone and that person would soon die without
reason, but no one ever said this to Maman-ti's face. Still, Satanta must have much faith in his power to say he could kill
all of those warriors. Big Bow had much medicine, had lifted
many scalps, and Fast Bear and Eagle Heart had counted
coup and proved their bravery in too many raids to count, including the one that had gotten The Principal People in so
much trouble. But why did not Satanta say he would kill
Lone Wolf and Kicking Bird? Satanta loathed Kicking Bird
and cared little for Lone Wolf. Big Tree blinked, understanding. Satanta knew those two chiefs were friends of the white-
eyes. That is why he did not say he would kill Kicking Bird
and Lone Wolf, although he surely wanted to. Yes, Satanta
was a great speaker, telling the *Tehannas* what he thought
they wanted to hear.

"I did not kill the *Tehannas*," Satanta said. That much was
true, as far as Big Tree knew, at least concerning the attack
against the wagon men. Satanta had come away with no
scalps, just a few mules, blankets, a musket, some corn and
sugar. "Why should I lie, since I have been under the control
of the white people? I came down the river you call the Pease
as a big medicine man to doctor the wounds of the braves."

No, thought Big Tree, the ancient *Koiet-senko* now traveling the Great Journey had been the medicine man, had
helped Red Warbonnet recover from the wound in his thigh
and washed out the bullet poison Tson-to-goodle suffered in
his knee, telling him that he would never walk the same
again but would live and have many wives to beat and copulate with.

"I have been abused by my tribe for being too friendly
with the white man. I have always been an advocate for
peace. I have always wished this to be made a country of
white people." Big Tree almost laughed at such an exagger-
ation. Satanta had scolded Kicking Bird for his dealings with
the shiftless white-eyes. Satanta had repeated over many
lodge fires that the only Principal People who profited were

those who took the true road of the warrior, that those who dealt with the white-eyes won nothing but trinkets and cloth. At first, anyway. Lately, as Satanta came to see just how plentiful these white-eyes were, and how rich they were, he had pressed for his own peace, his own trinkets and coffee and *Tehanna* beef.

Lifting his hands again to reveal the irons, Satanta continued. "I am wearing shackles because of my people and General Sher-Man. I am to suffer for what others did."

The chains sang as he lowered his arms, and he smiled at the crowd. "This is the first time I have ever faced the *Tehannas*. They know me not—neither do I know them," he said, taking a friendly step toward them, only the men with the shotguns did not think it harmless, and they brought up their weapons. One even thumbed back the metal ears. "It's all right!" Hor-Ace-Jones said urgently in the *Tehanna* tongue, then spoke to Satanta in Comanche, telling him to back up.

Frowning, Satanta decided to address the men in the corner and this judge-chief. He would likely not get shot speaking to these men.

"I am a big chief among my people and have great influence among the warriors of my tribe," Satanta said. "They know my voice and will hear my word." No one, neither white-eye nor *Gai'gwu*, would disagree with that statement.

"If you let me go back to my people, I will withdraw my warriors from the land of the *Tehannas*. I will take them all across Red River, and that shall be the line between us and the palefaces. I will wash out the spots of blood and make it a white land, and there shall be peace, and the *Tehannas* may plow and drive their oxen to the river.

"But if you kill me, it will be a spark on the prairie—make big fire—burn heap! No power can stop it."

That caused the crowd to whisper excitedly after Hor-Ace-Jones translated Satanta's statement into words the white-eyes understood, the first vocal reaction Big Tree had heard during Satanta's big talk. Even the great judge-chief in the dark robe lifted his head, suddenly interested, or perhaps

afraid, and the Mouth of the *Tehannas,* Lan-Ham, stopped
twisting the ends of his mustache. Were these good signs?
Big Tree did not know. Would The Principal People war
against the *Tehannas* harder than ever before should they kill
Satanta and him? Perhaps. Big Bow most certainly would
gather a war party. What would the white-eyes think of Satanta's words? He heard one man say "blackmail" and call
Satanta a "murderin' red bastard." Big Tree did not know
what those words meant, and Hor-Ace-Jones was too busy
translating, so he could not ask him, but he could tell that
none in the room cared for Satanta's words.

The whispers became louder, and one man yelled, pointing a long finger at Satanta and causing the judge-chief to
find his wooden hammer and shout for order. Only when silence fell across the room did Satanta continue his speech.

"If I could see my people, I pledge that neither I nor my
people will ever cross Red River again. That river shall be
the long line. I am willing to pledge myself for The Principal
People, that if you grant my freedom, I will make permanent
peace with the white man. Whatever mischief has been done,
has been done by The Principal People."

Big Tree did not like that last part. The Principal People
had not been alone in the mischief. *Tehannas* and bluecoats
and white-eyes in Kansas had done plenty of wrongs, not just
to *Gai'gwu* but to the Comanche, Arapaho, Kiowa-Apache,
and especially the Cheyenne, massacring peaceful camps on
the Washita and at Sand Creek only a few short years ago.
Satanta's speech began to sicken him. Perhaps the great Orator had become a squaw, as Big Bow, Red Warbonnet, and
the great *Koiet-senko* no longer walking the earth had accused him. He would sell the pride of The Principal People
in exchange for his life. Big Tree was not certain he was willing to walk the white man's road. Maybe, in time—if the
white-eyes did not hang him as they promised to do—he
would see things their way, but he was young and liked the
life of The Principal People.

The powerful Lan-Ham had been right. Satanta was nothing but a liar.

"This is the first time I ever entered the warpath against the white-eyes," Satanta said, and Big Tree shook his head. Satanta had led many war parties against the white-eyes. He had lifted white-eye scalps before Big Tree had been born during The Year The Captured Pawnee Boy Escaped And Returned To His People. Big Tree's heart sank. He did not think Satanta would resort to lying like the white-eyes to buy his freedom. Exaggerate, sure. Even the size of buffaloes killed or the number of points on an antler grew when The Principal People told stories. But Satanta's tongue had become forked. Perhaps he had been around the white-eyes too long. Big Tree would rather die than lie.

"If released, I will pledge myself on behalf of The Principal People for a lasting peace," Satanta said. "I have but little knowledge of the *Tehanna* people now. I have never understood them as a people. Release me, and your people may go on undisturbed with their farming and stock-raising—all will go well.

"When General Sher-Man and Yellow Hair had me arrested, they did not put upon me the indignity of wearing these shackles." He shook the chains again, but no one would step forward to free the locks. "I could go about with my limbs free. I have seen these people—men, women, and children in this council room—for two days, and I have said in my heart, 'I am willing to make peace.'"

Big Tree studied the *Tehannas* out of the corner of his eyes. Satanta's words did not move them. "I expect to hear of mischief done by my people on this frontier," the great Orator went on, but Big Tree no longer cared for his words. In that regard, he was already taking the white man's road. "I think they are now awaiting my return or anticipating my death. Stone Head is now anxiously awaiting to hear from me.

"Big Bow, Fast Bear, and Eagle Heart have been committing depredations in *Tehanna* land. I feel more enmity against them than I do against the *Tehannas*. I will kill them with my own hands if I am permitted to return to my home."

Satanta cleared his throat and returned to his seat. He Who Speaks The Black Robe Tongue started shuffling his papers while the white-eyes in the corner as well as those crowded in the long chairs began talking among themselves. The judge-chief reached for his wooden hammer but decided against using it.

"My words were strong," Satanta told Big Tree as he sat down. "The rains did not wash away my medicine. Our necks will not be broken and stretched by the coiled ropes. This is the way I see things. You may pay me in ponies when we return safely to our people."

Big Tree tried to stare ahead but could not. He jerked around to face Satanta, spitting out his anger. "You are a fool, old man!" he shouted, surprised at his voice. "You have made sure the *Tehannas* hang us." Satanta's eyes widened in shock, then anger, but before he could reply, Big Tree turned back to stare at the wall. He had seen white-eye pictures of the buildings without roofs or doors, the buildings with the ropes that would be wrapped around their necks. He had heard The Principal People describe the way the bodies of the white-eyes danced when dropped through the floor. He had heard them sing sad songs, heard the medicine men say how hard it would be for men who died such a death to travel the Great Journey.

Big Tree should have listened to the old *Koiet-senko*. He should not have stopped him when he tried to stab the blue-coat leader Greer-Son. He should have died with him there, died as a warrior, not as a squaw like Satanta.

He began thinking of the words to his death song.

Chapter 28

"The evidence was as pointed and positive that no other conclusion could have been reached."
—*The Daily Journal*, Austin, Texas, July 18, 1871

July 6, 1871
Jacksboro, Texas

"Guilty! Guilty! They'll hang Satanta, too!"

A pockmarked teen shouted the herald from the upstairs window to the crowd gathered below. Cheers erupted immediately, and M. J. Shelley smiled with satisfaction. She hadn't returned to the courtroom after the noon recess, hadn't wanted to hear the ghastly details again. Instead she went home, tried reading, quilting, even bathing, but idling around the house did nothing for her nerves, so, after the thunderstorm, she joined the throng outside and waited.

Blacksmith Ethan Gowdy broke out his jaw harp and started a tune, and two cowboys began a jig, passing a bottle back and forth while they laughed and danced, making up a song partly to the tune of "John Brown's Body," or maybe something else. They were so drunk it was hard to tell.

> *Big Tree and Satanta*
> *Will soon be barkin' with the hounds*
> *Chokin' on some hemp*
> *As the hangman sends 'em down*
> *No more scalps to be a-lifted*

> *No more kids to scream and yell*
> *'Cause them red niggers are goin'*
> *To Hell!*
> *Glory, glory, hallelujah*
> *Glory, glory, hallelujah*
> *Glory, glory, hallelujah*
> *Satanta and Big Tree's gonna hang!*

It was over. Well, mostly over. The judge still had to pass sentence on them, and he could set aside the jury's assessment of death, but Charles Soward had always been a fair man, and he'd do the right thing. The celebration began to expand. Hearing Soward's gavel and Sheriff McMillan's shouts, she knew it would be some time before order could be restored upstairs, or anywhere in town for that matter. Jacksboro would not sleep tonight.

She slid through the cheering, arm-pumping, singing, dancing mob and headed back home. A woman leaned against an empty hitching post across the street, and a moment passed before M. J. recognized her. The waitress at the Wichita Hotel, Amanda Doniphan, stood there like a ghost, pale, her high-button shoes covered with mud from today's rain. M. J. stopped to be sociable.

"They found Satanta guilty." M. J. immediately realized that had to be the most obvious statement ever made. Of course, they had convicted him and passed on the death sentence. Why else would hundreds of men, women, and children be singing and dancing in the mud in the middle of the afternoon?

"I know." Amanda's words came out as barely a whisper, and she dabbed her eyes with the hem of her calico skirt. Tears of joy, M. J. thought, although she certainly didn't look happy. M. J. left her alone. She wanted to get home soon and bake Peter Lynn a pie. God knows, Peter—and the eleven other men on that jury—deserved some type of reward.

*   *   *

July 7, 1871
Fort Sill Reserve, Indian Territory

Philadelphia
June 11

I write partly to express my sympathy with thee in thy responsible service for the Master—but more especially at this time to encourage thee to use every proper effort to secure for Satanta & his companions in crime a punishment consistent with the precepts of Christianity. I rejoice that there is a prospect of their trial by civil process, & that these unruly Kiowas are likely to learn that wrongdoing on their part will bring upon them the same penalties as like conduct would bring upon the palefaces. But how earnestly do I desire that their lives may be spared & Christian influences brought to bear for their conversion & salvation. Will not the effect upon the tribe be far better for these criminals to be held in close confinement during their natural lives than for them to receive the common penalty for murder in the first degree? I am quite unfamiliar with the law of Texas, but suppose it provides the death penalty for such crimes. But cannot thou, or cannot we, secure through the governor of the state, or otherwise, a commutation to imprisonment for life? I am apprehensive that the feeling of the white frontiersmen is such that they will demand immediate trial, conviction & execution—but in hope that I can strengthen thy hands in some little measure to use every exertion to secure for them a punishment more consistent with our sense of right, as well as more politic for the nation—& desiring the Lord's blessing upon all thy labors for the advancement of the Indian toward a Christian civilization—I pen this hasty note.

Your obt. servant,
John B. Garrett

Lawrie Tatum had never met John B. Garrett of Pennsylvania, but he could tell the man was a strong member of the Society of Friends, a better Quaker than Tatum had turned out to be. Sitting in his office near Fort Sill, he reread the letter for perhaps the thirtieth time since it had arrived last month. Garrett had not been the only man inspired to write; similar correspondence from men and women filled Tatum's desk drawer, all written by Friends he did and did not know. Oddly enough, no Texans had written him to praise his part in sending Satanta and Big Tree to Jack County or—he shuddered—Satank to his death. Nor had General Sherman or other military officers felt the urge to thank him.

The fact that he still held the title of Agent for the Kiowa and Comanche surprised him. Tatum felt certain the Indian Department and the Friends would force him to resign or just outright fire him upon learning that he had helped the Army capture his unenlightened wards and turn them over to Texas authorities, who would make sure the two surviving Kiowas never made it back to Indian Territory alive. But here he was.

He folded the letter and glanced again at the telegram on his desk.

BIG TREE SATANTA CONVICTED STOP JUDGE
TO PASS SENTENCE SAT STOP HANGING
EXPECTED STOP PLEASE ADVISE STOP M
LEEPER

Tatum stuffed Garrett's letter into the envelope and dropped it into the drawer atop the piles of correspondence. He found a handkerchief and mopped the pools of sweat accumulating on his bald head, pitched the wet rag onto his desk beside Leeper's telegram, and walked outside for fresh air.

Low, white clouds blanketed the blue sky like millions of balls of cotton, and a faint breeze from the north kept the afternoon cooler. A Kiowa boy and girl played with a litter of puppies beside a brush arbor near the corral while their mother's eyes smiled as she sang some heathen song and punctured leather with an awl. A few rods away stood Kicking Bird, dressed in an Army coat with the epaulets of an officer, breechcloth and moccasins, his hair braided and wrapped in otter skins. The great peace chief of the Kiowas was talking to Red Warbonnet, but the children's singsong laughter and the yipping of the puppies caused both men to turn. Red Warbonnet muttered something and pointed, and the two men broke into a hearty laugh.

They were all children, Tatum thought. Simple savages unfit for farming no matter how hard Tatum tried to teach them. He would have to talk to Kicking Bird eventually, tell him the news. Almost daily, Kicking Bird had visited Tatum, asking for the word from Texas. As much as Kicking Bird disliked Satanta, he cared for his people, and the Kiowas wanted Satanta and Big Tree returned alive.

A peace had fallen over the reservation since Satank's death, mainly because of fear. Fear was good, Tatum believed. It worked for God in the Old Testament, and it worked today against the Kiowas. But if the Army thought the Kiowas would remain acting like timid, frightened schoolchildren, they did not know the federal wards as well as Lawrie Tatum.

The Kiowa boy put his hand too close to a pup's mouth, and the dog bit him. He jerked away, stunned at first, then began bawling, and the mother picked up the child to comfort him. The little girl also began sobbing. Tatum watched in fear as Red Warbonnet, gripping a bow tightly, left Kicking Bird and limped to the brush arbor. Red Warbonnet had been favoring his left leg for some time now, and Tatum had a pretty good idea the warrior had been wounded during the Salt Creek Prairie massacre. Only Red Warbonnet had not been sent to stand trial and most likely hang. Tatum felt certain the warrior would kill the puppy—maybe the entire litter—for biting his son, or whatever the kid meant to him, but the brave stopped beside the mother and screamed at the two children.

Tatum cringed. Red Warbonnet continued to speak sharply, and both children stopped crying. The warrior shook his head and limped back to Kicking Bird.

Savages, Tatum thought. It was in their nature, their blood. And if the Texans hanged Satanta and Big Tree, the Kiowas would show just how savage they could be.

July 8, 1871
Jacksboro, Texas

The courtroom wasn't that crowded Saturday morning, probably because eight a.m. came far too early after celebrating until dawn. For the first time that week, Jacksboro resembled the quiet Texas town that had appeared so friendly and inviting to a relative newcomer from eastern Virginia. Thomas Ball still wore his gunbelt, though. No one had approached him or threatened him—few had even even talked to him—since Satanta's conviction, but he would not be caught unprepared again. He had spent the past two nights on the floor at Amanda Doniphan's, but he couldn't keep sleeping there, keep compromising her although they had done nothing except kiss. He'd have to find a new place to live soon.

Or take his shingle and move.

Would he even be able to find clients if he stayed in Jacksboro? Texicans, Ball had often been told, have long memories, but Joe Woolfolk had said not to worry. Woolfolk's remarks over breakfast kept running through his mind as Ball waited for Soward to enter the courtroom. "Texicans also like fighters, and they ain't likely to forget how hard you fit for Satanta and Big Tree. They'll figger that if you'd brawl that hard for two damned Kiowas who didn't stand a chance in hell, how hard would you fight for them?"

"You fought pretty hard, too," Ball had told his partner, and Woolfolk's smile had seemed genuine.

The bailiff entered from the anteroom, and the sparse

crowd of diligent reporters, Lanham, deputies, Army brass, witnesses, and a few town citizens stopped talking.

"All rise," the bailiff announced. "Court of the Thirteenth Judicial District of the great State of Texas is now in session, the Honorable Charles Soward presiding. Case Number Two-twenty-four, the State of Texas versus Satanta and Big Tree on seven counts of murder in the first degree."

The two Indians, still heavily chained, sitting next to the defense attorneys, did not need to hear Horace Jones instruct them in Comanche to stand. They had learned.

Soward followed the bailiff out of the room and took his seat, not so much as glancing at Ball, Woolfolk, or the men he was about to condemn. "Do the defendants wish to make any statements before I pass sentence?" he asked in a hoarse voice, staring at the paperwork before him.

Ball looked at the men he had failed as Jones translated the question. Satanta shook his head; Big Tree just stared at the Texas flag. "No, Your Honor," Ball answered.

"Very well." Soward rose, his dark eyes boring through the two Kiowas. Ball had expected Soward to make a lengthy speech. That's why he had not passed sentence immediately after Satanta's trial as had been expected. This way, his speech would be sure to make all the papers instead of having to share column space with Lanham's closing summation, although the prosecutor had kept his speech in the Satanta affair relatively short. So had Woolfolk during his closing argument.

"The jury having found the defendant Big Tree guilty of murder in the first degree and having assessed his punishment as death," Soward said dully, "it is therefore ordered, adjudged, and decreed by the court that the sheriff do take the said defendant into close custody and hold him to await the sentence of this court upon the judgment herein."

Ball exhaled and said, "Your Honor, the defense serves notice of its intent to appeal for a new trial. This was not a matter for the criminal courts of Texas."

"Denied," Soward said without looking away from Big

Tree. "The law is with the state." The judge coughed to clear his throat—too much celebrating, Ball guessed. Maybe that explained his curt sentencing. "Big Tree, do you have anything to say regarding why I should not pass sentence upon you?"

When Big Tree refused to respond, Soward continued. "It is therefore my solemn duty to order, adjudge, and decree that the sheriff of Jack County do take the defendant on the first day of September next to some convenient place near the courthouse at the town of Jacksboro in the county of Jack between the hours of six a.m. and one p.m., where he shall be hanged by the neck until he is dead, dead, dead. May the Lord have mercy on your soul. Amen."

He slammed the gavel before pronouncing the same sentence for Satanta, equally unmoved. Ball again requested a new trial, which Soward overruled.

"Exception," Ball said.

"Noted. I'll see counsel in chambers this afternoon at three o'clock. Sheriff, remove the prisoners."

Joe Woolfolk had always considered Charles Soward to be a pompous son of a bitch, the kind of gent who gave Kentuckians a bad name. He hadn't changed his opinion as he pulled three ten-dollar notes from his wallet and handed them to clerk J. R. Robinson to pay his contempt of court fine that afternoon in the judge's chambers. He shoved a receipt into his trouser pocket and stepped back to hear Ball cite precedent and argument and tell the good judge how and why he would appeal the conviction and sentence to the higher courts.

"You'll be denied," Soward said haughtily.

"I don't think so," Ball fired back.

Soward replied with a laugh while pouring three fingers of bourbon into a glass. "Sam?" he asked, holding out the bottle, but Lanham shook his head. The prosecutor hadn't said a word that afternoon. Shrugging, Soward slammed the cork into the bottleneck and dropped the bourbon into his desk drawer—never having offered the defense attorneys a drink.

Another reason to dislike the prig, thought Woolfolk, sending a mouthful of tobacco juice toward the spittoon but purposely missing and splattering the side of the judge's desk.

"I'll take it higher than the Texas courts if I have to," Ball said.

"They won't even consider it." Soward took a drink.

Exasperated, Ball unbuttoned his jacket, put both hands on his hips, and said, "What makes you so damned sure, Judge?"

"Because you have to have transcripts for the appeals courts to consider any mistakes that might have been made during the course of a trial, and we have no transcripts from Case Two-twenty-four."

Now Woolfolk stepped forward. "What the hell are you talkin' 'bout, Charles? I saw the stenographer you hired—"

"Lost," Soward said with a shrug. "I think they were burned this afternoon by mistake."

Woolfolk whirled. "Damn your hide, Sam Lanham. I never thought—" Lanham's expression stopped him. He didn't have to say a word. This had been Soward's idea, plain and simple. Lanham's face changed expression, and he shouted, "Ball! No!"

Woolfolk spun around, stepped quickly to the Virginian, and gripped his right hand before Ball could pull that hogleg from its holster. "You damn fool," Woolfolk said as the momentum carried Ball and him away from the desk. They slammed against the wall. Woolfolk spit out his plug of tobacco, afraid he might swallow the juice and lose his dinner. Ball put up a hell of a fight considering how badly he had been chewed up by those drunken Texicans the past few days, plus he had a bum leg to boot. Woolfolk clamped both hands on Ball's wrist, allowing Ball's left fist to jar his temple. Still, Woolfolk refused to let go.

Behind him, he heard footsteps and Soward's laughter.

Lanham grabbed Ball's left arm before he could land another blow, and Woolfolk twisted the right until the pistol dropped onto the floor.

"I don't want to try you for murder," Lanham whispered.

"I wasn't going to shoot him," Ball said in a rushed breath. "Just bend that pistol barrel over his head."

Still laughing, Charles Soward sank into his chair and drained his whiskey.

"I'm all right," Ball said, and the two lawyers released him. Woolfolk picked up the revolver and shoved it into his own waistband. He'd give it back to Ball later, when he was certain he wouldn't use it on Soward. The clerk just stood there ashen-faced. Lanham picked up his hat and dusted it off.

"I won't fine you for contempt, Thomas," Soward said, no longer laughing. In fact, his handsome face had turned solemn, as if he regretted his actions. "I understand your feelings."

"I should—" Ball began, but Soward shook his head.

"I did what I had to do," the judge said. "For the good of Texas. For Jack County. You'll see that someday."

"Go ahead and hang them, Soward," Ball said. "I'll put 'I did what I had to do' on your tombstone after the Kiowas rise up in revenge and kill every man, woman, and child in your damned district."

The shriek caused Sam Lanham to drop his grip and take off running down the alley. He had checked out of the Wichita Hotel that evening, had supper, and was on his way to catch the stagecoach to Weatherford. Most of the vagabonds who had come to Jack County to see the show had departed—Jacksboro looked practically deserted tonight compared to how it had been just a few days earlier—but a few riffraff remained.

He spotted the four men manhandling a pretty woman, and his rage detonated. Lanham pulled the Manhattan .31 pocket revolver from his shoulder holster and charged. At first, he thought the men were drunken loafers, but as he slammed the butt against one man's skull, he realized his mistake. Lanham sliced out with the barrel, breaking the second man's nose. The pretty girl slipped and fell into the mud.

These men weren't transients. He recognized the man whose nose he had just busted as blacksmith Ethan Gowdy. The other man writhing on the ground, holding his head, was a local cowboy. The third man, a drummer named Ed Perkins who roomed at the Widow Baggett's, stepped back, eyes widening at the sight of Lanham's gun, and sent his hands skyward. The final man, Deputy Sheriff Odell Dobson, drew a Remington .44 from his waistband.

Lanham shot him.

"You sons of bitches!" Lanham snapped, thumbed back the hammer and kicked the moaning cowboy in his face. "How dare you manhandle a woman like this? I'll have you all in Huntsville for five years!"

"No, no, no," Ed Perkins shot out. "You don't understand, Lanham. This girl—"

"The bitch," the deputy sheriff said with a groan. The bullet had struck him in his left shoulder and dropped him to his knees. He remained like that, his Remington swallowed by mud, right hand trying to stanch the flow of blood, tears welling in his eyes.

"One more word, Dobson!" Lanham leveled the pistol, and the deputy swallowed another curse.

Lanham felt lightheaded with fury. Realizing the danger had passed, he holstered his revolver and helped the young woman to her feet.

"Ma'am," he said gently, "my name is Samuel Willis Tucker Lanham, prosecuting attorney for the 'Jumbo' district, and I promise you that these four men will be sent to prison—"

"I know who you are," she said, and Lanham stared at her. Recognition came slowly, but now he remembered. She was the waitress at the Wichita Hotel.

"Miss . . ." He couldn't place the name.

"Doniphan," she said.

"Yes, of course. I'm sorry."

"She's an Indian lover!" Ed Perkins cried. "We was showin' her to the stage is all. Sendin' her south."

"Been consortin' with that sumbitch Thomas Ball!" Dobson added. "We seen 'em together."

"Jack County don't welcome no injun lovers," Ethan Gowdy whined through his bleeding, broken nose. "Or whores who—"

Lanham split his lip with a well-placed right.

"You miserable, stupid sons of bitches!" Lanham said, pacing back and forth in the alley, unable to control his rage. "Jesus Christ Almighty, how can you be so blind? How could I have been so stupid? Satanta and Big Tree aren't the savages! We are. You are." He singled out the four men, although the cowboy lying facedown in the mud likely didn't hear a word. "You and you and you and you! Satanta threatened a spark on the prairie, but you fools have already set it. You'll burn down everything the good men and women of Jack County have built with your damned hatred.

"No, by God!" His hands clasped the lapels of the whiskey drummer's vest and sent him crashing against the limestone wall of Glazner's Apothecary. "No, sir. All of you!" he roared. "Get out of my district. If ever I see any one of your faces, I'll kill you."

Other men appeared, dragging the unconscious cowboy and wounded deputy away and escorting the blacksmith and drummer out of Lanham's path. Only then did he notice the crowd—it had to be twenty or thirty men and women—that had gathered in the alley, likely drawn by the gunshot. No one said a word as Lanham picked up his grip, took the waitress gently by her arm, and escorted her to the stagecoach stop.

"Where's Thomas Ball?" Lanham asked Amanda Doniphan at the stagecoach station.

"Took the afternoon stage to Belknap. Wanted to see

Woolfolk about filing an appeal despite what Judge Soward said. Woolfolk left right after the meeting with Judge Soward. Tomball and me talked it over, and he ain't ready to quit."

Nodding, he almost smiled at Ball's persistence. "Do you have a place you can stay here in town?"

"I'll be all right," she said. "Those yokels . . ."

"There may be more like those . . ." He shuddered again, an aftereffect of his anger. "I think it wise if you accompany me. I'll pay for your ticket and put you up for the night. You can stay as long as you like, until this mess blows over or you make arrangements . . ." He stopped, not wanting to embarrass her.

She protested, but he insisted, and she shrugged, more afraid than she dared admit.

"You sure your wife won't mind, Mr. Lanham?"

"Of course not," he said while wondering: *Do I still have a wife?*

Chapter 29

"The killing for which these Indians were sentenced can hardly be considered . . . as coming within the technical crime of murder . . . but rather as an act of Savage Warfare."

—Governor Edmund J. Davis

July 9, 1871
Weatherford, Texas

They took their Sunday supper in silence. Usually, the Lanhams would critique the Methodist preacher's sermon, but it had turned too hot for such a forum, and they didn't want to bore their house guest, Amanda Doniphan, to tears. Besides, Sarah had not had much to say anyway and had barely even listened to Preacher McClure's commentary on Revelation and the recent frightful events just over the county line.

At least Sarah had been home. All during the jostling stagecoach ride, Sam Lanham had wondered if she might have changed her mind once reaching Weatherford, just packed up her clothes and whisked little Claude back to South Carolina. After church this morning, he had watched her out of the corner of his eye as the preacher, deacons, and just about everyone who had attended fellowship shook his hand and congratulated him on convicting Satanta and Big Tree. Sarah had said nothing, had not even tried to smile politely, and he understood why.

That scene in the Jacksboro alley between those cretins

and Amanda Doniphan—that had changed everything. Glory had smitten him; now it sickened him. What good would power and prestige be without Sarah there to share it with him? Yes, Satanta and Big Tree were murdering dogs, heathens, scoundrels, savages, everything Texicans and the Army said about them, but that did not mean they should be tried under white law. Hanging them would not settle anything, just escalate the bloodshed. Sam Lanham would be as much to blame as Sherman, Soward, and the twelve *disinterested* jurors for the violence sure to ensue after the hangman sprang the trap on those two damned Kiowas.

Lanham considered this while chewing on his potatoes, unpalatable this day, and Sarah was a fine cook. The silence had become uncomfortable. Neither had even brought up the trial and verdicts, except when he had briefly explained why he had brought the Wichita Hotel waitress home with him. That had required plenty of explanation. Now, however, Lanham felt the need to talk. His fork and knife rattled on the tabletop as he set them down, and he dabbed the corners of his mouth with his napkin. That reminded him of one of his first conversations with his wife.

"Why do men wear such big mustaches?" Sarah had asked.

Twisting the ends of his massive affair, he had quipped, "For a place to keep bread crumbs to snack on later."

Her eyes widened first, then she shook her head in mock disgust. "It's closer than a cummerbund," he had added, and she broke out laughing. He had joined her, pleased with the response. He hadn't been much for quick jokes then or now, so to have come up with such a well-received volley pleased him immensely.

He had no humor today, though.

"I read the letter from Agent Tatum," he announced, and both women looked up while his son moved piles of potatoes from one side of the plate to another. "The one waiting for me here." Sarah's eyes narrowed; Amanda Doniphan just stared blankly. Sarah looked away, and she scolded Claude to stop playing with his food and listen to his father, as though law held any interest to a three-year-old handful.

"I am thinking of carrying it to Judge Soward tomorrow."

His wife rose, and she opened her mouth as if to say something, then clutched her stomach. Sam swallowed down panic and leaped to his feet. Sarah's face turned ashen, and he caught her as she fell.

"Mama!" Claude screamed.

July 10, 1871
Weatherford, Texas

Lose this case, my friend, and it won't be Kiowas you have to fear, but every white man west of the Trinity River. Charles Soward recalled those words he had spoken to Sam Lanham the last time the prosecutor stood in the judge's office, presenting His Honor with a petition not to hold the term of court in Jacksboro. When was that? Third week of June or something like that. It seemed like a lifetime ago. Well, Lanham had won the case, had gotten his glory. So had Soward.

Soward thought about asking Lanham about his wife, but decided against it. Something troubled the "Jumbo" district prosecutor, but it wasn't his wife's health. Instead, Soward slid his humidor across his desktop and nodded. "Have a cigar, Sam," he said pleasantly.

"No, thanks."

Sighing, Soward leaned back in his chair. "I take it you are not here to discuss the next term of court."

"No." Lanham shuffled his feet, reached inside his coat, and withdrew an envelope. The paper crinkled as he pulled out the letter and handed it to Soward. "This was waiting for me at home," Lanham explained. "It's from the Indian agent, Tatum."

"The one that didn't have the balls to come down here and testify?"

Lanham didn't answer. Soward took the paper and quickly deciphered the Quaker's ungodly scroll.

> *In view of the trial of Satanta and Big Tree, permit me to remind thee that two great characteristic traits of the Indians are to seek revenge, and a great dread of imprisonment. From my knowledge of the Indians, I believe a more severe punishment would be to confine them for life than to execute them, and it would probably save the lives of some white people; for if they were executed it is more than probable that some of the other Kiowas would seek revenge in the murder of some white citizens. This is judging the case from a policy standpoint. But if we judge it from a Christian standpoint, I believe, we should in all cases, even murder in the first degree, confine a person for life, and leave to God his prerogative to determine when a person has lived long enough.*

He handed the letter back to the prosecutor. "You're having second thoughts about hanging those red bastards?" Soward tried to sound indignant.

"It isn't justice, Charles," Lanham replied. "I don't believe you think it's just, either."

Soward shook his head and let out a mirthless laugh. "You made a persuasive argument to make the jury see it your way."

Lanham shrugged. "I could have read the hotel arrivals printed in the *Dallas Herald,* and they would have voted to convict."

"Now you're sounding like Ball or Woolfolk."

"Burning those transcripts—"

Soward raised his hand to silence the attorney. "For the good of Texas. Remember?" He glanced at the clock. Too early for a sip of bourbon, even for him. "I've made my share of mistakes since being admitted to the bar, Sam," he said, "but having those transcripts burned was not one of them. I'm not a dunderhead. You know me better than that."

"I thought I did." Lanham's words came out as a sigh, and he sadly shook his head. "Satanta wasn't lying when he said it would be a spark on the prairie. The Kiowas will rise up to take revenge if you hang him and Big Tree. Tatum's right. Putting them in prison, with just the possibility of parole, could keep the Indians in check."

Maybe it wasn't too early after all. Soward opened his drawer, pulled out the Kentucky bourbon, and filled his glass, then slid it toward Lanham. The prosecutor certainly looked as if he needed a drink.

"I've already passed a sentence of death by hanging," Soward said. "It's out of my hands."

"But—"

"It's out of my hands because it was the only way, Sam. When I told Ball it was for the good of Texas, I meant it. The biggest mistake I made as judge of this district was assigning Ball and Woolfolk to the defense. I figured Woolfolk hated the Kiowas as much as anyone and wouldn't lift a finger to save them. I failed to consider just what a bellicose son of a bitch he is. As far as Ball, I thought he'd be too green to offer any defense. I thought they would offer some lame defense and lose, and drop the matter. Instead, they caught me in an ambuscade."

Lanham decided to take the drink. Soward let him finish before continuing.

"So the jury votes to convict despite the defense, only Ball doesn't raise up the white flag. He threatens to fight on, and that we could not afford. So I had to get rid of the transcripts. If by some sort of miracle—and after watching him in court, I wouldn't bet against him—he managed to get a change of venue and a new trial, maybe the jury wouldn't see things our way. Hell, over in Nacogdoches they've probably forgotten what it was like to be on the frontier, facing savages every day. Or Austin. Now there won't be an appeal, at least not one the defense can win."

"So they hang," Lanham said, "and Jack County runs red with blood. Is that it?"

"Not hardly. I never once thought Satanta and Big Tree would hang, but if I had disregarded the jury's verdict, if I had sentenced them to life in prison, my life wouldn't be worth two bits in Jack County. Or here, for that matter. You're interested in politics, Sam. So am I. Giving those Kiowas the death sentence saves my hide, but it doesn't condemn them."

"I'm not sure I follow you," said Lanham, looking more like the disheveled schoolteacher than an accomplished orator and barrister.

Laughing, Soward opened another drawer and pulled out his official stationery. "Tatum's not the only person who can write letters, Sam," he said, dipped his pen in the inkwell, and began:

To the Honorable E. J. Davis, Governor:
Sir:

> *I have the honor to say that the last term is regarded of more interest to our frontier than any court that has ever been held in the state. We obtained the necessary witnesses for the state, and after a fair and impartial trial, the defendants having the best counsel at the command of the court, the jury returned a verdict of murder in the first degree and fixed their punishment at death.*
>
> *Mr. Tatum expressed a strong desire that they should be punished by imprisonment for life, instead of death, but the jury thought differently. I passed sentence upon them on the eighth of July, and fixed the time of execution at Friday, September 1, next. I must say here that I concur with Mr. Tatum as to the punishment; simply, however, upon a politic view of the matter. Mr. Tatum has indicated that if they are tried, convicted, and punished by imprisonment, that*

*he would render the civil authorities all the
assistance in his power to bring others of those
tribes on the reservation who have been guilty of
outrages in Texas to trial and just punishment.*

*I would have petitioned Your Excellency to
commute their punishment to imprisonment for life
were it not that I know a great majority of the people
on this frontier demand their execution. Your
Excellency, however, acting for the weal of the state
at large, and free from the passions of the masses,
may see fit to commute their punishment. If so, I say
amen!*

*With many wishes for your good health, I remain
with much respect*

*Your very obt. servant,
Charles Soward
Judge, 13th Judicial District, Texas*

*July 11, 1871
Weatherford, Texas*

He slipped into the bedroom and sat in the chair, reached out
and took Sarah's hand in his own. Her eyes fluttered, focused, and she smiled.

"Miss Kinder says you're doing well," Sam Lanham told
her and brushed away a tear. "And the baby, too."

She mouthed the words, *I love you.*

He could no longer hold back the tears. "I love you," he
said, squeezing her hand harder. "Claude's all right. You
scared him out of a year's growth. Amanda Doniphan's with
him now. You need to stay in bed, dear." He had been talking
just to stay busy, but he settled down at last, leaned forward,
and kissed away his wife's tears.

Straightening, he told her, "I talked to Charles Soward
yesterday. It's out of our hands, but I think Governor Davis

will act, will commute the sentences of Satanta and Big Tree to life in prison."

She asked for water, and Lanham dipped a ladle into a nearby bowl, filled a glass, and lifted her head to help her drink. Finished, she slid back into the pillow and asked, "Did you threaten Soward, make him . . . ?"

He shook his head. "Nothing of the kind. Soward had this all planned from the start."

Sarah didn't believe him, even though he was telling the truth, but that didn't matter. Let her think he had blackmailed the honorable Charles Soward into asking the governor to commute the sentence. Let Woolfolk and Ball think their persistent badgering had made the judge see the light. They could take credit for everything if that's what they wanted. They could have the glory. Sam Lanham knew what he wanted, and he had it.

"I should be with the children," Sarah began. "School's—"

He cut her off sternly. "You are staying in bed. Miss Doniphan will see to that and tend to Claude. There's only this week left in school, and I will be the teacher." He leaned forward and kissed her. "I think I can handle that," he whispered. "One week of school. Less than a week, actually. You taught me enough."

He wiped his face with a handkerchief and added, "You taught me everything, Sarah. I'd be nothing without you." He leaned forward and kissed her lips, wanted to stay there a long time, but forced himself to stand, squeeze her hand once more, and head for the door. "I had best get to school," he said. "To teach those little bumpkins about division, Washington Irving, and history."

"Sam," she called out weakly.

Her smile pleased him as he turned.

"Are you sure you want to wear that shirt?" she asked.

Chapter 30

"Let it henceforth be understood, far and wide, that while our Government is making every effort to protect, civilize and Christianize the well disposed and peaceable Indians, those who still persist in deeds of robbery and murder will be . . . punished for their crimes, the same as are white criminals. With the inauguration of this policy our long harassed and bleeding border will at last have peace."
　　　　　—The Daily Journal, Austin, Texas, July 18, 1871

August 3, 1871
Washington, D.C.

William T. Sherman cussed out his orderly, kicked a trash can down the hall, and slammed the door to his office, rattling the windows and the portrait of himself hanging on the wall. Edmund J. Davis, that gutless, incompetent fat ass serving as governor down in Texas, had done it, gone and commuted the sentences of Big Tree and Satanta to life imprisonment, made all of the work Sherman and the Army had done meaningless.

"Would the general prefer to reschedule his meeting with the inspector general?"

The smooth voice startled Sherman, and he looked up, surprised at first to find Randolph Marcy sitting in a leather chair, cigar between his fingers, ashtray resting on the chair's arm. He had forgotten all about the appointment this morning and had kept Marcy waiting while carrying out his tirade down the halls of the War Department. If it had been anyone else, Sherman would have been embarrassed, but Marcy knew him well and had been with him during the whole miserable affair down in Texas and Fort Sill.

"You heard what they did yesterday in Texas?" Sherman snapped as he marched for the bar to pour a couple of glasses of Scotch.

Marcy flicked ash and took a long drag on the cigar, letting Sherman fix the drinks before answering. He looked at the clock in the corner. Ten forty-five, late enough for some of the general's single malt.

"I saw the telegram," Marcy answered. Sherman brought him a drink. Their glasses clinked, and Sherman took a sip before sitting at his desk.

"Satanta ought to have been hung," he said wearily. "That would have ended the trouble."

"Perhaps," Marcy said. "But life imprisonment is one hell of a gift."

Sherman laughed without humor and shook his head. "I learned a lot on our tour out west, Randolph, and I know the Kiowa well enough to see they'll be everlastingly pleading for his release."

Marcy did not disagree. He let Sherman continue his diatribe.

"He should never be released, and I hope the War Department will never consent to his return to his tribe."

The two soldiers stopped long enough to taste their drinks. "What about Big Tree?" asked Marcy, picking up his cigar.

"I would have preferred to see him hang, too, but I guess I do not deem his imprisonment essential, though he ought to keep Satanta company."

"Well, it's over and done with, General," Marcy said. He drained his drink, savoring the taste of good Scotch and a fine cigar. "Let Texas worry about it. Now, shall we discuss desertion rates and what can be done about them?"

October 15, 1871
Fort Richardson, Texas

Corporal John B. Charlton dropped the hammer to his side
and looked at the placard he had just tacked to the bulletin
board beside the day's duty roster.

The State of Texas
To all to whom these presents shall come:

> *Whereas, at the July term, A.D. 1871, of the*
> *District Court of Jack County, in said state, one*
> *Satanta and Big Tree, known as Indians of the Kiowa*
> *tribe, were tried and convicted of a charge of murder*
> *and sentenced therefore to suffer the penalty of death*
> *on the first day of September, A.D. 1871, and*
> *imprisonment for life will be more likely to operate*
> *as a restraint upon others of the tribe to which these*
> *Indians belong; and, where the killing for which*
> *these Indians were sentenced can hardly be*
> *considered as a just consideration of the animus as*
> *coming within the technical crime for murder under*
> *the statutes of the state, but rather as an act of*
> *savage warfare; now, therefore, I, Edmund J. Davis,*
> *governor of Texas, by virtue of the authority vested*
> *in me by the constitution and laws of the state, do*
> *hereby commute the sentence of Satanta and Big*
> *Tree to imprisonment for life, at hard labor, in the*
> *state penitentiary, and hereby direct the clerk of the*
> *district court of Jack County to make this*
> *commutation of sentence a matter of record in his*
> *office.*

Edmund J. Davis, Governor
James P. Newcomb, Secretary of State

"I heard that most of the soldiers here turned rabid at the news," the officer beside him commented. "You don't seem upset at all."

Charlton spit out his tobacco into his left hand, considering the quid for a moment before dropping it inside his hat to save for later. He tossed the hammer on the nearby bench, pulled on his hat, and looked at the redheaded infantry officer before answering.

"Most of the boys are fumin' they don't get to see a hangin'," he told the captain. "Me? I just foller orders, sir, like any good soldier." Good soldiers also knew better than to speak their mind to fancy infantry captains they did not know. Besides, Charlton was a cavalryman, and he had little use for infantry soldiers, officers or not, especially someone like Captain H. L. Chapman, who spent his time behind a desk down in San Antonio, far from the bloody frontier.

Captain H. L. Chapman, Eleventh Infantry, nodded and looked across the parade grounds. Chapman had arrived earlier that day, presenting his orders to Lieutenant Carter, as Colonel Mackenzie was in the field with a troop, making sure the Kiowas and Comanche were not about to start a war. That wasn't likely, though, with the death sentence revoked for Big Tree and Satanta, but those two Kiowas weren't safe yet. Fearing the mood among white settlers along the frontier, Governor Davis had requested a military escort for Satanta and Big Tree from Fort Richardson to the state penitentiary at Huntsville. Chapman had been given the assignment and orders to make sure his charges reached prison alive.

"How are the Indians doing?" Chapman asked.

"Fair to middlin'," Charlton replied, stepping off the boardwalk and pointing to the post guardhouse. "If the captain desires, I can take you to see them."

"Very good, Corporal."

As they crossed the parade grounds, Charlton explained, "They've been gettin' exercise when the weather ain't bad.

Satanta still likes listenin' to the regimental band. Big Tree
never says much. Kinda resigned, I guess."

"They know they won't hang?"

"Yes, sir. We told 'em when we learned back in August."
Of course, governments being governments, it took more
than two months for the poster announcing Davis's decision
to arrive from Austin.

"Must be happy then."

"I wouldn't say that, sir."

Chapman cocked his head. "Why not? I would be ecstatic
if I learned my life had been spared."

They had reached the guardhouse. "Beggin' the captain's
pardon, sir, but you ain't a Kiowa." The captain didn't press
the matter, and Charlton found his key ring and unlocked the
outer door. A few months ago, the two prisoners had been
under heavy guard, but now only one trooper stood in front
of the building.

Their boots echoed as they walked to the last cell, where
Charlton found another key and unlocked the iron door.
Chapman stepped around and stared at the two Indians. Satanta began talking immediately, holding out his handcuffed
wrists for inspection. Chapman moved closer, knelt, and examined the rash.

"Jesus," Chapman said, and Satanta pointed to his feet.

The officer stood and turned to Charlton. "How long has
he had 'guardhouse itch'?"

"Pretty much since he got here, sir," Charlton answered.
He had told Sergeant Varily, Lieutenant Carter, and even
Colonel Mackenzie about Satanta's rash, but no one had
cared. "It's gotten worse."

"It's as bad a case as I've ever seen, Corporal. I want Satanta's handcuffs removed, and his ankle bracelets. Have him
report to the post hospital, under guard, where a salve can be
applied. I won't turn over a prisoner about to come down
with gangrene to the warden at Huntsville. See to it, Corporal. Now."

Charlton fired off a salute and hurried outside with a new-found respect for Captain H. L. Chapman.

October 16, 1871
Fort Richardson, Texas

Wolf Heart and He Who Speaks The Black Robe Tongue met them outside the soldier-prison, which made Satanta glad. He proudly displayed his manacled hands and began talking in rapid Kiowa, saying how the bluecoat medicine man made his wrists and ankles stop itching, but the fool interpreter at this soldier-fort struggled with the Kiowa words. Satanta switched to Comanche, but the interpreter still stumbled. He was no Hor-Ace-Jones or Lee-Per, but both of those white-eyes had returned north, so Satanta would have to deal with this fool bluecoat on the journey to the prison in the *Tehanna* town called Huntsville.

Still, he thanked Wolf Heart and He Who Speaks The Black Robe Tongue for coming, thanked them for all of their help, for stopping the *Tehannas* from breaking and stretching their necks with the coiled ropes.

Wolf Heart patted Satanta's shoulder and shook Big Tree's hand, then walked back to the gathering of bluecoats and *Tehannas* underneath the flapping soldier flag. He Who Speaks The Black Robe Tongue also shook Big Tree's hand before the walk-a-heap bluecoats escorted him to the wagon that would take them away.

"I do not know if I will ever see my family again," Satanta told He Who Speaks The Black Robe Tongue, still speaking Comanche. "Tell The Principal People not to raid anymore. Tell them to do as Stone Head tells them."

The bluecoat tried to make sense of those words to the *Tehanna* lawyer who had fought for Satanta, but Satanta could tell the fool talker's translation was no good. Annoyed, Satanta shook his head, called the bluecoat a squaw, and fol-lowed Big Tree, only to stop after a few paces when He Who

Speaks The Black Robe Tongue said, *"Bene ambula et re-dumbula."*

Satanta looked back at the lawyer with his sad smile. *A safe journey to you.* Yes, He Who Speaks The Black Robe Tongue was wise, saying good-bye in the words of the old Jesus men. Satanta would have tried to express his wishes in that tongue, but he was not sure he could manage all of those phrases. After all, the black robes had never talked about such matters as Stone Head, *Gai'gwu,* family or raids, just about Jesus and the white-eye god and the place called Heaven.

Satanta walked back to He Who Speaks The Black Robe Tongue and embraced him warmly. He would never see this warrior again. *"Cum ut valeas,"* he said. *Farewell.* He pulled away, brushed away a tear, and quickly joined Big Tree in the wagon. The walk-a-heap bluecoats surrounded the wagon, the officer barked out something, and they began moving out of the soldier-fort.

Satanta patted Big Tree's knee. "It will be all right, my son," he said. "Satanta will see to that."

"Thank you, grandfather," Big Tree said without enthusiasm. Satanta's heart felt glad that Big Tree's anger with him had passed. Maybe he said more, but Satanta did not hear. The bluecoat men had started playing a song, their instruments much harsher, louder than the flutes and drums of The Principal People. Satanta smiled and turned back to listen. He hoped the *Tehannas* at this place called Huntsville played similar music.

"What did you tell Satanta?" Woolfolk asked as the two lawyers found a corner table in the empty Green Frog Saloon.

"Good-bye," Ball answered.

The bartender set two beers in front of them with a smile. "This one's on the house, gents," he said before heading back to the bar.

Woolfolk's eyebrows arched. "Times have changed," he said before picking up a mug.

Ball nodded and lifted his glass. The beer was warm and bitter, which suited his mood. The bartender had surprised him, though. Like Woolfolk, he had expected the people of Jack County to be enraged, to blame Ball and Woolfolk for sparing the lives of Big Tree and Satanta, but Jacksboro had converted back into another dusty, windswept town on the Texas frontier. No hordes of newspapermen and rabble. That was fine with him. He glanced out the window just in time to watch Peter Lynn ride by in a buckboard, M. J. Shelley at his side. That was all right, too.

"So you're stayin' put," Woolfolk said, and Ball turned back to face his friend.

"Looks like. You were right. I've been pretty busy the past month. Folks want to hire the lawyer who had the guts to defend two Kiowas."

Woolfolk grinned and pressed his mug against Ball's. The glasses clinked, and Woolfolk drained his beer in two more swallows.

"What about you?" Ball asked.

"Been a mite busy myself," Woolfolk answered. "Tendin' to a foal, butcherin' hogs for winter, workin' cattle." He flagged the bartender for another round.

Ball quickly finished his beer and set his glass on the table.

"You still seein' that waitress?" Woolfolk asked.

"Some," Ball said. "Amanda took a job at the Parker County Inn. After what happened here, I couldn't blame her for not wanting to come back. I only see her when I'm down in Weatherford, and like I've said, I've been busy up here." After spending more than a month at Woolfolk's ranch, Ball had found a new place to live in early September, a real house, in town, and had been settling in there while reestablishing his law practice. "But, yeah, I still see her."

"Good."

The bartender brought two more beers, picked up the

empty glasses, and left with another smile but no conversation.

"So." Woolfolk raised his mug. "We should be happy. We're in fine health, the lunacy has died down, you got a girl, I got a wife, family, and growin' ranch, and we spared the lives of our clients."

Ball's head bobbed slightly. They drank their beers in silence. Woolfolk started to pay for the second round, but Ball insisted, dropped a coin on the table, and the two men walked outside into the sunlight.

"You been thinking about Camp Chase?" Ball asked at last.

"Yeah," Woolfolk replied glumly. "Since Davis issued his commutation. You rememberin' Point Lookout?"

"Yeah." He shook his head, trying to block out the nightmares.

"We did what we had to do," Woolfolk said, speaking about the life sentences awaiting Satanta and Big Tree, not his own and Ball's stay in those damnyankee prisons during the war.

For the good of Texas, Ball thought, recalling Judge Soward's words. Huntsville prison would be a harsh adjustment for two Kiowas, so used to living free. Ball had only been to a circus once and had hated it, heartbroken at seeing the caged animals. That's how he envisioned Satanta and Big Tree in prison: stunned, angry, frightened, wanting to die. What was it Woolfolk had told him before the trial began? *A hangin's merciful.* Maybe hanging would have been better—certainly not for the people of Texas once the Kiowas retaliated, but more humane for Satanta and Big Tree. Life imprisonment would be a slow, painful death sentence for men like that. Hell, prison had damned near killed Woolfolk and Ball during the war. The conditions at Huntsville might be fifty times better than at Camp Chase or Point Lookout, but for two Kiowas it would remain unmerciful.

"I've thought 'bout that since Gov'nor Davis made his rulin' in August," Woolfolk said as he ducked underneath the hitching rail and grabbed the reins to his blood bay gelding. "Thought 'bout what prison'll be like for them two poor injuns. Hell, Sherman should have shot 'em back at Fort Sill."

"We didn't do them any favors," Ball agreed.

"Nope." Woolfolk shook Ball's hand and swung into the saddle. "Big Tree might be all right, him bein' young and all, but Satanta . . ." He shook his head.

"In pace requiescat," Ball said softly.

"What's that?"

"Nothing," Ball said, tipped his hat, and walked away.

Epilogue

"I cannot wither and die like a dog in chains."
　　　　　　　　　　　　　—Satanta, October 10, 1878

November 14, 1929
Elm Creek, Oklahoma

The reporter for the *Daily Oklahoman* tentatively approached the white-haired man in the wheelchair as soon as the funeral ended. He hadn't expected to find any white men, except Baptist churchgoers and perhaps a few old-timers from Lawton or Fort Sill, to show up to see an old-time Kiowa warrior planted, and this gent was a stranger. No one talked to him except his auburn-haired nurse. The reporter held out his hand, introduced himself, and asked, "Did you know the deceased?"

The old man shook his head and spit out tobacco juice. "Not really," he said, gumming out the words and motioning for the nurse to push his chair to the waiting Ford. He had to be well into his nineties. Sensing a story despite the man's reluctance, the journalist pulled out his note pad and followed. "His Kiowa name was Ádo-eete," the reporter said, "but everyone called him Big Tree. 'Big Tree was the last of all the old warriors,'—that's what my paper's going to say, unless that dern copy editor rewrites my stuff again. 'He, at the time of his death, was a leading member of the church at Elm Creek and held a creditable place in the esteem of his people.' I know you knew him, sir. Why else would you be at his funeral?"

"Because I'll do anything to get out of the home," the man snapped. The reporter detected a trace of a Virginia accent.

"You know his story, I bet," the reporter persisted. "He and Satanta were tried for murder down in Texas in 1871. Sentenced to hang, but the governor commuted the sentence. . . ."

Knowing the story better than most, the newspaperman recited the history to the old man.

Satanta and Big Tree were paroled on August 19, 1873, a move brought on by pressure from Indian agents and Eastern peacemakers and pleas from Kiowa leaders. When Edmund Davis issued the parole, William Tecumseh Sherman fired off a letter to the Texas governor saying, "I believe Satanta and Big Tree will have their revenge, if they have not already had it, and that if they are to have scalps that yours is the first that should be taken." Davis was trounced in the next election.

Prison officials said Big Tree had been a model inmate in Huntsville, and, paroled, he soon followed the white man's road. In 1897, he joined the Rainy Mountain Indian Mission, which he had helped establish with white Baptists, and became a deacon in the church. His wife had died about ten years ago, and yesterday, Big Tree had joined her.

The reporter recalled all this as the nurse wheeled the invalid to the Ford, helped him into the automobile, and stored the wheelchair in the back. The reporter took a chance. "Are you Captain Carter, the author?"

Robert G. Carter had made a name for himself around Fort Sill and in western American history circles. Promoted to first lieutenant in 1875, he had been forced to retire a year later because of wounds suffered during the Texas Indian Wars. In 1904, he received a promotion to captain on the retired list. Since then, he had become a writer and historian.

The old-timer laughed. "No, and I'm not J. B. Charlton, either."

John B. Charlton, promoted to sergeant, had also left the Fourth Cavalry in 1876. Charlton had then traveled the world before settling in south Texas, where he died at his Uvalde home in 1922. The fact that this old gent recalled Charlton's name tipped the reporter off. He had to know a lot more and could fill in the many gaps in the story of the trial and its aftermath.

The nurse cranked the Ford's engine and settled behind the steering wheel.

The journalist tried to think of the other officials he had learned about during his research of the great Kiowa trial. Mostly, he tried to think of who might still be alive. After all, the trial had ended fifty-eight years ago.

He quickly eliminated all of the military brass.

Sherman had continued to preach the extermination of Indians through the slaughter of buffalo and other means. He remained something of a celebrity, and his two-volume memoirs were published in 1875. Sherman retired as general-in-chief of the Army in 1883. In 1886, he settled in New York City, where he died on February 14, 1891, at age seventy-seven.

Easygoing Benjamin Henry Grierson served for nineteen more years in the Tenth Cavalry, overcoming prejudice to turn his black troopers into one of the most respected and well-disciplined Army units on the frontier. He campaigned against the Apache Victorio in west Texas, bought a ranch in the Davis Mountains, and retired as a brigadier general in 1890. In 1911, at age eighty-five, Grierson died at his Omena, Michigan, summer home.

With the Indian threat over in northwest Texas, Fort Richardson was abandoned by the military on May 29, 1878. Five years earlier, Ranald Slidell Mackenzie and the Fourth Cavalry had left Fort Richardson for Fort Clark in south Texas. Mackenzie would help subdue the Comanches and other tribes of the Southern Plains during the Red River War of 1874–75. He later served in Colorado, Arizona, and New Mexico, and was promoted to brigadier general on October

SPARK ON THE PRAIRIE

26, 1882. But hard drinking, syphilis, and a fall from a wagon in which he suffered a head injury strained his mental faculties. After a drunken brawl in San Antonio, Mackenzie was confined to an asylum. Placed on the retired list in 1884, Mackenzie was released from the asylum. In 1886, he moved to Staten Island, where his sister cared for him until his death, at age forty-eight, three years later.

Nor could the stranger have been one of the two interpreters.

Mathew Leeper and Horace P. Jones had traveled different paths after the trial. Leeper eventually quit the Indian Territory and became a practicing physician in Chicago, where he left public life before passing away some time back. A man who hated to see the coming of progress to the West, Jones continued on as post interpreter at Fort Sill, admired and respected by the Indians, who adopted him so he could be granted a land allotment when the reservation was broken up at the turn of the century. Jones, seventy-two years old, died in late 1901 in his farm shack near the fort and was buried in the post cemetery shortly before the first railroad arrived.

Who else? Not the old Indian agent. Having survived the turmoil caused by his 1871 actions, Lawrie Tatum disagreed with the Indian Bureau's decision to have Satanta and Big Tree released from prison, and it cost him his job. He was replaced by James M. Haworth in March of 1873 and returned to Iowa, where he helped establish a bank and Springdale Academy. He eventually became the young Herbert Hoover's guardian and published a book on his work as an Indian agent, *Our Red Brothers,* in 1899, one year before his death.

A jury member? No, they were mostly dead and gone, too. Peter Lynn had married M. J. Shelley on January 24, 1879. The couple had five children, P. S., Lucinda, Peter, Pearl, and Loma, rearing them on Lynn's Keechi Valley property about ten miles south of Jacksboro. M. J. and Peter were members of the Christian Church and, according to one historian, stood "high in their community and in the esteem of all who enjoy the honor of their friendship." If Lynn were still alive, and the reporter doubted that, he wouldn't likely come all the way from Jack County to Oklahoma for Big Tree's funeral.

That left the lawyers and judge, but . . .

Charles Soward had remained judge of the Thirteenth Judicial District comprising Parker, Jack, Palo Pinto, Hood, and Johnson counties until Governor Richard Coke appointed A. J. Hood to replace him in 1874. In addition to his terms as judge and district clerk, Soward also was mayor of Sherman, Texas, before opening an office as a land attorney in Weatherford and later retiring to Decatur. The reporter had read that the old judge had died a few years ago.

After the trial, Joseph Woolfolk had continued to practice law in Young County and held several county positions, but he concentrated on his family and his section of prime Brazos River land. He eventually left the public and legal life behind and spent most of his time with his wife and eight children while working on his farm just outside of Newcastle. He had died ten years ago and was buried in the family cemetery near Fort Belknap.

The trial of the Kiowas propelled Samuel W. T. Lanham to Washington and, eventually, the governor's mansion in Austin. From 1883 to 1893, and again from 1897 to 1903, he served in the U.S. House of Representatives. He left Congress to become the twenty-second governor of Texas, the last Confederate veteran to hold that position. He campaigned for—and succeeded in establishing—two colleges and stumped against boss rule and election corruption. Partly through his politicking, the Terrell Election Law of 1903 established primary elections and voting booths as well as the filing of campaign expenditures by candidates. He called his biggest success, however, his five children. On July 2, 1908, Sarah Meng Lanham died. Twenty-seven days later, her husband followed her.

Everyone had passed away, and now Big Tree, although he had never talked about the old days, and especially not the

Salt Creek Prairie murder trial and prison sentence. But what about Thomas A. Ball? The reporter had reached a dead end in his investigation of the defense attorney from Virginia. Ball had also entered politics. Still a bachelor, he was elected state senator in 1876, serving as chairman of the committee on the General Land Office, and was appointed assistant attorney general of Texas in January of 1879 before fading out of public life and history.

"Then you're Thomas Ball!" the reporter challenged, and the old man's eyes could not hide the truth.

Excited, the reporter fired off more facts, trying to impress the old guy, let him know he was not talking to some hack reporter for an Oklahoma rag. He knew as much about the trial, and the Kiowas, as anyone in these parts.

Although many Kiowas would take part in the Red River War, for all intent and purpose the conviction of Satanta and Big Tree spelled the demise of the Kiowa nation. Kicking Bird, T'ené-angópte, or "Eagle Who Strikes With His Talons" in Kiowa, would lead the peace movement. After the Red River War, government officials asked him to select Kiowa men to be sent to prison. He did, earning the enmity of his people. Only forty years old, Kicking Bird died on May 3, 1875, less than a week after the Indian prisoners were exiled to Florida. The Kiowas said he had been witched for betraying his people. Lone Wolf, Quey-pah-kah in Kiowa, and Maman-ti, "Man Who Walks Above The Ground," were among those sent to Fort Marion prison at St. Augustine. Maman-ti, who had led the attack at Salt Creek Prairie, contracted consumption in the damp, humid prison and died on July 29, 1875. Kiowa legend had it that he cast the spell that killed Kicking Bird and died for his sins. Lone Wolf was later returned to Indian Territory but died of malaria in 1879. Stumbling Bear became the leader of the peace movement after Kicking Bird's death. Crippled, blind, and a far cry from the robust man who had earned the Kiowa name Settem-ka-yah ("Bear That Runs Over A Man"), he died in 1903.

"Then I reckon you know what happened to Set-t'ainte,"

the old man said, spit again, and told the nurse to wait a minute.

The reporter smiled. The old man had used Satanta's Kiowa name.

"He was sent back to Huntsville after taking part in the Red River War," the reporter replied. "It's a pretty sad story . . ."

"It always is," the old man said.

In his sixties, Satanta watched his health quickly fade in the dreary confines of the state penitentiary. On October 10, 1878, he asked if he had any chance of being paroled again. Told he didn't, the Kiowa remarked, "I cannot wither and die like a dog in chains." The next day, he attempted suicide by cutting his wrists. Prison officials rushed him to the second-story infirmary and stopped the bleeding, but, left alone, Satanta jumped off the landing to his death.

He was buried in the Peckerwood Cemetery, the pauper's field near the prison.

"I'd like to write a book about the trial," the reporter said, "but no one can find the transcripts."

"You never will," said the man, nodding at his nurse. "Let's go."

"Can you help me with just one thing, sir?" the reporter pleaded. The man didn't answer, but the nurse didn't release the brake.

"After Satanta's death, that December, a marble tombstone was placed over Satanta's grave," the reporter began and recited the rest as if by rote.

Stonecutter Thomas Byrne of Houston said the one hundred twenty-seven dollar order was placed anonymously, and he followed the instructions, carving:

Satanta, Chief of the Kiowas

And, below that, he chiseled in something he couldn't translate:

In pace requiescat

"It's a mystery, and one I want to solve," the reporter said eagerly. "Who ordered that tombstone? And why? And what about the epitaph?"

"Know what it means?" the old man asked.

"No," the reporter answered quickly. "It's not Kiowa. I've asked a lot of the Indians. And it's not Spanish. My editor thinks it's Latin. I guess I should ask a priest."

As the car pulled away, the old man showed a toothless grin. "Balderdash," he said as the Ford puttered down the washboard road. "Why would anyone put Latin on an Indian's tombstone?"

Author's Note

Like the preceding novel in the Guns and Gavel series, *Arm of the Bandit,* this book is based on fact. With the exception of some minor players, including Amanda Doniphan and the Widow Baggett, the characters were actual people, although all personalities are my own creations. M. J. Shelley probably never dated Thomas Ball, but she did marry juror Peter Lynn, and I seriously doubt if Satanta ever urinated in the Jack County courthouse. If Thomas Brazeal's foot was amputated because of wounds sustained in the Salt Creek Prairie fight, I haven't read about it in any contemporary accounts or histories. The near-lynching of the Tonkawa scouts on the night of July 4 is also a figment of my imagination, but the precautions the Army and local civilian law enforcement used to bring the two defendants to court the following day are based on fact.

Transcripts of the trial no longer exist (though, as far as I know, not because Judge Soward ordered them burned), so I have relied on newspaper accounts, archival records, memoirs, and histories to re-create the scene, using actual quotes and letters when possible, although for convenience's sake I have corrected some misspellings. Unfortunately, the only speeches that have been preserved from the trial are Samuel W. T. Lanham's closing argument and Satanta's plea, while Thomas Ball's opening statement is briefly summarized in Robert G. Carter's *On the Border with Mackenzie, or Winning West Texas from the Comanches,* first published in 1935. So I have had to rely on my imagination in dealing with the other speeches and testimony. One other bit of literary license, I must note, is the testimony of William T. Sherman. He did not attend the trial, but he played such an integral part in the story—indeed, the case never would have been tried in a civilian courtroom if not for Sherman—that I wanted to let him speak under oath, using some of his own words taken from various letters. The Latin inscription on Satanta's tombstone—also lost to history (if the story is true)—is my own creation as well. If you insist, it means *May he rest in peace.*

A note on the novel's title: Satanta's courtroom speech has been interpreted in various ways by various sources. Austin's *Daily Journal* of July 18, 1871, recorded the statement as, "If you let me live, I feel my ability to control my people. If I die it will be like a match put to the prairie. No power can stop it." However, "a match put to the prairie" has also been translated as "spark in the prairie," "spark upon the prairie," and "spark on the prairie." I like "spark on the prairie" best.

I am indebted to many people for helping research this novel, including the staffs at the Center for American History in Austin, Texas; Combined Arms Research Library of Fort Leavenworth, Kansas; the state archives of Texas, Missouri, and Kentucky; the archives of the College of William and Mary and the University of Louisville; Oklahoma State Historical Society; Fort Sill Museum; Fort Richardson State Historical Park; Wise County Historical Commission; National Archives; and the Dallas Public Library; as well as Gregory Lalire at *Wild West* magazine; Marcus Huff, former editor of *True West* magazine; and my wife, Lisa, who managed to proofread my chapters despite caring for our newborn son, handling my publicity, doing charity work, keeping the house in order, and keeping me in line.

I would also like to point out my primary published sources: *Ninety-Four Years in Jack County, 1854–1948,* by Ida Lasater Huckabay; *Our Red Brothers and the Peace Policy of President Ulysses S. Grant,* by Lawrie Tatum; *Indian Depredations in Texas,* by J. W. Wilbarger; *The Kiowas,* by

Mildred P. Mayhall; *The Kiowas and the Legend of Kicking Bird,* by Stan Hoig; *Sentinel of the Southern Plains: Fort Richardson and the Northwest Texas Frontier, 1866–1878,* by Allen Lee Hamilton; *Five Years a Cavalryman; or Sketches of Regular Army Life on the Texas Frontier, Twenty Odd Years Ago,* by H. H. McConnell; *History of Jack County,* by Thomas F. Horton; three books by Charles M. Robinson III, *Satanta, Bad Hand: A Biography of General Ranald S. Mackenzie,* and *The Indian Trial: The Complete Story of the Warren Wagon Train Massacre and the Fall of the Kiowa Nation;* two by Robert G. Carter, *On the Border with Mackenzie* and *The Old Sergeant's Story: Fighting Indians and Bad Men in Texas from 1870 to 1876;* and the great books of Colonel Wilbur Sturtevant Nye, *Carbine & Lance: The Story of Old Fort Sill, Plains Indian Raiders,* and *Bad Medicine & Good: Tales of the Kiowas.* Although criticized by many historians for the late Benjamin Capps's frequent literary license, *The Warren Wagontrain Raid* was used as a secondary source.

Those are excellent starting points for anyone interested in reading more about Case Number 224, *the State of Texas vs. Satanta and Big Tree.*

Johnny D. Boggs
Santa Fe, New Mexico
June 20, 2002

SIGNET BOOKS   (0451)

JUDSON GRAY

RANSOM RIDERS   20418-2

When Penn and McCutcheon are ambushed on their way to rescue a millionaire's kidnapped niece, they start to fear that the kidnapping was an inside job.

CAYWOOD VALLEY FEUD   20656-8

Penn and McCutcheon are back! This third novel of the American frontier takes readers to the Ozarks, where a mysterious gunman has been terrorizing an Ozark family called Caywood—picking them off one by one. The gunman's description matches McCutcheon's good friend Jake Penn. And now, he must find Penn and prove him innocent before more blood is spilled.

To order call: 1-800-788-6262

S308